SPECIAL MESSAGE TO READERS

THE ULVERSCROFT FOUNDATION
(registered UK charity number 264873)
was established in 1972 to provide funds for
research, diagnosis and treatment of eye diseases.
Examples of major projects funded by
the Ulverscroft Foundation are:-

- The Children's Eye Unit at Moorfields Eye Hospital, London
- The Ulverscroft Children's Eye Unit at Great Ormond Street Hospital for Sick Children
- Funding research into eye diseases and treatment at the Department of Ophthalmology, University of Leicester
- The Ulverscroft Vision Research Group, Institute of Child Health
- Twin operating theatres at the Western Ophthalmic Hospital, London
- The Chair of Ophthalmology at the Royal Australian College of Ophthalmologists

You can help further the work of the Foundation
by making a donation or leaving a legacy.
Every contribution is gratefully received. If you
would like to help support the Foundation or
require further information, please contact:

THE ULVERSCROFT FOUNDATION
The Green, Bradgate Road, Anstey
Leicester LE7 7FU, England
Tel: (0116) 236 4325

website: www.foundation.ulverscroft.com

James Patterson is one of the best-known and biggest-selling writers of all time. His books have sold in excess of 375 million copies worldwide. He is the author of some of the most popular series of the past two decades, including Alex Cross and the Women's Murder Club. James is passionate about encouraging children to read. Inspired by his own son, who was a reluctant reader, he also writes a range of books for young readers. He has donated millions in grants to independent bookshops, and has been the most borrowed author of adult fiction in UK libraries for over a decade. He lives in Florida with his wife and son.

You can discover more about the author at www.jamespatterson.co.uk

TARGET ALEX CROSS

Men and women from across the nation line the streets of Washington, DC to mourn the unexpected death of the president. Five days later, a sniper's bullet strikes another devastating blow to the heart of Washington with the assassination of a prominent senator. The police are under huge pressure to deliver a speedy response, and as chief of detectives, Alex Cross's wife Bree Stone is given an ultimatum: solve the case, or lose her job. Meanwhile, the new president calls on Cross to lead an unparalleled FBI investigation to help capture America's most wanted criminal. The stakes have never been higher for Cross as his courage, his training, and his capacity for battle are stretched to their limits in the most important case of his life.

JAMES PATTERSON

TARGET
ALEX CROSS

Complete and Unabridged

CHARNWOOD
Leicester

First published in Great Britain in 2018 by
Century
London

First Charnwood Edition
published 2019
by arrangement with
Penguin Random House UK
London

A catalogue record for this book is available
from the British Library.

ISBN 978–1–4448–4256–2

Published by
F. A. Thorpe (Publishing)
Anstey, Leicestershire

Set by Words & Graphics Ltd.
Anstey, Leicestershire
Printed and bound in Great Britain by
T. J. International Ltd., Padstow, Cornwall

WHO IS ALEX CROSS?

PHYSICAL DESCRIPTION:

Alex Cross is 6 foot 3 inches (190cm), and weighs 196 lbs (89 kg).
He is African American, with an athletic build.

FAMILY HISTORY:

Cross was raised by his grandmother, Regina Cross Hope - known as Nana
Mama - following the death of his mother and his father's subsequent
descent into alcoholism. He moved to D.C. from Winston-Salem, North
Carolina, to live with Nana Mama when he was ten.

RELATIONSHIP HISTORY:

Cross was previously married to Maria, mother to his children Damon and
Janelle, however she was tragically killed in a drive-by shooting. Cross
has another son, Alex Jr., with Christine Johnson. He is now married
to Detective Brianna (Bree) Stone, who was recently appointed Chief of
Detectives for the Metro Police Department.

EDUCATION:

Cross has a PhD in psychology from Johns Hopkins University in Baltimore,
Maryland, with a special concentration in the field of abnormal
psychology and forensic psychology.

EMPLOYMENT:

Cross works as a psychologist in a private practice, based in his home. He
also consults for the Major Case Squad of the Metro Police Department,
where he previously worked as a psychologist for the Homicide and Major
Crimes team.

PROFILE

A loving father, Cross is never happier than when spending time with
his family. He is also a dedicated member of his community and often
volunteers at his local parish and soup kitchen. When not working
in the practice or consulting for MPD, he enjoys playing classical
music on the piano, reading, and teaching his children how to box.

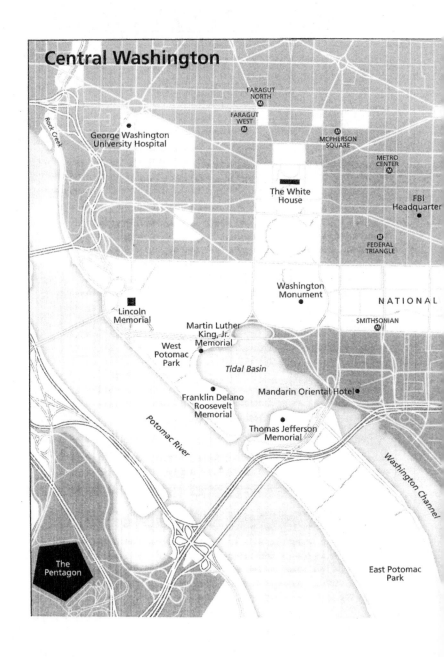

Central Washington

Rock Creek

FARAGUT
NORTH Ⓜ

FARAGUT
WEST Ⓜ

George Washington
University Hospital

MCPHERSON
SQUARE Ⓜ

METRO
CENTER Ⓜ

The White
House

FBI
Headquarter

Ⓜ
FEDERAL
TRIANGLE

Washington
Monument

NATIONAL

Lincoln
Memorial

SMITHSONIAN
Ⓜ

Martin Luther
King, Jr.
Memorial

West
Potomac
Park

Tidal Basin

Franklin Delano
Roosevelt
Memorial

Mandarin Oriental Hotel

Potomac River

Thomas Jefferson
Memorial

Washington Channel

The
Pentagon

East Potomac
Park

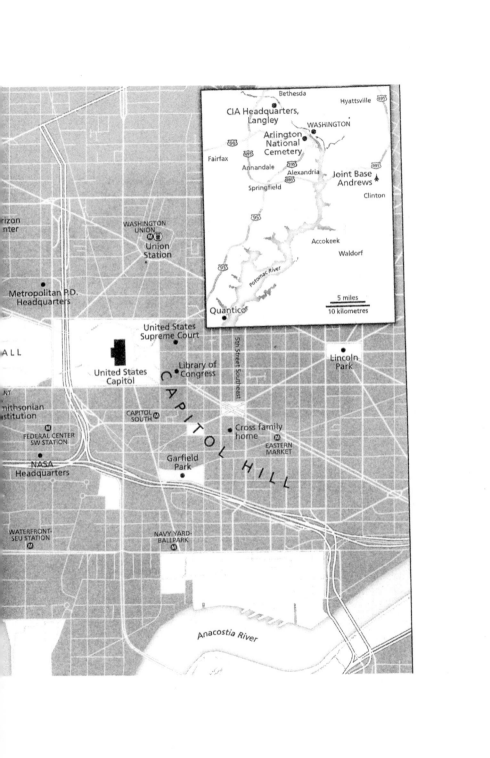

Prologue

1

Temperatures that late January morning plunged to four degrees above zero, and still people came by the hundreds of thousands, packing both sides of the procession route from Capitol Hill to the White House.

I was waiting at the corner of Constitution and Louisiana Avenues surrounded by my entire family. Bree Stone, my wife and DC Metro PD's chief of detectives, stood in front of me wearing her finest dress blues.

My twenty-year-old son, Damon, was on my right. He had flown up from North Carolina the night before and had on long underwear, a suit and tie, and a black down jacket. Nana Mama, my ninety-something grandmother, had refused to listen to reason and watch this on TV. Sitting in a folding camp chair to my left and wrapped in blankets, she wore a wool ski cap and everything warm she owned. Jannie, my seventeen-year-old, and Ali, nine, were dressed for the Arctic but hugging each other for warmth and stamping their feet behind us.

'How much longer, Dad?' Ali asked. 'I can't feel my toes.'

Over the soft din of the crowd and from well up Capitol Hill, I heard the four drum ruffles and bugle flourishes that precede 'Hail to the Chief.'

'They're leaving the Capitol,' I said. 'It won't be long now.'

The presidential anthem soon ended, and the cold crowd quieted.

I heard a man's voice call out, 'Right shoulder, arms!'

Another voice repeated the call. And then a third. One by one, every fifty yards and moving east to west, the soldiers flanking the route followed the command, bringing their rifles to their right shoulders and standing at ramrod attention.

The drums began to beat then, the slow cadence sounding muffled and somber from that distance.

One hundred West Point cadets appeared at the top of Capitol Hill, all dressed in gray and marching in unison. Similar contingents from the U.S. Naval, Air Force, and Coast Guard Academies followed, striding in precision, heads high, eyes focused straight ahead as they reached the bottom of the hill and passed us.

Up on the hill, the slow, steady beat of the drums continued, getting louder and coming closer. A color guard appeared bearing flags.

I heard the clopping of hooves before seven pale gray horses trotted from the Capitol grounds. Six of the horses moved in formation, two following two following two. The seventh horse marched at the head of the column to their left.

All seven horses were saddled, but only the left-hand three and the horse at the head of the column carried riders, uniformed members of the U.S. Army's Old Guard unit. The six horses in formation pulled the hundred-year-old black caisson that bore the flag-draped coffin of the late president of the United States.

2

The slow, steady clip-clopping of the horses came closer and closer, the noise building along with the somber beat of the drum corps.

Behind the caisson, a black, riderless horse, known as a caparisoned steed, shook its head and danced against the reins held by another member of the Old Guard.

The late president's personal riding boots were turned backward in the stirrups.

'Why do they do that?' Ali asked in a soft voice.

'It's a military tradition that signifies the fallen commander,' Nana whispered. 'They did the same thing at President Kennedy's funeral almost sixty years ago.'

'Were you here then?'

'Right where you're standing, darling,' Nana said, wiping her eyes with a handkerchief. 'I remember it like it was yesterday, just as tragic as today.'

I wasn't alive when JFK was president, but Nana had told me that it had been a time of great hope in the country because of its young leader and that hearing of his assassination had felt like a kick in the gut.

I'd felt the same way when Bree called me to say that Catherine Grant had collapsed in the Oval Office and died at age forty-seven, leaving behind a husband, twin ten-year-old daughters, and a stunned and grieving nation.

President Grant had been among the rarest of creatures in American politics, someone who actually managed to bring opposing sides together for the benefit of the country, and she'd done it by sheer force of her empathetic personality, her piercing brilliance, and her self-deprecating wit.

A former U.S. senator from Texas, Grant had won the White House in a landslide, and there'd been a real feeling of optimism in the country, a belief that the gridlock had ended, that politicians on both sides of the aisle were finally going to put their differences aside and work for the common good.

And they had, for three hundred and sixty-eight days.

Seventy-two hours after celebrating her first year in office, President Grant had been meeting with her military advisers when she suddenly complained of dizziness and seemed confused, then fell to the floor behind her desk. She died within moments.

Her doctors were stunned. The late president had been in top physical condition, and she had passed a rigorous physical exam with flying colors not two months before.

But the pathologists at Bethesda Naval Hospital said that Grant had succumbed to a fast-growing tumor that had enveloped her internal carotid artery, essentially interrupting the blood flow to most of her brain. No one could have saved her.

So there was a real sense of shared loss and

broken hope the morning of her funeral. As her cortege approached us, the mourners on both sides of Constitution Avenue turned sadly quiet.

Damon helped Nana Mama to her feet. Bree and I came to attention, and I had to fight against the emotion that built in my throat as Grant's coffin rolled by and the black riderless horse pranced and reared in the bitter-cold air.

But what really hit me was the sight of the limousine that trailed the black horse. I couldn't see them, but I knew that the late president's husband and daughters were inside.

I remembered how I'd felt when my first wife died tragically, leaving me lost, angry, and alone with a baby boy to care for. Those were the worst days of my life, when I thought I'd never be right again.

My heart broke for the First Family as they passed. I blinked back tears watching the drum corps march by, eyes straight ahead, the cadence of the funeral beat never wavering.

'Can we go now?' Ali asked. 'I can't feel my knees.'

'Not before we all hold hands and say a prayer for our country and that good woman's soul,' Nana Mama said, and she held her mittened hands out to us.

Part One

FIVE DAYS LATER

1

Snow fell as Sean Lawlor slipped into a narrow alley in Georgetown. A ruddy-skinned man with a salt-and-pepper beard and unruly hair, Lawlor was dressed in dark clothes, gloves, and a snap-brim cap with the earflaps down. As he moved deeper into the alley, he knew he was leaving tracks in the snow but didn't care.

Forecasts were calling for six inches before dawn, and he planned to be finished and gone long before the storm ended.

Lawlor padded to the rear gate of a beautiful old brick town house that faced Thirty-Fifth Street. After a long, slow look around, he climbed the gate and crossed a small terrace to a door he'd picked earlier in the evening after bypassing the alarm system.

It was four fifteen in the morning. He had half an hour at most.

Lawlor shut the door quietly behind him. He stood a moment, listening intently. Hearing nothing to disturb him, he brushed off snow while waiting for his eyes to adjust. Then he put blue surgical booties over his boots and walked down a hallway to the kitchen.

He pushed aside a chair, which made a squeaking noise on the tile floor. It didn't matter. There was no one home. The owners spent their winters in Palm Beach.

Lawlor went to a door on the other side of the

kitchen, opened it, and stepped down onto a set of steep wooden stairs. Shutting the door left him in inky darkness. He closed his eyes and flipped on the light.

After waiting again for his vision to adjust, Lawlor climbed down the stairs into a small, musty basement piled with boxes and old furniture. He ignored all of it and went to a workbench with tools hanging from a pegboard on the wall.

He shrugged off the knapsack he carried, traded his leather gloves for latex ones, unzipped the bag, and retrieved four bubble-wrapped packages, which he laid on the bench.

Lawlor cut off the bubble wrap and stowed the pieces in the pack before turning to admire the VooDoo Innovations Ultra Lite barreled action in 5.56x45mm NATO. *A work of art,* he thought.

He fitted the barreled action to a five-ounce minimalist rifle stock by Ace Precision and then screwed a SureFire Genesis sound suppressor onto the threaded crown of the barrel. Picking up the Zeus 640 optical sight, Lawlor thought, *A thing of beauty.*

He clipped the sight neatly into place. Overall, he was pleased with how the gun had turned out. He had ordered the components from U.S. internet wholesalers and had them shipped to the same nonexistent person at four separate UPS stores in and around the District of Columbia.

Lawlor had arrived at Dulles International two evenings ago on a flight from Amsterdam using a fake British passport. He'd picked up the components at the UPS stores yesterday morning, relying on a fake Pennsylvania driver's license he'd also bought online. He'd sighted in the gun yesterday afternoon in the woods of western Maryland. It was uncannily accurate.

It's the right tool, he told himself. *The perfect one for this job.*

2

Lawlor put the knapsack over his shoulder, took the gun up the basement stairs, and shut off the light before opening the door to the dark kitchen. He stepped out, pushed a button on the side of the sight, and raised the rifle.

The Zeus 640 was a thermal unit, which meant it allowed the user to see the world as heat images. When Lawlor peered through the scope, the interior of the house looked like it had been cast in pale daylight. Except for the heat registers. They showed in much brighter white.

The Zeus scope had been developed for hog hunters, and it had cost Lawlor more than eight thousand dollars. He thought it worth every penny, far superior to the kinds of rifle optics he'd been using just a few years ago.

Lawlor kept the gun stock pressed snug to his shoulder, climbed the stairs to the second floor, and entered the master suite at the front of the house. He ignored the antique furnishings and crossed to the window.

He lowered the rifle, opened the window sash, and looked outside. He saw the shadows of oak branches waving against the snowy background and the silhouette of a line of distinguished old townhomes across Thirty-Fifth Street.

He raised the gun again, peered through the sight. The snow-covered street and brick sidewalks turned dull black.

14

The heated town houses, however, were revealed in extraordinary detail, especially one to his right and down the street. A brick Georgian, it looked brilliant in the scope. The thermostat had to be turned up to seventy-five in there. Maybe eighty.

Lawlor swung the gun toward the front door of the hot house and studied the area, figuring he'd have four seconds, maybe less, when it counted. The brief time frame didn't faze him. He was good at his trade, used to dealing with short windows of opportunity.

Lawlor fished in his inner coat pocket and drew out a microchip that he fitted into a slot in the scope in order to record his actions for posterity. Then he relaxed and waited.

Ten minutes later, a light went on in the house to his far diagonal right, the hot one. He checked his watch. It was 4:30 a.m. *Right on schedule. Disciplined.*

Fifteen minutes after that, a black Suburban rolled up the street. Also right on time.

The wind was blowing stiffly down Thirty-Fifth from north to south. He would have to account for slight bullet drift.

The Suburban pulled over by the curb across from the hot house. Lawlor flipped the safety off and settled in, aiming at the front door and the steps down to the sidewalk.

The passenger, a large male wearing dark winter clothes, got out of the Suburban, ran across the street and sidewalk, climbed the steps, and rang the bell. The door opened, revealing a woman in a long overcoat.

15

Lawlor couldn't make out her features or determine her age through the thermal scope, and he didn't want to. He had seen several recent pictures of her, but through the Zeus 640, she was a pale white creature in a cold dark world, and he rather liked it that way.

Keeps things impersonal, like a video game, he thought, moving the crosshairs as the woman raised her hood and stepped out into the storm. He aimed at the right edge of the hood to account for drift. She followed the big guy, hurrying down the stairs, across the sidewalk, and into the street, eager to be out of the snow and get to her early yoga class.

Too bad, he thought as he pulled the trigger. *I heard yoga's good for you.*

The rifle made a soft thudding noise. The woman's head jerked and she crumpled on the street behind her bodyguard. Lawlor's instinct was to flee, but he stayed on task, moved the crosshairs to her chest, and shot her again.

He pushed down the sash and never looked back. After finding his spent brass, he rapidly disassembled the gun and placed three of the components back in the knapsack. He kept the thermal scope and used it so he could move fast back through the house.

After Lawlor slipped out the rear gate, he turned off the scope and pocketed it. Hearing the wailing of sirens already, he ducked his head and set off into the storm.

Too bad, he thought again. *Husband. Five children. Six grandkids. A real shame.*

16

3

Bree and I arrived in Georgetown shortly after dawn that first day of February. It was snowing at a steady pace with five inches on the ground already.

DC Metro patrol cars had blocked both ends of the street on Thirty-Fifth. We showed our IDs to the officer.

He said, 'There's U.S. Capitol Police, FBI, and Secret Service already up there.'

'I'd imagine so,' Bree said, and we went through the barrier and up the street, noticing many anxious residents looking out their windows.

FBI criminologists were setting up a tent around the victim and the crime scene. Yellow tape had been strung from both sides of the town house, across the street, and around the Suburban, where a big man in a black parka was engaged in a shouting match with a smaller man in an overcoat and ski cap.

'This is our case,' the big man said. 'She died on my goddamned watch.'

'U.S. Capitol Police will be part of the investigation,' the smaller man barked. 'But you will not, Lieutenant Lee. You are compromised, and you will be treated as such.'

'Compromised?' the big guy said, and for a second I thought he was going to deck the smaller man.

Then FBI special agent Ned Mahoney appeared from behind the tent.

'That's enough,' Mahoney said. 'Agent Reamer, please do not assume in any way that you are in charge of this investigation. The FBI has complete jurisdiction.'

'Says who?' Agent Reamer said.

'President Hobbs,' Mahoney said. 'Evidently, your new boss doesn't have much faith in the Secret Service these days. He talked with the director, and the director talked to me. And here we are.'

Agent Reamer looked furious but managed to keep his voice somewhat under control as he said, 'The Secret Service will not be cut out of this.'

'The Secret Service will not be cut out, but it will do what it is told to do,' Mahoney said, and then he saw us. 'Alex, Chief Stone. I want you both part of this.'

Quick introductions were made. U.S. Secret Service special agent Lance Reamer had worked Treasury investigations for the past ten years. The big guy was U.S. Capitol Police lieutenant Sheldon Lee. Lieutenant Lee had served on the victim's security team for six years.

With the snow and the wind, Lee hadn't heard the shots or the sound of sixty-nine-year-old U.S. senator Elizabeth 'Betsy' Walker falling to the ground behind him.

'I ran ahead and opened the rear door of the Suburban like I always do,' Lee said. 'I looked back and there she was. Lying in the snow, bleeding to death.'

His voice choked. 'My God, I had to go wake poor old Larry, her husband, to tell him. He's in there calling his children and . . . who the hell would do this? And why? That woman was a great person, treated everyone just right.'

That was true. The senator from California could be tough when she was fighting for a cause, and she had a first-rate mind, but she was one of those genial and compassionate women who had never met a stranger. Walker was also the second-most-senior member of the GOP in the Senate and a highly respected politician.

'Can we see the scene?' I asked as the snow slowed to flurries.

Agent Reamer said, 'Why exactly are *you* here, Dr. Cross?'

'Because I asked him to be here,' Mahoney growled. 'Dr. Cross used to be with the Behavioral Science Unit at Quantico, and he has more than two decades of exceptional service as an investigator. He's under contract to advise us on cases like these because the FBI thinks highly of him.'

Bree nodded. 'So does DC Metro.'

4

Reamer looked like he'd tasted something disagreeable and threw his hands up in disgust.

Mahoney called by radio and was told we could look at the crime scene from the flaps of the tent. We went as a pack of five past Lieutenant Lee's Suburban and around the other side of the shelter.

Inside, a team of Quantico's finest were working in baggy white jumpsuits pulled over their winter gear. Senator Walker lay twisted on her side in the snow. Her hood was half off her head, revealing a bullet hole beneath her right cheekbone.

'What do you know, Sally?'

Sally Burton, the chief FBI criminologist on the scene, stood up from beside the victim. 'The snow's making it tougher than tough, Ned, but so far, it looks like she was hit twice. The head shot killed her instantly. Shooter put a second round into her chest after she fell.'

'Like someone filled with hate would,' Lieutenant Lee said. 'A fanatic.'

'Or a professional,' Agent Reamer said.

'Or both,' I said. 'Who had reason to hate her?'

'Good question,' Mahoney said, and he looked back to Burton. 'Got an angle for the shots yet?'

The criminologist made a sour expression. 'The snow and no witness to her falling make

20

the first shot tough to call, but by the chest wound, I'm saying it's roughly this angle,' she said, gesturing high into the corner of the tent.

Mahoney thanked her, then turned to Lieutenant Lee. 'You have good rapport with the senator's husband?'

'Excellent rapport, sir. Larry's a sweet old guy, a real friend. Smart as they come too. He used to be a trial judge in San Francisco.'

'Go inside and talk to him frankly. Find out who didn't like or had a grudge against his wife for whatever reason. Names. Phone numbers if he's got them.'

'Wait,' Agent Reamer said. 'Lieutenant Lee is compromised.'

'He knows the family,' Mahoney said. 'Better than any of us. That helps.'

'But — '

Mahoney hardened. 'Do you honestly think Lieutenant Lee could be involved?'

'Well, no, but it's . . . it's gotta be against protocol,' Reamer sputtered.

'I don't give a damn about protocol,' Mahoney said. 'He's in.'

The lieutenant nodded. 'I can also get you a log of threatening calls and letters. Even Betsy got them from time to time.'

'Were they turned over to the FBI?' Mahoney asked.

'A few. They're in your files.'

When Lee left, the Secret Service agent said, 'Okay, then what am I doing?'

'Take several of your men, go to Senator Walker's offices, seal them, and then sit on them

21

and her staff until we get there,' Mahoney said. 'Dr. Cross, Chief Stone, and I are going to figure out where the hell those shots came from.'

It didn't take us long.

We knocked on the doors to the two town houses across and down the street that seemed likely candidates and found the residents home and upset. One, a prominent patent attorney, said her next-door neighbors Jimmy and Renee Fairfax were at their winter home in Palm Beach and had been for more than two months.

We called Mr. Fairfax's Florida residence to get permission to enter his house but got no answer. But when we found snowed-over tracks coming out of the rear terrace and discovered the rear door unlocked and the alarm system bypassed, Mahoney felt he had more than enough just cause to enter.

There was water in the hallway, probably melted snow, and smaller droplets crossing the floor to a door to the basement. There was no sign beyond that, certainly not of the footprints I'd expected to find, given that the shooter came in out of the weather.

We looked out the front window and decided the shooter had to have been higher, upstairs. We found a clear line of sight in the master bedroom, some hundred yards down the street from the evidence tent in front of Senator Walker's house.

'He was right here,' I said, looking around. 'Probably shot from his knees, using the windowsill as a rest.'

'No brass,' Bree said. 'The place is clean.'

22

Mahoney nodded. 'Either a fanatic or a professional.'

'Or both,' I said.

5

I had to leave at quarter to nine to make an appointment with a new patient, an attorney at the Justice Department. In addition to my law enforcement work, I have a PhD in clinical psychology and practice on a part-time basis out of an office in the basement of our house on Fifth Street in Southeast DC.

In the northern United States or out west, six inches of snow is no big deal. But in the nation's capital, it usually creates a state of emergency and near gridlock. I somehow managed to catch a cab, but I had to get out at the bottom of Capitol Hill and walk the rest of the way home.

The storm was clearing but a raw wind bit at my ears as I hustled along and thought about the late Senator Walker. Given her committee assignments — chairman of Energy and Natural Resources, and prominent seats on Appropriations and Agriculture — I was leaning away from the idea that a fanatic professional was behind the assassination.

As a matter of fact, I was tilting away from the idea of a fanatic at all. The entire thing felt surgical, or at least highly organized. Though I wasn't completely dismissing the idea of a terrorist, I was thinking a pro was responsible.

But why? Why a professional assassin? What had Senator Walker done to get gunned down in cold blood in front of her house? Who had she

24

crossed or destroyed?

Was the fact that she was shot outside her home meant as a statement, like a Mafia killing? Or was it merely a zone of opportunity?

I decided it was the latter. Before I left the crime scene, Lieutenant Lee had told me that the senator attended a yoga class Monday through Thursday. Every morning. It helped her clear her mind, he said.

It also helped her killer, I thought. *The shooter knew about the pattern through personal observation or because he had been told about it.*

Mr. and Mrs. Fairfax had been down in Palm Beach for two months. Mahoney believed it was possible the killer had been inside the house scouting Senator Walker multiple times and for extended periods. He had called for a second forensics team to comb the bedroom for DNA and microfibers, but I doubted they'd find much.

Making repeated trips inside the Fairfaxes' residence felt unprofessional to me. If I were a gun for hire, I'd want to spend as little time as possible in the kill zone. Whenever a human brushes up against something, he or she leaves tiny bits of skin and hairs that people like Sally Burton can gather and analyze. A trained assassin would know that.

No, I thought as I turned down Fifth Street and saw people out shoveling their sidewalks. *The killer went in there based on someone else's intelligence, so maybe once or twice, no more than —*

25

'Dad!'

I started, looked up, and saw a snowman in front of our house. Ali was beside it, excited and waving. I grinned. My youngest child had a real passion for life. Whatever he was into at the moment, he was fully there and usually having a heck of a good time.

'Nice one,' I said.

'I built it just since breakfast!'

'No school?'

'Snow day,' he said, beaming. 'I get to play.'

'Well, your dad gets to work. Have fun and don't get wet. You'll catch a cold.'

'You sound like Nana.'

'Maybe there's hope for me,' I said. I rubbed the top of his wool cap and went around the side of the house in fresh untracked snow up to my ankles to steps that led down to the basement door.

I used a key to open it and pushed the door in. Snow fell inside on the mat. So did a folded piece of paper.

I picked it up, unfolded it.

Alex Cross:
Stop Me, Please.

I turned it over. Nothing.

Behind me, in a trembling voice, a woman said, 'Dr. Cross?'

I pivoted to find a very attractive woman in her thirties looking down at me through the open door. Wearing a knit cap and mittens and

26

hugging herself in her baby-blue down coat, she had fresh tears on her cheeks. Her posture was hunched, which I read as more despondent than distressed.

'Yes, I'm Alex Cross,' I said, smiling. I stuffed the note in my jacket pocket and gestured her inside. 'I'm sorry about not shoveling the path in. Ms. Davis?'

Nina Davis smiled weakly through her tears as she passed me.

'I rather like all the snow, Dr. Cross,' she said. 'It reminds me of home.'

6

Nina Davis had been born and raised in Wisconsin, outside Madison, and she had always thought of snow as a bandage.

'You can't see the wounds and scars when there's snow falling,' she told me. 'I loved it as a child.'

We chatted while she filled out paperwork. Davis was thirty-seven, bright, attractive, and committed to her career at the U.S. Justice Department, where she was a supervising attorney working on organized-crime prosecutions.

'Once upon a time I was with the FBI,' I said.

'I know,' Davis said. 'It's why I sought you out, Dr. Cross. I figured you might understand or at least be sympathetic to my position.'

I smiled. 'I'll try to do both.'

Davis returned the smile without conviction. 'I don't know quite where to begin.'

'Tell me why you wanted to see me.'

She looked at her hands in her lap, shoulders slumped, and sighed. 'I don't think I know how to love, Dr. Cross.'

'Okay,' I said, and I settled in to listen, really listen.

Davis told me that in her entire life, she'd felt love for only one person: her father, Anderson Davis, a small-town attorney who had spent lots of time with his sole child. Katherine, his wife, had emotional problems and wasn't much interested in things physical. But Nina's father loved to hike and roam around the Wisconsin countryside.

'He called those walks tramps,' she said wistfully. 'He'd say, 'Come on, Nina, time for a tramp up to Beech Ridge.''

Davis blinked and wiped at a tear. 'Even now, I miss tramping with him. I was thirteen when he died.'

Tough age, I thought, and I made a note before saying, 'How did he die?'

'They were in the car, and my mother was driving. She was yelling at him about something, took her eyes off the road, and ran a red light. He was killed instantly.'

'I'm sorry to hear that. It must have been hard.'

Davis breathed in deep, pursed her lips, and shrugged. 'My dad was gone, and my mom killed him. What can you say?'

I absorbed that, then said gently, 'So you blame your mother?'

'Who else?' she said. 'She'd kept her eyes on the road, my dad would've lived to a ripe old age. She'd kept her eyes on the road, and I wouldn't have had a series of creepy men living in the house when I was a teenager.'

Davis had gone cold, and I decided to leave the statement for another time.

'She alive, your mother?'

'Last I heard.'

'When was that?'

'Three weeks ago, when I signed the monthly

check that pays for her assisted-living facility back home.'

'I'm hearing a lot of conflicted feelings,' I said. 'You blame her for all these things, and yet you stay involved in her care.'

'Yes, well, there's no one else to do it,' Davis said as another tear formed and slipped down her cheek.

The timer dinged. She looked disappointed.

'I promise you our next talk will be longer,' I said. 'When you're a one-man shop like I am, first sessions get taken up as much by paperwork as by real substance. And I charge your insurance for only a thirty-minute session rather than the hour. I can see you for a full hour tomorrow morning.'

Her knitted brow eased. 'That works.'

'Before you go, and just until we speak at our next appointment, I want you to remember those times when your mother made you happy, those times, maybe before your father's death, when you were grateful for her rather than resentful.'

Davis's laugh was short and sharp. 'I'll have to dig deep for memories like that.'

'I'd expect no less,' I said gently. We fixed a time for the next appointment, then I stood and opened my office door.

She walked through somewhat uncertainly, and I wondered whether she would ever return. I'd found over the years that a fair number of clients believed that they were going to get to the root of their problems in a session or two. When they realized that the process was less about cutting and more about peeling, some of them gave up. I never heard from them again.

'I'll see you tomorrow?' I asked as she opened the basement door.

'I'll be here, Dr. Cross,' she said, but she did not look back.

'I very much look forward to it, Nina,' I said, and I shut the door and the cold wind behind her.

Going back into my office, I wondered at the human brain's ability to seize on some terrible personal event and let that event define and control every action for years, decades, even lifetimes. I —

Three short, sharp knocks came at the basement door.

I was puzzled. I wasn't supposed to have another client until early afternoon.

When I opened the door, Ned Mahoney was standing there. Mahoney and I used to work together at the FBI, and he was normally as stoic a man as you'd find. But he was clearly upset as he came inside and shook snow off his pants legs.

I shut the door, and he looked at me. 'There's some kind of shitstorm brewing, Alex. We're going to need your help on this one, and more than part-time.'

7

Mahoney stared at me expectantly, waiting for an answer.

'I have just a few clients at the moment, Ned,' I said. 'The rest of my time is yours. Senator Walker's case?'

He hesitated before digging in an inner pocket of his coat. 'You've signed a recent nondisclosure form with us, the Bureau?'

'It's in the formal contract, but I'm happy to sign again if you think it's necessary.'

'No, no, of course not,' he said, pulling out his phone. 'It's just that this is sensitive in the extreme. You can't tell anyone, Bree and Sampson included.'

'John's on vacation in Belize, and I'll keep this close until I hear otherwise.'

'Good,' Mahoney said, and he looked at his phone. 'This was caught on a Dulles security cam a little more than two hours ago.'

He showed me a video still of a severe, dark-haired woman, more handsome than beautiful, who looked to be in her late thirties. She was dressed in denim, from her jeans to her blouse to her jacket. A shopping bag printed with a painting of the Eiffel Tower dangled off one arm. A leather knapsack hung from her other shoulder. She was pulling a carry-on roller and was in full stride.

'Who is she?'

'We believe her name is Kristina Varjan,' Mahoney said. 'A Hungarian-born freelance assassin.'

My mind raced. An assassin at Dulles International at 8:30 a.m., roughly three hours after Betsy Walker was shot?

I held up my hands. 'Wait. You *believe* this is Kristina Varjan?'

Mahoney paused, thinking, and then told me that two hours and twenty minutes before, a highly regarded and experienced CIA field agent was moving through crowded security lines en route to London and spotted her walking by. The agent had evidently had an up-close-and-personal run-in with Kristina Varjan in Istanbul several years earlier and had almost died as a result.

Having heard about the killing of Senator Walker, the agent got out of the TSA line and tried to pursue the woman to make sure. But the woman had vanished.

The agent missed the flight, made calls, pulled strings, and spoke to the Dulles security people. Camera feeds were rewound fifteen minutes, and they quickly found Varjan passing by the security lines. They tracked her, using footage from other security cameras, until she went outside into the snowstorm and walked off.

'So the agent had them track her backward,' Mahoney said. 'Turns out Varjan came off a Delta flight from Paris at eight a.m. That picture was taken in Customs. She's traveling using a Eurozone passport under the name Martina Rodoni.'

I studied the picture a long moment, then looked up at Ned. 'Which means she couldn't have killed Betsy Walker. The timing is off.'

'Correct.'

'Which means there are two professional assassins in the Greater DC area, one of whom killed a sitting U.S. senator.'

Mahoney nodded.

'Second assassin, second target?'

'I can't believe Varjan's here to see the monuments.'

'Put her picture in the hands of every cop within a hundred miles of DC.'

Mahoney looked conflicted. 'The director wants to keep this in-house with a full-court press to locate and pick her up for questioning.'

I cocked my head. 'He give you a reason?'

'National security,' Mahoney said though he didn't like it. 'Something about CIA intelligence-gathering methods. All above our pay grade. He did get the president to order heightened security for all members of Congress. In the meantime, you and I are supposed to find Varjan and bring her in.'

I thought about that a moment. Me and Ned in the field again. That felt good, so good that I put aside the questions about national security that kept popping into my head and turned to the task at hand.

'Can we get a file on Varjan? Something to help us put together a profile?'

'I can do you one better,' Mahoney said. 'We're going to talk to the CIA agent she almost killed.'

8

On the way to the Central Intelligence Agency in Langley, Virginia, I called Bree to tell her that the FBI had optioned my contract.

'Senator Walker's case?'

'Can't talk details.'

'The FBI's gain and Metro's loss,' she said. 'Remember, the game's tonight.'

'I haven't forgotten,' I said. 'I'll meet you there.'

'Promise?'

'Absolutely.'

Bree paused, then said, 'Got to go. The chief wants me in his office in ten minutes.'

Our connection died just as we pulled into the parking lot outside the CIA's security facility, a rectangular block built of bulletproof glass next to two solid steel gates that rose out of the ground to prevent unauthorized vehicular access.

We presented our credentials. The guards seemed to have been alerted to our arrival beforehand because, with no further ado, one of them took our photographs, printed visitors' badges with our faces on them, and clipped them to our jackets.

'Main entrance,' he said. 'Wait in the lobby. Someone will meet you there.'

'Someone,' Mahoney said after we passed through screening devices and were walking toward the main building. 'Do you think they always say that?'

'Makes sense.'

'I suppose.'

The wind picked up and blew granular snow at us, so we hustled to the entry. We entered a vaulted lobby with a large CIA seal set into the black-and-gray polished granite floor. We stood near the seal and watched as academic-looking folks in suits and others who were buff and more casually attired passed us.

'Analysts and operatives,' I murmured.

Before Ned could reply, a woman said, 'Special Agent Mahoney? Dr. Cross?'

We turned to find a trim, unassuming brunette woman in her thirties wearing a frumpy blue pantsuit walking across the lobby to us. She squinted at us through nerd glasses perched on the end of her nose, and she did not extend her hand.

'Would you follow me, please?'

She didn't wait for an answer but spun on her heel and marched off with us following close behind. We went down a long hallway, passing doors that had no identifiers. There were a lot of them, so I had no idea how she chose the right door to stop and use her key card on.

There was a soft click, and she turned the door handle and led us into a nondescript conference room with an empty table and chairs. She went around the table, took a seat, and folded her hands.

She squinted at us again. 'What can I tell you about Kristina Varjan?'

That surprised me. I thought she'd been taking us to see the spy.

Mahoney's eyebrows rose. 'You're the operative who spotted her this morning?'

'I am. You can call me Edith.'

'You look more like a soccer mom than a spy, Edith,' I said.

'That's the point,' she said dismissively.

Mahoney said, 'Tell us what we need to know to catch Varjan.'

'Catch her?' Edith said, and she laughed caustically. 'Good luck with that, gentlemen. God knows I tried. Here's what she gave me for my troubles.'

She took off her jacket and tugged a red sleeveless T-shirt off her left shoulder to reveal a nasty scar like interwoven spiderwebs below her collarbone.

Edith said she'd gotten the scar three years ago when the CIA began to suspect that Varjan had been responsible for the murder of two U.S. operatives in Istanbul. Edith's assignment had been to lure Varjan in, subdue her, and see her brought to an interrogation facility in Eastern Europe.

'I found her, and I thought I had her cornered entering an apartment building near the Bosporus,' she said. 'I was armed. She was not, or at least, not with a gun.'

Varjan surprised Edith and stabbed her repeatedly with a sharp pottery shard.

'I should have known better,' Edith said, shaking her head and crossing her arms. 'Varjan's an improviser. Invents weapons of the moment. Kills without hesitation.'

She told us that INS records showed that

37

Varjan had entered the U.S. that morning on a Eurozone passport under the name Martina Rodoni, a woman born in the former Yugoslavia who was now a resident of Ljubljana, Slovenia. Her occupation was listed as 'fashion consultant,' and she said she had come on business.

'Count on *not* finding her under that identity,' Edith said. 'She'll have shifted to another by now.'

'Then how do we figure out where she is?' I said. 'And what she's here to do?'

The CIA operative twisted her head to one side and pursed her lips a moment.

'I wish I could say I knew a habit of hers, a hotel chain she frequents or the kind of meals she likes to eat, but Varjan is a chameleon. She speaks eight languages and changes identity constantly. She knows it's her best defense.'

'So we've got nothing to go on?' Mahoney said.

'Well, you could do what I did to find her.'

'And what was that?' I asked.

'Figure out who she's here to kill and then lie in wait for her.'

I thought about that. 'Does she ever target politicians?'

'Dr. Cross, Kristina Varjan will target anyone if the price is right.'

9

Bree walked up to the closed double doors on the fifth floor of police headquarters downtown and knocked.

'Come in,' a familiar male voice called.

Bree opened the door and stepped inside the office of chief of police Bryan Michaels. The chief, a fit man with a thick shock of steel-gray hair, was on a cell phone, listening intently and nodding.

'I'm hearing you,' Michaels said in a firm tone. 'Loud and clear.'

He hung up, reached over to shake her hand, and gestured her to a chair. 'Where are we on Senator Walker's death?'

'Fourth in line, sir,' Bree said, taking the chair. 'FBI's got jurisdiction, with Secret Service and Capitol Police in support.'

He didn't seem to like that. 'So we're not even in the game?'

'I offered Ned Mahoney anything he needed from Metro PD,' Bree said. 'I'll be briefed on a daily basis.'

The chief said, 'I'm getting heat on this one, Bree. From the commissioner, the mayor, and the congressmen. They're all wondering how we're not out front on a murder in our own backyard. I'm wondering too.'

That surprised Bree. Chief Michaels was by nature a pragmatist, and he knew the command structure in a situation like this as well as she did.

Before she could reply, he said, 'Where's Alex in all this?'

'FBI snapped him up. I don't know exactly what he's working on.'

'Course not,' the chief said, shaking his head. 'I don't know if this consultant thing's going to work. It's . . . '

'Sir?'

'When Alex was on board full-time, I could count on Metro PD being out front no matter the case,' Michaels said.

'He's that kind of detective, sir,' Bree allowed.

'He is,' the chief said, and then he leaned across the desk. 'But he's unavailable. So I need you to step up, Bree. I want my chief of detectives to be hungry. Not a paper pusher. Not a caretaker. I want you to be bold, to take action, stand for something in the community. I mean, for God's sake, a U.S. senator was assassinated in *our* jurisdiction and we're not breaking ground?'

'Chief, again, and with all due respect, the FBI — '

'I don't give a rat's ass about the FBI or the Secret Service or the Capitol Police. This is *my* city, and *you* are its chief of detectives, Stone. Prove you still should be.'

Bree was taken aback for several moments before lifting her chin. 'And how exactly do I prove that, sir?'

'You find Senator Walker's assassin and deliver his head to Mahoney on a plate.'

40

10

Hands clasped behind his back, Sean Lawlor paced through a comfortable Airbnb apartment some five blocks from where he'd seen to the end of U.S. senator Betsy Walker.

Within hours of a successful strike on such a sensitive target, most other professional killers would have tried to leave the area, if not the city, if not the country. But Lawlor wasn't like most professionals. He was an elite practitioner, and he prided himself on thinking and acting outside the norm.

Given Senator Walker's stature, he had no doubt that the U.S. Citizenship and Immigration Services would be looking for people entering and leaving the country on a very short turnaround. That would have brought scrutiny he didn't need.

So Lawlor had decided to stay in Washington for three days before going to New York, where he planned to spend a long weekend. He would return to Amsterdam through Newark the following Monday.

He went to the kitchen and checked a laptop computer open on the counter. It showed a heavily encrypted internet browser linked in real time to one of his bank accounts in Panama. Nothing yet.

What the hell is taking so long?

Then again, Lawlor had sent an encrypted

copy of the thermal-imaging scope's memory file only three hours ago. He didn't know why that was necessary. Walker's death was all over cable news. It should have been enough.

He felt a buzzing in his pocket. He dug out a burn phone, checked the caller ID, and allowed himself a smile.

'I'm here, Piotr,' Lawlor said in Russian.

'Sergei,' Piotr replied. 'You've made my world happier.'

'I don't see the results in my account.'

'Large transfers take a while these days if you want them to move anonymously. In the meantime, are you free to meet and discuss your future?'

Lawlor checked his watch. 'If it's this evening.'

'That works. George Washington Hotel roof-top bar. Eight p.m. And you'll soon be receiving a token of appreciation for a job well done.'

Lawlor smiled, said, 'Thoughtful of you.'

'Even wolves have moments of kindness.'

Lawlor hung up and went to the bathroom to shower and shave.

When he was done, he padded back through the apartment, towel around his waist, and heard a *ding*.

He loped over to the laptop and was more than pleased to see that 1.4 million euros had just landed in his Panamanian account.

I like that, Lawlor thought. *I like that a lot.*

And who knew what Piotr had in mind for him now?

Someone in the lobby buzzed his apartment.

Lawlor stiffened. Very few people knew he was

in the United States, let alone in Georgetown, let alone in this apartment. Other than Piotr and the blokes he'd rented from, of course, and —

The buzzer went off again.

He shut the laptop cover, went to the front hallway, and pressed the intercom.

'Yes?' he said. 'Who is it?'

A woman with a Southern accent drawled, 'A gift from your happy agent.'

A gift from his happy agent? This kind of tip was unexpected but not unheard of in an assassin's line of work, especially if the strike had been of a sensitive nature, which this one had been. Still, he felt more than a little uneasy.

'Well?' the woman purred. 'Are you going to accept? Or should I go away and tell him you weren't interested?'

Lawlor hesitated, then thought: *How long has it been? Three, weeks? No, at least four.*

He thumbed the buzzer, said, 'Third floor, end of the hall.'

11

Excited but cautious, Lawlor hurried to the bedroom and pulled on dark slacks and a black V-neck T-shirt. He crossed to a suitcase and got out a small knife in a sheath hanging off a strap. He put it around his ankle, then found a small Ruger nine-millimeter pistol that he stuck in his waistband at the small of his back.

A gentle knock came at the apartment door. He slipped on running shoes, padded to the door, peered through the peephole, and saw a very chic woman in her thirties wearing a long black faux-fur coat that went well with her jet-black hair, high cheekbones, ruby lips, and pale skin.

Spectacular, he thought as he turned the door handle. *Bloody work of art.*

She stepped in. Lawlor smelled her perfume and her own intoxicating smell.

He closed the door, took her hand, spun her around, and pushed her firmly against the wall.

'Hey!' she protested, though she didn't struggle.

'Hands up against the wall,' he said. 'I need to check your purse and pockets.'

'For what?' she said, raising her hands.

'Things I don't like.'

He took the purse from her and set it aside. Then he patted her down from behind; he found nothing.

'Turn and open the coat.'

She sighed, pivoted, and undid the two hooks holding the coat shut.

The flaps fell away, revealing a very fit body in lacy black lingerie, stockings, stiletto heels, and nothing else.

'Surprise,' she said, smiling.

'Sorry, my sweet,' Lawlor said. 'Old habits.'

'You were a cop?' she asked, looking nervous.

'Soldier,' he said before picking up the purse and opening it.

'Where are you from?'

He didn't answer as he went through the purse, finding a cell phone, two condoms, a black elastic hair band, a small bottle of lubricant, a pair of thin latex surgical gloves, a small lint brush, a shower cap tucked in a sleeve that advertised the Willard hotel, a container of breath mints, and a tube of lipstick.

'Gloves?' Lawlor said.

She smirked. 'Some gents enjoy a little prostate massage.'

Lawlor grunted. 'None of that.'

She shrugged. 'Are we done or do you want to do a full strip search?'

'We're done,' he said, handing her the purse.

'You're not much for setting the mood,' she said, taking it.

'Give me time.'

She grinned saucily at him.

He gestured toward the hallway, said, 'Can I take your coat?'

'It's part of the show,' she said, and she giggled pleasantly as she headed down the short passage into the sitting area. 'Nice place.'

'Airbnb,' he said.

'No kidding?' she said, sounding impressed. She looked around before walking to the thermostat. 'Mind if I make it . . . hot in here?'

'By all means.'

She fiddled with the gauge and then turned to regard him. She seemed to like what she saw. 'You work out?'

'I do. You?'

'Every day. You're British?'

'Long time ago. You?'

'Florida. You an actor now or something?'

Lawlor cocked his head.

'Your 'happy agent'?'

'Oh, he's more like a broker. I do security work. He sets me up with the gigs.'

'Sounds dangerous,' she said, crossing the room to a small leather club chair and setting her purse on an end table. 'Stressful.'

'Sometimes,' he admitted. 'Can I get you a drink? Vodka?'

She smiled as she patted the chair. 'This is about your stress, not mine, baby. Be a doll, now, sit right here and let me take care of every little thing.'

Lawlor looked at her, thought, *Gotta be four weeks at least.*

He went and took the seat. She tugged off a lace-and-leather glove with her teeth, got out her cell phone, and tapped at it until Ariana Grande started to sing 'Love Me Harder.'

She set the phone down on the side table, slipped the glove back on, and danced with the

46

music, gliding her hips from side to side, gripping the lapels of the fur coat, and teasing him with more glimpses of what he'd already seen. She straddled his legs and ground ever so softly against him while leaning in for a kiss.

Under her weight, Lawlor felt his pistol press into his back, and he shifted slightly before letting her lips meet his. When she drew back, the assassin was already aroused. She ran her leather-clad fingers down his chest, stopped above his waist, then stood again, her humid eyes on him as the music picked up.

Singing the chorus, she took a few steps back and let the coat fall open. 'Like what you see?'

'I'd have to be an imbecile to not love what I'm seeing, lass.' He chuckled.

She liked that. She danced over, trailed her hands across his chest again, then slipped around the back of the chair. She leaned over and nuzzled his neck, letting her hair fall against him.

'This is going to feel so good,' she whispered in his ear. 'So good.'

He shivered when she ran the tip of her tongue along the top of his ear. 'It is good right now.'

'Just you wait, doll,' she murmured, then she straightened and flipped a loop of piano wire over his head.

12

During his search, Lawlor had not detected the length of piano wire that had been slipped into the lining of the right sleeve of Kristina Varjan's coat. But the instant Lawlor felt the wire touch his throat, he seemed to know what he was in for.

Like the professional he was, Lawlor did not thrash or reach up and try to grab at the wire as Varjan cinched the loop tight and wrenched it back. Instead, he arched hard in her direction.

Gun at the small of his back, Varjan thought, remembering the way he'd shifted when she'd straddled him. *Gun now!*

Lawlor's left hand came up with a small Ruger pistol; he twisted it her way and fired a split second after she flung herself to her right, still holding on to the wire. The pistol barked. The muzzle blasted so close to her ear, she thought her eardrum had ruptured.

Years of training forced her to swallow the pain and fight. As Lawlor choked and tried to aim at her again, Varjan let go of the wire with her left hand and used it to chop savagely at the curve of his neck, right where it met his shoulder.

The blow stunned his whole arm. The pistol went off a second time, but the bullet flew well wide of her. She chopped again and again until Lawlor dropped the pistol.

Varjan grabbed hold of the piano wire with both hands this time and threw her knee into the back of the chair; she heard Lawlor choke hard, and then the slick sounds of the wire cutting through his skin and into muscle.

Lawlor arched again, came up with a knife from somewhere, and tried to stab her. He missed.

She stepped away from the blade and wrenched and twisted the wire as hard as she could, then heard a noise like melon rind separating as the garrote broke through Lawlor's trachea. He made gurgling and gasping noises, stopped trying to stab her, dropped the knife, and began to thrash and try to dig the wire out of his neck with his right hand.

Every movement made the wire cut deeper; the struggle made the end come that much quicker. Thirty seconds later, Lawlor collapsed and died.

Varjan let go of the wire and fell to her hands and knees, chest heaving, her fingers numb, sweat boiling off her brow. She stayed that way, panting, for several moments before her instincts kicked in.

The gunshots had changed everything. She was aware of time and of the impending threat. She glanced at her watch: 4:12 p.m.

Still breathing hard, she went to her purse, which had fallen to the ground in the struggle, and retrieved the latex gloves and the shower cap. She stripped off the leather gloves as she hurried back to the apartment door and put on the latex gloves and the shower cap while taking glances out the peephole and listening. No doors had opened. No one was in the hall looking. *But what if people downstairs had heard? What if they'd made a call?*

She looked at her watch again. A minute and forty seconds had passed since she'd checked, and it had been perhaps a minute before that when the pistol was shot twice. She left the door, crossed to the drapes, and looked out; she saw a few pedestrians on the sidewalks below but heard no sirens.

Just in case, she pushed up one of the sashes so she could hear the street and returned to stand in front of Lawlor, who was bent over to his left, his eyes dull and bugged wide, his face a pallid blue.

The piano wire had severed his carotid at the end. The blood was all down the front of him, pooled in his lap.

She used the lint brush to quickly remove any strands of hair or flakes of skin she might have left on his clothes. Then she went to the sink cabinet and found kitchen garbage bags.

Varjan plucked out two and left one on the counter. She brought the other one to Lawlor's side, removed the piano wire from his neck, and bagged it.

She went to the front door and looked out the peephole. Nothing. She listened at the window. Quiet.

She found an abrasive cleanser with bleach in the bathroom, and she used it and a damp sponge to wipe down the places she'd touched the dead assassin, even those places already covered in blood. She also wiped the rug where she'd knelt and sweated, then she put the sponge in the bag with the piano wire.

Nearly fifteen minutes had passed since the shot, and still she heard no sirens.

Emboldened, Varjan quickly searched the rest of the apartment and found a high-dollar thermal-imaging rifle scope in the nightstand drawer. She put it in her purse along with Lawlor's cell phone and passport. She examined the contents of his wallet, took five hundred in cash, and left the rest.

Varjan was about to put Lawlor's laptop in the other garbage bag but decided to raise the lid first. To her surprise, the screen showed not a password prompt but a bank account in Panama that held more than one million euros and a million British pounds.

When she realized the link to the account was open and active, Varjan almost laughed out loud. Within five minutes, she had emptied the account and transferred the funds to an account of her own in El Salvador.

When she figured in the payment for killing Lawlor, it was easily the most profitable day of her career.

Her cell phone rang. She started, but answered.

'We are good?' Piotr said.

'We are good,' she said, dropping the Southern accent as she signed out of the bank's website and erased the history.

'I'm just about to leave.'

'The phone? His laptop?'

51

'Already packed. I'll drop them where you left the coat.'

'I like that.'

'Piotr, should I be looking over my shoulder now?'

'I do not understand.'

'Of course you do. He wasn't just here for fun, and I pay attention to the news.'

'You were strictly cleanup, and there's no reason to clean up the cleanup.'

Varjan didn't trust Piotr because she didn't trust anyone, but she let it slide. 'Payment?'

'Within the hour?'

'Fine.'

He cleared his throat. 'Are you committed to leaving the States, or would you consider other proposals?'

She thought about the money she'd just looted from Lawlor's secret account, the money she'd receive within the hour, and the money she had stashed in various places around the world.

'Depends on the time frame,' Varjan said. 'And the money.'

'Four days from now, seven-figure payday, specifics to follow,' Piotr said. 'I am sure you can amuse yourself somewhere on the East Coast in the meantime?'

She smiled and headed toward the door. 'Yes, this I am sure of.'

13

As a crowd of people moved past us toward the Verizon Center in Gallery Place, I looked incredulously at Bree.

'You're kidding me,' I said. 'Michaels actually told you to solve Walker's murder in order to prove you were worthy of being COD?'

'I'm supposed to serve his head to Ned on a platter,' Bree said, upset. 'I don't get it. I thought I'd been doing a solid job.'

'You've been doing a great job.'

'I think he wants me to replace you, and you're irreplaceable.'

'Well, thank you for that, I think, but you're a damn fine investigator, Bree. If he's redefining your job, go with it.'

'And how exactly am I supposed to find Walker's killer?' she said, crossing her arms. 'Charge in, tell you and Ned and the FBI and the Secret Service and the Capitol Police, 'Butt out, Chief Stone is here'?'

I grinned. 'I could actually see you pulling that one off.'

'Big help you are,' Bree said, and she looked so forlorn I hugged her.

'We'll get through whatever comes our way,' I said, rubbing her back. 'As long as we're together, we'll be — '

'Dad, c'mon! The game's gonna start!'

I looked up the sidewalk toward the Verizon

Center and saw Jannie in a blue down parka waving at me.

'Be right there!' I said, and then I put my knuckle under Bree's chin. 'Let's set this aside for the next hour and a half, okay? Our boy's in town.'

Bree nodded and smiled. 'And I'm grateful for that.'

'Me too,' I said, putting my arm around her shoulder.

We walked to the Verizon Center, a massive athletics complex in Northwest DC, and gave the ticket taker our tickets. Pounding techno music poured out of the speaker system. We found Jannie, Nana Mama, and Ali sitting in a cluster in the tenth and eleventh rows above center court.

'How's it looking?' I asked, taking a seat beside my grandmother, Bree sitting down behind me with Jannie and Ali.

'Davidson versus Goliath,' said Nana Mama, who'd been a basketball fan forever. 'And I hate to say it, but with a few notable exceptions, Davidson wasn't looking too strong during warm-ups.'

'Where's the faith, Nana?' Jannie said, sounding irritated. 'We could see the break-through tonight. Anything's possible once things start.'

'The way Georgetown's been playing?' said Ali, who watches a lot of basketball with my grandmother. 'Davidson's going to get stomped.'

The music changed, the recording taken over by a live pep band playing, 'Final Countdown.'

Members of the Georgetown University Hoyas men's basketball team charged onto the court with a full light show in progress.

The local crowd went wild, clapping and stomping their feet while the Hoyas went through a few last-minute layup drills.

'Here come the Wildcats!' Jannie said.

The Davidson College team ran out in their sweats and started their own final warm-up drills. As Nana Mama had said, with a few notable exceptions, the Wildcats looked nervous.

My oldest child, Damon, was one of the exceptions. A six-foot-five guard and three-point specialist who usually came off the bench, he entered the court looking all business and ready.

Damon had played at Division II Johns Hopkins, my alma mater. He played so well in a summer league that he attracted the attention of a Davidson coach, Jake Winston, who offered him a walk-on slot if he transferred.

Under Coach Winston's guidance, Damon had blossomed into a solid NCAA Division I player.

'C'mon, Damon!' Jannie cried as he dribbled in and made a nice jump shot. She whistled and clapped, and that made me happy.

My older son's basketball abilities came late and had been hard fought for. Athletically, Damon had long been overshadowed by Jannie's track exploits. He was the sixth man on a team ranked fifth in the Atlantic Coast Conference. She was being recruited by the top track schools in the nation.

So it was nice seeing my boy get his chance in the spotlight. It was even better seeing how much his little sister was supporting him.

14

Near Dupont Circle in Washington, DC, a man calling himself Pablo Cruz, a fit man with hawkish features wearing a Washington Nationals hoodie, jeans, and work boots, adjusted the shoulder straps of the heavy, black dry bag on his back.

He ambled down New Hampshire Avenue, then made a right on M Street. Near the bridge into Georgetown, he took a right onto Twenty-Sixth Street and went to the dead end.

Cruz glanced around before hurrying past a sign that said Rock Creek Park was closed after dark. Twenty yards down-slope, he left the path, cut to his right, and peered up at the lights in the nearest apartment building, focusing on two windows on the third floor on adjacent walls of a corner.

When he got the angle on that corner right, still watching those two windows over his shoulder, he backed down the slope woods. He shuffled his feet through the leaves and wondered if his read of the city's drainage schematics was correct.

His left heel found the edge of the corrugated drainpipe, and he smiled. Cruz got around and below it. He felt for the edge of the cover, found it, and retrieved a hammer, a chisel, and a headlamp from the dry bag.

Cruz turned on the lamp's soft red light

feature and waited until he heard a bus crossing the M Street Bridge over the park before attacking the spot welds that held the cover in place. Twenty minutes later, he pried the cover off and set it aside.

He turned the lamp off and returned it, along with his tools, to the dry bag, then sealed the bag and put it inside the drainpipe a few feet back. Then he replaced the cover and tamped it into place.

Done, he climbed above the pipe and looked at those windows on the third floor of the apartment building again. Cruz fixed the image in his mind.

He left then, angling back across the slope to the path up to Twenty-Sixth Street and telling himself he could find his way here again, even in the pitch-dark, even under the threat of death.

15

As both teams lined up at center court inside the Verizon Center, the overall height disparity was clearly in favor of Georgetown, then in first place in the Atlantic Coast Conference and ranked fourteenth in the nation.

The overall muscle disparity went the Hoyas' way as well.

Georgetown's center had two inches on our six-foot-seven pivot man, and he easily swatted the ball to one of his guards, who passed across the court to an attacking power forward, who went all the way in for a resounding slam dunk.

The Davidson players looked flat-footed in comparison to the Georgetown team. Damon was sitting on the bench when Kendall Barnes, the Wildcats' starting point guard, took the ball.

Barnes was as quick a young man as I'd ever seen. But coming up-court and cutting to his right, he failed to pick up a Hoya defender, who slashed in and fingered the ball out of Barnes's control.

The Hoya went the length of the court and let go with another thunderous slam dunk that threatened to shatter the backboard.

The people in the Verizon Center crowd went nuts, giving each other high-fives and taunting the Davidson players, who looked dazed. Coach Winston wisely called a time-out to try to calm his team. I twisted in my seat.

Ali said, 'This isn't David versus Goliath, Dad. It's more like prisoners fighting lions in ancient Rome.'

Jannie punched him lightly on the shoulder. 'You know too much.'

Ali shot her a superior look. 'I didn't know that was possible.'

Bree said, 'Anyone hungry?'

After getting a manageable order of hot dogs, chips, and sodas, Bree got up and left just before the teams retook the court.

'Damon's in!' Jannie said.

I looked out and saw she was right. Damon had been subbed in at guard to play opposite Barnes. Coach Winston had also replaced one of the starting forwards for a lanky true freshman from Missouri named Tanner Ott.

Barnes had the ball again. He acted as if he was going to make the same forward charge and cut right. When he feinted that way, the Hoyas bought it and shifted. Barnes flicked the ball behind him to Damon, who was set up in three-point range.

Damon received the ball, set, and sprang into his release.

'Nothing but net!' Jannie screamed before the ball even reached the hoop and swished through.

We were all on our feet cheering as Damon spun in his tracks, pumping his fist.

The Hoyas guard brought the ball up-court and tried to flick it to his center. But Tanner Ott intercepted the pass and drove the length of the court to an easy layup.

'We're ahead by one!' Jannie cried, leaping to

her feet and clapping.

That lead went to four when Damon dropped another three-point bomb, and the Hoyas called their own time-out.

Things got uglier for Davidson after that.

The Hoyas sank five straight field goals and then a three-pointer before Barnes worked to Ott, who drew a foul scoring inside. From then on, it was a real pitched battle.

Coach Winston had taught his Davidson team to use their superior speed to swarm on defense and to stay aggressive enough with their bigger opponents to draw fouls on offense. The Wildcats took a physical beating, but the free-throw shooters and Damon's third three-pointer kept the score a respectable 43 to 37 at the half.

'I can't believe the score's that low,' Ali said.

Jannie said, 'I bet Georgetown's thinking the same thing.'

'Davidson has a good defense, I'll grant you that,' Nana said between bites of the hot dog Bree had brought her.

'Think they can keep it up?' Bree asked me.

I smiled and shrugged. 'I think they can consider it a victory to be only six points behind a nationally ranked team at the half.'

Ali said, 'So you're saying if they lost by twelve points, it would still be a victory?'

'Okay, an achievement,' I said.

'It *is* an achievement,' Bree said. 'I'm impressed by their poise.'

The second half was harder fought than the first. Georgetown came onto the court trying to put Davidson away for good. But through the third quarter, the Wildcats chipped the Hoyas' lead to four and then to one when Damon fed to Barnes, who sank from three-point land.

Two of Georgetown's best players fouled out early in the fourth quarter. You could see the concern in the faces of the Hoyas when their coach called time-out. You could feel it in the crowd too.

The Wildcat players looked out of their minds, especially Ott, Barnes, and Damon, who was as pumped up as I'd ever seen him. Winston kept my son in the game and Damon delivered, dropping two more three-pointers, three field goals, and a free throw in the fourth quarter.

The game was tied with a minute left, and even skeptical Ali and Nana were on their feet cheering wildly for Davidson. The Hoyas scored on their first possession, an easy layup. Then Barnes fed Ott in the paint, and he laid the shot in and drew a foul.

His free throw dropped with twenty-nine seconds left. Down by one, Georgetown called its last time-out.

'I'm going to faint if this goes on much longer,' my grandmother said.

'We'll hold you up,' Jannie said. She took one of her hands and Ali took the other.

Bree's cell rang. She answered and listened.

'I'll be right there,' she said and then hung up.

'You can't leave now,' I said.

'I have to. Murder in Georgetown five blocks from where Walker was shot.'

'That was hours ago.'

'I'm looking for straws to grasp at.'

'Need company?'

'Can't; you're under FBI contract. Michaels would have my head if I let you in. Text me what happens?'

I nodded and kissed her. 'Be safe.'

She slipped down the aisle and disappeared before the referee blew his whistle. Georgetown brought the ball out-of-bounds and up-court in three long and precise passes. But the Wildcats' pesky defense kept them from getting an immediate shot.

When the Hoyas passed a fourth time, Barnes darted forward, intercepted it, and passed to Ott, who slammed the ball through Georgetown's hoop with eighteen seconds on the clock.

'We're up by three!' Ali squealed.

Neither team had time-outs left. Georgetown tried to break quickly up-court, but Barnes and Damon kept pressing the Hoyas.

When they tried to come inside with a lob pass to their center, Ott sprang and batted the ball. The Hoyas' guard snatched it up before Ott could steal, however, and passed it to Georgetown's best outside shooter.

He set to release, and I thought for sure we were heading into overtime. But Damon came leaping laterally and wind-milling his right hand.

After the shot, my son's fingers brushed the ball just enough that it caromed off the rim and into Barnes's able hands. He dribbled away from the Hoyas chasing and trying to foul him.

He was just too quick. The buzzer went off, and the Wildcats went crazy.

'Upset of the year!' Jannie cried, and we all cheered as if Damon and Davidson College had made the Final Four.

Part Two

TIME OF DEATH

16

Bree drank from a cup of hot black coffee as she surveyed the scene inside the apartment in Georgetown. The victim, a white male in his fifties, sat slumped in a club chair. Blood had spilled from his neck wound to his lap and clotted on his chest and belly like an apron.

'Time of death?' she asked Evelynn Kincaid, a top medical field examiner.

'Four or five hours ago?' said Kincaid, a tall lanky woman who used to play volleyball at Purdue. 'The heat was turned up, so I'll need more tests to be precise.'

'Nasty neck wound. The knife?' Bree said, gesturing to a switchblade on the carpet near the corpse.

Kincaid shook her head. 'That's his knife. There's a scabbard for it around his right ankle, and there's no blood on the blade.'

'So what was the weapon?'

The ME put on reading glasses, peered at the victim's neck. 'He's got bruising and skin abrasions above and below the wound. And the edges are ragged. Could be a thin rope, but I'm thinking small-gauge wire.'

'From behind?'

'I'd say so,' Kincaid said. 'The killer had to be plenty strong for the wire to cut deep like that. And smart. Victim got a shot off with that little Ruger in the corner, but it missed. Bullet hole is in the south wall, over there.'

'No one heard the shot?'

Natalie Parks, the detective on the scene, said, 'No one yet.'

'We have an ID? Who found him?'

Detective Parks said they'd found a driver's license and credit cards that identified the deceased as Carl Thomas of Pittsburgh, Pennsylvania, and business cards that pegged him as a medical-equipment salesman. A maid for the apartment's owners had arrived to bring clean towels around seven p.m. and found Thomas in his present state.

'I've already spoken with the owners,' Parks said. 'Thomas booked online nine days ago. He indicated in his application he was going to combine business with tourism and stay for three nights.'

Bree thought about that. 'Anything linking him to Senator Walker's killing?'

Parks and Kincaid both seemed surprised by the question.

'Two killings seventeen hours and five blocks apart,' Bree said. 'And this guy is armed not only with a pistol, but a knife he carries in an ankle sheath. So until we prove otherwise, we're considering these murders connected. Meantime, I want his prints run. Anything else? Itinerary? Phone? Computer?'

Parks shook her head. 'Nothing beyond the wallet and the IDs, Chief.'

'Killer took them. Clothes?'

'An overnight suitcase. A down parka, hat, gloves.'

'How'd he get here? Where's his car?'

'No idea yet.'

'Nothing that said 'shooter' in that overnight bag?'

'No bullets or rifle components, if that's what you mean,' Parks said.

Bree's phone rang. Dispatch.

Bree sighed and answered. 'This better be good. I'm running on fumes.'

'Chief, we've had officers under fire, a high-speed chase on Blair Road, and now an armed standoff in Takoma, multiple weapons involved,' the dispatcher said.

Bree started toward the door fast, barking questions at the dispatcher. She was told that it started when a Metro patrol unit had pulled over a Cadillac Escalade with California plates for failure to make a full stop at a blinking light. There were three males in the car. The officer ran the plates and found them registered to Fernando Romero of Oakland.

The name had rung bells.

'What kind of bells?' Bree demanded, leaving the apartment crime scene.

'Romero's a big gangbanger with ties to the Mexican drug cartels. He's got a long history of violence and three felony warrants out for his arrest, including one for threatening bodily harm to a U.S. senator two weeks ago.'

'Betsy Walker?' Bree said, running now.

'That's affirmative.'

17

We waited outside the Verizon Center until Damon emerged as happy as I'd ever seen him. And not just because he'd played an integral part in the upset of the NCAA season. He had his arm around a very pretty young Asian woman.

'This is my girlfriend, Song Li,' he said. 'She's from Hong Kong and goes to Davidson, a transfer like me.'

Girlfriend, I thought. *That's a first for Damon.*

'Song Li,' Nana said, walking up and taking her hand. 'What a beautiful name.'

Song smiled shyly and said in a soft British accent, 'Thank you, Mrs. Hope. Damon has told me so much about you, I feel like I know you.'

'You can call me Nana or Nana Mama like everyone else, dear,' my grandmother said.

Jannie appeared suspicious until Song turned to her and said, 'Are you the fabled Jannie?'

My daughter laughed. 'Fabled?'

'Damon brags on you almost every day.'

'That's not true,' Damon protested. 'Well, maybe almost every other day.'

'Dr. Cross?' Song said. She shook my hand and bowed her head. 'It is indeed an honor to meet you. My father will be most pleased.'

'It's nice to meet you too, Song,' I said. 'Your father?'

Damon said, 'He's a detective in Hong Kong.

It's how Song and I got to talking.'

Song smiled. 'When I told my father who Damon's father was, he got very excited. He has watched the tapes of your FBI seminars on profiling and homicide investigations. He says you are one of the best in the world.'

'I don't know about that. But it's very flattering and kind of him to say so.'

'I will tell him,' Song said. Beaming, she turned to Ali. 'Damon says you are studying Chinese in school?'

Ali rattled off something in Chinese that made Song laugh and clap her hands. She replied to Ali, and he started laughing as well.

'Okay,' Nana said. 'Fill the rest of us in?'

Song said, 'Ali said it was nice to meet a daughter of Hong Kong.'

Ali grinned. 'And she said it was nice to meet the brother of Mr. Basketball.'

'Mr. Basketball?' Damon said.

Song clapped again, laughed, and said, 'He has a very good ear. How long have you been studying, Ali?'

'A year?' he said.

'That's amazing!'

'Here's the Uber car, Dad,' Jannie said.

Damon looked at me. 'Can Song come with us? Stay at the house tonight?'

'Of course,' I said. 'She fits right in.'

Damon grinned and put his arm around her again. 'She does, doesn't she?'

'C'mon, then,' Nana Mama said. 'Get in, you two must be hungry.'

'Damon is always hungry,' Song said, shaking

her head and looking awed enough that we all chuckled.

We climbed into the car and set off toward home.

Damon said, 'Can Song sleep in your old attic office, Dad?'

I was slightly relieved to hear the plan. 'That's fine. You can blow up the mattress for her up there.'

On the ten-minute ride, Nana Mama gently interrogated Song, and we learned that she was born in Hong Kong, her mother worked in financial services, and her father had spent two years with Scotland Yard in London before returning home to head the detective and special investigations bureau for the Hong Kong police force.

'So he's like Bree?' Ali said.

I nodded. 'Sounds like it.'

Damon said, 'Where is Bree, anyway?'

18

When Bree reached the Takoma area of Washington, DC, patrol cars had blocked off both ends of Aspen Street between Seventh and Tenth.

'FBI here?' she asked a patrol officer.

'Not yet, Chief.'

'Secret Service, Capitol Police?'

'Negative; Metro SWAT's en route.'

That helped. Bree ducked under the crime scene tape and kept low as she hustled toward another patrol car up the block where two officers were crouched, their weapons drawn. The side windows of the cruiser were blown out. So was the windshield. Half a block beyond them, in the middle of the street, there was a midnight-blue Cadillac Escalade with California plates and an abandoned city snowplow.

'You the ones who pulled them over?' Bree said when she reached the officers.

'Wiggins and Flaherty, Chief,' said Officer Wiggins, a blonde in her thirties.

Flaherty said that getting the alert regarding Romero's felonies had taken long enough to make the gangbanger and his friends anxious.

'When they saw me climb out of the car, one of the two in the back opened fire, and Romero hit the gas.'

They gave chase for more than a mile before Romero saw the snowplow coming at them down

73

Aspen Street between Eighth and Ninth. They couldn't get around the plow, and they abandoned the Escalade in the middle of the street.

Armed with pistols and AR-style rifles, Romero shot at the snowplow, shattering the windshield and sending the operator scrambling out the other door and down the street. One of the other two opened up on the patrol car before the three of them forced their way into a yellow craftsman bungalow on the north side of the street.

'Time of last shots?' Bree asked.

'Nine minutes ago,' Wiggins said. 'And we've got officers watching the back of the house. They're still in there.'

'Hostages?'

'We're assuming so,' Flaherty said. 'According to city records, residents are Matthew Sheridan, his wife, Sienna, and their eight-year-old twins, Emma and Kate.'

Before Bree could reply, a gun went off in the house.

A woman started screaming, and then girls' shrill voices joined her.

Bree radioed dispatch, reported the shot and the hostages, and requested that the entire neighborhood be cordoned off.

Bree clicked off and her phone immediately rang. Chief of Police Michaels.

'What's happening?' he demanded.

Bree told him about Romero. 'He threatened Senator Walker two weeks ago in Oakland. Now he's here in DC armed to the teeth with two of his fellow bangers.'

74

'You think he killed Walker?'

'When pulled over nearly three thousand miles from home, he and his men responded with violence, and they've taken hostages. There's also a homicide victim in Georgetown who may or may not be involved.'

'Jesus,' Michaels said. 'What do you need from me?'

She looked down the street behind her, saw a big black SWAT van pulling up.

'The cavalry just arrived, Chief,' Bree said. 'I'll let you know if anything — '

More screams came from the house.

'Sorry, Chief, gotta go,' Bree said. She hung up and peeked over the hood of the patrol car.

Emma and Kate, the terrified eight-year-old Sheridan twins, came out the front door, followed closely by two of the gangsters. The men were wearing kerchiefs over their lower faces, holding on to the collars of the sisters' nightgowns, and pressing pistol muzzles to the backs of the girls' heads, using the children as human shields.

'We ain't waiting for no SWAT or negotiators,' one shouted. 'Get that plow the hell out of here. You let us move on, or we kill them and go out in a blaze!'

'No!' a woman screamed.

Bree peeked again and saw a brunette in a Washington Redskins jersey, jeans, and socks come out the door with the third man behind her. Bree recognized Romero from the picture that dispatch had sent. He held an AK-47 pressed to the back of a sobbing Sienna Sheridan.

He said something to her.

'Believe him!' she cried. 'He shot my husband. He'll kill us all.'

'So what's it gonna be?' Romero yelled as his men started down the front steps. 'A peaceful ending? Or a goddamned bloodbath?'

19

Bree took the bullhorn that Officer Wiggins offered her.

'This is Chief Stone of Metro PD,' she said, trying to sound calm. 'No one wants bloodshed here, Mr. Romero.'

'Then let us leave!' Romero yelled. 'Now.'

'You're going to have to give me time to clear the streets,' she called out. 'It's not like I have the keys to that snowplow at my fingertips.'

'Five minutes, then!' Romero said.

'Fifteen.'

'No. Ten! And after that we don't give a damn about no East Coast bullshit, and little girls and Mommy gonna start dying, just like that bitch Betsy Walker did!'

Betsy Walker. My God, Bree thought as they dragged the girls and their mother back inside the bungalow. *He did kill her. Romero is the shooter!*

She dropped behind the cruiser and keyed her radio mike.

'DC SWAT, this is Chief Stone.'

'Captain Forchek here, Chief. SWAT is armored and ready to deploy.'

A plan formulated quickly in her head. 'Captain, I need a team ready to push forward in support of my current location. I want quality shooters up high, with a clear view to that Land Rover. And put teams on porches on the southwest and northwest corners of Aspen and Tenth. Your best officers. Block off Ninth, north and south.'

'Roger that, Chief.'

From the house, Romero yelled, 'Seven minutes, Stone!'

'I hear you, Mr. Romero,' she said through the bullhorn. 'We're trying to find the snowplow operator.'

A rattle of gunfire went off inside before he shouted, 'There's no *trying*! We're about *doing* here, right?'

'Right, Mr. Romero,' she said, and then she ducked back behind the cruiser, still working out her strategy.

She looked at Officer Wiggins. 'Where *is* the snowplow driver?'

'With Barstow and Hayes,' she said. 'Other end of the street.'

Bree jumped up and started running east. She keyed her mike. 'Forchek, send your best driver to Aspen and Eighth.'

'That would be me,' the SWAT captain said. 'And I'm already on my way.'

Bree checked her watch as she ran. Six minutes.

Near the corner of Eighth, she cut right into an alley that wound back around south and then to the west, paralleling the hostage scene.

Bree triggered her mike. 'Where are we, Captain?'

'We are go at twenty-two hundred five, Chief. I'm driving the plow?'

'Roger that,' she said.

78

She checked her watch: 10:00. Five minutes. Was it enough?

It had to be enough. She focused on an image of Jannie and went from a run to a sprint, dodging trashcans and the odd stack of boxes for three blocks, trying not to slip in the snow. She turned back north on Tenth and raced toward the other cruiser blocking access to Aspen.

Captain Forchek, a rangy guy even in his body armor, stood there waiting with two uniformed officers and their cruiser blocking Aspen.

Gasping, she laid out her plan to the SWAT commander.

Forchek listened, thought, and then smiled. 'As long as the department backs me up afterward, I can do that, Chief.'

'Good,' she said, and she nodded to the other officers. 'Pull your car and retreat to Eleventh and Aspen. Park north on Eleventh. Stand ready to block Aspen on my command.'

20

Ninety seconds later, Captain Forchek ran crouched along the snow-packed south sidewalk of Aspen Street, sticking to the shadows until he was half a block from the snowplow.

Bree watched him through binoculars from the front porch of a town house at the southeast corner of Tenth and Aspen. Four SWAT officers awaited her command behind her, across Tenth. Another four waited on a porch across Aspen. The last of the twelve was diagonally across from her on the northwest corner of the intersection.

She keyed the bullhorn.

'Mr. Romero, we are moving the snowplow. I am assuring you safe passage as long as you leave the hostages behind.'

'You think I'm stupid?' Romero bellowed. 'They're staying with us until we decide to let them go. Just move the damn snowplow and get the hell out of our way!'

Suit yourself, Bree thought as she watched Forchek creep between two cars and angle onto the street itself, keeping the snowplow between him and the Sheridans' bungalow. He climbed in the open side door.

She keyed her mike. 'Nice and easy now, Captain.'

'Roger that, Chief.'

The snowplow engine turned over. Bree

swung her binoculars to the front porch of the Sheridans' house and saw Mrs. Sheridan and her daughters coming out. Romero and his two masked men were behind them.

'Move that goddamned plow!' Romero shouted.

Forchek lifted the snowplow's blade, turned on the headlights, and drove.

Bree watched Romero and his men hustling Sienna, Emma, and Kate Sheridan off the porch and down the short path toward the north sidewalk.

The moving snowplow blocked her view for several moments before Forchek drove past her, slowed, swung the plow in reverse, and backed it up onto Tenth Street heading north. He stopped the plow about fifty yards from the intersection, right where Bree wanted him. The plow headlights died.

Bree looked back at the Escalade and saw Romero already in the front passenger seat aiming his gun at a trembling Sienna Sheridan, who was behind the wheel. The other four were in the backseat, one girl at each window, Romero's men in the middle.

Real heroes.

Calling their positions into her radio, Bree watched the headlights on the Escalade go on, and the big SUV started toward her.

'Here we go,' she said. 'On my call, Forchek.'

'Roger that, Chief.'

The SWAT officers on both sides of Aspen ducked low. Bree pushed back into the shadows, watching through binoculars. For a moment, she held her breath as the Escalade approached

Ninth. She feared Romero might turn onto the side street but sighed with relief when he kept on coming.

'He's taking the easy way out,' she said into her mike. 'Ten seconds, Captain.'

The Cadillac's headlights swayed closer.

Bree dropped the binoculars, let them hang around her neck, and drew her service weapon. The snowplow's lights were still off, but Forchek had it moving in a slow roll toward Aspen.

She glanced from the accelerating SUV to the plow and said, 'Now.'

She heard the plow's big diesel engine roar and saw it barreling toward Aspen and the approaching Cadillac. The Escalade almost got through the intersection. But then the forward edge of the plow blade clipped the SUV's right rear quarter panel and tore off the bumper.

On the slick winter surface, the Cadillac was hurled into a sharp, clockwise spin. It smashed into two parked cars. Forchek skidded the plow to a stop, blocking their retreat but not her view.

Bree said, 'Take Romero.'

A rifle was shot from the rooftop diagonally across the intersection from her, shattering the passenger side of the Cadillac's windshield. The three SWAT teams exploded from their positions, and charged the Escalade.

Bree could see one of the girls screaming in the backseat of the SUV and feared the two other gunmen would execute them before the SWAT teams could set them free.

Romero opened fire with the AK-47 through the Escalade's passenger-side window, blowing it

82

out and hitting two of the SWAT men. They sprawled on the sidewalk behind parked cars.

Romero kicked open the Cadillac's door and sprayed bullets in a quick side-to-side arc, then he jumped out, crouched down, and fired another burst.

Three SWAT officers opened fire. All three hit the gangster, and he crumpled. Blood haloed around him on the snowy street.

Captain Forchek pushed open the plow door and leaped down, gun up and aiming through the Escalade's side rear window. The silhouette of one of Romero's men was sagged over on one of the Sheridan twins, who was shrieking in fear. The other gunman had her sister around the neck, a pistol pressed to her head.

'Don't do it!' Forchek shouted. 'I've got a dead shot at you from six feet! Drop the gun and put your hands up!'

The third gunman hesitated and then dropped the pistol.

Forchek yanked open the passenger rear door and pulled a sobbing Sheridan girl out.

Bree ran forward, calling into her radio for SWAT to raid the Sheridans' home. Other officers were helping Sienna Sheridan and her other daughter from the car. Inside the Cadillac, the third of Romero's crew stared straight ahead.

Even with the wool hat she wore down over her eyebrows, there was no mistaking her gender. Latina, mid-twenties, she had tattoos of lavender-colored teardrops on her lower cheeks.

There was blood all over her from the dead man beside her. There was a gaping wound in his throat from the SWAT sniper's shot, the one that missed Romero.

'Hands behind your head,' Bree said. 'Fingers laced, and slide to me.'

She did. Bree spun her around and zip-cuffed her wrists.

She keyed her radio and said, 'This is Chief Stone. Hostages are safe. Repeat, hostages safe. But I need ambulances. Over.'

She didn't bother listening to dispatch's reply but ran past Romero's corpse to check on the SWAT officers hit in that flurry of gunfire. Both men had taken the rounds to their bulletproof vests. They were shaken, but alive.

Her cell phone rang. Chief Michaels.

'Chief,' she said. 'I have Senator Walker's confessed assassin here. He's dead. Do you still want his head delivered to Ned Mahoney on a platter?'

21

The next morning, February 2, around seven, Damon and Jannie were ferrying plates of steaming scrambled eggs, maple-smoked bacon, and hash-brown potatoes with hot sauce, a Cross family favorite breakfast, to the table.

'You're sure you won't have coffee?' Nana Mama asked Bree, who had walked in the door only twenty minutes before.

'I'm going to sleep once Damon and Song leave,' she said, and she yawned.

'Orange juice, then?'

Bree smiled. 'That sounds wonderful, Nana.'

As we dished breakfast onto our plates, I said, 'We're proud of you, by the way. All of us, Bree.'

Ali and Song started clapping and whistling, and we all joined in.

'Stop!' Bree said, holding up her hands in mild protest but smiling softly. 'I was just doing my job.'

'Just doing your job?' Song said in disbelief. 'You caught Senator Walker's killer less than twenty-four hours after she was shot. You did it before the FBI was even on the scene, and all four hostages survived!' SWAT team members had entered the Sheridans' bungalow, found Mr. Sheridan wounded but alive, and rushed him, his wife, and their daughters to the hospital.

I wanted to say that Bree had also handled the pressure from Chief Michaels admirably, but I kept that to myself. She'd called me the night before shortly after talking to Michaels, who'd been forced to eat crow, and said that he was recommending her for citations.

'I got lucky,' Bree told Song. 'And, for the record, I think Damon did too.'

Song grinned, glanced shyly my older son's way, then gazed at each of us in turn. 'Thank you. All of you. You've been so kind, and I want to say how very much I appreciate it.'

'You're more than welcome here,' Nana said. 'Anytime.'

We ate our fill. Bree's eyes were fluttering shut before she agreed to my offer to help her to bed. She sleepily said her good-byes, and we disappeared upstairs. I tucked her in with a promise to wake her at three so she could participate in the FBI interrogation of Romero's female accomplice.

Downstairs, I found Damon and Song already in their coats and carrying their small travel bags.

'Sure you don't want me to drive you to the airport?'

'I have a per diem from school, Dad,' Damon said. 'It will cover the Uber.'

'Okay, then,' I said, and I gave him a big hug. 'You did great last night.'

'Thanks,' he said.

'The first of many more great games,' I said.

'Definitely,' Song said, and she hugged me. 'Again, Dr. Cross, it was an honor to meet you and Chief Stone. My father will be most, most pleased.'

'Give your dad my best,' I said. 'All our best.'

Song and Damon hugged Nana and Jannie. Song and Ali said their good-byes in Chinese, which delighted them both. And then my oldest and his girlfriend waved and went out to the Uber car to return to their lives too many miles away.

I felt sad for myself and excited for them all in the same moment.

'C'mon, Ali,' Jannie said. 'Or we'll be late for school.'

'And don't forget you've got an early patient, Alex,' my grandmother said.

I glanced at my watch. It was twelve minutes to eight.

'Thanks for the reminder,' I said, and I gave Nana a kiss and my kids high-fives and then went back through the kitchen.

Taking the stairs down to my basement office, I realized once again how lucky I was and how grateful I was to have good kids and a wife who was damn near a superhero. I laughed at that and at the fact that she'd be embarrassed to hear me say anything remotely like —

At the bottom of the staircase, I saw an envelope had been pushed through the mail slot. I went over and picked it up off the carpet. My name was printed in block letters on the front. No address. No return address.

Tearing the envelope open, I walked to my office, then I pulled out a folded sheet of unlined paper. Spelled out in letters cut from magazines, the note read:

Alex Cross, stop me, please!

22

I read the message twice more, feeling inexplicably angered.

Stop who from doing what? Why not just tell me?

I started to ball up the paper, intending to toss it, but then stopped.

Who's sending them? And why?

Taking a deep breath after these questions popped in my head, I realized the message was a form of manipulation, a way of toying with me.

It was in my nature to help people whenever I could, either through my practice or through my investigative skills.

The message asked me to help but didn't say how. I sensed that was deliberate and designed to irritate me, to get me asking myself unanswerable questions like *Who's sending these messages? And why?*

The mind is an ancient contraption controlled by questions, which is both a positive and a negative. Ask yourself a good, definable question, and your mind will do everything in its power to answer it, and it probably will be able to if given enough time.

But if the question is unanswerable, the brain spins, hearing the question over and over and over and getting no response. *Why does this always happen to me?* Or *Why can't I get over this tragedy?* Or *Who's sending these messages?*

Like twisting the key in the ignition of an engine that won't turn over, the brain whirls on these unsolvable or as-yet-unsolved queries. Eventually, without answers, the brain gets agitated, angered, and then ground down. Eventually, it burns its way into a crisis or stalls entirely.

Is that what these messages are meant to do? Get me wondering and then fixated on who is sending them and why? Get me —

I heard a knock at my outer basement door. After putting the message in the top drawer of my desk, I went to answer the door and found Nina Davis, the Justice Department attorney, waiting.

'I'm glad you decided to come back,' I said.

She smiled weakly. 'I didn't know if I would until just a few minutes ago.'

Nina made her way to my office and took the same seat she'd occupied during our first appointment.

I sat opposite her. 'How are things?'

'Oh, you know, busy, busy, busy.'

'Did you have the chance to do that exercise we discussed yesterday? Where you looked for good memories of your mother?'

Her face fell. 'You know, Dr. Cross, work's been so crazy, I . . . no, actually, I didn't go there.'

I noted that, said, 'Because those memories don't exist?'

Nina shrugged. 'Because it's a waste of time. If they did exist, they were blotted out by other memories, but really, that's not what I'm here for.'

'Okay.'

She struggled, said, 'I told you I can't feel love, but that's not totally true. I . . . '

She looked at her lap.

'As I've said, Nina, this is a safe place. You'll get no judgment from me, and nothing you tell me ever leaves here. And honestly, I've heard so much and seen so much over the years, very little shocks me. I've found that most behaviors and problems, they aren't all that unique once you talk them out, get to the root of things.'

She crossed her arms and seemed offended, which didn't surprise me.

'You have no idea the things I've done, Dr. Cross,' she said. 'The things I do when I'm not at work.'

I kept quiet and gazed at her expectantly. I'd intentionally broken her pattern of thinking by intimating that her story, whatever it was, was not unique.

Why? People in mental crisis are often convinced that they're the only ones in the world suffering like this, which simply isn't true. Once they abandon that notion, after realizing that most people have thoughts just like theirs, it's often easier to get them to open up fully.

'I do feel something like love,' Davis said at last. 'Not the real thing, but close enough to crave it.'

'When does that feeling happen?'

Davis hesitated, glanced at the floor, then stiffened her shoulders and looked back up at me. 'When I put myself in extreme situations. Sexually, I mean.'

Over the course of the next forty-five minutes, Nina Davis told me of Kaycee Janeway, her dark side and alter ego when it came to sex.

Nina liked to stalk men, big strong men who could dominate her.

She would see a man like that, usually outside of work, and actually feel something, a tingle of attraction, perhaps, a twinge of risk, or a more primitive reaction to his particular musky smell. Whatever it was, there was always something else about him that took it further, triggered fantasies, and changed her fully from Nina to Kaycee.

'I follow them when I can,' Nina said, staring off. 'The men. At night, mostly, in bars, restaurants, even movie theaters. With their wives and girlfriends, or without. And the entire time I'm thinking of having sex with them. Rough stuff, mostly, but other times tender and sweet, and everything it's supposed to be.'

After several nights of stalking, Nina would try to ambush or accidentally encounter her prey and lure him in.

'Once I know the fantasy I want to fulfill, I've never had problems attracting the men, or anyway Kaycee hasn't,' Nina said. 'And once the men know what I want, it's not hard to convince them to give it to me, or at least try to give it to me.'

No judgments, I reminded myself.

'And you feel something like love during these encounters?'

She brightened then, became almost radiant, and for the first time I realized just how beautiful

Nina Davis was. Those eyes, those lashes, her dazzling smile. I understood in that moment that most men she stalked would indeed succumb to her.

'Yes,' she said. 'I feel . . . desperate emotion, during the sex and after. Other than the brief happiness I get from a job well done, they're the only times I feel deeply — when they're rough and domineering and . . . especially when they're strangling me.'

'So you engage in asphyxiation sex?'

'As often as Kaycee can get it,' she said matter-of-factly.

Nina said that when the blood flow to her brain was cut off by strangulation during intercourse, she almost always orgasmed and almost always felt flooded with warm feelings and positive emotions afterward.

'But they don't last,' she said. 'After a few hours, I'm back to Nina, and there's nothing to really feel again.'

I said nothing, took a few notes.

'So I'm a basket case, right?' Nina asked as the hour ended.

'No,' I said. 'Not in the least.'

'But you've never heard of something this weird, this disturbed, have you?'

I smiled, determined to break her of the idea that her issues were unique, and said, 'Actually, I've heard stranger, and much more disturbed.'

She blinked. Her face tightened. 'Well, then, I guess . . . '

'You guess?'

After a moment's struggle, she stood and said,

'Nothing, Dr. Cross.'

'Maybe something to talk about next time?'

She hesitated again. 'Maybe. Do you think I could come back tomorrow to talk about this?'

I checked my schedule. 'Yes, tomorrow at one thirty.'

'Thank you. And, again, thank you for listening without judgment. I'm still trying to understand myself.'

'We *all* are. Thank you for sharing. It had to have been difficult.'

She knitted her brow. 'You know? Not really.'

When Nina Davis had gone, I let myself admit again how very attractive she was before thinking how defensive Nina had been when I'd challenged her. It was a clear sign to me that she was heavily invested in the role of a hypersexual woman.

This was beyond sex with strangers as a way to unlock emotions. This was some deep, dark story she told herself or tried to forget, a story I didn't think I'd come close to hearing all of yet.

23

El Paso County, Texas

After seeing to his two horses, Dana Potter picked up the last plastic storage box from the bed of the white Dodge Ram pickup with Kansas plates that he'd stolen in Abilene the evening before.

Potter lugged the boxes across the dusty yard to the back of an old ranch house surrounded by steep, rocky, and hills in the middle of a nowhere that began thirty miles to the east and went on all the way to the New Mexico border.

A tall, wiry, and weathered man in his early forties, Potter toed open the kitchen door with his cowboy boots and went inside.

'That's the lot of it,' he said.

Mary, his wife, looked up from the ultralight rifle she had mounted lengthwise in a portable gunsmith vise set up on an old wooden table covered in grocery bags.

'Put them there,' Mary said, gesturing with a screwdriver to the floor.

He put the boxes down and went over to his wife. 'She come through zeroed?'

'Only one way to find out,' she said.

He hugged her. 'I'll do the basic check if you want to call on the sat phone. We can shoot her tomorrow.'

She hugged him back. 'Thanks. I've been worried.'

'I know. Go on, now.'

Potter leveled the bolt-action rifle in 6.5 mm Creedmoor using a bubble level he placed on the elevation turret of the gun's Schmidt and Bender tactical telescopic sight. Then he dug in an open box of tools next to the gun vise and came up with a hard plastic case that contained a bore-sighting system precisely calibrated to the gun.

Mary was on her phone. 'Jesse?'

She listened, smiled, said, 'Long drive, but it'll be worth it. How're you feeling?'

In the silence that followed, Potter leveled and taped a custom cardboard chart to the kitchen wall. Then he got out the bore-sighting device itself.

It had a long tapered front end that fit snugly down the barrel of the rifle. The rear of it was the size of a Bic lighter and featured a laser.

Mary listened intently, and then her face clouded. 'Put on Patty.'

Potter said, 'What?'

His wife held up a finger.

Potter threw up his hands and turned around to peer through the scope. He adjusted the gun and the vise until the crosshairs were dead on a similar set of crosshairs printed on the chart taped to the wall.

Mary said, 'Patty, I'm thankful for you being there. What's his temperature?' Her expression darkened further. 'Well, no matter what happens, he has to take his meds. Okay? Tell him his dad and I will call again later.'

She hung up, angry. 'Jesse refused two doses of

96

his medicine, and he's running a steady low-grade fever because of it.'

Potter felt himself tighten, and then he sighed.

'Look at it from his perspective. He's a fifteen-year-old who's been told he's going to die unless he can get access to an insanely expensive treatment his government doesn't believe in and won't pay for. He's trying to get some control over his life, and refusing meds is his answer.'

Mary tried to stay angry, but then she let it go, appearing more sad than convinced. 'I don't like being away from him like this. Every moment, it's . . .'

'Did we have a choice?'

'No,' she said, and her expression hardened. 'We didn't. We don't. It's no use wishing we had the money any other way. How's my doll looking?'

He went to the gun and flipped on the laser sticking out of the barrel. A glowing red dot appeared on the chart three inches above the printed crosshairs.

'Perfect,' he said. 'You're three high at a hundred meters, dead on to three hundred. Two turret clicks and you're zero at five hundred.'

'I do like precision.'

'It's everything,' he said, taking her rifle from the vise and setting it aside.

Potter picked up his own rifle. Green custom stock with a nice grip, the gun was also chambered in 6.5mm Creedmoor, but it carried a Leica sniper scope with an illuminated reticle.

When properly sighted in, Potter's rifle was

more than capable of handling a five-hundred-yard shot. He just wanted to make sure it would when the time —

The sat phone blinked and beeped before he could start testing the rifle.

It was a number he recognized, and he answered.

'Peter here,' said a male voice with a slight British accent. 'How was the drive?'

'Just beat that storm coming.'

'Any trouble entering the country?'

'None.'

'I told you the passports and veterinarian papers were solid.'

'We didn't even need them. You going to give us our assignment?'

'It's all there, in the closet in the back bedroom. Everything you'll need.'

Mary left the kitchen, heading toward the back bedroom.

Potter stayed where he was. 'You'll deposit the down payment?'

'As soon as you tell me you're taking the job.'

'We're here, aren't we?'

'Just the same.'

Mary came back into the kitchen carrying a thick manila envelope. She'd lost several shades of color.

'I'll call you back,' Potter said, and he clicked off. 'What's the matter?'

'Jesus Christ, Dana,' she said, handing him the envelope. 'What the hell are we into now?'

24

Handcuffed and wearing an orange prisoner jump-suit, the only surviving member of Romero's crew glared at the tabletop as Bree followed Ned Mahoney into an interrogation room at the federal detention facility in Alexandria, Virginia.

I was in an observation booth with U.S. Secret Service agent Lance Reamer and Capitol Police lieutenant Sheldon Lee.

'She still hasn't said anything?' Special Agent Reamer asked.

'She's asked for an attorney,' I said.

'Course she did,' Lieutenant Lee said bitterly.

Mahoney and Bree took seats opposite her. She raised her head, saw Bree, and acted as if she'd sniffed something foul. She had spiderweb tattoos on both hands and another climbing the left side of her neck.

'Your prints came up,' Mahoney said, sliding a piece of paper in front of her. 'Lupe Morales. Multiple arrests as a juvenile. Four as an adult, for solicitation, drug dealing twice, and abetting an armed robbery. Looks like you did three years in the California Institution for Women at Lompoc for that one.'

'Eighteen months,' Lupe said, and she yawned. 'I've asked for a lawyer. Twice now.'

'The federal defender's office has been notified,' Bree said. 'In the meantime, you can do yourself a whole lot of good by talking to us.'

99

She sniffed. 'I've heard that one before.'

Bree showed no reaction. 'The U.S. attorney is preparing to charge you with four counts of kidnapping, three counts of attempted murder, and two counts of firing on police officers in the course of duty. Oh, and co-conspirator in the plot to murder a sitting U.S. senator. I'm thinking life without parole times two, maybe more.'

'If not the federal death penalty,' Mahoney said. 'The new administration's big on taking that road whenever possible. Or hadn't you heard?'

Lupe sat forward, her upper lip curled. 'I'm guilty of nothing but being stupid and going along for a ride I shouldn't never have been on. Know what I'm saying?'

'No, actually,' Bree said.

'Spell it out,' Mahoney said.

'Check my gun,' she said. 'That little Glock? No bullets, and not because I ran out. It's clean because I've never shot it. I didn't shoot at no one. Never have. Never will. And especially no senator.'

In the booth, I put a call in to the FBI lab at Quantico and asked a tech to check her assertion about her gun. He put me on hold. As I waited for an answer, I heard Lupe denying knowing exactly why Fernando Romero had decided to drive across country from Oakland to Washington, DC.

'Only thing I knew is he said he was gonna set some things straight and make a pile of Benjamins doing it,' Lupe said. 'I was just along for the ride.'

'Armed to the teeth?' Mahoney said.

'Not me. Like I said, that piece was all show.'

'Tell us about Senator Walker,' Bree said.

She shrugged. 'Fernando hated her.'

'Enough to kill her?'

Lupe thought about that and then nodded. 'But he'd have to have been seriously messed up on meth and Jim Beam and have her, like, show up at the door when he was all hating the world and shit.'

Mahoney said, 'C'mon, Ms. Morales. Romero or his other man or you shot Senator Walker early yesterday morning from an empty town house in Georgetown.'

'The hell I did,' Lupe said, sitting up, indignant. 'Fernando didn't either, or Chewy. We might've hated Walker, but we sure didn't kill her.'

'Romero confessed,' Bree said. 'I heard him. So did two other police officers.'

'No way!'

'Way,' Bree said. 'When you were out on the porch with the girls, when Romero and I were negotiating for time, he told me we had ten minutes and after that he didn't give a damn, that little girls and Mommy were going to start dying, quote, 'just like that bitch Betsy Walker did.''

'So?' Lupe said. 'That's no confession. He was just, like, comparing it.'

'That's not the way I heard it.'

'You hear it any way you want, that don't make it so. Was Fernando happy Walker was dead? Totally. He went out into the damned snow and did a dance when he heard. But he did not kill Betsy Walker. None of us did. Early yesterday morning? When she was shot? We were stuck in a shithole motel 'cause of that ice storm. The Deer Jump Lodge or something in, like, Roanoke. You go on and check. We gotta be on security cams there. People can't be two places at once.'

Bree started to say something but Mahoney beat her to it.

'We will check, Ms. Morales. But again, if you weren't here to kill Senator Walker, why did you and Mr. Romero and this Chewy come to Washington in the first place? And armed to the teeth?'

'Like I said, I don't know for sure,' Lupe said evasively. 'I came along for the ride, mostly. I always wanted to see like the Lincoln Monument. Know what I'm saying?'

Bree said, 'But Mr. Romero was coming for other reasons, to set things right and make a lot of money? Is that correct?'

'That's what I'm saying.'

'Were *you* going to make money?'

Lupe didn't reply for several beats. 'I dunno, maybe. It hadn't been decided if I was in or out yet, like, if I was needed. Necessary, I guess.'

'To do what?' Bree asked.

Lupe's face scrunched up. 'No clue, I said.'

There was a sharp knock at the door. A tall, willowy blonde in a fine blue pantsuit and a pearl necklace came in carrying an attaché case.

'Perrie Knight, counselor-at-law,' she said crisply. 'I'll be representing Ms. Morales. And

102

this interview, I'm afraid, is over.'

Bree exited the interrogation room looking agitated. She was openly angry when she reached the observation booth. I was still on hold, waiting for the lab tech.

'Romero confessed,' she said. 'I heard it. Wiggins and Flaherty heard it too.'

'Lupe says it was just a manner of speaking,' Agent Reamer said.

'Sure, she says that,' Bree replied. 'She wants off death row.'

'What's Perrie Knight doing involved in this case?' Lieutenant Lee said. 'She's not with federal defenders. She's high-dollar, white-collar crime cases.'

The tech at Quantico came back on the line. I listened, thanked him, and hung up. 'Morales was right about her gun being empty. In fact, the FBI lab says it's never been fired.'

'That doesn't absolve Romero of the murder,' Bree said.

'I agree,' Lieutenant Lee said.

'You're both right,' I said. 'Until we check with that motel, an empty gun doesn't absolve anyone. But you should also know that the ballistics folks at Quantico say that none of the weapons recovered last night remotely match the bullets that killed Senator Walker. I think we have to consider the senator's case open again.'

25

Marty Franks whistled an old Kansas tune, 'Carry On Wayward Son,' as he drove east toward an oncoming winter storm. It was already getting late. The sun barely showed in a gunmetal sky. Less than an hour of daylight left.

Few people were on the highway in this mountainous part of West Virginia. Dead of winter. No reason to be out and about if you didn't have to be, especially with a blizzard forecast.

Franks liked to whistle. He was good at it, and he kept whistling that Kansas song until the burn phone rang on the seat beside him.

He pressed Answer on the Bluetooth connection. 'Talk.'

'Peter here. How you coming along, Conker?' said a man with a British accent.

'Five, maybe six hours out of DC, if I'm lucky,' Franks said.

'There's a room for you at the Mandarin Oriental under Richard Conker. Everything else you'll need is in the safe. Code 1958. Repeat, 1958.'

'Got it.'

'I'll talk to you in the morning, then.'

The line went dead. Franks ate a carrot, took a gulp of water, and thought about a bed at the Mandarin. But that was hours away.

He took his mind off the long drive by

focusing on the pleasant soreness in his shoulders and legs. A welterweight in his thirties with a smooth shaved head and a disarming smile, he kept his body in prime condition by pushing it hard, and often.

Earlier in the day, just west of Cleveland, he'd stopped at a park and in twenty-degree temperatures put himself through a brutal hour-long routine of gymnastics, calisthenics, and body-weight plyometric exercises, followed by his own meld of yoga and the various martial arts he'd studied over the years. He'd burned twenty-five hundred calories, easy.

Since then, Franks had been engaged in a near nonstop, slow-motion binge of various shakes, protein bars, and raw vegetables and fruits.

And yet, after his phone call with the Brit, after knowing he had a high-dollar job waiting, he felt a different kind of hunger. One that couldn't be sated with food.

Franks saw a sign ahead: ROUTE 16, IVYDALE — MUDFORK.

Despite the storm coming, despite the long drive ahead, he ran his tongue along his lips, went with his gut, and got off at the exit.

West Virginia State Route 16 ran north and south. He took a left and headed toward Mudfork. The road was narrow, snow-covered, and potholed in places, but Franks drove fast in his white Chevy Tahoe. Wyoming plates. Radial studded snow tires. Heavy-duty shocks. Registered to Richard Conker.

Franks pressed on the gas, his head swiveling as he scanned the area. He didn't have a lot of time to find what he was looking for. Once darkness fell, he'd be done.

North of the hamlet of Nebo, the land on both sides of the route turned hilly; it was forested in bare oaks and clad in four inches of fresh snow. Franks passed a short driveway and saw an opportunity that made him smile.

Beyond some pines, two hundred yards farther on, he came upon the relic of a farmhouse, windowless, siding peeled to bare board and rotten. The barn's roof was caved in. No sign of life anywhere.

Even better.

Franks pulled into the overgrown lane and parked the white Tahoe behind a gnarled old spruce and crab-apple trees laden with snow. His wiser, more experienced self said to sit there a few moments, breathe, and consider other options.

But then, even with the window closed, he heard the buzz of a chain saw. It almost took his breath away. Throwing caution to the wind, he reached around beneath the seat behind him, grabbed a few things, and climbed out.

The snow came up over Franks's ankles, running shoes, socks, and the bottom of his leggings. His feet felt cold and wet almost immediately, but he didn't care.

He pulled up the hood of his black fleece jacket against the wind and broke into a jog, passing an old chicken coop in the overgrown farmyard as he headed toward a stand of mature pine trees and the revving, biting sounds of that saw.

26

Franks ducked into a pine break planted ages ago.

No doubt meant to block the view of nosy neighbors, he thought, ignoring the fluffy snow that sloughed off the boughs and clung to his hood, shoulders, and sleeves. He welcomed the snow and knew he had to have been almost invisible in those firs, frosted as he was, and moved toward the chain saw.

Creeping up to the edge of the muddy work yard he'd glimpsed from the road, he spotted a stack of long logs to his left and a steel shed to his right.

The chain saw and its operator worked by an idle log splitter set up near the base of a low hill of firewood. The logger had his back to Franks and was lopping fifteen-inch sections off a stripped tree trunk braced and strapped between two sawhorses.

He had on an orange helmet with a visor and ear protectors, and he wore thick leather chaps and gauntlet gloves over a quilted canvas coverall. By the ease with which the man wielded the twenty-four-inch Stihl saw, Franks understood that beneath all that heavy gear, there was someone of formidable strength and power.

That thrilled Franks. He forced himself to breathe deeply for a count of three before stepping from the pines, plucking up a short length of discarded tree limb about the thickness of his fist, and running right at the logger.

He slowed at ten yards, glanced toward the road, saw nothing, and then threw the piece of wood at the man's back.

It smacked him. The logger started. The Stihl chain saw bucked and jumped, almost coming free of his grasp.

He released the throttle. The saw idled. The blade stopped cutting a quarter of the way through the log. Only then did the logger look over his shoulder.

Franks was in a fighting crouch not six yards away. He showed the sawyer the eight-inch blade of the Buck hunting knife in his right hand before lunging toward him.

Franks slashed at the logger's left upper arm, felt the razor-sharp blade slice through the canvas jacket and several layers beneath. The sawyer screamed out in pain. Franks leaped back into that fighting crouch, the Buck knife weaving in the cold air, the blade showing a film of bright blood.

The logger let loose a bellow of rage then. He hit the gas on the chain saw and wrenched it free of the log. He swung it sideways and moved toward Franks, who jumped away nimbly, just out of reach of the chain saw's ripping blade.

Franks grinned at the logger, who'd swung too hard with the heavy saw and staggered left in the mud before regaining his balance. Now he squared off as he faced him, the cutting machine growling in his hands.

Franks looked the sawyer in the eye then and

saw no fear. That made Franks even happier. Somehow, somewhere in the past, in the military, perhaps, the logger had faced death, and with that two-foot chain saw in hand now, he had the confidence of a warrior who knows his enemy holds an inferior weapon.

'I'll cut you in half, shit-brains,' the logger shouted from behind his helmet's visor. 'I'll put you in two pieces.'

'Do it, then,' Franks said calmly. 'You can claim self-defense.'

The logger thought about that, smiled, and pulled the butt end of the saw tight to his pelvis so the blade stuck out in front of him like some motorized sword. The logger charged at Franks, feinting this way and that with the spinning head of the saw.

At each feint, Franks stepped back, one foot, then the other, and then again, staying just inches from the whirling teeth and seeing his enemy grow more and more frustrated at not being able to cut him to pieces.

The logger took his finger off the gas. His shoulders and chest were heaving from the exertion of flinging the heavy saw around.

Franks stood his ground, watching everything about the man, trying to see him as a whole enemy rather than just eyes or legs or arms, and definitely not as just that saw.

'What the hell are you doing this for?' the logger yelled.

'Practice,' Franks yelled back.

'Practice? You insane?'

'Just hungry.'

'Hungry? Hungry?'

The logger's expression turned murderous. He exploded then and charged forward, wielding the saw like a bayonet that he intended to drive straight through Franks.

Franks stood his ground. At the last second, he flung his body sideways and sprang at the logger. The chain saw's teeth passed inches from his belly before he drove the Buck knife up under the visor and deep into the logger's neck.

The logger dropped the chain saw, which bit into the mud and flipped away from them, sputtering, coughing, and then dying.

Franks was barely aware of the sounds. He was watching and feeling the logger's quivers and shakes as more of his blood spurted against the inside of the visor. He grabbed the knife handle with his other hand just before the logger died and sagged against the blade and hilt.

Franks used all of his strength to heft the dead man's weight, then pushed hard against it and yanked back on the knife handle. The blade came free. The logger fell in the mud beside his saw.

Franks stood there for several long moments, gasping for air, feeling exhilarated beyond words, soaking up the whole scene, until a snowflake hit his face. He looked up into a sky heading toward dusk, seeing more and more flakes coming at him, thick ones, swirling down.

He felt giddy. A part of him wanted to stay and relive the last few amazing minutes. But his wiser self knew when to walk away.

Franks never wavered as he hustled through

the pine break into the old farmyard. The snow showers had turned into a squall by the time he reached the Chevy.

When he drove past the logger's work lot, Franks could make out the small hill of firewood through the falling snow but not the log splitter or the man he'd killed in mortal combat. He felt neither pity toward nor interest in the logger beyond the memory of their encounter. The logger had been a thrill, a challenge, training against a worthy opponent, and nothing more.

He started to whistle, and then to sing. 'Carry on, my wayward son, there'll be peace when you are done.'

As he sang on, the wind picked up. So did the snow. It was a full-on blizzard by the time he reached I-79 and turned east again toward Washington.

27

Chief Michaels gave Bree a withering glare as he worried a pen in his hand.

'You told me we had him!' Michaels said. 'Self-confessed, you said! I told the mayor. I told the congressmen. I . . . shit.'

He plopped in his chair and tossed the pen on the desk in disgust.

Bree took a deep breath before saying as calmly as she could: 'Chief, at the time, I believed I had Senator Walker's killer. Romero had threatened the senator recently. He referenced Senator Walker's murder as evidence he would not hesitate to kill Mrs. Sheridan or her daughters. His accomplice says he came three thousand miles to, quote, 'set some things straight and make a pile of Benjamins.' He was a prime suspect even before he started shooting.'

'But Romero's on this motel security tape in Roanoke?'

'I haven't seen it,' she said, deflated. 'But evidently Romero, Lupe Morales, and this Chewy character are all on motel video checking in and out. With the snowstorm, there definitely was not enough time for them to get from Roanoke and back.'

'So the senator's killer remains at large,' Michaels said. 'There's still an asshole out there we don't know about.'

'Or a dead one we do know about.'

Michaels cocked his head. 'I'm not following.'

Bree opened the manila file in her lap. She handed over photographs taken at the strangulation scene in Georgetown.

'This man, carrying the ID of one Carl Thomas of Pittsburgh, was throttled five blocks from the senator's crime scene about seventeen hours after Walker was shot.'

'Loose proximity,' the chief said dismissively. 'Where's the hard connection?'

'The victim was able to get two shots off at his killer with a gun recovered at the scene,' she said, and then she pushed a paper across the desk. 'The rush report says there's gunpowder residue on the victim's right hand and wrist that matches the pistol.'

'Okay?'

Bree handed him a second document. 'Results for gunpowder on his clothes.'

Michaels studied the lab results, which had come in moments before Bree was set to speak with the chief.

He glanced at the first report. 'Different gunpowders?'

Bree nodded. 'It's all being sent to Quantico for confirmation, but it will be interesting to see if the blast powder on his clothes matches the residues found in that apartment Senator Walker's assassin used.'

'That's a pretty big leap, isn't it?'

'I don't think so, Chief, even without the lab results,' she said. 'I had Thomas's prints run. We got no hits in the FBI databases, but we did in Scotland Yard's files.'

113

Michaels sat forward. 'Scotland Yard? I thought the victim was from Pittsburgh.'

'I said his driver's license said he was from Pittsburgh.'

'And Scotland Yard says different?'

'Not in so many words.'

'What the hell does that mean?'

'It means that when we ran the prints, we definitely got a hit in Scotland Yard,' she said. 'There's a file there somewhere, but we were denied access to it.'

Michaels shook his head. 'So let me get this straight. A man with a Pittsburgh ID dies violently five blocks from Senator Walker's murder scene, and Scotland Yard won't tell us who he really is?'

'That's correct.'

The chief thought about that. 'So he's a spook or something? Someone protected, anyway. Or someone Scotland Yard doesn't want us to know about?'

'Any or all three, sir,' Bree said.

'What if he was working with the Brits? What if he shot Betsy Walker on orders *from* the Brits?'

Bree had not considered that last idea, and the implications shocked her.

'It would be a political assassination ordered by a foreign power,' she said. 'An act of war. By an ally.'

28

My son Ali hustled ahead of me toward the front door of Fong and Company, the best Asian market in the District of Columbia.

'I think this will be fun,' Ali said, looking at me over his shoulder. 'You know, kind of like that show I like. *Weird Foods?* I *love* that guy. He's always eating the grossest things and makes it sound like he's in heaven doing it.'

'Okay, what's weird in this recipe?'

'Nothing. I don't think. But there's bound to be weird food in the store, right?'

He sounded so desperately hopeful that I laughed. 'I'm sure we can find something weird if we look hard enough.'

Ali brightened and pushed into Fong's, a sprawling, happy warren with narrow aisles and shelves stacked high with mysterious boxes that threw sweet and spicy smells into the air.

Ali went off through the maze, hunting. He pointed to several live tanks by the fish counter and said, 'Okay, that's weird.'

'Live crabs?'

'No, the eels,' he said, and he shivered. 'I couldn't eat those.'

I saw them slithering about in the tank next to the crabs and lobsters. 'Yeah, I'm not big on eels either.'

'I'd eat just about anything else, though,' Ali said.

That lasted until he spotted a sign for Burmese peppers, five thousand degrees of heat.

'Okay, so I wouldn't eat those either,' he said. 'Why do some people like their food so hot that it makes them cry?'

'I don't really know. Ask your grandfather.'

'Yeah, he's always putting hot sauce on things.'

We found a nice clerk in her twenties named Pam Pan and showed her Song's list of ingredients.

'Judging by the ingredients, those are going to be yummy rolls,' Pan said.

'Old Hong Kong family recipe,' Ali said.

'Really?' Pan said.

'My girlfriend-in-law's grandmother's recipe.'

'Your girlfriend-in-law?'

'My brother's girlfriend,' Ali said, smiling. 'Makes sense, right?'

The clerk laughed and looked at me. 'Is he like this all the time?'

'Twenty-four/seven.'

Ali went on to prove it as the clerk took us around, peppering her with questions about the ingredients and whether there were any 'really weird' foods in the store. He got a kick out of pickled chicken's feet, which, to his credit, he tried.

The faces he made caused Pan and me to crack up, and I felt like we'd made a friend by the time she'd found every ingredient in the recipe. Ali and I left the market and called for an Uber to take us home.

'I like that place,' Ali said as we stood out on the sidewalk.

'I could see that, especially when you ate that chicken foot.'

'I did it.'

'You did it. With style, I might add.'

He liked that and gave me a hug. 'I love you, Dad.'

'I love you too, buddy,' I said, hugging him back. 'Pickled chicken feet and all.'

29

An hour later, Nana Mama's kitchen was smelling outrageously good as she and Ali stir-fried the stuffing for the rolls. My cell phone rang.

It was Ned Mahoney.

'Alex?' he said before I could greet him. 'You alone?'

'Give me a minute,' I said, and I hit mute. 'I have to take this.'

'Dinner's at seven,' my grandmother said. 'Bree said she'd be here by then.'

I went down to my office and shut the door behind me.

'Okay, I'm good,' I said.

'We've got a new potential suspect in Senator Walker's murder case.'

Mahoney went on to describe Viktor Kasimov, a Russian businessman closely allied with the Kremlin. Kasimov acted as an envoy between Washington and Moscow from time to time. Back-channel stuff carried out under a diplomatic passport.

'He's also a degenerate, a hypocrite, and possibly a rapist.'

Ned said that Kasimov had been a suspect in a string of rapes in the United States and Europe, starting during his graduate years at UCLA. Kasimov was smart, cunning, and unafraid to use cash and lawyers to shut women up, and he used the diplomatic passport to keep himself out of the hands of authorities.

Kasimov was also believed to be a liaison between Moscow and factions in the Middle East who were looking for an arms deal, an accusation he had emphatically denied.

'He's slippery,' Mahoney said. 'Half the time he lives out on a yacht in international waters where he can't be arrested or detained. Two weeks ago, he made a mistake. After a night of partying in Mexico City, he flew on a private jet to Los Angeles. Guess who was waiting for him.'

'I can't answer that.'

'California state troopers, the California state attorney general, and Senator Betsy Walker. Seems the last time Kasimov was in town, he forcibly raped Senator Walker's best friend's daughter after giving her a date-rape drug.'

I said nothing.

'He squealed diplomatic immunity, but he ended up in LA County Jail. He spent almost a week in there until his army of attorneys paid for by the Russians got some state judge to grant him a two-million-dollar bail.'

'There's an idiot savant born every minute.'

'You know it. Kasimov came up with a check for the whole nut. No bondsman. But here's the thing. He left jail seriously pissed off at Betsy Walker. He said that in Russia, she'd be in jail or shot.'

'In that same Russia, he should have his balls chopped off,' I said.

'You're probably right,' Mahoney said.

119

'So, let me guess. He skipped bail on the full two million?'

'That's the thing, Alex. He hasn't left the country.'

'No surveillance post-release?'

'Sure,' he said. 'Kasimov and a small entourage flew domestic charter from LA to DC last week. He had a meeting at the Russian embassy and took a suite at the Mandarin Oriental. He hasn't been seen outside since. Six days. His people claim he's fighting a nasty flu he picked up in jail courtesy of Senator Walker.'

'He's not wearing an ankle bracelet?'

'Not a stipulation of bail.'

'An even more savant judge.'

'Or more corrupt.'

'You think Kasimov was angry enough at Betsy Walker to have killed her?'

'Or have her killed? Yes. That's the word I'm getting. And there's another thing.'

'What's that?'

'He's a hell of a marksman with rifle and pistol. He came in eleventh overall at the last Olympic Games.'

'Was he in town when Betsy Walker died?'

'He was indeed.'

'Then I think we need to talk with him sooner rather than later.'

'Meet me at the Mandarin in an hour?'

I looked at my watch. It was 6:20.

'Ali and Nana are making a special dinner, and I know Bree would like to be there. Better make it two.'

30

At twenty past eight that evening, Ned Mahoney used a key card we'd gotten from the head of security at the Mandarin Oriental hotel to unlock elevator access to the suites-only fourteenth floor.

The doors shut. My mind was still processing what the security chief had told us.

Kasimov and his entourage of four were occupying the Jefferson Suite: three bedrooms, a kitchen, and a stunning view of the Jefferson Memorial. The Russian businessman had evidently been sick for days with an intestinal bug. A concierge doctor had been making twice-daily calls to his suite, and he was up there now.

Ned, Bree, and I got off on the fourteenth floor. The carpet was lush, like walking on spongy wool, and the air was scented from flowers in a vase on a table opposite the elevator.

'I kind of like this,' Mahoney said. 'The ambience.'

'Who wouldn't?' I said.

Bree laughed and shook her head.

We found the door to the Jefferson Suite and saw that the light near the bell was red, indicating the inhabitants did not wish to be disturbed. Mahoney rang it anyway.

When there was no answer, he rang it again, and then a third time, until a man barked in a thick accent, 'Go away.'

'FBI. Open up please,' Mahoney said, showing his credentials through the peephole.

The locks were thrown open and the door moved to reveal a shaved-headed man built like an Olympic weight lifter wearing a pair of bulging gray slacks and a blue dress shirt.

'What do want?' he asked in the same thick accent.

'Who are you, sir?' Mahoney said.

'Boris,' he said.

'We'd like to speak with Mr. Kasimov, Boris.'

'Impossible. He has medical issues. Contagious.'

'We'll take the chance.'

'No,' Boris said, his eyes dully locked on ours. 'He is weak. They're giving him the IV liquids and drugs. What is this about? More lies?'

'Just a few questions about Senator Walker,' Bree said. 'She's dead.'

Behind Boris, at the other end of the entry hall, a handsome, tall, and athletically built man in his late thirties appeared. He wore a Dallas Cowboys baseball cap over dark wavy hair and carried a large shoulder bag.

'Dr. Winters?' a voice called weakly.

The man in the Cowboys cap stopped and looked back. Another man dressed like Boris appeared, pushing a wheelchair. Kasimov sat in the chair under a blanket. An IV line ran from a pouch on a pole into his arm. He looked like death warmed over.

'Yes, Mr. Kasimov?' the doctor said.

'You will return tomorrow?' the businessman said.

'Yes. But the change in medications should help you tonight.'

'Thank you,' the man behind Kasimov said.

Dr. Winters started toward us again. Mahoney called out, 'Mr. Kasimov? I'm with the FBI. Could I have five minutes of your time?'

'I said he's sick,' Boris said loudly.

Kasimov peered down the hall a moment, blinked slowly, and then said, 'No, Boris, let them in. Let's see what they're trying to frame me for this time.'

31

Two floors below Kasimov's suite, Martin Franks paced in his room. He whistled that Kansas tune again. *Carry on, my wayward son . . .*

He just couldn't get the damn thing out of his mind.

But every time Franks passed his unmade bed, he glanced at the FedEx envelope lying there, bulging with documents regarding his target. He was always up for a challenge and never a man rattled by the implications of an assignment.

But this?

This was . . .

He couldn't bring himself to say it.

But it was, wasn't it?

He picked the envelope up, shaking his head in disbelief. *I'd never have to work again.*

Franks's heart raced a bit at that thought before excitement was replaced by anxiety. Being a hired gun had made life simpler, turned his darkest impulses clean, orderly, and paid for. What if he stopped after this, made it his last for-hire job?

After several long moments he decided he could stop professionally and yet sate his particular hunger by continuing to look for those moments of chance, those prime targets of opportunity, like the logger.

Franks smiled. *The logger.*

124

He closed his eyes and let his mind dwell on the instant where he'd dodged the chain saw and driven the knife deep into the sawyer's neck.

Wasn't that something?

But wouldn't this be something else again?

My biggest Houdini takeout ever.

Franks opened his eyes and read the payment schedule once more. With that kind of money, he could vanish into Bolivia or Uruguay, and . . .

He shut off that line of dreaming then, turned cold and professional, and forced himself to focus entirely on the assignment and whether or not he could get it done. He started by setting aside the target's name and title and all the potential implications of the hit.

None of that meant a thing to Franks, at least for the moment. He drew out more documents from the FedEx envelope and studied rather than scanned them, as he had the first time through, seeing patterns and possibilities, the risks and the penalties.

An hour later, Franks believed that he was up to the task from a technical perspective. Only then did he pull out the photographs and biography of his target. Only then did he consider the idea of being tried and hung for his crimes.

Is it worth it?

He immediately knew the money alone was not enough. But Franks closed his eyes and imagined getting the job done and seeing himself slip away clean, and the sum of the payout plus the thrill of achievement *was* enough.

He opened his eyes. He felt a familiar want

tickle and churn in his stomach. He looked to the photographs of his target again and started to whistle the Kansas tune.

In Franks's mind, the job was already done. He picked up the burn phone from the bed and dialed. The phone rang twice before a computerized voice told him to leave a message at the beep.

'This is Conker, Peter,' Franks said. 'I accept.'

32

Somewhere in Kasimov's suite, a phone rang twice, then stopped.

Boris was unhappy, but stood aside. Dr. Winters nodded to us uncertainly as we passed him in the hall.

Kasimov sagged more than sat in his wheelchair, his eyelids lazy, but he studied us when we held out our credentials.

'What's this about?' the man behind the wheelchair said.

'And you are?' I asked.

'Nikolai,' he said. 'Mr. Kasimov's personal assistant.'

'I'm not dead, Nikolai,' Kasimov said weakly. 'I can answer their questions.'

'I think it is unwise. Better to wait for the attorney.'

'I'll be the judge of that,' Kasimov said, watching us all closely.

'Where were you around four thirty a.m. the day before yesterday?' I asked.

He let loose a phlegmy chortle. 'You mean at the time Senator Walker died?'

'Exactly,' Mahoney said.

'See?' Kasimov said in a weak, sardonic tone. 'I told you I'd hear about that sooner or later.'

'Please answer the question,' I said.

Kasimov was obviously not used to being talked to like this and glared at me a moment before saying, 'I was in bed, here, Dr. Cross, sicker than a Siberian dog.'

'Can anyone corroborate that?'

Boris raised his hand. So did Nikolai.

Boris said, 'And the hotel maid who was sent to clean up. And Dr. Winters.'

'Mr. Kasimov has not left this suite in six days,' Nikolai said.

'What's got you so sick?' Mahoney said.

'My doctor says flu and food poisoning at the same time,' Kasimov said. 'Worst illness I've ever had.'

'Did you consider Senator Walker an enemy?' Bree asked.

He coughed a laugh, said, 'Certainly not a friend.'

'But you had nothing to do with her death?'

He blinked slowly, then turned his lazy attention on each of us in turn. 'I had nothing to do with her death,' he said, and he smiled weakly. 'Doesn't mean I wasn't happy about it, just that I had zero involvement.'

'Just a coincidence you being in town?' Mahoney said.

'As a matter of fact, yes. I came to visit my embassy, and I got sick. End of story. And now, please, I'll ask you to leave. I'm feeling the need to sleep. Good night.'

Nikolai turned the wheelchair away from us. Boris gestured toward the door.

We said nothing in the hallway, but I noted the positions of the security cameras before we took the elevator back down to the lobby, again in silence. Only in the crowded lobby near the

128

sound of the piano playing and the hubbub of the bar did we speak.

'He looked like hell,' Mahoney said.

'I agree,' Bree said. 'He's been through something rotten.'

Mahoney gestured ahead toward the lounge. I looked and saw Dr. Winters sitting at the bar drinking a martini and chatting up a very attractive woman whom unfortunately I knew fairly well.

I said, 'I have a conflict here. The woman talking to Winters is an active patient of mine. You're going to have to flush her out of there before I join you.'

'I'm going home,' Bree said. 'I'm too wiped out to be much good. Let me know how it goes.'

I gave her a kiss and watched her go. Mahoney walked over and showed his credentials to Dr. Winters and Nina Davis. The Justice Department attorney was dressed for the hunt, her ash-blond hair swept back to reveal her high cheekbones, and her body stuffed into a strapless black cocktail dress that looked like a thousand bucks.

Davis peered at Ned's badge, listened to him say something, and looked disappointed. She picked up her clutch and slid off the barstool. She moved confidently to the coat check, retrieved a coat, and then spotted me.

'Sorry about that, Nina,' I said, walking up to her. 'I'm here with Special Agent Mahoney. My other life. We just needed to talk to the doctor alone.'

Davis watched me a moment, trying to see if I

129

was judging her, then said, 'What's he done?'

'You know him?'

'Sure,' she said. 'Chad Winters. He's an . . . old acquaintance.'

'Trustworthy?'

She hesitated. 'I'd ask the medical board. See you tomorrow afternoon?'

I nodded.

When I reached Mahoney and Winters, the doctor was acting the defensive professional. 'There is still such a thing as doctor-patient confidentiality,' he complained.

'We're not asking about Kasimov's medical history,' Ned said. 'Just trying to corroborate his statements. He says he was sick early Tuesday morning and that you were there.'

'That's true,' Dr. Winters said. 'He was projectile vomiting. High fever. I had to give him a shot of trimethobenzamide so he could keep food down.'

'He said a combination of the flu and food poisoning?' I said.

The doctor nodded. 'Simultaneous viral and bacterial infections. He's over the bacterial thing, but that's a nasty strain of flu he's fighting. It's been a killer across Africa and Asia and can go on for a full two weeks.'

Mahoney and I looked at each other. The Russian's alibi sounded bombproof. He wasn't the killer. But he still could have been involved.

'Thank you, Doctor,' Mahoney said. 'We appreciate it, and we're sorry to interrupt your talk with the lovely lady.'

'No worries,' Dr. Winters said, and he

130

laughed. 'That lovely lady's got a dark side, and it's probably better for me to keep clear of her, if you know what I mean.'

33

West Texas

At the first hint of dawn on February 3, Dana Potter looked over at Mary. His wife was staring through the windshield of their pickup truck as he drove along a red clay range road that cut through more of that scrubby, broken West Texas country.

The horses shifted in the trailer behind them, causing the truck to sway.

Mary swore under her breath.

'You okay?' Potter asked.

'Just processing,' Mary said, but she didn't look at him.

'It's the only answer.'

'I get it, and I'm here, aren't I?' she said, and she paused to brood. 'I just can't help thinking what we're risking, eh? We might never see . . . '

'It's a job, just like every other job we've ever done,' Potter said.

'No, Dana, it's not.'

'You have to think that way or we should have turned it down.'

There was a silence before she responded with raw emotion, 'I love my boy.'

Potter choked up. 'And we're going to get him the help he needs, and then some, give Jesse the life he deserves.'

Mary teared up. 'I'm so frightened for him.'

'We do this, he's got a real chance. You saw the reports.'

'I keep wanting to believe, but . . . '

'We can do this,' Potter said. 'We're professionals, eh?'

She wiped at her tears and smiled, but it was weak. 'Keep reminding me of that over the next two days.'

'Course I will. Just keep thinking: It's a game. A game we always win. I mean, when it's come right down to it, have we ever been close to losing?'

Mary smiled more broadly then and shook her head. 'Not once.'

'There you go. We'll just play our game, and things will go fine.'

She sighed and squeezed his hand. 'How much farther?'

'Twenty minutes?'

'Peter should have put us closer,' she said.

'Better to be far away,' he said, glancing at a Garmin Montana GPS unit mounted on the dash. 'Keeps things simpler.'

The GPS was loaded with a topographical map and an overlay that identified property ownerships. Texas was largely privately held, but there were slivers of federal land in the wilder sections of the state.

When it was almost full daylight, Potter spotted a two-track leading to a heavy steel gate with a sign from the Bureau of Land Management saying the road was closed. He stopped, said, 'I cut the lock. Close it behind us.'

Mary did, and they quickly pushed on up the

track and down the other side of a rise where they could not be seen from the country road. He parked, turned the truck off.

It was cold, just above freezing, when they climbed out, both wearing dull tan camouflage that matched the vegetation. They got the horses from the trailer. After shouldering heavy day packs, they climbed into the saddles and set off up a game trail that climbed the flank of a low mesa covered in scrub oak and creosote that grabbed and tore at them.

The temperature rose with the sun. The horses began to sweat. Two miles in they dropped off the mesa into a dry wash, an empty streambed that crawled off through a maze of brush and low trees. Two more miles on, they climbed a rocky outcropping and stayed high and trending southwest for another mile.

One hour and nine minutes after they had started out, they dropped into an arroyo. They left the horses in shade. Potter got out a handsaw and cut boughs of thin green leaves from a paloverde tree and set them in a pile on the bank when they left the sandy riverbed.

The hill beyond was steep, with little vegetation and loose rocks everywhere.

'Take our time,' he said. 'No noise to set the dogs off. And wind's in our favor.'

Mary nodded and followed him slowly up the hill, putting her boots where he'd put his. They reached the crown of the hill and heard a cock crow in the distance, then a cowbell or two followed by the neighing of horses.

They dropped their packs and dragged them

134

as they crawled across the hill and caught the first glimpse of the long, narrow valley beyond. Strips of cultivated ground separated by thickets cut the valley floor from side to side all the way past barns and corrals to a low, Spanish-style hacienda with whitewashed walls, a terra-cotta-tile roof, and a terrace bathed in warm sun even at that early hour.

Lying on his side, Potter opened his pack and removed a pair of Leica Geovid binoculars. He trained them on the terrace and saw twelve people at the three tables, all middle-aged men, having breakfast and drinking coffee. Most of them wore canvas jackets, some with hunter-orange fabric across the shoulders.

'Right where he said they'd be,' he said.

'I see them,' Mary said, looking through her own set of binoculars.

Potter pressed a button on the binoculars that activated a range-finding system. He aimed the red glowing square on the nearest man and clicked the button a second time.

'Five hundred and twelve meters to the first table,' he said.

'Five twenty-six to the doors,' Mary said.

He put his binoculars down after taking several more distance readings and memorizing them.

'I'm good.'

'I am too,' she said. 'This spot will do nicely.'

'Perfect line of sight.'

They sneaked out backward and didn't stand until they were ten feet down the other side of the hill. Back at the arroyo, they took the paloverde boughs and used them to brush out their tracks going into the sandy bottom and all the way to the horses.

'Ready?' Potter asked when they were saddled.

Mary nodded. He set his watch to stopwatch mode, started it, and said, 'Go!'

The Potters kicked up their horses and took off back the way they'd come, pushing their rides hard and taking chances where they could have slowed.

It had taken them sixty-nine minutes on the way in, but only twenty-eight minutes had passed when they reached the truck and trailer. Five minutes after that, they pulled out on the country road and headed north.

Ten miles farther on, Potter drove through another BLM gate, this one open, and again stopped out of sight of the road at the back of an escarpment overlooking a big dusty flat. He and Mary gave the horses water before walking down onto the flat carrying two milk jugs filled with a special punch.

Using range finders, they placed one jug at 512 meters and the second at 526.

Back at the truck, they took out the components of their ultralight rifles from their packs, put them together, and finished the process by attaching bipods and screwing in matte-black sound suppressors.

They walked to the edge of the escarpment, extended the bipod legs, and lay prone behind the rifles before finding their targets. Potter settled the crosshairs of his telescopic sight on the jug at 526 meters.

'Green?' he asked.

'Green. On five,' she said. 'Four, three, two — '

Both rifles went off in unison, making thumping noises, and the bullets smashed into the jugs. They erupted into thin, billowing pillars of flame.

34

Inside a large storage unit in Fairfax, Virginia, the man calling himself Pablo Cruz smiled when a bell dinged. He reached into an Ultimaker 2+ desktop 3-D printer and retrieved an appliance made of translucent high-detail resin that looked like a spider's web that was about nine inches long and six wide.

The long edges of the appliance were turned toward each other, forming a shape that failed to connect by two inches. The resin was warm to the touch, and as he flexed the web he found it strong but malleable in all directions.

When it had cooled more, he squeezed open the edges and slipped the entire web onto his right forearm. It extended from just below his elbow over and around his wrist and fit snug, as if it had been crafted specifically for him, which it had.

Cruz slipped it off and set it beside its twin on a workbench he'd brought in to the storage unit the week before. There were two small, translucent brackets on the bench that were made of Kevlar-reinforced nylon, a material stronger than block aluminum and neutral when scanned with a metal detector.

The underside of the brackets held swivel balls in sockets attached to tiny, T-shaped valves. The brackets fitted to the underside of the forearm appliances.

Cruz put on reading glasses to attach small hoses made of translucent carbon fiber to the T-valve. An inch long and three-eighths of an inch in diameter, the hose was designed to handle sudden and extreme pressure.

He picked up a piece of clear Kevlar-reinforced nylon the shape and size of a .25-caliber bullet. Cruz placed the projectile in the head chamber of a clear three-inch barrel, then screwed the barrel into the free end of the T-valve. To the other end of the hoses, he attached Kevlar-reinforced nylon canisters the size of small cigarette lighters that fit snugly in the webbed appliance as well.

His burn phone rang. He answered.

The man he knew as Piotr spoke Russian. 'We are good, Gabriel?' he asked.

Cruz replied in Russian. 'Actually, there is a problem with compensation.'

A cold silence followed. Cruz waited him out.

'We had a deal,' Piotr said at last.

'Until I knew the subject.'

'I thought you were the best.'

'I am the best. It's why you came to me.'

There was another long pause.

'How much?'

'Thirty-five million. Ten now, twenty-five when the job's done.'

'I can't authorize that.'

'Then get it authorized. Now.'

Piotr, sounding furious, said, 'Hold on.'

Cruz switched the phone to speaker and set it on the bench. While he waited for a reply, he squeezed the appliances onto his forearms and fitted the crowned ends of the barrels through loops on the webbing below his wrists.

Piotr came back on the line. 'Deal,' he said. 'Final payment upon deed accomplished.'

Cruz hung up the phone, put it on the bench, and took a deep breath before picking up a hammer and crushing the device.

Only then did he turn his attention to the fashion mannequin he'd set up at the other end of the storage unit. He walked to within ten feet, raised his right hand, and flicked his hand sharply back, arching his fingers toward his upper forearm.

He felt the webbed appliance stretch. The ball pivoted in its socket and tripped a trigger in the valve that, with a thud, released a powerful burst of highly pressurized helium from the carbon canister.

The gas drove the nylon bullet out of the barrel at fourteen hundred feet per second. It hit the mannequin in the chest, blew through the foam, and disintegrated into shards that hit the steel back wall of the unit.

Cruz smiled, raised his left arm, and flicked that hand back, triggering the second of his hybrid, undetectable derringers. This bullet struck the mannequin on the bridge of the nose and blew out the back of its head.

35

Nina Davis was right on time. She knocked on my basement door at half past one and swept in with a smile that was, well, beguiling, not at all the troubled woman who'd showed up yesterday.

'Hello, Dr. Cross,' she said pleasantly as she moved by me toward my office.

Nina wore a hint of jasmine perfume that lingered in the air as I followed her. Inside, she shrugged off her trench coat, revealing a clingy black cashmere turtleneck sweater and snug matching slacks and heels. Gold earrings dangled from her earlobes.

When she sat, she looked at me with a sparkle in her eyes. 'I must say, you lead an exciting life, Dr. Cross.'

'How's that?'

She adjusted her position, crossed her legs, smiled, said, 'Last night. Chad Winters and a Russian honcho?'

'Winters told you about the Russian?'

'It was all he talked about, how he and the Russian were tight.'

'He told us the Russian had been very sick.'

Nina studied me in amusement, as if she knew something I did not.

'The honcho was sick. But not his men. They come and go all the time. Chad's seen them do it.'

'Okay?'

'They have disguises. Makeup. Latex prosthetics.'

'Why?'

'To fool the CIA. Chad says they're watching the honcho and his men.'

I didn't doubt it but said, 'You'd swear to the FBI about that? What Dr. Winters told you?'

She gave me a look that suggested I was daft and said, 'I do work for the Justice Department. If it helps, of course I'd swear.'

'I'll have Mahoney — the agent you met last night — call you after we're done.'

'Sure. After we're done.'

'What am I going to find if I look into Winters?'

She paused. 'I believe there was an issue with overprescribing pain meds that he managed to beat.'

I let that sink in. 'Okay, can I ask you something? You don't have to answer if it makes you uncomfortable.'

Nina cocked her head. 'You said this is a safe place. No judgments, right?'

'Correct,' I said. 'Last night, before Special Agent Mahoney approached you, was I seeing Nina or Kaycee?'

The barest of smiles crossed her lips. 'Guess.'

'Kaycee.'

'She hadn't decided,' Nina said. 'Kaycee, I mean. She hadn't decided she wanted him. Winters.'

'Because?'

She laughed. 'He's easy. Kaycee stalked him a long time ago.'

'So no risk, no reward?'

'What's the point to anything if there is no real challenge?' she said, and she shifted again so her sweater moved across her breasts.

'No danger?'

'From Chad? I suppose. There are rumors he's into pain. Sexually.'

'But you enjoy the dangerous aspects of stalking men like Chad and seducing them.'

Nina tapped a fingernail against her lips and thought about that.

'Maybe,' she said. 'But then again there's always danger when you're a woman venturing into the unknown.'

'You like the unknown.'

'I'm comfortable there, if that's what you're asking.'

'Not wary?'

Nina shook her head, causing her ash-blond hair to come loose and fall gracefully across one shoulder. 'No, Kaycee is oblivious, but I have a sense for creeps. And besides, as I said, I study them for quite a while before I make my move.'

'You do understand that some people might find a woman stalking men as disturbing as a man stalking women?'

'Would they? I suppose. But it's not like I'm obsessive or violent. Ultimately, they have free will. The guy always has to make the final move in my little game.'

'You enjoy that moment, when they make the final move?'

'Very much so.'

'What do you feel right then?'

'Desire, of course.'

'Beyond desire?'

Nina twisted her chin slightly, gazed downward and diagonally a few moments, then met my eyes and said, 'I guess I feel liberated, a primal woman in her essence.'

'No guilt. No remorse.'

'None,' she said firmly. 'No boundaries. I am in the feminine and free.'

'Kaycee is, you mean,' I said.

'I know Kaycee's spirit.'

'Is that the moment when you feel closest to love? When the man becomes the aggressor?'

'No. That's later. During.'

'When he's choking you?'

Nina's eyes shimmered ever so slightly, as if she were replaying a memory.

'Not always,' she said at last. 'But often enough.'

'Where did that come from? The choking?'

Nina frowned slightly. 'Where? I don't know. I think I read about it in a book, *The Joy of Sex*?'

'How old were you?'

'When?'

'When you read the book.'

Her frown deepened. 'I . . . I can't remember. In my teens?'

'And when did you first experiment with asphyxiation?'

She turned defensive. 'What does this have to do with an inability to love?'

I held up both hands. 'You've told me that the closest you come to feeling love is during rough sex when you're choking to orgasm. I'm trying to

144

understand why that turns you on so much.'

Nina looked past me. 'I . . . I don't know. I just tried it once, and it felt so good, I wanted to do it again. And again.'

'How old were you when you first tried it?'

She squinted, blinked, and then looked at me with slight puzzlement. 'Twenty-three? Twenty-four? Sometime in law school, I think. There was a guy, Bill. We used to hook up, more for stress release than anything romantic. And I just asked him to do it, choke me, and he did, and the rest is history.'

I sat there, giving no response, aware of the clock ticking away and chewing on what she'd told me.

'Let's change direction,' I said at last. 'Tell me about life with your mother after your father died.'

Some of her billowing female essence seeped away. Her skin paled, and her face sagged, weary.

The alarm on my phone rang, ending the session.

Nina looked relieved, brightened, and then beamed at me. 'Saved by the bell.'

'Saved by the bell.'

By the time the Justice Department attorney stood up from the chair, she was radiating the feminine again, from her smell to her beauty to her confidence as she put on her coat. Nina extended her hand. I took it, surprised at how delicate it was. She gazed at me with a sweet, intoxicating expression.

'Thank you, Dr. Cross,' she said softly. 'Kaycee and I look forward to the next time we meet.'

36

Around three in the afternoon, Martin Franks flipped the blinker on his pickup truck and turned right off a state route south of Charlottesville, Virginia. Franks headed west. On the pickup's navigation screen, he saw that the road ahead climbed into rural, forested country, and he started to whistle 'Carry On Wayward Son.'

The ex-Special Forces operator liked this scenario. The rural ground. The woods. It brought back waking-dream images of the logger.

Places like abandoned farms, big tracts of timber, they tended to isolate people. That was always good, in Franks's opinion. Fewer eyes meant more latitude in the games he liked to play.

Franks crossed a bridge above a stream lined with leafless hardwood trees. On the other side of the stream, he crossed a railroad track, and the road surface changed to hard-packed dirt and gravel.

Now it was up to chance, synchronicity, serendipity, three powers Franks was used to cultivating. Franks had once dated a beautiful young woman named Ella. She was his opposite in almost every sense, a pacifist given to hippie clothing who taught him the power of imagining what he wanted and then asking the universe for

146

some sign that his vision was being seen and shared.

This unorthodox approach to life had saved Franks more than once when he was operating in Afghanistan. Every morning and every night on tour, he asked the universe for a warning if danger loomed.

Twice, he had been on the verge of walking into a Taliban ambush. The first time, a kid goat scampered out of hiding, blatting as if a dog were after it.

The second time, Franks had seen vultures flying above a village they were about to enter.

Both times he'd halted his team and waited and watched. In the first case, he saw human movement among the rocks where the goat had run from, and in the second, he'd realized that the carrion birds were there because Taliban fighters had already killed enough civilians in the village to attract them.

'C'mon,' Franks said to the sky and the universe beyond. 'Give me a sign here. Tell me I was right to come up this road. Show me a worthy opponent.'

He passed a bungalow in a clearing. A young woman was hanging sheets in a raw wind. Her bundled-up little child, a toddler, really, was booting a little soccer ball.

Franks passed. He had a rule about killing women for sport. He wouldn't do it. Especially young moms with kids.

He drove on and passed a steel building that housed a machine shop and several smaller homes before hitting a long stretch of forest. He kept hoping he'd see a car or a truck pulled over, and tracks going off into the trees.

That would make things easier. He had a pang of guilt knowing that he shouldn't have been there at all, that he should have stayed hunkered down at the Mandarin Oriental, focused on his task for the next, what, fifty-six hours?

Franks had found over the years, however, that the closer he got to a commercial job, the more he felt compelled to hunt on his own, almost as if he were —

A Virginia State Police cruiser was pulled off the road just ahead. The lights were on but not blinking. Franks slowed as he passed by and saw a big Asian, late thirties, early forties, with a thick neck holding a coffee cup and a sandwich.

Franks smiled, waved. The trooper lifted his cup.

Franks glanced in the rearview, thinking, *What's he doing way out here? So far from the highway?*

And then an idea hatched in his head, and the questions didn't matter. Whistling, he drove around a bend in the road and turned around. He took off his sunglasses, rolled down the window, put his hand out, waved again, and pulled to a stop opposite the cruiser.

The trooper acted slightly annoyed, but he set his coffee cup and sandwich down and lowered his window.

'I'm sorry to interrupt dinner, sir,' Franks said. 'But my nav system committed suicide this morning, and my cell's not picking up data for

Google maps, and I can't figure out where the heck I am on the real map.'

Franks held up a Rand McNally atlas of the Eastern Seaboard, climbed out of the truck cab, and said, 'Could you help orient me, Officer?'

'Sergeant,' the trooper said, opening his door. 'Sergeant Nick Moon.'

'I appreciate it, Sergeant Moon,' Franks said, opening the atlas to Virginia and putting it on the hood of the cruiser.

Moon climbed out. Muscular, athletic, he wore a bulletproof vest, had a large black Beretta pistol in his holster, and outweighed Franks by twenty pounds.

'Where y'all from?' Sergeant Moon said.

'Born in Arizona, but the past couple of years I've been jumping between Wyoming and South Dakota.'

'Oil fields?'

Franks smiled. 'I do emergency welding work. You know, fix what needs fixing.'

'Good money in that?'

'Enough that I don't work winters. I travel all over, taking a look around at things while I have the freedom.'

'Sounds like a nice life,' the trooper said. 'Nothing tying you down.'

'Not for the next six weeks,' Franks said. He gestured at the map. 'Can you help?'

'Sure,' Moon said, leaning toward the map and squinting.

Franks glanced around and saw no cars, then he smashed his right elbow up into the trooper's voice box.

149

Moon reeled backward and sideways, gagging as he hit the open cruiser door and fell to the ground. Franks was almost disappointed the trooper was down already, but he jumped forward to finish the drama.

He kicked Moon's right hand as he struggled for his service weapon. Franks's steel-toed boot broke several fingers. Moon gasped and choked. Franks stooped, reached for the trooper's pistol, and had almost slipped it free of the holster when a meaty fist smashed into the right side of his face.

Franks staggered and went to his knees. He saw dots, felt woozy, but not enough to dull instincts honed for years in the Arizona desert and the bigger sandpit.

Through sheer will, he threw himself forward, scrambling to get out of range of Moon's left fist, and spun to his feet. Franks's right eye was swelling shut, and he tasted blood on his lips, but the fog of the blow to his head was lifting.

The trooper was still on his back, reaching across his body for the gun. Franks took one fast step and with his steel-toed boot kicked Sergeant Moon on the top of his skull. He heard a crunch. The trooper's body went rigid.

Franks kicked him again, this time in the temple, and then a third time, this one to Moon's exposed neck. He felt vertebrae snap. The trooper sagged, dead.

For four long, heaving breaths, Franks felt that shaky adrenaline clarity he always got after a challenging kill, that hyper-confidence that empowered him when he realized he'd cheated death again. But there was no time to linger. No time to revel in it.

After wiping his prints off the sergeant's pistol, he reholstered it, picked up the road atlas, and crossed to his truck.

Franks took one last look at the tableau of Sergeant Moon's death scene, committed it to sweet memory, and drove off. He didn't look back and did not whistle a single note.

37

I left my office shortly after darkness fell, my mind still returning to Nina Davis.

She was one of the most devastatingly beautiful women I'd ever met. She seemed to ooze sensuality from her pores and suggested forbidden adventure with every gesture. And she had predatory instincts. She stalked her sexual prey.

What was that about? She intimated she'd stalked Dr. Winters before, and successfully. But what else did she say? That there were rumors that he was into pain? Wouldn't she have known that for certain?

As I climbed the stairs, smelling the aromas of Nana Mama's latest triumph wafting through the door, I could not avoid the growing trepidation I felt. Nina Davis was making me nervous. I was the therapist. I was supposed to keep the inner lives of my clients at arm's length, where they could be dispassionately observed.

But since Nina had left, close to four hours before, I'd been thinking about her, imagining her stalking me, imagining her bringing me right to the edge of a decision.

The guy has to make the final move in her little game. Isn't that what she said?

I felt guilty for even considering that possibility. Not only was I a happily married guy, but my job demanded I keep my feelings out of her game.

But I was also a man, an alpha male if ever

there was one, and Nina was so . . . how did she describe it? *Free in her* —

On the other side of the door, the sound of a cooking spoon banging against a pot startled me back to reality. I opened the kitchen door and sighed with relief at the familiar sight of Nana Mama at the stove, her back to me.

'That smells excellent,' I said.

'A lamb stew I whipped up,' she said.

'How long until dinner?'

She glanced at the clock. 'Forty minutes?'

'I'm going to take a walk,' I said. 'Clear my head.'

'Don't get hit by a bus.'

I laughed and kissed her on the cheek. 'I'll try not to.'

I grabbed a jacket, cap, and gloves. I was putting them on when Bree came through the door looking like she'd taken a pummeling.

'Are you going for a walk?' she said. 'I need one.'

After putting my arms around her and kissing her on the lips, I said, 'I would love to go for a walk with you.'

That pleased Bree. She snuggled into my chest for a long hug before we went outside into the chill air and headed north toward Pennsylvania Avenue. As we walked, she told me about her frustration at her inability to make headway in the Betsy Walker murder case and about how Chief Michaels was calling her twice a day for updates.

'I don't know what's behind this pressure he's putting on me.'

153

'Sounds like he's up for a big job or he's going to run for elected office.'

Bree thought about that. 'So he needs a coup, and I'm the one who's supposed to manufacture that?'

'I'm not saying I'm right. Just conjecture.'

She rubbed her temple, then stopped and fell into my arms.

'Hey,' I said, patting her back.

'I just need a hug, that's all.'

'I love you,' I said. 'And you can have as many hugs as you need.'

'Thank you, baby,' Bree whispered. 'I love you too.'

Someone called out from behind us, 'C'mon, get a room, why don't you?'

We broke our embrace to see John Sampson hustling toward us. It had been a while since I'd seen my oldest friend and former partner at DC Metro.

'When'd you get back?' I asked, shaking his hand.

'Four hours ago,' he said.

'Good trip?' Bree asked.

'The best,' Sampson said. 'I was ready to go back to work tomorrow completely refreshed, but I guess I had to start early.'

We both looked at him with puzzled expressions.

'I just got a call from a friend with the Virginia State Police,' Sampson said. 'A mutual acquaintance of ours, Sergeant Nick Moon — '

'I know Moon,' Bree said.

'I do too,' I said. 'He's a guest instructor in

mixed martial arts and submission techniques at Quantico.'

'That's him,' Sampson said. 'Good guy. And he's dead.'

'What?' Bree said. 'How? Line of duty?'

'He was in uniform,' Sampson said. 'A couple of teenagers found him lying dead beside his cruiser, which was still running.'

'Shot?'

Sampson shook his head. 'Looks like he'd been in a fight. Three of his right fingers were broken. His larynx was crushed. The knuckles of his left hand were split and bloody. The top of his skull was fractured from kicks, and his neck was broken.'

'Jesus,' I said. 'His service weapon?'

'Snapped in his holster.'

'So he was surprised,' Bree said. 'Hit without warning.'

'Still,' I said. 'The Sergeant Moon I remember was a fighting machine. You'd have to be one hell of a warrior to kill him.'

'That's exactly what my friend said: a professional killed Moon.'

Thinking about the sniper who'd killed Senator Walker and then about Kristina Varjan, the Hungarian killer for hire spotted at Dulles Airport, I said, 'As in an assassin?'

'He said Special Forces kind of badass, but sure, assassin would fit.'

Bree said, 'No one saw the fight?'

'Happened way out in the middle of nowhere,' Sampson said. 'But the state police may have gotten lucky.'

155

'How's that?' I asked.

'Moon's left hand, the one with the split knuckles. It had to have connected with one hell of a punch. There was blood evidence at the scene that wasn't Moon's.'

Bree said, 'And there's probably DNA on his knuckles. That helps.'

That did help, but in my gut, something churned, a sensation that grew the more I thought about the shooting expertise of Senator Walker's killer, the CIA's concerns about Kristina Varjan, and how one of law enforcement's best self-defense men had turned up beaten and dead by his cruiser in a way that suggested a pro.

'Alex?' Bree said. 'What is it? What are you thinking?'

I licked my lips before gazing at Sampson and Bree in turn.

'I'm thinking it's odd that we've had two, maybe three professional killers around suddenly, and I'm feeling like they're all here for some reason beyond Senator Walker and Sergeant Moon.'

38

Shortly after nine in the morning, Pablo Cruz pressed down the last strip of blue painter's tape on the floor of an abandoned factory in the far northwest corner of Maryland. It was a vast space that had once held huge textile looms and massive cutting machines.

The machines had been removed and sold for scrap a long time ago, leaving the silhouettes of their footprints on the filthy concrete floor. Cruz barely glanced at them. He studied the maze of tape he'd been laying down since the afternoon before.

The maze stretched almost the entire length of the space, more than one hundred and twenty-five yards by the range finder Cruz had brought in to. help him transfer dimensions from old blueprints onto this factory's floor.

Looking from the blueprints to the tape diagram, he thought he'd come close, probably within inches of the actual spaces he'd be dealing with the day after tomorrow.

Day after tomorrow, Cruz thought, feeling a thrill go through him and checking his watch.

Cruz tried to ignore the second thrill that shivered up his spine. This would no doubt be the pinnacle of his career. The crowning achievement.

If he survived.

That last thought sobered him, yanked him

out of fantasy and back to the task at hand. He zipped his down coat up under his chin and saw his breath in the cold air as he studied the maze once again. Then he closed his eyes and tried to see it in his mind, tried to imagine himself moving through all the various hallways, rooms, and passages.

When he'd gotten halfway through, he stopped imagining and opened his eyes.

He'd been studying the diagrams so much, Cruz felt ready to go at least that far. Halfway. Just to see what he'd already memorized. He got out a phone, found the stopwatch, and started it.

He walked confidently to marks indicating steps and climbed them to a guarded door. He would have the proper identifications. They would put him through a metal detector and find nothing.

They would pat him down, probably find the resin webs around his forearms and wrists, but he had a perfect excuse. They would search his bag, but they would recognize nothing. They would let him through.

With that certainty firmly in mind, Cruz proceeded, still at that steady, relaxed pace, until he reached a large square room in the maze. He slanted to the opposite corner of the room, and another passage. There he broke into a jog, as if he'd needed to be somewhere five minutes before.

When he reached a T, he broke left, crossed the mouth of an even larger space, and started to slow as he moved toward the mannequin from the storage unit. He'd set it up at the intersection of two passages.

If he had to shoot early, it would be here.

Cruz walked confidently, hands out, palms up, toward the mannequin. Ten feet shy of it, he snapped the fingers of his left hand back toward his wrist.

A Kevlar-reinforced nylon bullet slammed into the mannequin's throat and blew out the back of its neck.

Cruz did not stop to admire the destruction. Instead, he pushed on, reloading the graphite derringer and trying to see if he remembered the diagram past midpoint.

He went to a closet in the maze, gave himself sixty seconds to change clothes and credentials, and then hurried up another long passage. He hesitated at a door on the right and looked ahead a moment before going inside.

After waiting for ninety seconds exactly, Cruz exited the room, turned right again, then took two lefts and went through imaginary double doors into the largest space yet, so big he hadn't bothered to tape it all in. He made his way toward the far-right corner, where a second and a third mannequin stood. In his mind, Cruz imagined the place packed and him shifting and slipping his way forward.

Cruz stopped fifteen feet to the right of the mannequins and waited, a smile on his face, his left hand poised as if resting on the shoulder of someone in front of him.

Cruz laughed, bobbed his head, extended his right hand in welcome, and then snapped his fingers back sharply. The web stretched and triggered the second single-shot gas derringer. It fired with a thud, and the nylon bullet penetrated the mannequin's chest and knocked it to the ground.

A moment later, he fired the left-hand derringer at the rear mannequin and hit it square in the chest.

Cruz clicked the stopwatch on his phone and saw that nine minutes and eleven seconds had elapsed. He started the clock again, stayed cool as he backed up, slow, deliberate, then turned and headed back through the maze the way he'd come.

In the long hallway, Cruz broke into a slow jog. When he reached the mannequin with the hole in its neck, he stopped for fifteen seconds, then moved on, running fast now, and was soon back at the entrance to the schematic.

Cruz stopped the clock; his hard breathing left clouds pluming in the frigid air. Six minutes and fourteen seconds coming back. Fifteen minutes and twenty-five seconds total.

That will do it, he thought, and he stared at the door that led outside the factory.

Cruz shook off the idea that he was ready and told himself to run the route at least twenty more times. He had enough time to practice until he could do the whole thing blindfolded or in the dark. Before resetting the stopwatch and starting again, he decided he would do both.

39

Ned Mahoney pulled over at the curb and pointed diagonally across a busy street past a dingy strip mall to the Happy Pines Motel in suburban Gaithersburg, Maryland.

The Happy Pines was one of those no-tell joints you could rent by the hour, day, week, or month. A thirty-unit, two-story affair, the motel was badly in need of renovation, and the rain and gray skies made the place look even drearier than it was.

But according to Mahoney, a woman named Martina Rodoni bearing a Eurozone passport had registered at the Happy Pines two days before. Even though our contact at the CIA said there was zero chance Varjan would use the identity again, we decided to drive out to see if they were one and the same.

I said, 'What are the odds she's here?'

Mahoney turned off the car, said, 'The clerk I spoke with said she's in and out and hasn't let them service the room.'

For a moment, I thought about Kasimov, the Russian, and how he'd been holed up at his hotel while his men put on disguises to go out on clandestine missions.

But I tucked that away and focused on the motel parking lot, seeing aged Ford pickups and beater Chevy sedans with tailpipes held on by coat hangers. Nothing newer. Nothing that screamed rental. Then again, Kristina Varjan could have parked on the street or in the alley behind the motel, where Mahoney had a squad of junior FBI agents moving into position.

When they radioed us that they were ready, we spilled out of the car, all of us dressed in jeans, work boots, and oversize rain jackets that hid our Kevlar vests. Remembering what we'd been told about the Hungarian assassin, I wondered if I was wearing enough armor.

As we crossed the street, I said, 'You don't find it odd she used the same name she used coming into the country? Edith, that spook we spoke with at the CIA, said she switches identities constantly.'

Mahoney shrugged. 'She didn't know she'd been spotted, so she stuck with it.'

We went into the office where we were met by the owner, Vash Yasant, a young, nervous Indian immigrant who'd bought the motel three months before.

'What's this about?' Yasant said. 'What's she done?'

'Let's make sure of something first,' Mahoney said, and on the counter he put a still from the surveillance footage at Dulles airport.

'Is that her?' I asked.

Yasant studied it, stroking his chin, then nodded vigorously. 'Yes, that's her. I'd swear on it. Especially that bag. She had it with her when she checked in.'

'She have a car?'

'She said she came by Metro and bus.'

'Room?' Mahoney said.

162

'Number fifteen, right above us,' Yasant said, pointing upward. 'She wanted a room facing the street.'

I sighed. 'She saw us coming in.'

'If she was looking,' Mahoney said.

'She went out two hours ago,' the motel manager said. 'What has this Martina Rodoni done?'

'Nothing so far,' I said. 'We just want to talk to her.'

'I will take you to her room,' Yasant said. 'I'll bring the master key.'

I thought that was a mistake, but Mahoney said, 'You'll stay well behind us, and you will move only when told to.'

'Yes, sir!' the innkeeper cried, and he stood up straight.

'Yes, what?' his wife said, coming out from behind a curtain. She was dressed in a colorful sari and was very pregnant.

Her husband said, 'Rani, these men are with the FBI, and that woman up in fifteen, she is very, very dangerous. They have asked me to assist them with the key!'

Mrs. Yasant looked at her husband, at us, and then at her husband again. 'You will do no such thing, Vash! The baby comes any day, and you cannot go playing policeman!'

The innkeeper looked ready to argue, but Mahoney said, 'On second thought, Mr. Yasant, your wife's probably right. Why don't you just give us the key? We'll drop it on the way out.'

The father-to-be looked chagrined and deflated, but he handed us the key from a hook

163

on the wall behind him.

'You will report what you find up there?' he asked. 'This is my place, yes?'

'Absolutely,' I said.

We went out of the door and drew weapons and put them in our raincoat pockets before climbing the near staircase and walking back toward the main drag and room 15. It was mid-morning, no new hourly customers, and the long-termers had gone off to scavenge their lives.

Every room we passed was quiet. Even room 15, which had a Do Not Disturb sign hanging from the door handle.

Mahoney stood to the side of the door, looked at the window and tight curtains beyond it, then knocked sharply.

No answer. After thirty seconds, Mahoney knocked again.

Again, no answer.

Mahoney took his pistol out. I did the same. He fitted the key in the lock and turned it.

I pushed the door inward, revealing twin beds, unused, still crisply made. Dead center of the bed deeper into the room was the same roller bag we'd seen Varjan wheeling in the Dulles airport security footage.

Beside it was a cheap cell phone.

Mahoney went over to the bag, but I stopped him.

'Why leave it like this?' I said. 'Why not put it in the closed closet?'

Ned did not have time to answer before the cell phone on the tacky bedspread began to ring and buzz.

164

I was closer, so I picked it up and answered on speaker.

'Hello?' I said. 'Kristina? Kristina Varjan?'

There was a moment before Varjan said, 'Good-bye. Whoever you are.'

The phone went dead.

My eyes darted to the bag.

'Run!'

We spun and bolted toward the open door. I was behind Mahoney and one step onto the balcony when the phone in my hand began to ring with a different ringtone.

I threw myself completely out of the room a split second before the bomb went off behind us, blowing out the windows and blasting the metal door off its hinges.

40

Two hours later, the blast was still ringing in my ears as I looked down on the carnival that had descended on the Happy Pines Motel. Two fire trucks. Five police cruisers. Four vans bearing a small army of crime scene techs and special agents from the FBI and the Bureau of Alcohol, Tobacco, and Firearms.

Mahoney was standing next to me, elbows on the balcony railing, still shocked by how close we'd come to death.

'Wish I'd never quit smoking,' he said, and I heard a quiver in his voice.

'Close,' I said, equally shaken. 'That's the closest I've ever come.'

I'd called Bree to let her know what had happened, and Mahoney and I had already spoken about Varjan with a parade of agents assigned to the case. Our theory was that she suspected she'd been spotted after arriving at Dulles and had tested that suspicion by renting the motel room under the name Martina Rodoni.

'She sat on us, waiting,' I said. 'For two days.'

'She's disciplined, I give you that,' Mahoney said.

'Is she? Why try to kill us? It only increases the heat on her.'

'I'll set aside the why for now. She did it is all I need to know. We have to get her face everywhere. She's got other business planned.'

'I agree. Enhance and enlarge the security photo of her. She'll be recognized.'

He nodded and took out his cell phone.

Almost directly below us in the parking lot, Rani Yasant was yelling at her husband, who was looking up at the smoldering hole that had once been room 15.

'You see?' Mrs. Yasant cried, hands on her belly. 'If you had been brave and gone up there, you would have died, Vash, and then where would I be? Answer me that, where would I be?'

Yasant put both hands to his head as if squeezing it in a vise. 'Why do you always think this way, Rani? I did not go up there. I am alive. And you wish me to be a coward in every aspect of my life!'

He shouted this last bit, and it caused his wife to step back and start crying.

'What are we going to do?' she said, sobbing. 'I told you not to buy that extra fire insurance. I said it was too expensive!'

Her husband softened and walked over to her. He put his arms around her.

'It's okay, Rani. I did not listen to you.'

His wife looked up at him through tears. 'Is that true?'

'We're covered,' he said, and he kissed her forehead.

'Agent Mahoney?'

Mahoney and I turned to find Tim Schmidt, the supervising special agent with BATF, coming toward us. Mahoney finished his call and hung up.

Schmidt said, 'Preliminary results say you had plastic explosives in that bag with a frequency trigger set to trip at the phone's ringtone. Where is the phone, by the way? We'd like to take it if possible.'

Mahoney said, 'It's already on its way to Quantico, but we will share everything with BATF as soon as we have it.'

Schmidt puffed up his cheeks and blew out his mouth. 'Fair enough. It's cooled down enough in there to look around if you want.'

We walked back to room 15. The walls were scorched and blackened. So was the ceiling. There was an inch of dark water on the floor.

The near twin bed had been thrown over. The mattress lay in the slurry, coated in soot. The mattress of the far bed, the one where the bag and phone had been, now had a gaping charred hole in it almost the entire width and three-quarters of the length.

I stared at the blast hole. So did Ned, who said, 'Darn happy to be here, Alex.'

I nodded, still stunned and thanking my guardian angel for helping me put the phone, the bag, and Varjan's words together fast enough to clear the room and survive. I felt humbled and then desperate to go home and be with my family.

But I overrode that desire with the need to do my job. I turned from the mattress and looked at a table lamp, bent and twisted on the floor, and then at the night table flipped over on its left flank. The right side was caved in and scorched.

The drawer was closed.

Beside the table on the floor was an open and partially burned Gideon Bible.

I looked at the closed drawer. I supposed it was possible the blast had driven the open drawer shut. Or that Gideon Bible had been out before the blast. Had I seen it?

I didn't remember. If it was out, why? Would a professional assassin like Varjan seek spiritual solace in a motel Bible?

After putting on gloves, I picked the Bible up. A charred chunk of pages fell out from the back. I flipped through the Bible but found nothing tucked in it.

I was about to set it aside when I noticed that soot from the burned pages had streaked and smudged across the mostly white inside of the Bible's back cover. Then I noticed that the soot had raised the impression of letters there. An e and an r.

Someone had obviously scribbled on the front of the back page, and the pressure had gone through to the cover. I was about to set it aside to be bagged again, but then I thought, *What if Varjan scribbled there?*

What were the odds of that? Hundreds of people must have used the room in the past twelve months, let alone years.

Still, I did not want to leave any stone unturned. I broke off the charred edges of the pages that had fallen on the floor, crumbled the charring into dust, and spilled it around the two visible letters and across the page.

Words appeared, a stack of them:

169

Celes Chere
Prelim 2 sharp
Marstons, same
Gabriel, same
Conker 3

Conker? Below that, there were other letters but they were indistinct. A *b* and an *i* or a *t* and then a *c*. Or an *o?*

I had no idea when the words were written or what significance they held. I took a picture of the list with my phone and left the Bible for the criminalists to bag and analyze further.

'Not much here that wasn't here before she planted the bomb,' said Schmidt, the ATF agent.

'This was a kill zone for her, nothing more,' Mahoney said. 'But we've got her phone, and we'll be inside it in hours.'

'Why the hell is she here?' Schmidt said. 'Who the hell is she trying to kill?'

'Besides us?' I said. 'No clue. But when we find her, I sure plan to ask.'

41

Kristina Varjan drove a beater Dodge sedan she'd bought off a lot in College Park. It had a shimmy in the front end and almost a hundred and fifty thousand miles on it, so she kept on at one mile under the speed limit, heading up I-95 toward Atlantic City, New Jersey, and an Airbnb apartment she'd rented online.

Varjan had cut her hair shorter, spiked it, and bleached the tips blond. She'd changed into skinny jeans, a fleece-lined denim jacket, and a long-sleeved Sex Pistols T-shirt. Her makeup was heavy on the mascara. She'd pierced her own nose the night before, and her upper right lip and tongue too.

When she glanced at herself in the rearview, she looked nothing like Martina Rodoni, the fashionable European in for a week of sightseeing. Now she was Elena Wolfe, rebellious nonconformist over from Great Britain to play a few games.

Varjan shifted. She was sick of sitting, especially in this seat. She'd sat in it for almost two days, watching the Happy Pines Motel from well down the street.

She'd almost quit her surveillance the evening before, tried to tell herself that thirty-six hours watching her back trail was enough, that she'd been wrong, that she hadn't seen the CIA op she'd fought with in Istanbul standing in the line

171

for security at Dulles only minutes after her own arrival in the U.S.

Take off, Varjan had thought. *You're good. Get your game on. Leave everything else behind you.*

Varjan had almost driven to the Happy Pines to retrieve the bomb, check out, and carry on with her more pressing plans. But some difficult voice in her head insisted she'd been spotted and that she needed to keep up her vigil.

The difficult voice had proved to be the right one.

What happened then had been reflexive, nothing she could have controlled. She hadn't meant to blow the bomb unless that CIA agent, Edith, was with them. But then that guy who'd answered the phone, he'd known her real name.

He called me Kristina, Kristina Varjan.

The very words made Varjan feel exposed and angry, made her want to lash out. She preferred to go through life playing roles, only rarely showing her true self to anyone and never using her given name in any context.

But that man had known her. He'd used her real name!

And then it had been reflexive. Uncontrollable. She'd set off the bomb.

Varjan understood she needed to inform Piotr, or whatever his real name was, and explain the situation.

However, maybe the less he knew, the better. Given the contracts he'd assigned her the day before, she understood that any weakness would likely change their arrangement and make her a

172

target for elimination at some point in the near future.

That was too complicated. That was just too much to handle while trying to execute multiple plays as fast as possible.

No, Varjan decided as she passed the exit for Baltimore's Inner Harbor area. She'd keep her employer in the dark, get the jobs done, collect, and then vanish once and for all.

42

What *was* Varjan up to?

That question and others like it ran laps in my head as I got out of an Uber at my house. The sun had set. The lights glowed in the front room. So did the big screen, which was tuned to the news.

I climbed the front steps, thanking my Savior once again.

When I opened the door, I heard Bree cry, 'Alex?'

'Dad!' Ali shouted.

They all came running to the front hall, Bree, Ali, Jannie, and Nana Mama too. Bree had tears in her eyes. 'It's so good . . . you're here.'

I hugged her, kissed her, whispered in her ear, 'I'll always be here.'

She squeezed me tight, then stood back while I hugged my daughter, son, and grandmother.

'The local news says an assassin set off the bomb, a lady assassin,' Ali said.

Jannie said, 'They showed her picture. Did you see her, Dad?'

'No,' I said. 'But she saw us. She called the phone for the first time *after* we were in the room, so we figure she had to have been in range, watching, when she made the second call to trigger the bomb.'

Nana Mama patted her heart. 'Thank God, you got out of there in time.'

'I've been weak-kneed and grateful a thousand times since it happened,' I said.

We went into the kitchen, where my grandmother had a steaming pot of soup made from chicken, celery, onions, basil, garlic, oregano, and halved cherry tomatoes. She'd also made two big loaves of garlic bread slathered with lots of butter.

While Jannie helped Bree ladle the soup into bowls that Ali ferried to the kitchen table, I was feeling almost overjoyed. It was such a simple thing, being with family, preparing for dinner, but that evening, it made me want to cry.

'What else, Dad?' Ali said. 'Do you know where she went? Varjan?'

Ordinarily I would have deflected further conversations about an ongoing case, but since Mahoney had let the cat out of the bag with the media, I shared with them what I knew. I explained Varjan's reputation as a ruthless killer for hire, her recent arrival in the U.S. under the name Martina Rodoni, and our belief that she was in the country to kill someone other than me and Mahoney.

Nana came to the table and we all held hands to say grace.

My grandmother finished with 'Thank You for getting Alex out of that motel room this morning. And bless him in the days ahead.'

'Amen,' we all said.

After I'd eaten two slices of homemade bread, finished a bowl of the delicious soup, and gone back for seconds, Bree said, 'I don't suppose there was any evidence left in the motel room?

Other than the bomb material, I mean.'

I started to shake my head, but then I remembered something. I dug in my pocket for my phone.

'About the only thing I could find that survived was a Bible, and I don't know if this has a thing to do with anything, but there was this list of . . . '

I found the picture on my phone and tapped it to open it. 'Here.'

I turned it and showed them the list raised by the soot:

Celes Chere
Prelim 2 sharp
Marstons, same
Gabriel, same
Conker 3

'What does that mean?' Jannie asked, passing the phone to Nana. 'Did she write it?'

'Who knows?' I said. 'It was just there on the inside back cover, so I shot it.'

Ali took the phone from Nana Mama, who shrugged, said, 'What's a Conker?'

Staring at the screen, Ali said, 'Well, a Conker is this . . . ' He looked up at me. 'Dad, Kristina Varjan. No doubt about it.'

'How do you know that?' Jannie asked, her brow knitted.

'So, first, Conker? He's like this crazed squirrel. Drinks. Smokes. Likes to smack people in the face with a frying pan.'

'What?' my grandmother said.

176

'In a really good video game, Nana,' Ali said. 'Conker's the hero avatar in Conker's Bad Fur Day. Check it out, Dad, for real.'

'I will, but *how* do you know that Varjan wrote the list?'

He pointed to the list. 'Marstons? Gabriel? Those are avatars in other video games made by the same company, Victorious Gaming.'

Bree said, 'I still don't see how that links — '

Ali held up his hand, said, 'Celes Chere? I swear to God, she has her own Victorious game too. I've got friends at school who are obsessed with going to — '

He grabbed up his phone, started tapping with his thumbs.

'Oh my God, I think it starts tomorrow!'

'What does?' Bree asked.

'Just let me make sure,' Ali said, and then he looked up at us, grinning, and pumped his fist. 'Victorious promotes these big e-sports tournaments where people obsessed with the games go to play for like a gazillion in Bitcoin. The biggest tournament of the year starts tomorrow in Atlantic City! Prelims for Blade Girl, featuring Celes Chere, start at two p.m. Same thing for the Marstons. And Conker prelims get under way at three!'

43

At 1:40 the next afternoon, February 4, a Thursday, techno music pulsed and blared through the Atlantic City Convention Center. The raucous crowd was not at all what Mahoney and I expected. Yes, there were lots of eager tweens and doughy adolescent males who looked like they tended toward the stoner-slacker end of the spectrum. But there were also young women and grown men and women, many dressed as their favorite avatars in a Victorious game. We saw six or seven Conkers in the kind of squirrel outfits you might see at a rave concert, several women dressed as glam avatar Celes Chere, and two couples sporting the sort of futuristic cowboy garb the Marstons supposedly favored in their game.

Vendors sold fast food. Hawkers offered tournament programs and other Victorious-branded souvenirs.

Mahoney said, 'Feels like we're going into a combination of a prize fight, a rock concert, and a Star Wars convention.'

'With three million in Bitcoin to the winner,' said Philip Stapleton, Victorious Gaming's security director.

'Why Bitcoin?' I asked.

Stapleton shrugged. 'My bosses think it's edgy.'

Stapleton was in his early forties, a former

navy NCIS investigator who'd been shot in the hip in the line of duty, left the military, and joined Victorious two years ago.

We'd given him the gist of what had brought us to the event and a copy of Kristina Varjan's photograph to distribute via text to his team. He'd been concerned that a wanted bomber might be in the complex, but we told him it was unlikely she was there.

He took us through open double doors into a sprawling exposition space. There were five raised stages, four of them set up to look like boxing rings but without the highest rope around their perimeters.

There were seats surrounding the rings and the main stage, fifty rows deep and filling with fans. Above each ring were four large screens facing the growing crowds. The pulsing techno grew louder.

Stapleton explained that during the preliminary rounds, each of the four rings would serve as a battleground for one of the four big Victorious games.

The first ring would feature contestants in Conker's Bad Fur Day, the game Ali described the night before. The Ruins would play in ring number two, starring the Marstons, a couple in a dystopian world searching for their lost children.

Competitors in ring three would vie in Avenging Angel, which featured the avatar Gabriel in a fantasy scenario. Ring four's contestants were looking to advance in Blade Girl, starring Celes Chere, a badass with mad martial arts skills facing danger in an unnamed urban setting.

I wanted to head straight to the Blade Girl ring but was stopped by a booming voice over the PA system: 'Let's get ready to rumble! Let's get ready to be Victorious!'

The fans jumped up, raised their fists overhead, screamed, whistled, and stomped their feet. The music took on a frenetic, infectious pace and beat.

Stapleton led us to the central stage where Austin Crowley and Sydney Bronson, the young co-founders of Victorious, were dancing and imploring the crowd to join them. They were dressed like hipsters, Crowley in thick black glasses and a nerd cut and Bronson in a black-and-white-checkered jacket and a red porkpie hat.

I'd read up on them on the way over. Crowley and Bronson had met by chance at a party in Boston. Crowley was a sophomore and standout student at MIT who spent his free time gaming. Bronson was a bored freshman at Harvard who also spent most of his free time playing games.

In their first conversation, both said they thought they could come up with better games than any on the market. They decided to try, and they had enough success with their first effort that they both quit school. The rest was history. According to *Forbes*, six years after they left academia, they were worth a quarter of a billion dollars.

The music died. Bronson went to the mike, said, 'That's the energy we want in this room! Am I right, right, right?'

The crowd hooted and howled back its approval.

'We hear you,' Bronson said. 'We see ya, and we feel ya too!'

The fans erupted again.

Over their clapping, Bronson said, 'I am Sydney Bronson, chief visionary officer at Victorious! And I'd like to introduce my partner and our chief geek, the man who takes my ideas and makes them come alive, Austin Crowley!'

Crowley came somewhat reluctantly to the mike. His eyes swept the crowd, hesitated, then pushed on. He looked like he was suffering from stage fright as he said, 'Well, do they make you happy? Our games?'

The crowd cheered. He gained confidence, threw his fist overhead, and roared, 'Will Victorious rule the gaming world?'

The fans went wild.

'All right!' Bronson said, coming back to the mike and throwing his arm around his partner. 'Austin and I welcome you to the Victorious world championships, the richest e-sports event on the planet, an event that is only going to get bigger and richer in the years to come!'

The men gave each other high-fives and then shouted in unison, 'We declare these games open!'

Crowley threw both hands over his head, and Bronson pumped his fist and crowed, 'First bouts start in five minutes!'

They waved and walked offstage.

Fans started to push toward the various rings.

I was about to suggest to Ned that we take a walk around when, across the sea of people moving in all directions away from the stage, I saw a woman dressed as Celes Chere gazing back at me. She had a green lanyard around her neck and a green badge that identified her as a contestant.

Pretty face, short, spiky blond hair, shiny white coat, and pale skin. She looked away, put on cat's-eye sunglasses, and merged with the fans heading toward rings one and two. I stared after her, seeing the structure of her cheekbones, jaw, and nose in profile before the crowd blocked my view.

'Alex,' Mahoney said. 'Let's — '

I started pushing into the crowd, calling over my shoulder, 'I think I just saw Varjan!'

44

The current in the river of fans was moving against us, and we didn't want to pull our badges and set off a panic. It was slow getting through, but we finally reached the left side of the stage and entered into a flow of people moving in the direction I had seen her.

'There she is,' Mahoney said.

I stopped to see him pointing at a woman about thirty yards away, also dressed as Celes Chere. But she had thirty pounds on the woman I'd just seen.

'Not her,' I said, catching sight of another Celes Chere, but she was too tall. In frustration I looked at Stapleton, who'd followed us. 'Can we get up on the stage?'

He hesitated, and then nodded. 'You're sure it was her?'

'Not one hundred percent, no,' I said, climbing the stairs.

On the stage, I pivoted to scan the crowds on the north side of rings one and two. Mahoney climbed up beside me.

I spotted a third Celes Chere with her back to us, and then two more, and then six or seven others just entering the venue in a pack.

'They're everywhere!' Mahoney said.

'We'll have to check every one.'

A voice behind us said, 'Who are these guys, Phil?'

Mahoney and I turned to find the founders of Victorious looking at us. We pulled out our credentials and introduced ourselves. They were alarmed when Stapleton said we were searching for an assassin and bomber.

'In here?' said Bronson, the one who'd left Harvard. 'Why would he come here?'

'She,' Mahoney said. 'And we don't know. Maybe she's a fan of your games.'

I said, 'She was wearing a contestant's badge.'

Crowley, the one who'd dropped out of MIT, had a mild stammer. 'What d-does she look like?'

'She's dressed as Celes Chere.'

Bronson laughed. 'Good luck finding her. There'll be two hundred of them in here by the time we get to the semifinals.'

Crowley studied me. 'Do we need to clear this hall? Sweep the place?'

'We can't do that,' Bronson said. 'We're not doing that. It's all we'd need to — '

Over the crowd noise, the first explosion was muffled. The second was louder but nothing like the bomb that had torn apart the motel room the day before.

Still, gray and brown smoke boiled and billowed from the northeast corner of the space. People there began to scream and run toward the exits.

That set off a stampede. The smoke rolled forward and swallowed the crowd, which turned hysterical. Fire alarms went off. The sprinkler system was triggered.

That set off more hysteria, and people began

184

to slip and fall as they scrambled toward the doors.

Stapleton grabbed Bronson and Crowley. 'Until we know what's going on, we need to get you both out of here, now!'

The video-game creators looked frightened but nodded.

Bronson said, 'You don't think this assassin woman did this, do you?'

Peering through the mist and the smoke at the knots of fans fleeing the building, I said, 'There's not a bit of doubt in my mind she did it. The question is why.'

Part Three

BLACK FRIDAY

45

At one a.m. mountain time on Friday, February 5, Dana Potter parked his truck out of sight on a spur into BLM land off a desolate road in rural El Paso County, West Texas, hard by the New Mexico border.

'Check your phone,' he said as he put on an ultralight communication unit with a jaw microphone.

'It's off for a reason,' Mary said.

'Let's triple-check.'

His wife looked irritated but did as he asked while he got out into the cold air and retrieved their packs from the back of the pickup.

'Nothing, no service,' she said. 'Dark hole.'

'Thank you.'

'You sure that thing's going to work on sat phones?'

'Supposed to shut down a mile around,' he said, hoisting his pack onto his shoulders. 'We'll see.'

Mary looked uncertain as she put her pack on, put her boot in the stirrup, and then climbed onto her horse. She sighed.

'What's the matter?' Potter said once he was in his own saddle.

'I was just thinking of what could go wrong.'

'I plan on seeing my boy day after tomorrow, tell him his life is saved.'

She gazed at him and nodded slowly and then sharply. 'Me too.'

'Happy to hear,' Potter said.

They each tugged down infrared glasses that lit up the scrub and the low mesa before them. They kicked their horses and moved in silence and at a steady pace as they cut cross-country along the same route they'd used before.

At two-twenty, one hour and eleven minutes after they'd started out, they reached the arroyo, retrieved the still green paloverde boughs, and, as before, set them in a pile on the opposite bank of the sandy dry riverbed. They tied up the horses well upriver.

It was still pitch-dark, a moonless night, and the stars shone brilliantly when the two crested the hill above the agricultural fields and the ranch.

Potter felt a steady breeze hitting the back of his neck.

'Wait,' he said. 'Wrong wind.'

They stood there, calmly waiting, for five, maybe six minutes before dogs barked in the distance.

Wordlessly, they backed down the side of the mesa and removed their packs. They each found an Ozonics device about the size of a thick paperback. The Ozonics was a miniature ozone generator that would destroy their scent; not even dogs would be able to detect them.

They turned the machines on, dressed warmer, and assembled their rifles. With their packs up on their shoulders again and carrying the weapons and the ozone machines, they climbed back up the hill and stood there waiting, listening.

When no dogs had barked after five minutes, they moved quickly forward to their chosen hides. Mary lay belly-down behind her rifle at 2:40 a.m. mountain time, almost ninety minutes before first light. Her husband laid a rectangle of camouflage material over her, from her boots to her head, where it draped across the top of her telescopic sight.

'Good?' he muttered.

'Real solid,' she said. 'Night-night.'

'I'll wake you.'

'Mmm,' his wife said.

Potter set up less than a foot away, got beneath another length of camouflage cloth, and put the Ozonics out in front of him downwind. He got behind his rifle, settled, and heard Mary rhythmically breathing. He still marveled at his wife's ability to shut the world off at will and find refuge in catnaps that almost always made her sharper.

A match made in heaven, he thought, closing his own eyes. *I still believe that.*

46

I couldn't sleep that night. I tossed and turned, my mind working in circles. Each trip through the puzzling events of the past week, cycling over and over, made me anxious and stirred up a metallic taste at the back of my throat.

That taste is a sure sign that you're going to throw up or that you're so tense you're burning adrenaline. At four twenty a.m., I said good-bye to any notion of real sleep and got up slowly and quietly so as not to wake Bree.

She'd had a tough day and was back to making little headway in the Senator Walker murder investigation while dealing with Chief Michaels, who was renewing pressure on her.

I eased into our closet, shut the door, and turned on the light. Three minutes later, dressed in long underwear, FBI sweats, and a pair of New Balance running shoes, I shut the bedroom door behind me.

I stood there a moment at the head of the stairs, aware of the ticking of the furnace, the hum of the fan in Jannie's room, and the squeak of a mattress in Ali's. Behind the near door, I could hear Nana Mama's gently rasping breathing.

Those familiar noises calmed me as I walked down to the front hall, where I put on a black watch cap, a headlamp, a windbreaker with reflective stripes front and back, and a pair of thin wool gloves. Outside, it was a clear, moonless night. The temperature hovered just above freezing, and I could see clouds of my breath while I went through some ballistic stretches.

At four forty, I turned on the headlamp, jogged down the stairs to the sidewalk, and took off at an ambitious pace toward Capitol Hill. I hoped vigorous physical activity would take my mind off that vicious circle of incidents, thoughts, and half-baked theories that had been plaguing me since Ned Mahoney and I left Atlantic City.

But no such luck. By the time I crossed Pennsylvania Avenue and started chugging uphill toward the Capitol, they were back again. This time the facts, memories, and ideas flipped through my brain in near chronological order.

Senator Betsy Walker is ambushed and shot by a pro just feet from her front door. Shortly after Walker's murder, Kristina Varjan, known assassin, enters the country with a fake passport and is spotted by a CIA operative.

Carl Thomas, the medical-equipment sales-man from Pittsburgh, is found hours later and a few blocks away, garroted to death in an Airbnb. Access to his files is blocked by Scotland Yard.

Fernando Romero, sworn enemy of Senator Walker, drives cross-country to make a pile of Benjamins, gets caught in a snowstorm the night of Walker's murder, and drives on into Washington only to die in a firefight with police.

Sergeant Nick Moon, one of the toughest, most skilled martial artists I've ever known, is killed in a hand-to-hand fight by another professional not two hours south.

Varjan tries to blow up me and Mahoney. Then she appears dressed in a costume at a video-gamers' extravaganza. Was she going to be a contestant?

I tried to discount that idea, but then thought, *Maybe she's good at the game.*

But then why set off a smoke bomb? She had to have recognized me somehow and was using it as diversion to make her escape.

But why? Why would she do that? She'd already gotten away from me. Why didn't she just leave the building?

I thought about Austin Crowley and Sydney Bronson, how rattled they'd been to hear that a bomber, assassin, and fugitive from justice had been a registered contestant. They'd promised to turn over their data from all entries into the tournament.

As I ran between the Capitol and the Supreme Court Building, heading north toward Independence Avenue, none of it made any clear sense. The circular thinking started again, upsetting me, and I ran faster, picking up the pace to a virtual sprint. Pumping my arms, lengthening my stride, I reached Independence and was going to run downhill all the way to Union Station before turning back toward home.

But then, right there at the corner of Constitution Avenue, just north of the Supreme Court Building and the Library of Congress, I was hit with a sense of foreboding so strong that I came to a full stop and stood there panting, sweat pouring off my brow and trickling down my back. I was overheated, but I shivered so hard my headlamp beam slashed back and forth, and my teeth chattered.

I looked down the hill and in my mind I saw the riderless black horse from President Catherine Grant's funeral procession. It was so real, I could hear the stallion's hooves clopping.

I'm not much for premonitions or gut instincts. For me, for the most part, it's all about the facts and the way they fit together or don't.

Standing there, however, sweating and shivering in the cold in the middle of the night and seeing that black horse so vividly in my mind, there was no denying the ominous sense I felt all around me. I couldn't point to its source, and then, suddenly, I could.

Kristina Varjan. Senator Walker's sniper. The gangbanger Romero. The strangled guy, Thomas. And Sergeant Moon's killer.

What if they were all connected? What if every one of them was a professional assassin, including Thomas, the one Scotland Yard was keeping under wraps? What if they were co-operating? What if someone was directing them?

The sense of menace and apprehension kept building the more I thought about those questions, and finally I decided that a prudent man had to go forward on the assumption they were all trained professional killers.

Five professional killers, maybe more, and they were all within a hundred miles of Washington, DC. What they were here for was unclear, but the fact that one of them might have assassinated a U.S. senator came front and center in my thoughts.

This isn't over.

I heard horse hooves in my memory and felt at a deep gut level that something bad was about to happen. Something very bad.

I pivoted and started sprinting back home.

I could feel the threat in my muscles and in my bones.

47

At 4:30 a.m., Pablo Cruz encountered heavy security at the Washington, DC, arena that was the main venue for the World Youth Congress, which was opening that morning.

Cruz had shaved his head and the goatee and wore a blue work coverall embroidered with the DC arena's logo. He carried a District of Columbia driver's license and an arena employee ID card that identified him as Kent Leonard, a member of the setup and maintenance crew assigned to work the three-day event.

Cruz put thirty dollars, a cheap wristwatch, a key ring, reading glasses, sunglasses, a pack of gum, and three alcohol wipes in small foil packages in a tray and then turned to a U.S. Secret Service agent standing there. He gestured to his ears.

In a nasal, almost Donald Duck voice, he said, 'I'm wearing bilateral hearing aids. Do I take them out?'

'If you don't mind, sir. No cell phone?'

'They said no phones, and besides, I can't hear for nothing on those things,' Cruz said before removing the hearing aids, placing them in the bin, and walking through a metal detector.

He'd used the IDs and worn similar hearing aids when entering the arena three times in the past two days, and he fully expected the venue's security guards, DC Police, and members of the

U.S. Secret Service to wave him through.

But after he'd cleared the metal detector, he was met by a Secret Service agent carrying a wand. Special Agent Crane, according to his ID, told Cruz to extend his arms and spread his legs.

Cruz acted as if he didn't hear the order. Agent Lewis, Crane's partner, went to the bin and got out his hearing aids.

The assassin put them on and this time followed Crane's orders as the agent moved the detection wand over him. He ignored the cheeping noise when it passed the two hearing devices.

When he was done, Crane handed the wand to his partner, who had been typing on an iPad, and said, 'I'm going to have to pat you down, Mr. Leonard.'

'Whatever,' Cruz said.

Agent Crane checked the assassin's legs and pockets.

Lewis said, 'He checks out.'

Crane nodded before patting both of Cruz's arms. His expression changed.

'Please pull up your sleeves, sir,' he said.

Cruz calmly rolled back the sleeves of the jumpsuit, revealing the translucent spiderwebs wrapped around both forearms.

'What are those?'

'Braces for a repetitive-strain injury,' Cruz said in that quacking voice. 'My cousin invented them. Did the same design for knees.'

'I could use one of those,' Agent Lewis said. 'They on the market?'

'The website's going up and the knee brace is

coming out I think, like, next month? Spiderweb Braces,' Cruz said. 'These are prototypes.'

'Work well?' the agent said, stepping back to let him pass.

Cruz smiled. 'First day. I'll let you know on my way out, even before I tell my cousin.'

'Have a good day, Mr. Leonard.'

'God willing, sir,' Cruz said, and he walked on.

Feeling like he'd already won a major battle and remembering the schematic maze he'd taped to the abandoned factory floor, Cruz worked his way through the perimeter corridors surrounding the arena and then used a key he'd stolen, copied, and returned to a janitor two days before to unlock an unmarked door.

He looked around, saw the hallways largely empty at that hour, and slipped into a utility stairwell. He clambered quickly down two flights of steel stairs, exited into a subbasement with narrower halls, and went through them confidently until he reached a T. He turned left and, to his relief, found the passage in front of him empty.

Cruz went straight to a door marked with an electrical warning symbol, unlocked it, and went through it into a small, very warm space with meters running on the wall, recording the energy the facility was consuming.

He removed his left hearing aid and tugged the ultrathin wire that linked the amplifier to the earbud. Four more inches of wire came out of the amp. He wound the cord around a connector that joined the largest electrical meter to the big power line feeding the facility. Then he opened one of the alcohol wipes and carefully cleaned the aid and everywhere he'd touched the meter.

He did the same to the doorknob in and out of the room before moving back toward the stairwell. Just shy of it, Cruz used his key to open a door on his right and went into a storage closet that held toilet paper, napkins, coffee cups, and the like.

Behind a stack of paper towels, he found the things he'd smuggled in two days before beneath his work clothes: the disassembled parts of his graphite derringers, a sandy-blond toupee, contact lenses, a set of clothes, and an ID.

Cruz stripped out of the jumpsuit, folded it, then assembled the weapons and attached one to the belly of each spiderweb. He put the contact lenses in; they made his eyes a dazzling blue. Then he donned black pants, black shoes, a black dress shirt, and a black V-neck sweater.

He set the white cleric's collar and the toupee next to him on the floor at the back of the storage unit and sat on several rolls of paper towels in total darkness, meditating and dozing while he waited for his moment.

Anxiety was not allowed to enter his brain.

Neither was fear. Or thoughts of the plan. Or dreams of the future.

Cruz became like death: nobody, nowhere, in no time.

48

At 4:50 a.m. on Friday, Kristina Varjan got in an empty elevator in George Washington University Hospital and pushed the button for the fourth floor.

Wearing hospital scrubs, glasses, hazel contact lenses, and a long auburn wig gathered into a ponytail, she carried a blood-draw kit in her left hand and sported an excellent fake GW badge that read TERRI LE GRAND, PHLEBOTOMIST. A near-perfect forgery of an official GW employee pass hung from a clip at her waist.

As the elevator began to rise, Varjan was still debating whether she'd done the right thing by lighting two M-80 firecrackers taped to two smoke bombs and dropping them in a trash can at the Victorious tournament.

She'd gotten out of there clean, hadn't she? There was that, and more. Those were FBI agents in the tournament hall, the same FBI agents who'd gone to her motel room. She'd known that the second she'd laid eyes on them.

But what else was she going to do? She'd had to send a message, hadn't she?

Yes, of that Varjan was certain. She'd been smart to use the smoke bombs for many reasons. But how had the FBI agents gotten there?

Before she could dwell any longer on the thought, the elevator slowed and dinged. The doors opened, and she exited.

Varjan ambled down the hall, yawning and covering her mouth with her sleeve.

She saw a nurse working at a computer at the dimly lit nurses' station.

'Hi,' Varjan said, smiling at the nurse. 'I'm here for Jones and Hitchcock?'

The nurse, a Filipina in her forties, wore a white sweater over her scrubs and a badge that said BRITA. She cocked her head. 'You're kind of early.'

'I'm working an early shift,' Varjan whispered. 'Moonlighting. I'm usually at Georgetown Friday afternoons and I needed a double.'

Brita put on reading glasses, typed on the computer. 'Who's the draw for?'

Varjan looked at a clipboard, said, 'Meeks for Jones. Albertson for Hitchcock.'

The nurse nodded. 'Shame to wake them. Hitchcock had a rough night.'

'I could go upstairs and do my business and swing back if that would help.'

'No, go ahead. I have to deal with our shift change in five.'

'Thanks, Brita,' Varjan said, and she moved down the hall toward Hitchcock's door. When she looked back, she saw the nurse busy at her computer again.

She went past Hitchcock's door and the next one, took a deep breath, and used her elbow to push open the third door to a private room occupied by Arthur Jones.

Jones lay in bed, his gray skin lit by various monitors around him. In a chair on the far side of the bed, covered in a blanket, an older woman snored softly. Varjan swallowed. It could have been worse, but the woman did complicate things.

Varjan was flexible and adaptable, however. As she slipped toward the bed and the tangle of medical lines hooked to the old man, she was already spinning lies to use should the woman wake.

But the old woman showed no sign that she heard Varjan setting her kit on a table and opening it. Jones, however, stirred when she slipped a device on his finger to check his pulse ox and then put the blood pressure cuff around his upper arm.

'What the hell time is it?' he whispered grumpily.

Varjan held his gaze, smiled, whispered, 'Little before five, sir.'

'Couldn't this have waited a couple hours?'

The assassin acted sympathetic as she pumped the cuff. 'I'm just following doctor's orders.'

Varjan put on a stethoscope and took Jones's blood pressure.

'Don't tell me how bad my numbers are,' he grumbled. 'Don't mean a damn thing anyway, I'm going under the knife this afternoon.'

'People live through cardiac surgery every day,' she said, removing the cuff.

'That's what they say. Where you poking me now?'

'Inner left arm.'

Without responding, Jones closed his eyes, adjusted the IV line sticking in the back of his left hand, and exposed the inside of his elbow.

Varjan wrapped a length of tubing around his weak upper arm and felt for a vein.

She took a needle, attached it to a vacuum tube, and —

'Who the hell are you?' the woman in the chair said.

49

Varjan started, said, 'Sorry, Terri Le Grand. The phlebotomist. You?'

'Eddie, the sister,' the woman said, studying her critically. 'He had blood taken last night.'

The assassin gazed at her. 'And I'd think there'll be more drawn before surgery.'

Eddie sniffed. 'You'll drain him before he can get on the table.'

'Surprise,' Jones said, his eyes still shut. 'Dear sister woke up on the positive side of the bed again.'

'They're taking a lot of blood, Arthur,' his sister said.

'Some of it's being stockpiled for surgery,' Varjan said as she slipped the needle toward his arm. 'Little pinch.'

'Ow,' Jones said, his eyes flashing open. 'That hurt!'

Varjan, flustered, said, 'I . . . I'm sorry. That never happens.'

'Torture him, why don't you?' Eddie said.

'Eddie,' Jones said, looking away from Varjan. 'Please.'

His sister sniffed again. 'Just saying.'

Varjan watched blood flow into the vacuum tube and got a second tube ready. This one was not a vacuum but the barrel of a syringe. She set it into the back of the needle and pressed the plunger. The syringe contained a high dose of

205

propranolol, a drug used to slow the heart rate and lower blood pressure.

Once the full dose was in, Varjan tugged back on the plunger until it was partially filled with blood. She slid out the needle, put cotton on the wound site, and taped it in place.

'There,' she said, smiling brightly. 'Not so bad.'

Eddie said, 'Do you get off on sticking people like that?'

'That's it,' Jones said. 'Can you have the nurse call Rebecca, my wife? Tell her to come early before I'm driven mad?'

Eddie acted offended. 'What? I slept in a chair for you, Arthur.'

Varjan did not know what to make of the siblings and didn't much care.

'Well,' she said awkwardly, 'I hope surgery goes well.'

'If I don't die from my sister's bleak outlook on life,' Jones said.

'Rational outlook on life,' Eddie said. 'The cold hard facts.'

Varjan smiled half heartedly and left. She could hear them bickering softly as she walked down the hall toward the nurses' station, where the shift change was under way. Brita, the Filipina nurse, looked up from her chart.

'Good?'

'Better than good,' Varjan said. 'Have a nice sleep.'

She walked directly to the elevator and pushed the down button. Several moments passed before alarms began to sound in the hall.

Eddie ran out of her brother's room, yelled, 'He's not breathing!'

Nurses and orderlies from both shifts grabbed crash carts and raced toward Jones's room. The elevator doors opened.

Varjan took one last look at the team racing past Eddie, who trembled at the doorway. She looked in at the doctors and nurses and then glanced down the hall at her brother's assassin. 'You bled him dry!' she cried. 'I knew that would happen!'

Varjan vanished inside the elevator, keeping her face turned away from the cameras while the doors slid shut behind her.

50

I was drenched when I ran back up the front steps to my home. Inside, I didn't bother taking off my jacket or watch cap; I just went straight to the kitchen and punched Redial on my cell.

'C'mon, Ned,' I said. 'Pick up.'

I'd tried to call Mahoney six or seven times on the run home, but every call to his personal phone immediately jumped to voice mail. And every call to his work phone ended with a federal robot telling me his voice mail was not yet set up.

That was impossible. Mahoney had had the same work number for eight years. We talked all the time on the work phone.

Five assassins, I thought as I started making coffee. *No, three.* If Thomas was an assassin, he was a dead one. So was Romero.

Were there more than the three left?

It could have been just the three at that point, but that seemed unlikely to me. If there were three, there could be four or five or even six.

Five or six. I knew those numbers were a pure guess, but that didn't matter. A prudent man should assume the worst and prepare for it.

Was five or six the worst-case scenario? Or were there even more than that?

Or was I just imagining this? A tired, frazzled brain searching for answers?

Pouring myself a cup of coffee, I decided to go

with my instincts because I did not have enough facts. After trying both of Ned's phones again, I poured coffee into a second cup and took it and mine upstairs to our bedroom, where I flipped on the lights.

Shutting the door, I said, 'Bree, wake up.'

She groaned and pulled the pillow over her head. 'Go away. I need to sleep.'

I walked over and grabbed the pillow away.

'Alex!' she shouted angrily. 'Bree needs to — '

'I know Bree needs to sleep,' I said. 'But I need to talk to Chief Stone. Or do you want me to leave you out of the loop and go straight to Chief Michaels?'

Her brow knitted and she squinted at me and some of the stiffness in her shoulders eased. 'What time is it?' she grumbled.

'Just after five,' I said.

'You've been out running already?'

I put her coffee on the night table. 'Couldn't sleep, figured I'd go for a run and think some things through.'

Bree yawned and struggled to sit up. 'Okay?'

'I think there's a conspiracy going on,' I said. 'A conspiracy of assassins.'

She sipped the coffee, listening and saying nothing as I tried to explain the fractured logic of my theory.

'Something bad is about to happen. I know this doesn't sound like me, but I can feel it.'

Bree was quiet for several moments before saying, 'This doesn't sound like you at all, Alex. Seeing riderless horses. How much sleep have you been getting?'

'This has nothing to do with sleep, and I didn't see the horse. I just remembered it. This really has to do with Senator Walker getting killed, probably by Thomas, who was then killed either by Varjan or whoever beat Sergeant Moon to death.'

'Alex, there's a lot of conjecture in what you're saying. Especially the idea that there are more assassins than we know about.'

'I'm saying we should be proceeding based on that assumption. If I'm wrong, I'm wrong. But I don't think I am.'

Bree was quiet again but studying me. 'What do you think these assassins are going to do?'

'I . . . I don't know. But if they were part of a plot that begins with the killing of a sitting U.S. senator, draw your own conclusions.'

'I can't draw any conclusions,' she said. 'We don't have enough facts.'

'I'm telling you, something brutal is going to happen in the District, maybe today.'

I could see her getting more frustrated by the moment. 'What do you want me to do? Put all my detectives on the streets? Ask Michaels to double the shift? Put every cop on patrol because your gut says so?'

'That would be a start,' I said.

She threw up her hands. 'Well, I'm not in a position to do that.'

'You should at least tell Michaels.'

'Tell him what? That a consultant to the department wants a small army to take over the District of Columbia because of a gut feeling?'

I could see I was getting nowhere fast. 'Okay,'

I said, heading toward the door.

'Where are you going?'

'To my office to see what patients I can cancel and then to find Mahoney to see if he can understand what I'm saying.'

'Alex,' Bree said as I opened the door. 'Just because I don't agree with you doesn't mean I don't love you.'

I felt the skin around my temples relax. 'I know. I love you too. Go back to sleep.'

'That's not happening,' she said ruefully, and she took another sip of coffee.

I went out the door and back down the stairs, feeling confused and wondering whether this was just a theory cooked up by my tired mind. But by the time I reached the kitchen, I was certain again that I was right.

After pouring another cup of coffee, I went down the stairs, hitting Redial on my cell. Again I heard that infuriating recording about the voice mail not being set up.

I reached the bottom of the stairs and I was about to dial Ned's personal phone again when I noticed an envelope on the floor below the mail slot. I picked it up, saw my name and address and a stamp but no postmark and no return address.

I slit the envelope open as I walked to my office. There was a single piece of white paper inside. Across the page, scrawled in lurid red crayon, it said:

stop me please, Alex Cross

51

Two time zones to the west of DC, Mary Potter whispered, 'Dana?'

Hearing his wife's voice in his earbud, Potter jerked awake, saw the hillside and the valley floor below in a pale gray light. A rooster crowed.

'Shit,' he said. 'Time is it?'

'Time to get ready,' she said. 'There's lights on in the hacienda.'

Twenty minutes later, the winter sun crested a hillside to the east and behind them. Warmth swept in over them and continued across the valley to the terrace they'd watched two days before.

It was broad daylight before the first person appeared, a young man wearing a sweater and apron who laid out dining service at the four tables on the terrace. He also switched on a tall portable heater. They could see the steam rising off the top of it through their scopes.

'Let's go hot,' Potter said. He extracted from his pocket three 6.5mm Creedmoor cartridges that he fed into the magazine of his rifle and a fourth that he seated in the chamber before closing the bolt and engaging the safe.

Only then did he reach in his pack for the signal jammer. The device was anodized black, about the size of a paperback, and made of some light alloy. Potter didn't know where the jammer had come from or how it worked, and he didn't much care. It had been with their briefing package in the ranch house when they arrived.

He set it in front and to the left of the Ozonics, where his forward hand could reach it in a hurry. Eight minutes later, the first to breakfast, a polished, fit blonde in her late thirties, came out onto the terrace wearing dark sunglasses and canvas bird-hunting gear that she made appear stylish.

Potter reached into a side pants pocket, retrieved his cell phone, and thumbed it on. No service. Excellent.

'Here comes my baby,' Mary sang softly. 'Here he comes now.'

Her target, a man in his sixties wearing canvas pants, a vest, and a ball cap, walked to the now-seated woman, engaged in some pleasantries with her, and then moved on to a table closer to the heater. He settled into a chair facing the length of the valley.

'Green,' she said. 'Five hundred and nine meters. The right ethmoid bone.'

The ethmoid bone. The perfect aiming point if you meant to shatter a skull and drop a man in his tracks. Or in his chair, as the case may be.

'Adjust your turret four clicks and stay right there,' Potter said. 'No drift in this tailwind.'

They waited fifteen minutes while five more people, all middle- to late-middle-aged men, came slowly streaming onto the terrace for breakfast. Two sat with the polished woman. Two sat by themselves. One sat to the left of Mary's target.

He was peach-skinned, heavyset, and gregarious. Mary's target seemed to enjoy the man's presence and threw back his head to laugh twice.

Then a tall woman in her forties, big-boned with short dark hair, appeared. She was wearing a green down vest over her canvas jacket.

'That's the missus,' Mary said. 'You're on deck.'

52

The missus seemed to know everyone, and she worked the terrace before taking a seat at the empty fourth table with her right shoulder to the heater and in full profile.

Potter instinctively didn't like her in that position and had to ponder why before he understood that her husband was likely to sit to her left, facing the full view of the valley, obstructed by his wife.

Potter's target, who was five six in his hunting boots, ambled onto the terrace and greeted the eight folks already drinking coffee and giving their breakfast orders to the waiter. Potter had his crosshairs on the man from the second he appeared and he kept them there as he moved across the terrace to shake the hand of Mary's target. The crosshairs stayed with him even as he went over to his wife, kissed her forehead, and took the exact wrong seat.

The missus was so tall and broad-shouldered that her husband was all but blocked. Depending on the angle at which she faced him, Potter could only find small parts of the man's body to aim at, none of them lethal.

'Red,' he said.

'Change angle?' Mary said.

'Wait.'

He deliberately tensed and relaxed his shoulders, calmly watching through the scope as the waiter brought espresso to his target's table. The wife took a sip and sat back, crossing her legs and exposing the left side of her husband's body and head.

'Green,' he said. He reached forward and flipped the switch on the jamming device.

Mary said, 'Same.'

Potter adjusted his upper body and the gun. The crosshairs of his scope found the bridge of the man's nose and settled there.

He pushed forward the three-position safety on the rifle to fire and brought the pad of his right index finger to the curl of the trigger. No pressure. Not yet.

'Green,' he said, and they both went into a pattern of thinking and action that had been pounded into them.

'Breathe,' Mary said.

Potter took a deep breath and let a quarter of it out, saying, 'Relax.' He dropped all tension in his body. 'Aim.' His crosshairs were exactly where he wanted them.

'Sight picture,' Mary said.

Potter's attention leaped from his target to his target's wife and behind them. He was about to say *Squeeze* when the missus leaned forward for her espresso, blocking the shot.

'Red,' he said, and he exhaled.

'Still green,' Mary said.

Potter said nothing until the wife reclined in the chair again, though not quite as far. Still, he had a clear look at the target's frontal bone just above his left eye.

'Green,' he said.

They went back into that sequence again, both of them in sync: breathe, relax, aim, sight picture . . .

'Squeeze,' Potter said.

Their triggers broke crisply. Their bullets made thudding noises leaving the suppressors at the same instant the wife sat forward. Seeing the vapor trails of both their projectiles rip over the fields and the treetops, Potter knew even before impact that Mary's shot was true, and that he had screwed up big-time.

The 127-grain bullet smashed into his target's wife's lower right cheek. Her head and torso whipped around left and seized up. Beyond her, Potter's target was half on, half off the chair. There was blood on his right chest wall, but he was very much alive and looking dumbly around.

People were screaming and shouting. Their voices carried to the assassins.

But Potter paid them no mind. He cycled the bolt on his rifle, thinking that the bullet must have gone through the wife's mouth, ricocheted, exited, and slammed into her husband's chest.

Those thoughts vanished when he found his target's sternum in his crosshairs, skipped shooting protocol, and tapped the trigger. The Creedmoor cracked. He stayed on the scope, watching the vapor trail all the way to the center of his target's chest.

'Dead man,' Mary said.

Potter came off the gun, took his spent cartridge, pocketed it, then grabbed the gun, pack, and camo netting. He scooted backward, still hearing faint shouts, dragging his rifle, pack, and netting with him. Mary was already out of sight of the hacienda and pulling a spray bottle full of bleach from her pack.

After stuffing the camo net in the pack, she took the bottle, crouched, and duck-walked forward right in her tracks. She got to where she'd lain for the shots and sprayed pure bleach on the Ozonics device, which she left running in place to keep destroying scent after they left. Then she retreated, spraying the whole time.

Potter took his Ozonics but left the signal jammer to keep all communications with the ranch cut off as long as possible. He sprayed the jammer and where he'd lain and all along his exit path, sweeping his gloved hand back and forth through the loose dirt, mixing it with the bleach.

Back over the side of the mesa, they shouldered their packs and guns before scrambling down and to the arroyo. They swept their way up the dry riverbed, jumped on the horses, and kicked them up hard.

They rode northeast toward the truck and trailer as fast as they could go, their jobs done, and already thinking of home.

It was 7:32 a.m. mountain time.

53

At 9:40 a.m. eastern time, Martin Franks whistled as he glanced at his reflection in the window of a car on South End Avenue in Battery Park, Manhattan. Franks looked nothing like the man who'd checked out of the Mandarin Oriental the morning before and taken an afternoon Amtrak train to Penn Station.

Franks's hair was cut military-short now. His dark blue suit, white shirt, and tie fitted him well, but not impeccably. Aviator sunglasses and the bud in his ear screamed law enforcement. On a chain around his neck, he carried the badges and identity cards of a U.S. Treasury Department special agent.

He had makeup on to tone down the bruising he'd received when the trooper had punched him, and a story to explain that bruising.

Carrying a cardboard tray with three Starbucks coffees and a stack of napkins beneath, Franks walked to the Gateway Plaza Garage and entered just as it started to rain. He took an elevator to the third floor and got out with every bit of badass, walking-boss bravado he could muster.

To his right, he saw a custom black Chevy Suburban parked sideways across three spaces. Two men dressed in dark suits and wearing earbuds stood outside and immediately fixed their attention on Franks, who balanced the coffee with one hand and held up his agent's badge with the other.

'You Penny and Cox?' he said in a soft Southern drawl.

'Cox,' said the redhead.

'Penny,' said the thick-necked guy.

'Kevin Stoddard,' Franks said, dropping the badge and holding out his free hand. 'On temporary assignment to the New York office. My boss said I should come out to spell you if you need to take a leak and at least get you some coffee.'

Penny shook his hand, took a cup, looked Franks in the eye. 'Who's your SAC?'

'Warner,' Franks said. 'I'm on the assignment sheet.'

Cox pulled out his phone, started typing with his thumbs. Franks acted serene but inside he was praying the hacker had done his work the right way. Otherwise, Franks was going the wrong way and fast.

Cox looked up and nodded. 'Where you based usually, Stoddard?'

'Big Easy,' Franks said. 'Past nine years.'

'Counterfeiting?' Penny asked.

'Mostly,' Franks said. 'But you get threats now and then you have to investigate. Some of those backwoods-bayou boys got tempers and go spouting off about killing the Fed chairman. That kind of thing.'

Penny laughed. 'I've heard a few of those. What're you doing up here?'

'There's a flood of well-crafted bogus fifties down our way,' Franks said. 'Two months ago,

220

the same quality bills started showing up in Queens. We're trying to trace the common denominator.'

Cox took a coffee, said, 'Those guys are getting damn good with the digital stuff.'

Penny said, 'What happened to your cheek?'

Franks made a show of looking disgusted and amused. 'My eleven-year-old nephew, my sister's kid, he's been taking tae kwon do? He asked me if he could show me some moves the other night. I wasn't expecting a spinning roundhouse to the side of my head. Almost knocked me cold!'

Penny and Cox started laughing.

Franks did too, said, 'So much for my badassery.'

He set the cardboard tray and napkins on the hood of the Suburban, took the third cup of coffee for himself. 'What time are you boys in the air?'

Penny looked at Cox, said, 'Wheels off the ground at eleven.'

Franks said, 'Helps when you have a motorcycle escort clearing the way to JFK.'

Cox shook his head. 'No escort. Bowman doesn't like them, prefers to blend in.'

Penny said, 'I think she's right. Once she's in and we're rolling, we're just another mobile master of the universe heading toward the corporate jet.'

Franks drank from his coffee. He liked these guys. Salt of the earth, as his mother used to say. Ex-military. Wife. Kids.

Deep down, however, he felt no pity, just building anticipation and thrill.

221

At four minutes to ten, the agents put their hands to their earbuds.

Cox said, 'Roger that.'

Penny headed toward the passenger door. 'Thanks for the designer mud, Stoddard.'

'Glad to be of service,' Franks said. He picked up the empty coffee carrier and stripped off a .25-caliber Ruger pistol taped to the bottom.

He shot Penny through the skull from three feet away, then turned the gun on Cox and said, 'Don't.'

54

Cox's hand froze in mid-reach for his weapon.

'Both guns on the hood,' Franks said. 'Don't screw around. I can do this with you living or dying. Doesn't matter to me.'

Cox reached in, got out his service weapon, then took a backup from his ankle. He put them on the hood.

'Steady,' Franks said, still aiming across the hood as he took the smaller weapon and put it in his pocket, then squatted and tore Penny's earbud and radio off his corpse.

'Get in,' Franks said, opening the passenger-side door. 'You're driving.'

Cox said, 'Whatever you're planning — '

'Save it for someone who cares.'

Cox hesitated but then climbed behind the wheel.

Franks got in, nudged aside a closed umbrella on the floor, and shut the door.

'Drive.'

'Where?' Cox said.

'Don't be cute,' Franks said. 'I know the plan. Follow it.'

The Treasury agent made a show of putting the Suburban in gear and then tried to backhand Franks.

The assassin anticipated the move and swatted the blow away, then put the Ruger against Cox's temple. 'I'm so far ahead of you, Agent Cox. Do what I say, and you get to live to see the wife and kids. One more dumb move like that, you won't.'

The agent was furious but put both hands on the wheel. He drove. His service weapon slid off the hood and clattered onto the parking-garage floor.

They exited the garage into drizzle that had turned to steady rain by the time Cox turned on Broadway, heading south into the financial district.

In Franks's earbud, a man said, 'This is Thomas. Shamrock wants to move.'

'Roger that,' Cox said.

'Minute out,' Franks said.

'Copy.'

Franks said, 'When you get there, pull over smooth, put it in park.'

'What the hell are you going to do?'

The assassin said nothing as they rolled to a stop in front of Trinity Episcopal Church. The second Cox put the SUV in park, Franks put his finger in the agent's free ear, aimed behind Cox's jaw, and shot him through the top of his spine, killing him instantly.

The shot sounded loud to Franks, but it was buffered by the bulletproof glass; people on the sidewalk, rushing to get out of the rain, didn't seem to notice. He grabbed the umbrella, stepped out, shut the door, and put the umbrella up just before the front door to the church opened.

A big black man in a suit and trench coat came out, carrying an umbrella above a short, dark-haired Caucasian female in her fifties

224

wearing a long blue rain jacket and pumps. The muscle was taking pelting rain to his eyes.

Franks kept his umbrella tilted to block his face. As the pair crossed the sidewalk, he reached as if to open the rear door and then swung toward the woman and shot her in the face at point-blank range.

The agent exploded toward Franks, slashing the umbrella at him and then getting his shoulder into the assassin, driving him back against the SUV. Franks went ragdoll, as if he'd been stunned.

The second he felt the agent go for the submission, he aimed through the umbrella and fired. He heard a grunt before the man fell at his feet, wounded but not dead and going for his weapon.

Franks aimed at the middle of the agent's forehead.

He pulled the trigger.

Click.

Franks whipped the empty gun at the wounded man's face, hitting him. He pivoted, raced around the SUV to the driver's side, pulled Cox's corpse out, and left him there sprawled in the bus lane.

He threw the car in drive, put on his blinker, and started to pull out into traffic just as the agent started firing. The first round punctured the rear window, blew through both seats, and shattered the radio display.

The second shot . . .

55

As nobody lost in nowhere in no time, three hours passed like minutes for Pablo Cruz. His watch beeped at 8:00 a.m.

He woke feeling deeply rested and ready for the task at hand.

Cruz got up, dusted off his pants, put the cleric's collar on, and then put on the excellent toupee. Then he exited the darkened storage facility into the basement hallway.

He put on a pair of conservative black-framed glasses fitted with photochromic lenses that adapted to changes in light, darker in sunlight, almost clear inside. Walking quicker now, Cruz left the subbasement and climbed the staircase. Beyond the door, he heard the din of a gathering crowd.

Cruz crisply opened the door and eased out into a stream of earnest youth from all over the world and their adult leaders and chaperones. He smiled at a young woman guiding a group of Asian teens, and she grinned back.

He got nods and smiles for the next five minutes as he circled the arena, taking note of all law enforcement before heading inside. Cruz entered from the rear, farthest from a stage set in a rainbow of bunting.

Many of the seats off the floor were already taken. To get on the floor, Cruz showed badges identifying him as the Reverend Nicholas Flint of the First Baptist Church of Nebraska, part of a church group that included a choir from Omaha that was set to sing as part of the congress's opening ceremony.

He showed his badges three more times, moving past television cameras, and soon found himself at the back of a throng of people, young and old, who were pressed up against barriers set well back from the stage. His glasses kept lightening in tint until they showed just a hint of gray.

Cruz reached up to adjust his collar and withdrew a sliver of translucent graphite as sharp as a sewing needle.

The assassin fitted it between his right index and middle finger, waited until more people filled in tightly behind him, then used it to prick the rear end of a young woman in front of him. She yelped, grabbed her butt, and spun around. Cruz looked at her through the glasses.

'I just got bit too,' he said. 'Someone told me the place is infested.'

That made her frown. 'Really?'

'Just heard it,' he said. 'Can I get by? I'm supposed to get pictures of the choir. They're in my group.'

She brightened. 'Sure, Reverend.'

'Bless you, child,' he said, and he slipped past her.

Forty minutes later, the arena was packed, and Cruz was where he needed to be, one row of bodies off the front and to the far right of the stage behind a contingent of teenagers rallying around a sign that said FLORIDA. There were signs from fifty states and one hundred countries all over the arena.

Cruz kept looking around in wonder and awe, as if he couldn't believe how lucky he was to be there. The stage began to crowd with dignitaries. The small church choir from Kansas filled the risers to stage left, almost directly in front of the assassin.

At 9:57 a.m., a silver-haired woman with a big smile on her face walked to the dais and tapped the microphone.

'Welcome to this year's meeting of the World Youth Congress!' she cried, and the arena erupted in applause.

Cruz clapped his approval, keeping his eyes fixed on her, not glancing at any of the eight burly men wearing suits and earbuds with their backs to the stage who were scanning the audience.

When the clapping died down, the woman said, 'My good young friends, I am Nancy Farrell, chairman of this year's congress. Today, I have the distinct honor of introducing a new friend who will open your congress with an exciting announcement. Young ladies and gentlemen of the world and of the future, it is with great pleasure that I introduce the president of the United States, James B. Hobbs.'

56

The U.S. Marine Corps band came onto the stage playing 'Hail to the Chief.'

Secret Service agents came out from behind curtains at floor level, followed by President Hobbs, in office now less than two weeks. The president strode out, waving and smiling the way any good politician will when the crowd is sure to be on his side.

Tall, silver-haired, and lanky, Hobbs had grown up on a cattle ranch in Wyoming. He had weathered good looks and a reputation in the U.S. Senate as a man of integrity and geniality, traits that had attracted the late president Catherine Grant.

On paper, you couldn't ask for a better guy to lead the country, Cruz thought.

But as the president began to work the barricade, shaking hands with kids and adults, Cruz could see Hobbs was showing signs of being uncomfortable with the job, or at least with the way the Secret Service men moved in a tight protective phalanx around him on three sides.

Two tall agents walked behind Hobbs. Each of them had one hand resting gently on the president's back and the other close to his weapon. Two more agents moved laterally off his left shoulder. The one closest to Cruz was scanning ahead.

Cruz forced himself not to look at the lead

agent but beyond him and his partner to the president. The assassin grinned broadly as if one of the higher points of his life was coming his way.

He reached up to his hearing aid, pressed on it for ten seconds, then turned it off. He watched the nearest television camera, to his right about ninety feet. It appeared to be trained on the president. The green light on the front of the camera flickered and died. The cameraman's head popped up, his expression puzzled.

Cruz looked around and saw the other camera operators doing the same.

He stood up on his toes and made a show of clapping as Hobbs and his entourage came closer. He glanced around, caught young person after young person's excited eyes, and nodded to them, mouthing, *Isn't this incredible?*

Still clapping, still up on his toes and delighted, Cruz saw how the lead agent was already peering past him and how the agent closest to the president was signaling when each person could reach out to shake Hobbs's hand. Only then did the assassin glance beyond the president to the ramrod-straight man following the entourage.

Military bearing. Tight haircut. Gray business suit.

Those things instantly registered in Cruz's mind before his happy attention snapped back to Hobbs, now less than six feet away, so close the assassin could hear him saying, 'So glad to meet you. Wonderful. Wonderful to see you, young ladies.'

The three teens directly in front of him pressed forward. Cruz did too, saw the lead agent putting his hand on the arms of the kids. Still clapping, Cruz smiled, looked at the Secret Service agent, and raised his brows quizzically.

The agent held up a finger. Cruz nodded, glanced at Hobbs shaking the hand of a fifteen-year-old girl and then posing for a selfie with a pimply boy before moving directly in front of him.

The kids that separated them shook the president's hands before the leader of the free world looked up and directly into his killer's eyes. Cruz gave him nothing but heartfelt admiration as he reached over the heads of the kids and extended his hand.

Hobbs grabbed it, shook it, and winked at him. As the president released his grip, the assassin snapped his hand back and felt the thud of the air gun going off, felt it vibrating through his retreating forearm, no noise at all in that din.

The 90-grain graphite bullet hit the president square in the chest. Hobbs lurched backward, wild-eyed, not understanding what had happened as he collapsed into the arms of the bodyguards behind him.

Cruz reacted with immediate shock, drawing his head and upper body back with an exaggerated gape of disbelief as the agents grabbed the president and lowered him to the floor. Kids began to scream.

Hobbs's assassin watched, mouth wide in puzzlement. He swung his attention to his left, hands to his head as if he wasn't sure of what he'd seen. The crowd around him surged back as more agents and a doctor rushed to the stricken president.

Cruz saw the man with the military bearing, tight haircut, and business suit eight feet away, looking scared and incredulous. He was standing sidelong to the assassin, offering a narrow profile, not the broadside shot Cruz wanted, but Cruz believed in taking the first solid opportunity he had at a target.

He raised his left hand, snapped his wrist back. Again, he felt the thud but heard no report of it. The man twisted at the graphite bullet's impact, spiraling, tripping, and sprawling onto the concrete floor.

People near him started yelling and ducking down. More in the crowd were trying to get away from the stage. Cruz went with them.

Then medics rushed in. As quickly as the hysteria had built, it lulled and died in the arena. All the assassin could hear was children crying as he kept slowly retreating, trying to act in fear and bewildered disbelief.

Fifteen seconds later, when he'd moved far enough to see a clear path to an exit, he reached up to the hearing aid and pressed the on button three times.

Twelve seconds after that, the lights in the arena wavered, dimmed, and then died.

57

'Alex!'

Nana Mama screamed so loud I heard her in my basement office. I had been unable to get hold of Mahoney, so I decided not to cancel my office hours.

'Alex, come up here now!'

I was between patients and heard the horror in her voice. I bolted up the stairs into the kitchen.

My grandmother was standing by the kitchen table, her mouth open, tears streaming down her cheeks. 'They just interrupted my *Rachael Ray*,' she said. 'They think the president's been shot.'

'What?' I said, my stomach plunging as I moved around to see the television. 'Where? When?'

'The DC arena,' she said. 'Some youth congress. Maybe ten minutes ago.'

Nana had the screen tuned to CNN, which was in full alert mode. Wolf Blitzer was talking nonstop over looping video that showed President Hobbs entering the arena and working the rope line, upright and smiling, before the camera went dark.

'Every network feed was hacked and cut just a few moments before the president collapsed,' Blitzer said. 'Witnesses said Hobbs appeared to jerk as if shot before falling back against his Secret Service agents. There have been no reports of guns seen or fired inside the arena, which has lost power and is under lockdown.

'We have confirmed reports that President Hobbs is being rushed to Walter Reed. We also have confirmed that Secretary of Defense Harold Murphy, widely considered the top candidate to be named Hobbs's vice president, was also wounded and en route to . . . hold on.'

The feed cut to Blitzer, who was listening to his earbud, his expression turning graver and graver before he looked up into the camera and said, 'We have just confirmed that U.S. treasury secretary Abigail Bowman has been shot and killed near the New York Stock Exchange along with two of her bodyguards.'

'Jesus,' I said, shocked, even though I'd suspected something terrible was in the works. 'The president? Treasury? Defense?'

'It's a plot, a conspiracy!' Nana Mama said. 'Just like JFK! Someone's trying to overthrow the government!'

Before I could agree, Blitzer announced that trading at all U.S. financial markets had been suspended, and the U.S. Capitol Building, the U.S. Supreme Court Building, and all federal buildings in the District of Columbia were being locked down.

My cell phone rang. Bree.

'Are you seeing this?' she said, sounding unnerved.

'I'm watching with Nana,' I said.

'I should have listened to you.'

'Doesn't matter, and I'm not happy about being right. What's going on there?'

'It's chaos. We're deploying around the DC

arena. I'm heading there now.'

'Keep me posted. I'll try Ned again.'

I hung up and hit Mahoney's number on speed dial even as I watched the feed jump to Walter Reed and footage of an ambulance racing through the gates.

Blitzer said, 'That was the scene two minutes ago as the president's medical team tried to keep him alive and get him to an operating room. We're awaiting a statement on President Hobbs's condition, but early reports indicate he was badly wounded.'

The screen jumped to the scene outside the DC arena, where FBI SWAT officers were piling out of vans armed with automatic weapons.

Blitzer said, 'No one is being allowed in or out of what has become without a doubt the biggest crime scene in the world. CNN will be focused exclusively on this fast-breaking story and — '

Mahoney's work cell rang and didn't go to that robotic voice. I went into the other room, listening to the ringing. He never answered. I left a message, went back to the kitchen. 'What's going on?'

Nana Mama said, 'Capitol Hill Police are ordering congressmen and senators to stay in their offices while dogs are searching all federal buildings.'

On the screen, Blitzer sent coverage live to the White House, where the press corps was in pandemonium, shouting questions at Dolores St. Mary, President Hobbs's shocked and rattled press secretary.

'What's the president's condition?' one yelled.

'Who's in charge, Dolores?' shouted another.

'Who's running the country?' a third demanded.

58

The press secretary held up her hands, said, 'Please, we are going to handle your questions as best we can, but today's events are unprecedented and evolving at a rapid pace. We don't yet know the president's condition other than he is alive, as is the secretary of defense. We're waiting and praying for them just like everyone else.'

She took a deep breath. 'I'm going to introduce U.S. attorney general Samuel Larkin, FBI director Derek Sanford, and chairman of the Joint Chiefs of Staff General Alan Hayes.'

The three men looked like they'd been through a firefight when they climbed onto the dais. Attorney General Larkin went to the lectern.

Larkin, a powerfully built man in his fifties, was no stranger to controversy or conflict. He'd had a reputation as a crusader and social climber when he was U.S. attorney for Lower Manhattan, and he often was accused of grandstanding in events. The late president, Catherine Grant, had named him to the post, and he'd had to survive a difficult nomination and confirmation process.

Since then he'd been an attorney general with remarkably good approval ratings, so good that James Hobbs had kept him on after taking the oath of office.

But that day Larkin was profoundly somber as he put on reading glasses and glanced at a prepared statement before looking straight at the cameras.

'President James B. Hobbs was shot by an unknown assailant this morning. Seconds before that attack, treasury secretary Abigail Bowman was shot and killed in cold blood in New York. Seconds after the president was shot, Secretary of Defense Harold Murphy was also severely wounded.'

He paused, looked down as if he could not believe what he was about to say, and then raised his head up and went on in a commanding voice. 'Under the Twentieth and Twenty-Fifth Amendments of the U.S. Constitution and by the Succession Act of 1947, with the president incapacitated and the office of vice president vacant, power passes to the Speaker of the House, and if that office is vacant, to the Senate president pro tempore, and if that office is vacant, to the secretary of state. If that office is vacant, the secretary of the treasury assumes power. If that office is vacant, the secretary of defense is president.'

Larkin swallowed hard then firmed the set of his jaw. 'It is my miserable task to inform the nation that West Virginia senator Arthur Jones, the Senate president pro tempore, died of a heart attack at GW Medical Center earlier this morning.'

He held up his hands, shouted, 'Let me speak!'

The rabble quieted.

Larkin said, 'I must also inform the nation that about an hour ago, at a quail-hunting ranch in West Texas, Speaker of the House Matthew Guilford and Secretary of State Aaron Deeds were assassinated by long-range snipers. We've only just gotten word.'

Gasps went up from a shocked press corps.

'It's a coup,' I said in shock and awe. 'A coup attempt in the United . . . '

'What does this mean?' a reporter shouted. 'So who takes office?'

The attorney general said, 'Under the order of succession, with the secretary of defense incapacitated, I do.'

More shouting. 'You're assuming the office of presidency?'

'I am,' Larkin said. 'I did not seek this role, but our nation is under attack. Make no mistake, our country, our Constitution, our way of life, it's all under attack, and because of that I will take the oath of office as acting president, working closely with General Hayes and FBI director Sanford in defense of our country.'

Before the reporters could yell anything, Larkin said, 'To that end, after my swearing-in, I will sign executive orders giving full authority to Mr. Sanford and the FBI to implement the U.S. Justice Department's assassination-contingency plans and to lead the investigation to uncover who was behind this coordinated attack on our democracy. I will also sign orders instituting a state of martial law in the United States of America for the next one hundred hours.'

'What?' I said. 'Holy ... has that ever happened?'

'Nothing like this has ever happened,' Nana said.

Larkin ignored the reporters freaking out in the White House press room and left.

Chairman of the Joint Chiefs General Hayes went to the microphone.

'All travel in U.S. airspace is suspended for the duration of martial law. All planes currently in the air out of New York, Washington, and Texas are being ordered to the ground and impounded. All other flights in the air will proceed to their destinations.

'All public-transit systems will halt. Drive if you have to, but know that your vehicle, especially in and around the District of Columbia, is subject to search. We will find whoever is behind these assassinations, and we will find them — '

I heard the doorbell before the front door opened and I went to the hall to see Mahoney rushing toward me. 'Let's go, Alex,' he said. 'We've got work to do.'

59

Sitting in the Suburban in the driving rain, snarled in traffic trying to get on the Brooklyn Bridge leaving Manhattan, Martin Franks was listening to 1010 WINS all-news radio about the attacks.

Franks swallowed hard against the searing pain in his upper right arm. Waiting for the narcotics to kick in, he checked the belt he'd placed as a tourniquet just below his shoulder and just above the gaping wound.

The treasury secretary's bodyguard's second shot had blown through Franks's upper right shoulder, shattering the humerus bone and destroying nerves. Years of training was the only thing that kept Franks from blacking out in agony.

At the first stoplight south of the church, the assassin had looked in the rearview, saw no flashing lights, and dug with his left hand in his pockets for the two things he always carried into battle: commercially made foil packages that contained bandages treated with clotting agents and antibiotics and a small envelope containing forty OxyContin pills.

Franks shook six pills into his mouth and chewed them as he tore open his shirt. Swallowing the pills, he used his teeth to rip one clotting bandage free of the foil.

He slid it in under his shirt. When he stuffed

the bandage in the entry wound, he almost fainted. When he got a second bandage and used it to stuff the exit wound, he'd dry-heaved and moaned.

The light turned green. Shaken, woozy, not thinking straight, Franks drove on rather than trying to take a left onto John Street.

His original escape plan called for him to abandon the Suburban as soon as possible, then get off the streets and use the subway to get uptown to Penn Station, where he'd catch an Amtrak to Albany and points north.

But being wounded like this changed everything.

Franks had to use the car to take him someplace far away where he could call for a specialist to help. The specialist would cost Franks hundreds of thousands of dollars, no doubt, but he'd live. He'd live and he'd . . .

In his daze and looking through the slapping windshield wipers and the driving rain, Franks tried to stay in his lane and focus on his options. He could get to the Carey Tunnel from here. But there was a toll, wasn't there? Brooklyn Bridge, then.

He moaned when he realized he'd just missed another chance to go east. The intensity of the rain made traffic crawl as he drove farther south toward Battery Park and finally got on Water Street, where he turned and headed north.

When traffic came to a stop, Franks checked the wound again. The bleeding was slowing, and he didn't feel like his lung had been damaged. The drugs kicked in like a warm fountain, going up his spine and into his head. He swooned.

A car honked. Franks came around, feeling better, sweeter. Traffic rolled forward half a block and stalled again. Then, on the radio, he heard the attorney general, now acting president, Larkin describe the scope of the conspiracy.

Five of them, Franks thought in awe. *Coordinated attacks on the top five. Who does that?*

Traffic started to move before he could consider his own involvement. He was a traitor, wasn't he?

'Yes, that's what I am,' he said, and he laughed bitterly and ate two more painkillers. 'Just like dear old dad.'

Two minutes later, he heard Larkin institute martial law. The drugs became a wave, then, that washed over the assassin, and he barely kept the SUV in the lane.

The rain came in sheets. The windshield wipers swept wildly back and forth. He tried to use that visualization method that had served him so well in Afghanistan, tried to see what he was about to do, and he asked the universe to signal him if he was in danger.

Franks felt hypnotized and numb when he finally took a left on Beekman Street and crawled toward the right turn on Park Row and the entrance to the Brooklyn Bridge.

Traffic slowed to a halt again.

On the radio, some army general was ordering people to get off the streets.

Where do they expect people to go? Franks thought, and he laughed at the absurdity of it.

Looking ahead through the rain and the wipers, he saw cruisers with lights flashing at the bridge entrance. He thought he saw dark figures walking between the cars, coming at him. And then he didn't need a sign from above. He was positive that the police, five of them, guns drawn, were knocking on car windows and speaking to drivers and passengers alike.

Franks started to whistle 'Carry On Wayward Son' and then pushed the button that popped the rear hatch. He yanked the car into park left-handed and grabbed his pistol. He forced himself over the front seat and then over the backseat, then rolled out into the pelting rain.

A young woman was driving the Land Rover behind him. She was peering at Franks through the windshield. He ignored her and took two steps, figuring out the route he would take, when the woman started honking her horn.

Franks considered shooting her but instead lowered his head to the rain and hurried diagonally away from the police across Park Row. He made the sidewalk by City Hall Park, and kept moving away from the bridge. The woman kept honking her horn.

He never looked back and thought he'd make the corner onto Vesey Street.

Twelve steps from being out of sight, he heard a woman shout, 'Stop where you are. Show me your hands!'

For some reason, Franks thought of the logger, then he stuffed the barrel of his gun under his right armpit, lifted the Treasury agent badge up with his left hand, and turned to find a young female uniformed cop about thirty feet away.

She was shakily aiming her service pistol at him, and he could see doubt and fear all about her.

'Federal agent!' Franks cried, showing her the badge and ID. 'Don't shoot!'

'Down on the ground!' she shouted.

'You're making a mistake, rookie,' he warned her as he started to lower himself down. 'I was chasing the killer. He's getting — '

A squall of rain hit them. He dropped to his knees, went for the gun, snagged it expertly, and whipped it out, intending to shoot the young cop.

She shot first and hit Franks square in the chest. He staggered back in disbelief but still tried to aim at her. She shot him twice more.

He fell on his back, dying.

Franks's last vision was of the cop standing over him, aiming at him.

'No rookie mistake, man,' she said, her voice taunting and quivering both. 'No rookie mistake at all.'

60

Roughly two hours after President Hobbs was shot, Mahoney and I lifted off the roof of FBI headquarters in a helicopter bound for Joint Base Andrews, which used to be known as Andrews Air Force Base.

Looking down on the nation's capital, I saw tanks flanking the bridges and armed soldiers amassing on every corner. There were cops and FBI agents searching every vehicle trying to leave Washington. In all my years in DC, I had never seen this level of military presence, not even after 9/11.

The media was painting the mood of the country as bordering on panic. There were reports of runs on grocery stores and on guns and ammunition. People were frightened and desperate to know what was happening.

'We'll catch him,' Mahoney said, breaking into my thoughts. 'With or without professional footage of the actual shooting.'

'Krazy Kat said he thought he could do something,' I said.

Ned cringed. 'Did we have to bring him in?'

'Rawlins is the best there is,' I said. 'I figure he's our only chance of getting a look at the killer anytime soon.'

Mahoney grunted and looked at his phone screen. We flew within sight of my home, and I looked toward it, wondering when I'd return.

For a moment, I shut my eyes and prayed it would happen sooner rather than later.

We landed on a helipad at Andrews, not far from Marine One, the president's helicopter. Air Force One was there, but it looked different to me. There were three other planes just like it, all unmarked, all Boeing E-4s, sitting on the tarmac along with ten fighter jets and half a dozen private jets.

Armed airmen inspected our FBI identifications. Everywhere we looked, we saw battle-ready soldiers and airmen.

For the first time, it felt to me like we really could be a nation at war.

My generation of Americans had never experienced political assassination. And nothing of this magnitude had ever happened in U.S. history.

That shook me. It really did. I understood why people might feel on the verge of panic. No one knew who or what was behind the attacks or what might be coming next. That dread and uncertainty were enough to push people right to the edge psychologically, and I expected to hear about looting and civil unrest before too long.

A soldier led us into an open hangar, and we entered a space big enough to hold a C-130 cargo jet or two. As we crossed the hangar floor, I looked down at my casual clothes and felt underdressed to meet the president, even given the circumstances. Nana Mama would have been appalled.

The soldier stopped and stood aside, and I

followed Mahoney into a large room with six long rectangular tables.

Around the tables sat perhaps twenty people, several of whom I knew at a glance. Samuel Larkin, the acting president, was huddled at the far end of one table with FBI director Sanford, General Hayes, and Homeland Security director Elaine Monroe as well as CIA director Felix White.

I recognized the upset faces of enough other people at the table to realize they were the surviving members of the cabinet. John Watts, the chief justice of the U.S. Supreme Court, was there as well. So were the leaders of both parties in both houses of Congress.

'What in God's name am I doing in this room?' I whispered to Mahoney.

'I was thinking the same thing,' Mahoney said.

'Mahoney, Cross,' FBI director Sanford said, waving us toward the president.

We shook hands with Larkin.

'I've heard a lot about you, Dr. Cross,' he said in a grave voice. 'Director Sanford said you and Special Agent Mahoney were the people he wanted involved in the investigation immediately.'

'Well,' I said, taken aback. 'I'm honored to be here to help in any way I can, and please excuse the clothes.'

Larkin put his hand on my shoulder and gazed at me evenly. 'We've got more dire things to deal with.'

'Yes, Mr. President.'

He held my gaze a moment and then nodded

and said softly, 'Good. Take a seat, Dr. Cross. And keep your eyes and ears open.'

'Yes, sir. I'll do that.'

61

As Mahoney and I took seats, we saw members of the cabinet, one of the congressional leaders, and several others I did not recognize sizing us up. My first inclination was to ignore them, but then I realized that all of the people in the room feared for their lives but were also probably jockeying for position in the power vacuum created by the assassinations.

The killings were an act of war or a coup, something huge and sinister — I was in such a deep state of shock that for the moment I couldn't do anything *but* heed Larkin's advice to sit down, listen, and watch.

The acting president said, 'The purpose of this meeting is twofold. All members of the current cabinet are to serve through the period of martial law at least. You will be separated, however, and flown with your families aboard one of the E-fours, the advanced airborne command posts, to secure locations.'

Several of them started to protest. Larkin held up his hand and said, 'There is no discussion. This is being done for your own safety and for the good of the country. I will be doing the same thing in the near future.

'In any case, we will stay in close contact via secure satellite transmission. You will be involved in all major policy debates and made aware of decisions in real time.

'Chief Justice Watts and leaders of the majority and minority parties, I ask that you remain readily available in the coming days. In an emergency like this, I will need clear legal guidance on what I can and cannot do to try to defend the nation.'

The chief justice hesitated but then said, 'It's highly unorthodox, but I think in this time of crisis, it's a smart idea, Mr. President.'

Larkin nodded, leaned forward, and looked around the table.

'Let me be clear about something,' he said. 'In this case, no one is above the law or outside our jurisdiction. I am instructing Director Sanford and all intelligence agency leaders to follow the investigation wherever it leads.

'If this is the work of a hostile nation, we will declare war. If this is the work of any ideological group, domestic or foreign, we will root them out and bring them to justice. I will not have these heinous acts wreck the country, not on my watch.'

Many at the table nodded and voiced their approval.

Larkin started signing executive orders that put the Justice Department's assassination-contingency plan into effect. In line with that plan, he sought and received approval from the congressional leaders and from the chief justice to temporarily amend the rules of Congress to limit members' access to classified information as the investigation rolled forward.

The plan also called for a rapidly deployed investigative group answering to the FBI director, the AG, the president, and those gathered in the room. Larkin asked the majority leaders of both houses to form select committees on the assassinations that would provide independent oversight and reports.

'I will not allow this to be like the JFK investigation,' Larkin said. 'I will not have some future panel judge us deficient in our investigation. This is no lone gunman. These coordinated assassinations are clearly the result of a massive conspiracy, the most outrageous attack on our democracy since Pearl Harbor, and I plan to tell the nation just that when I address them later in the day.'

For a moment Larkin seemed excited by that prospect, the idea of speaking to the nation in a time of great crisis, and I wondered whether he'd ever imagined himself president of the United States. He certainly had been a brilliant careerist.

I knew his resume; he'd been a decorated army captain before going to Yale Law School and then joining the Justice Department. It was almost as if he'd planned his rise. And now here it was, his moment, probably a lot sooner than he'd expected.

The acting president looked down the table at me and Mahoney. 'Dr. Cross, SAC Mahoney, for the next one hundred hours I am allocating unlimited resources to bring to bear on these crimes. Advise us on how best to proceed.'

62

Metro police chief of detectives Bree Stone and Metro detective John Sampson walked the perimeter of the DC arena as a mix of FBI, Secret Service, and Metro investigators manned a system to get the children out of the venue while interviewing anyone with any information, anything at all.

The main security checkpoint was clogged with kids and their parents and chaperones trying to get out of the arena. Bree spotted Secret Service Agent Lance Reamer, who looked beyond agitated.

'Anything?' she asked.

He shook his head. 'They cut the — '

'Please, coming through!' a woman called out.

Bree looked up to see two paramedics flanking a man on a rolling gurney who had bloody bandages all over his head and face. A DC SWAT officer trailed them.

Several of the children got upset at the sight of the wounded man.

The paramedics pushed the gurney through. Bree walked with them toward a waiting ambulance. 'What happened?'

The SWAT officer said, 'We found him in the basement in a pool of blood from four different head wounds. Name's Kent Leonard. Works here. Lost some teeth, probably some broken bones in his face. Looks like he was hit with a piece of iron. They destroyed his hearing aids too. Guy's stone-deaf without them.'

'Hearing aids?' said a Secret Service agent coming their way.

Another agent came over too. 'We know this guy.'

They introduced themselves as Agents Crane and Lewis, then Agent Crane went to the wounded man's side, made eye contact, and nodded.

Leonard looked at him fuzzily, then reached his hand up to the side of his head and said in a duck-like voice. 'Where are my hearing aids?'

Bree tugged out a notebook, scribbled: *They're broken. Do you sign?*

He shook his head no.

'Can we do this later?' the EMT said. 'He could have a skull fracture.'

'And the president's been shot,' Bree said to him, scribbling again. 'I just want him to answer one question.'

She flipped the pad around. *What happened?*

He gazed at the question a moment before coughing and saying in that nasal quacking voice, 'I was down getting paper towels from storage when the lights went out. I used the light on my watch to go to the room with the big electrical panels. I got there and started to open the door. Someone hit me from behind. I bounced off the door, and then fell to the ground, and he just kept hitting me until I blacked out.'

He? Bree wrote. *You saw him?*

He nodded. 'In the watch light. Blond guy.

Weird blue eyes. I . . . ' His eyes fluttered, and he moaned. 'My head hurts.'

The EMT said, 'I need to get him to a level-one trauma center.'

Bree wanted to ask him more questions, but Reamer said, 'Go ahead.'

She looked at the man's face, which was swollen and an angry purplish color.

'Load him,' she said. 'But I want someone with him in case he remembers anything else. He's the only one who's come in direct contact with one of the assassins.'

'You think there were two?' Sampson said.

'Someone shot the president upstairs in the arena. A blond man with weird blue eyes cut the lights. Mr. Leonard surprised that person and got beaten.'

'I'll go with him,' Agent Crane said.

'No,' Reamer said. 'I need you here. The Secret Service may not be in charge, but we are involved.'

'I'll go,' Sampson said.

'I need *you* here,' Bree said. 'I'll get a uniform to go with him.'

'I'm off,' Reamer said as he turned away. 'I'm still looking for an eyewitness to the shooting.'

63

In the conference room off the hangar at Joint Base Andrews, I looked at the president and the country's leaders and saw them all studying me.

I said, 'If I had unlimited resources, I'd bring in the best investigative coordinator the FBI has to oversee four distinct teams. One team should focus on forensics and generating swift, accurate test results. The second team should be composed of the Bureau's best investigators dispatched into the field, starting at the three assassination sites. Intelligence analysts from the FBI, CIA, NSA, and Homeland Security should staff the third team and should have an eye on every piece of evidence that comes in.'

President Larkin nodded. 'And the fourth?'

I said the last team should be composed of a smaller group of elite investigators, analysts, and forensics specialists assigned to look at the crimes from a loftier perspective. What was the purpose of the assassinations? Why did they have to happen? Whom and what did they benefit? Whom and what did they destroy?

Mahoney agreed with my rough design but added, 'That fourth team should also be charged with identifying and arresting the person or persons in government who helped coordinate the attacks.'

There was dead silence in the room.

Finally, Director Sanford said, 'You believe

there's a traitor, Agent Mahoney?'

'Without question, sir,' Ned said. 'Probably several.' An older man with a professor's manner whom I later learned was NSA director John Parkes leaned forward and said, 'Or whoever is behind this has completely compromised our cybersecurity system. You'll want to consider this as well.'

Parkes typed on a laptop. A screen on the wall flashed, then showed a map of the world with continents and countries connected by strands, streams, and rivers of tiny shimmering lights.

Parkes said, 'You're looking at the data flow on the dark web forty-eight hours ago, then twenty-four hours ago, and now.'

The lines of sparkling light ebbed and flowed. Roughly thirty-six hours ago, a big dense river of data connecting the United States, Russia, North Korea, and China had appeared, then widened and deepened, building toward a flood.

Linda Johnson, the Senate minority leader, said, 'Are we looking at the start of World War Three?'

Before anyone could reply, Director Sanford looked at his phone, said, 'Abbie Bowman's assassin was killed ten minutes ago. New York rookie cop shot him. He was carrying perfect forgeries of Treasury Department IDs. They're fingerprinting him and checking dental records as we speak.'

Mahoney said, 'That's a big break.'

'Here's another,' Felix White, the CIA director, said, gesturing at his laptop. 'We've picked up satellite chatter, Russian satellite chatter. Three-quarters of the Kremlin think the motherland is behind the assassinations.'

'Maybe it is,' I said. 'Maybe through Viktor Kasimov.'

'Son of a bitch,' White said, and he threw a pencil on the table. 'We keep an eye on Kasimov when he's not here assaulting women. We were alerted this morning that his pilot filed flight plans to London. Kasimov and his crew took off around nine.'

'Right before the shooting started,' General Hayes said.

President Larkin said, 'Have our agents waiting for Mr. Kasimov at Heathrow. I don't give a damn about his diplomatic status. The second he touches down, grab him and put him on a return flight in handcuffs and ankle irons.'

'Yes, Mr. President,' the CIA director said. 'With great pleasure, Mr. President.'

There was a soft knock at the door. It opened, and a flustered air force captain said, 'Excuse me. There's a Keith Karl Rawlins, an FBI contractor, who just landed from Quantico. He says he might have figured out who shot the president.'

64

Keith Karl Rawlins, AKA Krazy Kat, entered the room a few moments later. Rawlins usually worked in a subbasement at Quantico; he was a very highly paid contractor who offered his unique expertise exclusively to the FBI.

Rawlins had dual PhDs from Stanford, one in physics and a second in electrical engineering. In his spare time, he was working on a third doctorate from MIT in computer science.

The last time I'd seen him, he'd cut his hair in a Mohawk and dyed it flaming red. That was all gone now. He'd shaved his head, grown a beard and braided it, and he wore camo fatigues, sandals, and two new nose rings.

You could tell from the expressions on the faces of the people in the room that they didn't know what to make of Rawlins, even if Director Sanford had described him before he came in as 'possibly the smartest person on earth when it comes to harnessing data.'

Rawlins nodded to me, said, 'Good idea, Dr. Cross.'

'It worked?'

'Well enough,' Rawlins said as he got out a laptop and started typing.

'What are you talking about?' President Larkin demanded.

'Dr. Cross asked if I could harvest pictures and videos from cell phones in the DC arena being posted on social media. The challenge was putting it all together in a meaningful way. But even that wasn't like learning to speak Cantonese in ten days.'

Rawlins hit a button and looked up at the screen on the wall. The NSA director's map showing the ballooning dark-web activity among the U.S., Russia, North Korea, and China vanished.

In its place we saw a digital, somewhat disjointed, almost 3-D rendition of the inside of the DC arena and the crowd of excited youngsters as President Hobbs came down the rope line surrounded by Secret Service agents.

Rawlins slowed it after Hobbs took a selfie with a young boy, then spun the view around so we were looking over shoulders and around heads at the president, who shook hands and talked with three tween girls.

A grinning blond man, camera left, reached over the girls to shake President Hobbs's hand. Hobbs smiled at the man, who wore a cleric's collar and tinted glasses.

President Hobbs released the blond man's hand, moved toward the next person, and then suddenly fell backward into his bodyguard. The blond man's smile turned puzzled and then alarmed before the screen froze.

'I didn't see a gun,' Chief Justice Watts said.

'Swing us around,' I said. 'Let's see him from the front.'

Rawlins gave his computer an order. The media swept back in time and went around again before zooming in on the blond man reaching for the president's hand. We watched the same events unfold: the handshake, the release, President Hobbs stumbling.

'I still don't see it,' the chief justice said.

'I think I did,' I said. 'Take us in super-slo-mo. Watch his right hand, his loose shirt cuff, and the belly of his coat sleeve right after the president ends the handshake.'

They all leaned forward as Rawlins rewound the footage and stayed on President Hobbs, still smiling as he released the blond man's hand. When their fingers had drifted ten, maybe twelve inches apart, the minister arched his hand backward as if to wave. The belly of his sleeve billowed. The cuff distorted.

A split second later, President Hobbs staggered back into his Secret Service agents. Rawlins froze the image.

'No one heard a gunshot,' Director Sanford said.

'Because there was no gun,' I said. 'No conventional one, at least. Can we see him shoot the secretary of defense?'

Rawlins said, 'I didn't look.'

He stayed with the suspect as he moved with the crowd past the fallen president. Then the shooter shifted his hips toward the stage and raised his left hand toward Harold Murphy.

The footage got a little jerky, but you saw the blond man's hand arching again, and the secretary of defense going down.

'What's he doing with his hand?' President Larkin said.

'I think he's triggering an air gun of some sort,' I said.

Sanford looked up from his phone. 'Which explains the pieces of bullet they took out of President Hobbs twenty minutes ago.'

The FBI director forwarded an image to Rawlins, who put it on the screen: a photograph of dark gray pieces lying in a steel pan.

'It will have to be analyzed, but I'll bet that's graphite or carbon,' I said. 'His weapons were probably made out of polymers that are undetectable by current methods.'

Rawlins typed again. The screen filled with a clear shot of the blond man in the tinted glasses.

He said, 'I'd get this picture in the hands of all law enforcement at that arena and everywhere else in the country.'

'Wait,' I said, studying the picture. 'He's posing as a cleric, presumably. Who says he really has blond hair and wears glasses?'

Rawlins smiled. 'I'm barely a half a step ahead of you, Dr. Cross.'

65

Bree and Sampson were still working outside the main entrance to the DC arena, interviewing kids, parents, and guardians, when Bree's phone buzzed.

After she had finished talking to a young girl from the Philippines, she got out her phone and found a text from Alex. He'd sent a link labeled Hobbs's shooter.

She clicked on it, saw the blond minister, and remembered Leonard, the guy found beaten in the basement. He'd said he was hit by a blond man.

But how did that work? Did the blond have time to shoot Hobbs and the secretary of defense and then go down to club the maintenance man?

Or were there two assassins, both dressed similarly? One in the basement cutting the lights, one upstairs trying to kill a president?

Her phone buzzed; another link from Alex: Shooter in left profile.

She clicked it, saw the same blond minister reaching out his right hand toward President Hobbs, The next link showed his right profile, but it was blurry. Bree tried to blow it up, but the resolution got too grainy.

The fourth link showed him from behind, arm stretched out toward Hobbs.

The fifth, sixth, seventh, and eighth images came in with a note that read Shooter with disguise digitally removed courtesy of K. K. Rawlins.

She thumbed the first new image. The blond hair and glasses were gone, leaving the man bald and blurry about the eyes. The two profile pictures were of interest, but it wasn't until she opened the eighth link that she really paused.

With the blond hair gone, as she looked at the shooter from behind, she could see something odd about his right ear. She zoomed in on it and felt her stomach drop.

It was a hearing aid. No doubt.

Feeling confused, then certain, and then panicked, Bree yelled at Sampson, 'We're leaving, John!'

Sampson apologized to the woman he was interviewing and ran after Bree as she barked into her radio. 'This is Stone! An ambulance left the arena forty minutes ago. Where'd it go?'

'GW,' the dispatcher said. 'EMTs handed him off twenty-five minutes ago.'

'Who's the officer with him?'

'Pettit. You want me to raise him?'

Bree stopped at the car and tossed the keys to Sampson, weighing the pros and cons of alerting a young patrol officer that he might be sitting on a would-be presidential assassin. And what if the shooter was with Pettit and heard her warning?

'Chief?' the dispatcher said.

'No,' Bree said, climbing into the front seat. 'Get me Pettit's cell phone number.'

Sampson threw a bubble on the roof and hit the siren. They roared off across town, running red lights in virtually zero traffic as they closed in on George Washington University Hospital in the Foggy Bottom neighborhood of the District.

'What'd he do?' Sampson said. 'Beat the snot out of himself? Knock out his own teeth?'

'It worked,' she said, furious. 'His own mother wouldn't have recognized him.'

'And being deaf?'

'No idea.'

The dispatcher came back with Officer Pettit's cell phone number.

'Good,' Bree said. 'How many patrol cars available to respond?'

'Four. FBI's using the rest to keep the city tied down.'

Bree gave orders to move the four cruisers to the roads that formed the perimeter of the medical center, and then she called Pettit.

It went immediately to voice mail. She tried again. Same thing.

Bree still didn't want to call the officer on the radio for fear he'd be in range of Leonard, or whoever the shooter really was. After trying a third time, she called Alex.

'Hi,' he said, sounding out of breath.

'Where are you?'

'About to get on a military jet at Andrews.'

'Going where?'

'West Texas.'

'Why? The president was shot here.'

'We want to see every crime scene.'

She heard the heavy whine of a jet engine on his end.

'When are you coming back?'

His voice was almost drowned by the noise. 'I don't know.'

'I think we've got Hobbs's shooter,' she said. 'He's at GW.'

'What's that? I can't hear you.'

The engine roar got worse and the connection died just as Sampson pulled over at the entrance to the GW emergency room. It had started to rain again.

'Chief,' Sampson said. 'You need to tell the FBI he's here.'

Bree had intentionally delayed, but now she nodded and told dispatch to notify FBI command that she and Sampson were investigating a possible suspect at the hospital. She didn't give any more than she had to, figuring if she and Sampson made the collar on Hobbs's shooter, she'd never hear another discouraging word from Chief Michaels — or anyone else, for that matter.

Inside, they showed their badges and IDs to the charge nurse and asked where Leonard was being treated. The nurse looked it up, said, 'Multiple facial cuts and fractures. He was stitched, bandaged, and moved to radiology. He's getting a CT.'

She gave them directions to the CT scanner, which had been temporarily moved to a lower level in an older part of the complex while new facilities were being built.

Bree and Sampson followed her directions, getting off an elevator just as a male doctor in scrubs, Crocs, a surgical cap, and a hooded rain jacket entered the elevator next to theirs. Bree caught a glimpse of an older man with gray, loose skin, wavy dark gray hair, and glasses.

He wore headphones but was also talking on his cell phone. Bree heard him complaining about the number of autopsies he had to do before he could go home.

'They're stacked like cordwood in there,' the pathologist said as the elevator doors shut.

Walking down a hallway with an industrial feel, Bree and Sampson passed pathology and the morgue. They pushed through double doors at the far end of the corridor and took a right into an empty passage with a small sign that read RADIOLOGY.

Bree got her badge out and loosened her service weapon in its holster.

Sampson opened the door.

'No!' Bree said, staring in disbelief at Metro PD Officer Walter Pettit who was lying on the floor with a neck that looked broken and his service revolver missing.

They tore out their pistols. In the room where the CT scanner was still running, they found two female techs in hospital scrubs sprawled on the floor, dead.

Bree called dispatch for backup from the FBI and all available law enforcement.

'Surround George Washington University Hospital,' she said. 'The president's shooter is in here somewhere.'

66

Bree listened to the radio chatter as FBI and Metro Police descended on the medical center.

Sampson said, 'They're going to have to clear every room in this place and get all nonessential personnel out of here before they do it.'

'We can get that started down here,' Bree said.

She took a long look at Pettit before she followed Sampson, feeling her stomach churn at her role in the young officer's death. There would be time for regret and guilt later, she told herself. Once the man who'd killed Pettit and shot the president was caught.

With pistols still drawn, they exited the radiology suite and retraced their steps. They went into the pathology department and found no one at the front desk.

They went around the desk and into a short hallway with autopsy rooms to either side. All were empty, and the stainless-steel equipment inside was spotless.

They reached the door at the end of the hall and found it locked with an electronic key-card slot.

'Probably goes to the morgue,' Sampson said.

That made sense to Bree, and she led them in the opposite direction, past the autopsy rooms and into a separate hallway with office doors on both sides. The first three were empty.

As they headed toward the fourth office, a

woman in surgical scrubs crawled out of the door, bleeding from her ears and nose. Bree and Sampson ran to her and called for help from the ER.

A name tag identified the woman as CHRISTINE WILLIS, MD, DEPARTMENT OF PATHOLOGY. She was rambling and in pain, but they figured out that while listening to music, she had been attacked by someone from behind and knocked out.

She said she came around and saw her attacker, who had bandages all over his face, leaving her office with her key card.

'He's gotta be hiding in the morgue,' Sampson said. 'Or was.'

Dr. Willis told them where to find another pass key in a drawer at the front desk. On her radio, Bree heard that nurses and a doctor were arriving from the ER.

Only then did she leave the pathologist and follow Sampson back to the morgue door. He slid the key card in the slot and heard it click.

He opened it slowly. The lights were off.

Sampson reached around, groped for a moment, then flipped a switch. The morgue lights lit, and they eased inside, backs to each other.

Bree saw nothing but rows of cold-storage lockers.

'Over there,' Sampson said.

She turned and peered around him to see a male, Asian, in boxers slumped against the far wall. Sampson went to the man, checked for a pulse, looked for breathing, then shook his head at Bree. She called in the homicide and started opening the cold lockers.

Every one she opened was full. Corpses were stacked like cordwood in —

She opened the second-to-last locker and gaped at the corpse of an obese man.

Three surgical scalpels lay on his chest. From the base of his neck to the crown of his head, he'd been skinned.

67

Pablo Cruz stepped off a maintenance elevator that put him in a narrow hallway behind the hospital cafeteria. Despite the opiates the ER docs had given him, he was in ferocious pain from the broken teeth and facial bones.

And it was taking everything in his power to block out the clammy, sticky feel of the cowl of cold, dead skin that he'd pulled down over his head to cover the bruising and bandages on his face. That's who they'd be looking for if they were looking. The guy with the bandages. Not some old man with saggy gray skin.

Cruz had tied on a surgical cap to hide part of the incision lines he'd had to make to skin the corpse's head. He'd put the female pathologist's headphones on to hide another four inches of cut skin. The hooded rain jacket covered the incisions down the sides of the neck. So did an ID on a chain he'd taken from the dead pathologist in the morgue.

But he was worried about how it looked around his eyes, nose, and lips. Did they sag too much? Would someone know?

He put the hood of the rain jacket up and cast his eyes down while he walked along the hallway, nervous that a hospital worker might appear; he didn't want to test his disguise up close in any way.

Cruz passed the cafeteria, hearing pots and

pans banging and a woman singing in Spanish. Then he smelled garbage.

He followed the smell out a door onto a loading dock. To his right there were men unloading a linen-service truck. Cruz paid them no attention, just bounded down the stairs and trotted out the open overhead door into chill pouring rain. He zipped the jacket to the collar and tugged on the hood strings to tighten it before lowering his head and walking very fast south on Twenty-Third Street.

A knot of four or five people in raincoats or carrying umbrellas hurried ahead of him on the sidewalk, medical personnel, judging from the way they were talking. They were worrying about how they'd get home with all the public transit shut down.

A block away, a police cruiser was parked across the intersection, its blue lights flashing. The shooter moved closer to the group ahead of him.

When they were near the intersection with H Street, Cruz held the hood tight and turned his head briefly toward the police car, as if he were curious.

Then he looked away, having given them just enough to know his face wasn't bandaged but not enough to see he wore a dead man's skin.

Cruz crossed the street behind the others and heard no one call out. He stayed with them as the rain fell harder, and still he heard no one yell after him.

It wasn't until he was a block and a half south of the medical center that he heard a symphony of sirens start up, all of them getting closer, trumpeting and wailing their way toward a hospital where the president's shooter wasn't anymore.

68

I had taken off from Andrews sitting in the rear seat of an air force F-15E Strike Eagle fighter jet, as stunning and exhilarating an experience as I've ever had.

Mahoney had gone in a second one. With U.S. airspace empty, the pilots were free to fly near the Strike Eagles' blistering top-end speed of more than eighteen hundred miles an hour. We covered the 1,624 miles to an air force base west of San Antonio in less than fifty-five minutes.

As the planes were coming in for a landing, Director Sanford told Mahoney that Kasimov had not arrived in London. Ned relayed the information to me over my headset.

'Where'd he go?' I asked.

'Toward North Africa,' Mahoney said. 'Before he disappeared off the radar.'

'No,' I said as we touched down.

'Yup. His jet was picked up crossing Majorcan airspace, and then nothing.'

Was this an act of war? With Kasimov on the inside, choreographing the attacks from his suite at the Mandarin Oriental?

A Texas National Guard Apache helicopter flew us thirty-five minutes southwest of the air base over dry, broken country pocked with scrub brush to the remote Garand Ranch, reputed to be one of the Lone Star State's finest quail-hunting lodges.

We flew in over harvested agricultural fields. Deer scattered and bounded from the stubble as we dropped in altitude and landed near a barn and a hacienda-style lodge.

A small contingent of local law enforcement waited for us along with an FBI forensics crew that had just arrived on the scene from the Dallas office. To my surprise, I recognized someone in the crowd right away: U.S. Capitol Police lieutenant Sheldon Lee looked shell-shocked when I walked up and shook his hand.

'What are you doing here, Lieutenant?'

Lee shook his head in disbelief. 'Bill Johnston, Speaker Guilford's usual body man, got sick, and I got assigned to come down and watch Guilford and the secretary of state take a much-needed break and hunt quail. First Betsy Walker and now Guilford, both on my watch? I . . . it makes me look — '

'Dr. Cross?'

I looked to Terrance Crown, the U.S. Diplomatic Service agent who'd been assigned to protect secretary of state Aaron Deeds and his wife, Eliza.

'I'm glad you're here, sir,' Crown said, shaken. 'I've heard you're the best, and we need the best right now.'

Eldon Pritchard, a lean man in his forties with a waxed mustache who was wearing a white cowboy hat, boots, jeans, and the badge of a Texas Ranger, was also there, but he seemed thoroughly unimpressed by our presence.

They took us out on the terrace, where the bodies of the Speaker of the House and the

275

secretary of state were still lying where they'd fallen, covered with clear plastic sheeting. It was warm in the sunshine, but they were in shade. Eliza Deeds, the secretary of state's wife, had been medevaced to a hospital in Dallas hours ago.

'We haven't touched a thing,' Lieutenant Lee said. 'I insisted. And the staff is waiting to talk.'

'Take us through it,' Mahoney said.

We heard about breakfasts on the terrace in the morning sun, a Garand Ranch tradition even in winter. We heard about soft, distant thuds, and how the Speaker had been hit first and the secretary of state wounded and then killed with another shot.

Mahoney said, 'And that was at roughly what time?'

Both Lieutenant Lee and Agent Crown agreed it was 7:28 a.m. local time when the shooting ended, plus or minus thirty seconds.

'Why did it take so long for word to reach Washington?' I asked.

Lee said, 'This whole area is a dead zone as far as cell service. They usually have satellite coverage, but it was out too. We had to drive twenty miles on dirt roads to call it in.'

Mahoney said, 'Which gave the other assassins back east time to act.'

'The coordination in this is breathtaking,' I said.

'Who knew the Speaker was coming?' Mahoney said. 'And the secretary of state?'

Lee said Guilford's wife knew about the trip, of course, and his two sons, his chief of staff, and his personal secretary. Other than that small circle, the Speaker tended to keep his hunting life quiet.

Likewise, Secretary of State Deeds had told few people that he and his wife were going off for a few days with the Speaker of the House. But Deeds's bodyguard did say the secretary's top tier of foreign policy advisers all knew he would be at the ranch.

'They were in a tizzy, afraid there would be no cell service,' Crown said. 'I guess they were right.'

I said, 'We'll come back to that. Do we know where the shots came from?'

One of the FBI forensics techs said, 'Haven't gotten that far yet.'

Pritchard, the Texas Ranger, spat tobacco into a Styrofoam cup and said, 'I already eyeballed it. They came from out on that bluff beyond the ag fields. I'm figuring five hundred to five twenty-five meters out.'

'You don't know that,' the tech said.

Pritchard shot him a sour look as he smoothed his mustache. 'Son, I promise you, I can walk you to within ten feet of where those snipers were lying.'

Mahoney said, 'So you've been out there to look already?'

Pritchard smiled. 'I may be a hick, Special Agent Mahoney, but I am not stupid.'

69

Pritchard had us climb into his truck. A black Malinois shepherd paced behind a screen in the back of it.

'My boy Samba back there's an asset to you,' Pritchard said. 'Best man-tracker in the state, and that's no BS. Won down to Houston, fair and square.'

Mahoney said, 'You don't think they've left the county by now?'

'Probably so,' the Texas Ranger said. 'But at least Samba can tell us the way they went and where your forensics team should focus.'

It made sense to me. Pritchard drove a ranch road to the base of the bluff. We got out and climbed a rocky, sandy wall through sage and other desert plants blooming.

It smells too good for a murder scene, I thought as we crested the rise. Mahoney puffed up beside me, with the Texas Ranger, his dog, and the FBI forensics crew trailing.

Pritchard adjusted his belt and then released the Malinois. 'Seek, Samba. Seek!'

The dog's ears went up. He bounded forward, arcing across the wind with his tail up. We watched him dodge sage plants and then slow, his muzzle raised and his nostrils flaring. I didn't know dogs that well, but he seemed confused.

'Seek!' Pritchard said again.

The Malinois's vigor renewed. He trotted

forward again some forty yards, looking confident, then looped back toward us. His tail was all we could see for a few moments, wagging there above the brush.

Samba halted. He started to wheeze, then whimper, then shriek in pain. He exploded away from the spot and spun in circles, digging frantically at his nose and muzzle with his paws.

'Damn it!' Pritchard said, running after the dog. 'He get into a porcupine?'

When the Ranger caught up to Samba, the dog was still crying and scratching at his face.

'Damn it,' the Ranger said again. 'No quills,' he called back to us. 'They must have sprayed the place with bleach or cayenne or both!'

I held up a hand, telling the forensics team to stay put. Mahoney and I donned blue booties. Ten feet apart, we walked abreast, searching the undergrowth separating us from Pritchard and his dog, which was still whimpering.

'I got something,' Mahoney said just as my eyes came to rest on a rectangular box lying in the sand.

'I do too,' I said, easing around a bush and putting on latex gloves.

I squatted down and picked up the box, which was about the size of a paperback novel. It had slits on the front, a fan on the bottom, a complicated control panel, and a logo.

'Anyone know what an Ozonics is?' I asked.

Pritchard had calmed his dog and reclipped his lead.

'Portable ozone machine,' he said. 'Hunters use them to kill odor. Makes sense.'

'Why's that?' I asked.

'Wind's blowing from us to the hacienda,' the Texas Ranger said. 'If the ranch dogs had smelled them out here, they'd have barked, probably come to investigate. Sumbitches really thought this through, you know. Contingencies.'

Before I could agree, Mahoney held up a smaller, thinner metal box. 'Any idea on this one, Mr. Pritchard?'

He told his dog to stay and came over to look. After several moments, he looked over at one of his deputies.

'Got your radio, Devin?'

The deputy nodded.

'Call me.'

He did, but Pritchard didn't get the transmission on his end.

'Jammer,' the Ranger said. 'No wonder the satellite phone wasn't working.'

Mahoney said, 'Looks like the ground's been swept for a ways,' he said.

'Samba good enough to pick up scent back there?' I asked.

Pritchard shook his head. 'His nose is toast for today.'

Mahoney said, 'You know this country?'

The Ranger nodded. 'Lot of it.'

'Where would their natural line of travel be? How would they likely go if they were heading, say, roughly north?'

Pritchard thought a moment. 'Straight north, there's a whole lot of nothing but BLM land, broken country, and box canyons for twenty miles, maybe more.'

'Northeast? Northwest?'

The Texas Ranger thought about that, then said, 'Northeast, maybe four, five miles, there used to be an old road into a mining claim on the federal land, but I want to say its gated or blocked.'

'I'm betting it's not anymore,' I said. 'How long to drive there?'

'We'll have to loop all the way around. Forty minutes?'

'We'll fly,' Mahoney said.

We did. Following Pritchard's directions, the helicopter took us to a heavy-duty gate off a spur of a country road. A sign said ROAD CLOSED. BUREAU OF LAND MANAGEMENT. The lock had been cut. We opened the gate and started on foot up a terrible, washed-out rock-and-sand road.

'No tire tracks,' Ned said.

'But look at all the little lines in the sand,' I said, kneeling. 'It's like whoever drove in and out was pulling brooms behind them.'

'Special Agent Mahoney?' the copter pilot called from the other side of the gate. 'We just got the call, sir. President Hobbs is dead.'

70

Darkness had fallen when Mahoney and I touched down at Andrews. With the tailwind, we'd made even better time on the return flight.

As we climbed out of the Strike Eagles, it seemed surreal that we'd been in West Texas less than an hour before. We hustled across the tarmac. My phone beeped, alerting me to several calls from Bree.

I slowed, told Ned I'd be right along, and called her back.

'Thank God,' she said. 'Have you heard?'

'That Hobbs died?'

'No, that we had his assassin on a gurney right in front of us and let him slip. Then we had him almost cornered in GW Medical Center, and he got past us again wearing a dead guy's facial skin.'

That struck me as gruesome. 'For real?'

'I found the skinned body myself! Someone's keeping him just ahead of us. I think there's a traitor, Alex.'

'Ned does too,' I said.

'Maybe Lance Reamer with the Secret Service,' she said, her voice hardening as she recounted how Reamer had waved the bleeding assassin through the checkpoint over her protests and then balked at providing an agent to accompany the killer to the hospital.

'I know you lost an officer, but you're going to

have to do better than that.'

'I know,' Bree said, and she exhaled hard.

I told her about the old mining road north of the hunting ranch that looked swept.

'But we found some fresh tire imprints about three hundred yards up the road when whoever it was bounced over rocks and hit sand,' I said. 'Looks like a big pickup pulling a horse trailer. Trouble is, those happen to be everywhere in Texas and all points north, south, east, and west of it. Mahoney's got agents and police canvassing in a fifty-mile radius around that ranch, but nothing yet.'

I told her I'd text if I thought I could make it home, and then I went inside the hangar.

In the hours we'd been gone, the vast space had been transformed into a teeming hive. There were several hundred people inside, uniformed and not. At least a hundred of them had already been assigned workstations complete with ultra-secure computers linked to the databases of the FBI, the CIA, the NSA, and Homeland Security. Four huge TV monitors hung above the work area.

They were tuned to CNN and the network news. The nation was in shock at the four assassinations. People were fearing an attempt to topple the government altogether, and they spoke of potential anarchy and despair. President Larkin was due to speak to the country in less than an hour.

I spotted Keith Karl Rawlins, and then I saw Mahoney talking to a trim, fit woman in a business suit. I vaguely recognized her as a high-ranking FBI official. She didn't look happy and seemed to find my arrival a cause for more sourness.

Mahoney introduced her as Susan Carstensen, the Bureau's deputy director for investigations. Carstensen shook my hand and said, 'We won't be jetting about at supersonic speeds like that again unless I give the go, are we clear, Dr. Cross?'

'Director Sanford ordered us to go,' I said.

'Just the same. I won't have this spin out of control with cowboys riding off on a whim.'

Mahoney gritted his teeth. 'With all due respect, ma'am, that was no whim, and we're hardly cowboys. We were able to see the entire crime scene as well as find the odor destroyers I described, a signal jammer, and the tire prints.'

Carstensen lost the attitude, became all business. 'The jamming device. Russian-made?'

'On its way to Quantico for testing,' Mahoney said.

'Kasimov?'

'Nothing,' she said. 'But you should know that NSA is reporting we're getting scores of attempts to hack us coming out of Russia, China, and North Korea.'

'You mean they're trying to hack us in here?' I said.

'The word is out. They seem to know this is the center of the investigation.'

'Feeling us out,' Mahoney said. 'Seeing if we can be compromised.'

'What's Larkin going to say tonight?'

'We don't know.'

An agent rushed up. 'Sorry to interrupt, ma'am, but we've got a positive ID on the treasury secretary's killer.'

Ten minutes later, on all four screens, a photograph went up of a burly man with a shock of unruly dark hair, a thick beard, and sunglasses. He was standing on a high point somewhere, rock and desert behind him. He wore faded military camouflage and a black-and-white-checked scarf around his neck. A black assault rifle hung from his chest harness, and he was smiling over ten dead bodies at his feet.

'Martin Franks,' Carstensen said through a microphone so everyone in the hangar could hear. 'Former U.S. JSOC operator, former Marine MARSOC operator, honorably discharged under an odious plea agreement four years ago. His COs came to suspect Franks had psychopathic tendencies. He liked to kill.

'This picture shows the result of his unauthorized one-man foray into a suspected Taliban village. He claimed he was discovered and had to fight his way out. There was an investigation, but it was one live man versus ten dead, and it had happened at night. No one else in the village could say exactly what had happened. Or would. The JAGs cut a deal to let him walk out and save the country further embarrassment.'

The screen split, and a photo appeared showing an older man among saguaro cacti. He wore green work clothes and carried an AK-47.

'This is Morris 'Moe' Franks,' she went on.

'Martin Franks's father. Moe has been on and off our watch list for more than two decades. Lives off the grid in southwest Arizona. Been involved in various militia groups over the years and has published tracts espousing anti-globalist views and stating his belief that only an armed uprising will cure the country's ills.'

'So Moe is alive?' an analyst asked.

'Far as we know,' Carstensen said. 'I've dispatched a team to his compound. In the meantime, I want everything you can find about his son's activities since his discharge. You have an open warrant to search. Dismissed.'

She turned to me and Mahoney. 'Thoughts?'

'I think homing in on Franks and squeezing the old man are smart moves,' Mahoney said.

'I'm sensing a *but* coming,' she said, crossing her arms.

Ned said, 'We just can't lose track of the big picture in all this. The assassinations. The hacks. This all could be provocation to war.'

'I think President Larkin has that covered.'

I cleared my throat. 'I think there's also the possibility that this is not state-sanctioned, that we have a single, ruthless Machiavellian mind at work behind the scenes. In light of that, I keep asking myself, *Who benefits here?*'

'And?' Carstensen said.

'There's no way around it,' I said, lowering my voice. 'Who benefits? Larkin. He most certainly benefits.'

Carstensen shook her head, incredulous, and laughed. 'You think Sam Larkin orchestrated the assassination of all the people above him in the succession chain so he could take over the country?'

'I think we have a duty to investigate that possibility, don't you?'

71

President Larkin spoke to the nation from Air Force One at nine p.m. eastern time.

Mahoney and I watched it on the big screens in the hangar. In the immediate run-up to the speech, the media noted that in city after city across America and despite the imposition of martial law, tens of thousands of young people had shown up in public places carrying flags and waiting to watch Larkin on their mobile devices.

When Larkin came on, he was grave, not at all the crusader he'd once been.

'My fellow Americans,' he began. 'I come to you in a time of peril. We have been attacked in an effort to destabilize our great nation. The assassinations of our president, Speaker of the House, the secretaries of state and the treasury, and the assassination attempt on the secretary of defense are acts of war on America and its people, and those acts will not go unanswered.'

Larkin said this last with such deep intensity and resolve that I was having trouble seeing him as part of a great plot to take power. But he'd been such a brash and ambitious man when he was younger. Could leopards change their spots?

The acting president went on, outlining the steps being taken to identify the assassins and the people behind them. He asked for calm while the investigative team did its business.

'I know the idea of martial law in the United

States is a frightening one,' Larkin said. 'But I believe it is necessary if we are to get to the heart of the matter fast and understand the identity of our common enemy. Until then, we cannot respond. Until then, we are in pure defensive and investigative modes.

'I never sought this office. I believed I had reached the pinnacle of my career as your attorney general, and I was proud of my performance there. But now this responsibility has come to me, and I promise each and every one of you that I will try to make the best decisions for the survival of our great nation and our way of life.'

He paused to smile a bit and nod his head. 'Now, I'm not saying I won't make mistakes or act in ways that you disagree with. But if I make a mistake, I'll take responsibility, and if I act in ways that you don't agree with, I'd ask you to give me a little time. There's a method to my madness.

'Good night, and God bless the United States of America.'

The screens went dark and then jumped to various anchors and commentators, who were quick to describe the nation as being 'under siege' and 'ramping up for combat.'

'What'd you think?' Mahoney asked.

'I thought it was a little odd that he said there was a method to his madness, but otherwise, it was calming. I felt like the guy was trying to do what he said he would.'

Ned glanced up at the screens, where pieces of Larkin's short speech were being replayed. 'I hope you're right, Alex,' he said. 'Because if you're wrong, whatever trust people have left in Washington will evaporate, and God only knows what could happen after that. Riots. Chaos. Lawlessness.'

'Not if we catch who's behind it all,' I said.

72

Past midnight and beneath a chill, driving rain, a pile of leaves stirred in a gully in Rock Creek Park, below Twenty-Sixth Street. A hand emerged slowly and pushed the sopping dead leaves off the cowl of dead skin Pablo Cruz still wore.

The skin and the jacket had kept his upper body mostly dry, but when Cruz sat up, he was drenched from the waist down and using every breathing skill he knew to keep his core warm.

His feet were numb, and when he stood, his knees were stiff. The narcotics the doctors had given him were wearing off. His face ached. His broken teeth screamed.

An ordinary man might have succumbed to hypothermia by now. A weaker man might be focused on finding drugs to kill the pain.

But Cruz was neither ordinary nor weak. He'd long ago trained himself to be a superior man, one who could control his emotions, mind, and pain. Whatever it took to survive, he would do, and he would deal with the physical damage later.

The assassin peeled off the cowl of skin and buried it before he crawled out of the gully about three-quarters of the way up the slope above the creek bed. Blue lights flashed far to the northwest, down through the trees, down there on the parkway.

Forcing his mind to his contingency plans, Cruz figured he had only one chance of getting out of the nation's capital alive. He'd heard all the sirens heading toward the hospital and seen the roadblocks at the bridges to Virginia from a distance.

Cruz expected that all major and minor roads leading out of the District were now closed. The Metro was down. He hadn't heard a plane in the sky in hours. Few cars had passed, and even fewer helicopters were flying in the relentless rain.

He traversed north along the muddy slope, using the shadows thrown by streetlights and buildings up on Twenty-Sixth to make out downed logs and low-hanging tree branches. He reached the M Street bridge and crawled through the brush and up the side of the embankment by the abutment.

Above him on the bridge, he heard two distraught-sounding women hurrying toward Georgetown and talking about President Hobbs's death. Cruz allowed himself a moment of congratulation, a mental pat on the back for a job not only complete but well executed. All in all.

He considered climbing the rest of the way up to the street and just crossing it with his head down to the rain, the way he imagined the women who'd just passed him had done. But instinct overruled the idea. He scrambled back down and beneath the bridge.

Cruz stopped there when he heard a mechanical noise in the distance. Tanks!

They were bringing in soldiers and tanks. Of

course they were. Larkin had declared martial law, hadn't he?

For a moment, the assassin felt unnerved. It was one thing to evade police and even federal agents, but an army?

It won't be an army, he told himself. *They'll be brought in as a presence, a threat. There won't be a soldier on every corner. Or will there?*

Cruz shook off the questions. In dire situations such as this, he'd always found it better to stick to the plan and execute it rather than ponder it to death.

He kept on to the north of the bridge where Twenty-Sixth hit that dead end. When he climbed up to the edge of the park, he could see back to M Street, where one tank had blocked the entrance to the bridge. A second was continuing on toward Georgetown.

Cruz crept across the slope, peering up at the lights in the nearest apartment building, then focusing on two windows on the third floor on adjacent walls of a corner. When he got the angle right, and still watching those two windows, he slid down the hill and shuffled his feet through the leaves, wondering if the dry bag could have been found by a kid exploring in the park or by a nosy dog. Or maybe the rain had flushed the drain cover off and then out and . . .

His heel found the edge of the corrugated drainpipe, which was belching water. Cruz got around and below it, felt for the edge of the cover, and pried it off. The dry bag slid out and fell at his feet before he could reach inside. He knew smiling would be torture, but he grinned anyway.

Cruz did his best not to moan at the pain as he stooped to pick the dry bag up, thinking, *Now? Now I've got a real chance.*

73

Cruz sidestepped slowly down the steep slope, the rubber bag held out in front of him to block the branches he couldn't see in the darkness and rain. Several hundred yards to his north and down on the parkway, those blue lights were still flashing, and behind them he saw the bulk of yet another tank.

He stopped in a thicket above Rock Creek itself and opened the dry bag. He found the headlamp, but he did not use it. And he tossed the hammer and chisel before feeling around for and tugging out a Bare X-Mission dry suit made tough enough and warm enough for cave divers.

Black, and made of nylon ripstop, the suit could withstand extreme climates and still keep the wearer alive. He stripped out of his wet clothes, and, teeth chattering, he struggled into the suit, booties, and gloves.

From neck to toe, he almost immediately started to warm.

Only then did Cruz fish in the bag for the hood, a dive mask, and a smaller dry bag that contained a brick of cash in various currencies, several identifications, and a small book with critical phone and account numbers. He also got out a combat knife in a sheath on a nylon-webbed belt and a small Ruger pistol in a holster before finding the first-aid kit and the antibiotics and painkillers.

Cruz figured the massive dose of antibiotics the doctors at George Washington had administered were enough to hold him for a while, but ate four painkillers and then a fifth before strapping the Ruger and the knife to his waist.

He got his arms in the shoulder straps and hoisted the smaller bag onto his back. Carrying the hood and the dive mask, he eased in the shadows, going tree to tree, until . . .

The assassin stopped, catching movement no more than ninety yards away. Across the creek, up on the parkway, a soldier stepped beneath a street lamp, and then more soldiers. A squad of them were moving on patrol and slowly coming his way.

With a dog.

A black and tan German shepherd.

Even in the rain, Cruz knew, the dog would alert to his scent sooner rather than later. He yanked the hood down over his battered face, fought off the urge to curse at the agony that caused, and then tugged the dive mask on. He sat and then slid feetfirst down over mud and slick leaves, losing sight of the soldiers before plunging into the rushing muddy Rock Creek itself.

With the bag on his back causing drag, Cruz had difficulty keeping his feet out in front of him. He got sideways quickly, hit a submerged rock with his hip, and was swept over it.

Then his arm snagged on a branch, and he had to struggle against the current to get free; he turned around on his back, feet leading again. It was all he could do to keep his head above the water as he searched downstream for the shape of rocks and sharper obstructions.

He hit several, all unseen, but took the blows without a sound. The raging creek was doing its job, whisking him farther and farther from that patrol.

Ahead, however, up on the parkway to his right, Cruz soon saw flashing blue lights. Above them, on the M Street Bridge, soldiers were shining powerful spotlights down into the park.

Other flashlights appeared behind the cruisers on the parkway. Another patrol of multiple soldiers were headed north toward him, shining their beams down into the creek bed, crisscrossing like so many light sabers.

When the president's assassin realized he could die in the next few moments, he turned reptilian, cold-blooded, as he took and released several deep, sharp breaths and then plunged his head back and under the raging water. Rather than fight the current, he relaxed, let the flood have its way with him, smashing him against a boulder and then flinging him into deeper water just as the flashlight beams cut across the surface of the creek eighteen inches above him. He was soon past the soldiers on the parkway, but he remembered the ones on the bridge and stayed submerged.

Forty seconds. Fifty seconds. Sixty.

His lungs were close to bursting, but he did not lift his head until those lights had passed over him, and he was looking up through the heavily silted water at the dark underside of the bridge. Cruz surfaced, took four deep breaths, and ducked back down beneath the water.

The creek was straighter there, and he went with the flow out from under the bridge and down a long dark stretch away from prying lights. Feeling the current slow as the creek widened and deepened, he surfaced and breathed deep again.

It was remarkable just how warm he was. The suit was lined with material that reflected and trapped his body heat. The water was probably forty-five degrees, judging from the way it felt on his chin and lower cheeks, but the rest of his body might as well have been in Florida.

Twenty minutes later, he floated beneath the off-ramps from K Street and the Whitehurst Freeway. Over the thrum of rain, Cruz could hear tanks clanking up on the overpasses, and he could smell their burning diesel.

The current slowed even more as he approached the Swedish embassy, which was up on the western bank of the creek and lit up like a fortress. He swam to the opposite side of the waterway and stayed tight to its east bank until he was well clear of the place.

Beneath the Virginia Avenue bridge, he stopped and crouched in the shallows.

The lights were on ahead of him at the Thompson Boat Center. He could see Humvees and soldiers in the parking lot and imagined that others would be guarding the docks on the Potomac side.

Cruz peered down the east bank of the creek and decided he'd hang tight to it, maybe even crawl up into the brush if it looked like a better —

'Hey, what?' a man's drunken voice said from

Cruz's left, high up the bank below the bottom of the bridge. 'Frick's that, Mikey?'

'Huh?'

'Down there, bro!' he said, and a flashlight went on.

Before Cruz could move, the beam found him. He took two strides and dived toward midstream, hearing shouts behind him.

He swam deep, let the current take him for a count of twenty, then cut left, trying to make it back to the vegetation overhanging the eastern shore. He reached it, grabbed onto roots, and lifted his head for air.

The two drunken bums under the bridge were still yelling.

'Hey! Hey, soldier man! There's a frickin' frogman in the creek! Frickin' frogman in the water, dude!'

Soldiers were running toward the creek, guns up, shining their lights. They were all to Cruz's right, and looking back toward the bridge and the men shouting. He didn't notice the two coming from the dock side of the boathouse until their lights had found him. The assassin wasn't sixty yards from the confluence of Rock Creek and the Potomac when the soldiers started shouting at him to freeze and put his hands up.

Cruz dived again and swam deep and blindly downstream, wishing for a surge of storm water to speed him into the Potomac.

Even submerged like that, a good six feet under, he heard the rat-a-tat-tat of automatic-weapon fire and the shrill whine of the bullets cutting through the water all around him.

Part Four

A NATIONWIDE MANHUNT

74

A door banged open that Saturday morning.

I startled awake, dazed and unsure where I was, and Ali rushed to my bedside and broke down crying.

'Dad,' he blubbered. 'We're all gonna die!'

I sat up, bleary-eyed, still in my clothes, and remembered I'd gotten home past three a.m. and collapsed into bed beside Bree.

I looked over at my wife, who was just stirring, and then back at my son, who was weeping with a pitiful expression on his face.

'We're all gonna die, Dad!'

'Stop. What are you talking about?' I said, fighting a yawn.

'It's what they're saying on the news,' he insisted. 'Larkin, he did something against Russia, China, and, like, North Korea. They think it's war and, like, going nuclear.'

'What?' Bree said, shooting up.

I was already out of bed. I snatched up Ali and carried him downstairs into the kitchen to find Nana Mama in her robe and Jannie in her University of Oregon sweats, both staring at the big screen in the outer room where some talking head was babbling about the entire world being on the verge of war.

My grandmother looked at me, grayer than pale, and said, 'It's like the Cuban missile crisis all over again, Alex.'

Bree hustled into the room. 'Explain what happened.'

Jannie said, 'Larkin attacked Moscow and Beijing.'

'No,' I said, horrified. 'Missiles?'

'No,' Ali said. 'Cyberattacks, Dad.'

Nana Mama said, 'Larkin ordered CIA hackers to shut down electrical power for ten minutes in those cities and whatever the name of the capital of North Korea is.'

'Pyongyang,' Ali said.

'We can do that?' Bree asked. 'Shut down all power?'

'We've already done it,' Jannie said.

Up on the screen, the feed cut to President Larkin aboard Air Force One.

He stared into the camera with deep resolve and said, 'To authorities in Russia, China, and North Korea, my message is simple. If you continue to hack us, we will be forced to counterattack on a larger scale than what you've already seen. If you send missiles, we will respond with quick and devastating force. Your move.'

The screen went blank for a moment and then returned to a flustered morning-news anchor used to delivering fluff. She couldn't speak at first, and then she broke down. 'What's the point? The nukes could be coming, and I'm sitting in Washington while the president's off in a jet somewhere trying to start World War Three!'

'See!' Ali said, and he started crying again. 'We have to get out of here, Dad!'

'We can't,' I said. 'They've still got the city cut

304

off, trying to catch President Hobbs's assassin.'

Jannie started to cry. 'No, Dad, they think he's already dead.'

'What?' Bree said, shaking her head in confusion.

We'd both been asleep less than five hours, and the world felt like it had changed completely in that time.

Nana Mama was watching the poor news anchor who was being led off camera; her co-anchor looked like he wanted to follow her. My grandmother muted the TV.

She said, 'He was in Rock Creek in a wet suit. Some homeless guys living under the Virginia bridge spotted him trying to swim to the Potomac. Multiple soldiers guarding the Thompson Boat Center opened fire on him with machine guns. They feel sure he's dead. They're dredging the . . . there.'

She unmuted the TV. The feed had shifted to a camera on Virginia Avenue aimed at the Thompson Boat Center. Beyond it, police and Coast Guard boats were plying the Potomac, looking for a body.

'Who cares?' Ali said, and he hugged me fiercely. 'The Russians are going to nuke us, aren't they? Or the Chinese?'

Feeling how terrified he was, I kissed him and hugged him back. 'No one wants a war like that. Not even our enemies.'

'Then why did the president shut their lights off?'

'Because they were attacking us in the wake of the assassinations. They were trying to see if we were weakened. President Larkin was showing them we aren't.'

'I'm scared, Dad,' Ali said.

'We're going to be okay. No one wants a war like that,' I repeated. 'You just have to have faith in — '

'But when we can leave, can we?'

I turned to Bree. 'Maybe it wouldn't be a bad idea for Nana Mama and the kids to go see my dad in Florida until things settle down.'

'What?' Jannie said. 'No, Dad. My spring season's coming up.'

'How would we get there?' my grandmother asked. 'No planes. No trains.'

'We'll cross these bridges when we — ' My phone buzzed. Ned Mahoney.

'You rested?' he said.

'Barely. You see what's going on?'

'Yes, which is why they want us back at Andrews ASAP.'

75

The rain had stopped at last, temperatures were rising, and the clouds were breaking up when a Gulfstream jet landed at Joint Base Andrews at 2:15 p.m. on Saturday, February 6.

As the jet taxied toward me and the hangar, I kept looking over my shoulder, back inside, to see hundreds of people trying to do their jobs as best they could. But the strain and worry showed.

Ever since President Larkin's act of brinkmanship, the media had been going crazy, declaring the country on the verge of all-out war with two superpowers and a rogue regime. Protests were breaking out. People were panicking, and there were reports of widespread food shortages, violence, and looting. We were hearing of clogged highways as people fled the country's larger cities.

But the threat of the entire Eastern Seaboard being leveled as mushroom clouds rose above it was what hung over everyone at Andrews, including me.

All morning I had tried to stay focused on what I could do: review all the new evidence coming in and look for something that would help us get a break. But then up on the screens, there would be some update on the secretary of defense's status or a piece on CNN about the proper use of gas masks, and I'd be thrown into a loop of what-if questions that destroyed my concentration.

I could see the same happening to many others working the investigation. On the whole, it felt like we were making little if any progress.

Despite hours of searching, dredging, and diving near the confluence of Rock Creek and the Potomac River, there'd been no sign of the guy in the dry suit that the Virginia National Guardsmen had shot at in the early-morning hours.

Had 'the Frogman,' as the media was calling him, been the president's assassin? Why else would someone be in Rock Creek when the city was in total lockdown, the air temperature was in the thirties, and the water temperature was in the forties at best? Plus, he hadn't been all that far from where Bree had had him almost cornered inside GW University Hospital.

In my gut, the Frogman *was* the blond minister who killed the president, shot the defense secretary, killed the pathologist, and skinned a corpse. And we'd lost him.

Mahoney tried to convince me that the cold river water could have sunk the corpse, that the body would surface downriver sooner or later. But I wasn't so sure.

As the Gulfstream rolled to a stop and was surrounded by armed airmen, an alarm started whooping long and slow somewhere in the distance.

Time seemed to stand still.

Many of the airmen had taken their eyes off the jet and were searching the sky. You could see the fear in their faces. I could feel it in mine.

Was there a missile coming?

The alarms were sounding, but would that make a difference? I tried not to think about my family, but it was impossible not to.

I had an image of all of us at Sunday dinner, kidding one another, laughing, and debating the chances of Damon's team surging enough to make the NCAA championships in March.

But in the next moment, as the Gulfstream's hatch opened and the ramp unfolded, I was imagining a nuclear blast, fire, and devastating scorching gusts of wind that would leave everything in my life in smoke and ruin.

Had President Larkin made the right decision as a show of power? Or had he provoked our rivals and enemies to take unthinkable actions?

I kept wondering if Larkin was too rash to be leader of the free world. I kept asking myself if he would ever have come remotely close to occupying the Oval Office if President Hobbs, the Speaker of the House, and three members of Hobbs's cabinet had not been shot down in cold blood.

Agents in SWAT gear exited the Gulfstream, leading a grizzled-looking, sunburned man in denim and handcuffs. Morris Franks, the father of the treasury secretary's killer, was in his sixties with gray hair and an untamed silver beard. Despite the show of force all around him, Franks didn't seem frightened as they led him past me. He didn't seem angry either.

Indeed, when our eyes met for the first time, his affect was so flat, I thought I was looking at a man who had no real emotional center, a man who was dead inside.

Mahoney tapped me on the shoulder. 'Let's go, Alex. The director wants us to interrogate him.'

As I turned to follow him, I felt my phone buzz, alerting me to a text.

I didn't recognize the phone number, but I understood the text.

Dr. Cross, please, I need to talk to you. It's Nina Davis.

I texted her back immediately, telling her that I was part of the investigation into the assassinations and unavailable for the moment.

After hitting Send, I hurried after Ned.

76

After attending a short briefing with the FBI agents who'd raided Morris Franks's compound in Arizona and reviewing the list of initial evidence gathered there, Mahoney and I entered a makeshift interrogation room off the main hangar floor.

His handcuffs had been removed, but the professed anarchist was in a restraint belt and ankle irons. Chains ran from both to a steel desk freshly bolted into the concrete floor. Franks was drinking a Dr Pepper and smoking a filterless cigarette.

In my pocket, my phone buzzed.

I pulled it out, saw it was Nina Davis again.

This is important! An emergency!

Can't. Sorry. Emergencies here as well, I messaged back. I sighed, pushed aside the guilt I felt putting a client off, and forced myself to stay focused on Franks.

'You good, Mr. Franks?' I said after Mahoney introduced us.

Franks took a drag on his cigarette and then a swig of his Dr Pepper, blew out cigarette smoke, burped, and said, 'Been better. Been worse. I could use something to eat. Oh, and a Miranda warning if you don't want the ACLU crawling up your shorts. And an attorney ASAP.'

Mahoney said, 'Haven't you heard, Mr. Franks? Martial law's been declared. Things like

311

Miranda warnings, habeas corpus, and the right to an attorney have been suspended along with all other rules of a free civilization.'

Franks blinked and looked at me.

I nodded to him, said, 'Kind of ironic, isn't it?'

'What's that?'

'The tyranny and government oppression you've always predicted — they're happening, and you know what? You're one of the first victims.'

I saw a slight tic in the corner of his mouth, but that was all he gave me.

'What's this about?' Franks demanded. 'No one will tell me a damned thing.'

Mahoney slid a picture across the table to him. 'That's Abigail Bowman, the U.S. treasury secretary, lying dead in the rain there.'

He studied her, shrugged. 'Yeah? So what's that got to do with me?'

'Your son, Martin, killed her. Shot her down in cold blood.'

He looked at me and then Mahoney before saying, 'That's bull.'

I pushed a second photo across the table at him. 'Nope. He killed Bowman and a Treasury agent and wounded a second one, but not before that agent got a slug in your son. Martin tried to flee Manhattan, but a rookie cop gunned him down.'

Franks stared at the image of his son sprawled on the rain-soaked sidewalk. His lower lip quivered, and then he appeared disgusted.

Oozing contempt, he said, 'You looked for a scapegoat, and you found my boy.'

'Your son was an assassin,' Mahoney said. 'He was wearing fake Treasury identification and a badge when he was killed.'

'Planted.'

'We didn't even have to do that,' Mahoney said.

I switched topics. 'Tell us about Martin. Where had he been living?'

'I'm not saying anything. And take that picture away. I don't want to see it.'

I left it where it was, said, 'Your son's dead, Mr. Franks. Unless you want us to believe you were part of the assassinations, I suggest you start talking.'

'I got nothing to say. I haven't seen Martin or been in contact with him in . . . gotta be two years now.'

'Not a peep?'

'*Nada.*'

Mahoney said, 'That's funny. The agents who arrested you said your place was full of new solar technology, appliances, sat dish, and stacks of cash.'

'So? I don't trust banks, and I got an inheritance at the same time as a guy who owed me money paid up.'

I sighed. 'The cash was in mailers with fake return addresses, and three of them had notes signed by your son. One said he'd see you again soon.'

'Turn of phrase,' Franks said. 'And the cash? He was just helping his old man. Other than that, like I said, we hadn't been in touch.'

'Where'd he get the money?'

'Can't say. But last time I saw him — couple years back, after he left the Marines — he said he was getting into contract security work overseas. He said there's real money in that these days.'

'You declare that cash to the IRS?' Mahoney asked.

Franks chuckled and picked up another cigarette. 'What do you think?'

I lit the cigarette for him, waited until he'd had a few puffs.

'Was Martin political?'

'Hell no.' He snorted. 'I swear to you, I never heard him once talk about politics unless I was baiting him. Even then, he'd change the subject.'

'To what?' Mahoney asked.

'Anything. When he was in it, you know, combat. He liked to talk about that.'

That last bit did not jibe with my own experience, which was that people who'd been in combat rarely talked about it. Then again, Martin Franks was given the soft boot out of the Marines because his superiors thought he had psychopathic tendencies.

My cell buzzed, alerting me to a text. I chewed my lip in frustration, figuring it was Nina Davis again. But I slipped the phone from my pocket, glanced at the screen, and saw a text from Bree:

Scotland Yard coughed up Carl Thomas's file! Call me ASAP!

Mahoney said, 'Your son ever mention going to Russia? China? North Korea?'

Franks screwed up his face as he took a drag off the cigarette, then said, 'Never. But you

314

know? More I think about it, it sounds to me like my boy maybe came around to his pop's way of seeing things. In my mind, Martin died to free us from tyranny. He sacrificed himself for the ideals of his country, and I salute him for his bravery. I predict Martin will go down in history as being as much of a patriot as one of them minutemen.'

I stood up to leave the room. 'I hate to break this to you, Mr. Franks, but I am absolutely certain your son will go down in history as a coward and a traitor to his country. I have the distinct feeling you will too.'

77

When making any long road trip, Dana and Mary Potter liked to travel around the clock. One would sleep while the other drove. Switching off every two hours and gassing up every four, they could cover close to eighteen hundred miles in a single day.

Indeed, they'd left Texas as fast as they dared, crossing on back roads into New Mexico in a stolen truck with stolen plates before any word of the assassinations surfaced in New York, Washington, or El Paso County.

But by the time they'd made the Colorado line, around five that afternoon, the news was full of the killings, with new, shocking developments almost every minute, very little of it coming out of the Lone Star State, which was exactly how they wanted it to stay.

The roads were dry. They made good time. Wyoming had come and gone before midnight. But the weather had turned sour south of Billings, Montana. Wind, snow, and bitter temperatures had plagued them in the long hours before dawn.

Shortly after daylight on Saturday morning, the storm intensified to near whiteout conditions. A prudent couple would have pulled off the road in Lewistown or Malta and waited it out.

But Mary wanted to be home, and her

husband wanted as swift an escape as possible. And the storm wasn't a bad thing when it came right down to it.

No one would be looking for assassins in a blizzard on Montana's desolate Hi-Line highway. A killer could drive right by you, and you'd never know it because you'd be keeping your eyes on the white-knuckle road.

So the Potters had driven on toward Glasgow in northeast Montana, listening to the news coverage on the satellite radio. Word of President Larkin's retaliatory cyberattack on the other nations had shocked them both.

'I want to get home, Dana,' Mary said in a fretful voice. 'Before the world goes all to hell on us. My God, what have we done?'

He got angry. 'We did a job to save our son's life. That's what we did.'

She got angrier. 'They're saying we may have helped start World War Three!'

'I'm a professional. You're a professional. I did a job, and so did you. And we did it for a noble purpose.'

Mary said nothing, just stabbed off the radio. 'I want to call home.'

'No sat phone,' he said firmly. 'Radio silence until we're in the . . . '

On the GPS navigation screen in the truck's central console, he saw what he was looking for and slowed, feeling the trailer slide a little behind him before he came to a full stop and turned north onto Frenchman's Creek Road.

The gravel road had not been plowed. They spun and almost jackknifed the trailer in nine inches of snow. But before they could go in the ditch, Potter wrestled the pickup and trailer back to the middle of the road.

When he was a full mile north of the Hi-Line, he stopped in a spot out of the wind, and they donned wool hats, quilted Carhartt parkas, and heavy leather mitts lined with sheep fleece. Both of them had already changed into insulated bib overalls and boots at the last gas stop.

While Mary saddled and fed the horses grain, he chained up all four tires and changed the stolen Wyoming plates for Montana tags. Despite their heavy clothes, they were cold to the bone when they climbed back in the pickup and started north again.

An hour later, the road doglegged and dropped down beside Frenchman's Creek itself. The vague outlines of a ranch house and barns appeared through the snow.

Potter stopped and used binoculars to look at the windows for lights inside.

'She's still in Arizona, right where she should be this time of year,' he said after a few minutes.

'Let's get it over with, then,' Mary said. 'We've got a cold ride ahead of us.'

They rolled into the ranch yard. Potter saw no tracks anywhere.

He stopped near a shed between the house and the barn, said, 'Good a place as any. You clean up inside, and I'll get the horses unloaded. We'll put the truck and trailer back where we found them, and we're out of here. No one the wiser.'

His wife nodded absently and put on latex

gloves. The windows were already caked in rime, and Mary was spraying and wiping down the interior of the pickup when Potter climbed out.

The wind howled through the ranch yard. With the wind chill, it had to be fifty below.

Potter ducked his face away from the wind, went around the back of the horse trailer, and opened it. He got the horses out one by one and tied them to a tree on the leeward side of the ranch house.

The wind gusted. As he came around the porch to shut the trailer, he put up his arm to shield his eyes and face from snow.

At first Potter didn't see the old woman in the wheelchair on the porch, buried under wool clothes and quilts, wearing ski goggles, and aiming a lever-action hunting rifle at him.

When he finally spotted her, he threw up his hands and said, 'Don't shoot!'

She wiggled her lower face out from beneath a scarf, revealing sagging gray skin and an oxygen line running to her nostrils. She glared at him venomously.

'That's my damn truck!' she shouted in a thin, bitter voice. 'That's my damn trailer too!'

78

Potter raised his leather mitts higher, thought fast, and said, 'Please, Mrs. Linney, I work for the Montana Department of Justice. The truck and trailer were found abandoned down the Bitterroot Valley. Didn't anybody call to tell you I was coming?'

The old lady's glare did not diminish, but she lifted her head a few inches off the rifle sights before saying, 'Phone's been out since the storm hit. And the electricity. And the furnace.'

'I'm sorry, ma'am. Don't you have anyone to help you?'

'My son's coming for me.'

'Could you lower the gun, Mrs. Linney? It's making me nervous.'

'You got ID? Badge?' she said, keeping the rifle trained on him.

'ID, no badge,' he said, lowering his arms. 'The company I work for does contract delivery work for the state. I have papers for you to sign too. Can we go inside? Get out of the wind?'

Mrs. Linney hesitated until a frigid gale hit them. She grimaced and gestured with the rifle toward the closed front door. 'You first.'

'Thank you, ma'am,' Potter said. He bowed his head into the biting, whistling wind and started toward the door.

She's an ornery old cuss, he thought, but he made sure he smiled at her over the barrel of her gun, which followed him in a way that let him know she knew how to use it. He twisted the knob, pushed the door open, and stepped into a center hallway with old wide-planked wood floors.

There was a modern kitchen at the far end. He walked past a room with a television to his right and an old-fashioned formal parlor to his left. Both rooms were neat, tidy.

He stopped and pivoted to look back at Mrs. Linney, who was driving her motorized wheelchair with her left hand while her right gripped the rifle, which was now in her lap. That helped.

'Here,' Potter said, starting toward her. 'I'll shut the door for you.'

'No need,' she said, and she threw the chair in reverse and pushed the door shut.

She stared at him a moment, then pulled down her scarf. Her breath came in clouds. Even without the wind, it had to be near zero inside.

'Your pipes freeze?' he asked.

'Drained them, poured antifreeze down the lines,' she said. 'I know how to survive up here.'

'I bet you do.'

She drove a few feet toward Potter and then stopped.

'Let's see that ID and those papers,' she said.

He smiled again, unzipped his parka, and reached inside for his wallet. He dug out his fake Wyoming driver's license and started toward her.

Mrs. Linney directed the gun toward him. 'Just hold it up from there.'

Potter did.

'Wyoming?' she said.

'We deliver to both states and Idaho too. I kept my residence in Cheyenne because there's no state income tax.'

'Montana takes ten percent of what's mine,' she said, sounding disgusted. 'What about those papers?'

Potter patted his chest, acted confused, said, 'Darn, they're in the truck. Can I get them?'

Mrs. Linney raised the rifle, aimed at his chest, said, 'You do that.'

She put up the wool scarf, retreated, and reached around to twist the doorknob. The wind blew the door open. She drove a few feet toward him so the door was pinned against the wall, and then started to back out onto the porch.

Potter was beginning to regret his decision to borrow Mrs. Linney's truck and trailer to bring his horses to Texas. But she was supposed to be in Tucson all winter.

Before Mrs. Linney's wheels crossed the doorway, Mary stepped up behind the old bird, reached around, and tore out her oxygen line before clamping a leather mitten across her mouth and nose.

Instead of screaming and struggling, Mrs. Linney aimed wildly at Potter and pulled the trigger. The gun went off. Plaster exploded off the wall next to him.

She tried to run the lever. But he took two big strides and pinned the rifle against her thighs. Mrs. Linney showed no terror at being trapped and smothered. She just glared at him, making sputtering noises of hatred in her throat.

'Poor thing,' Mary said, keeping her grip firm.

'Chair battery ran down in the cold. Oxygen tank empty.'

Potter nodded to his wife and to the old woman, who'd begun to struggle now and show fear.

'Poor thing froze to death, right on her front porch,' Potter said, more to Mrs. Linney than to Mary. 'Her son found her.'

They left Mrs. Linney like that, sitting there in her wheelchair, dead on her front porch, eyes open, with the gun in her lap and her oxygen line back in place. By the time they'd dropped the trailer, put the truck in the barn, and mounted the horses, the snow was already collecting on the quilts in the old woman's lap.

They trotted out of the ranch yard, heading true north along the creek. The cold and the wind were beyond bitter. But they forged on. The snow and the gales would soon obliterate their tracks. And they hadn't far to go.

Seven miles farther on, the Linney ranch road became a cattle trail that snaked another three miles to a gate in a barbed-wire fence cutting across a vast, empty, broken prairie.

Beyond the fence, they'd be in Saskatchewan.

Beyond the fence, the Potters would almost be home.

79

Out in the hangar at Joint Base Andrews, I called Bree back. She answered at the first ring.

'Read the file I just sent you,' she said, sounding breathless. 'I'm positive he's Senator Walker's killer, and wait until you see who's mentioned in there!'

'Who?'

'Read it.'

I told her I'd call her back, went to my workstation, and downloaded the file.

It turned out that Carl Thomas, the medical-equipment salesman from Pennsylvania, was actually Sean Patrick Lawlor, fifty-four, a former member of the British elite SAS counter-terror team. Lawlor was a long-range sniper who'd gone rogue during the first Gulf War and shot forty-one of Saddam Hussein's palace guards as they retreated from Kuwait toward Iraq.

Lawlor was court-martialed for mass murder. The prosecutors said he had acted mercilessly in the killings of the retreating Iraqi forces. His defense argued that he'd been given no written orders of engagement beyond stopping any Iraqi soldiers from using the road, north or south.

The British military court decided that Lawlor's judgment at shooting forty-one of the men may have been beyond the pale, but given the lack of clear orders and the fact that he had been in a war zone engaged in mortal combat with the enemy, he was not guilty of mass murder, or of murder in any way.

Lawlor's superiors let him know, however, that he'd never again return to the field for Britain, and he was offered an honorable discharge. He took it.

Afterward, Lawlor was approached by MI6 agents to engage in contract work as a killer for hire. He did so for more than a decade, but then he became too expensive, and they severed their relationship with him.

At that point, in his early forties, Lawlor became a shooter for hire, rumored to have worked at times for Russian, Chinese, and North Korean interests.

I scrolled down the names with which Lawlor had been associated and recognized none until three-quarters of the way down the list.

'There he is!' I cried. I jumped up and pumped my fist.

I turned to find Mahoney and FBI deputy director Carstensen coming toward me.

'There who is?' Carstensen said.

'Viktor Kasimov,' I said, my heart still beating fast. 'At least twice, Kasimov seems to have hired a man named Sean Lawlor, a former British SAS operator who assassinated Senator Walker at the beginning of all this.'

'Where did you come by all that?' Mahoney said.

'DC Metro chief of detectives Bree Stone,' I said to Carstensen. 'My brilliant wife, who got it from Scotland Yard. I think Kasimov has disappeared for a reason. As in a Kremlin reason.'

I shared the file with Carstensen and Mahoney. While they read it, I called Bree back to congratulate her.

'This could be the big break we needed,' I said. 'Everyone here knows that if we find Kasimov, we might find the other assassins.'

'Good,' she said, sounding pleased. 'Do me a favor? Have whoever's in charge there drop a line to Chief Michaels to that effect?'

'Done,' I said.

'I love you,' she said. 'It's been only a few hours, but I can't wait to see you.'

'I can't wait to hold you,' I said, and I flashed for a terrifying split second on that threat of a nuclear bomb going off before adding: 'And the kids. And Nana.'

'Talk soon,' she said, and she cut the connection.

I walked back toward Mahoney and the deputy director, who were no longer reading Lawlor's file but standing with their eyes on the big screens overhead.

Mahoney saw me and shook his head in disbelief. 'As if this whole thing couldn't get any crazier.'

80

Up on the screens, veteran NBC journalist and anchorman Lester Holt appeared doing a standup on the steps of the U.S. Senate.

'Is Samuel Larkin the legitimate president of the United States?' Holt asked. 'Or, according to the arcane rules of Congress and presidential succession, should someone else be in the Oval Office with a finger on the cyber and nuclear buttons?'

The broadcaster asked us to recall that, prior to the attacks, the late President Hobbs had been in office less than two weeks and had not yet nominated a new vice president.

'That's important to understand,' Holt said. 'The president nominates his vice president, who must then be confirmed by two-thirds of both houses of Congress.'

The anchorman said this was different from the Speaker of the House, normally third in line to the presidency, in that the most powerful person in the House of Representatives had to be *elected* by the members of the majority party.

Like the vice president, members of the president's cabinet, including the secretaries of treasury, state, and defense and the attorney general, were *nominated* to their posts by the president. The Senate had to *confirm* their nominations.

'We *nominate* and congressionally confirm a

vice president,' Holt said, ticking off points on his gloved fingers. 'We *elect* a Speaker. And we *nominate and confirm* cabinet members at the Senate.'

Holt started to walk up the Senate steps. 'Only one position in the immediate order of succession to the Oval Office is automatic. The person fourth in line to the presidency, the Senate president pro tempore, is always the most senior member of the majority party. When that senator dies, the next in seniority automatically and immediately inherits the position and title.'

The scene jumped to inside the Senate, with Holt standing outside the chambers.

'In the chaos of the hours that have passed since the attacks, a single fact seems to have been forgotten, or perhaps ignored,' he said. 'When the Senate president pro tempore, West Virginia senator Arthur Jones, had a heart attack and was pronounced dead, the next senator in line automatically and with zero fanfare became Senate president pro tempore.'

The anchorman paused for effect. 'This all happened a good four hours before the assassinations. In light of this obscure but very real rule, should Samuel Larkin be running the country? Launching attacks against the power grids of other nations? Provoking nuclear war? Or should the new Senate president pro tempore — Bryce Talbot of Nevada — be president of the United States?'

The screen cut to show archival footage of Senator Talbot, a slick, smart, silver-haired former prosecutor from Reno in his late sixties. I knew Talbot, or knew of his reputation, anyway, and it made me slightly unsettled.

The senator from Nevada was one of the top fund-raisers on Capitol Hill, and he held the power of the purse strings as chairman of the Senate Appropriations Committee. Talbot was reputed to be in the back pocket of, among other special-interest groups, the gambling industry. Then again, what senator from Nevada wouldn't be?

The screen cut to Senator Talbot in his office. Talbot looked genuinely stunned when Holt said that according to the Constitution and rules of the Senate, he should be the president of the United States.

'Is that true, Lester?' he asked, shocked.

'I believe it is, Senator,' Holt said. 'Will you seek to remove Mr. Larkin and take his place in the Oval Office?'

Talbot looked deeply conflicted but said, 'Well, I'll have to talk to people smarter than me about this before I make any firm decisions. But if what you're saying is true, Lester, then it is my solemn duty to take office, regardless of the high esteem in which I hold Sam Larkin.'

81

Shortly before six that Saturday evening, I was on my second cup of coffee at the Mandarin Oriental bar when the man I was waiting for entered, looking harried and jittery, a backpack slung over his shoulder.

I left my coffee cup to cut across the lobby to intercept him.

'Dr. Winters?' I said.

The concierge doctor started and seemed puzzled and then threatened by my presence.

'Dr. Cross? What are you doing here?'

'Can I have a few moments of your time?'

'I have a patient waiting.'

'The patient's me.'

He looked confused. 'What's wrong?'

'Just a few questions we need answered sooner rather than later.'

Winters, who was in his early forties, scratched at his hand. 'I get paid for this, you know, making calls.'

'The FBI will cover your fee. Can I get you something to drink?'

'Bourbon,' Winters said.

A few minutes later, a waitress set a tumbler with two fingers of Maker's Mark in front of Winters; he raised it, drank it down, and ordered another.

'What do you need?' he said.

'What was your relationship to Viktor Kasimov?'

330

'I was his doctor.'

'Nothing else?'

'No. What do you mean?'

'I've read the file on your medical-license review,' I said.

Winters got disgusted and then angry. 'I'm clean, and I have been clean for almost four years.'

'You were reprimanded for overprescribing pain medication,' I said.

'Four years ago,' he said.

'So you didn't give Kasimov a script for Oxy?'

'No. He had a stomach bug. Why would I?'

'What about seeing makeup and masks? You neglected to tell us about that when we spoke.'

Winters ducked his chin, and you could tell he was wondering how the hell I knew that, and then he did know.

'That psycho bitch tell you that?' he asked. 'Kaycee?'

I was almost going to correct him, tell him her real name, but instead I nodded. 'She did. She thought it was the right thing to do.'

'I'm sure she did,' the concierge doctor said, almost sneering. 'But so what? Is it a crime?'

'Depends,' I said. 'If Kasimov's men donned disguises to go to a liquor store, no. But if they went out and were involved in a conspiracy to assassinate the president, it's quite a different story. A case could be made for your aiding and abetting murder.'

Winters's hands flew up in surrender. 'No way. They told me they just needed to be able to visit the Russian embassy without attracting attention. I swear to God.'

I studied him, thinking that I didn't trust him. 'Kasimov or his men mention where they were going the last time you saw them?'

'London,' the doctor said. 'I told him to see a doctor there if he was feeling dehydrated after his sickness and the flight. That's it. End of story.'

'Okay,' I said. 'If you think of anything else, here's my card.'

He took it without enthusiasm, didn't look at it, and stuffed it in his pocket.

The waitress came with his second drink. I threw down two twenties and got up.

'My address is on the card,' I said. 'Send your bill there.'

'No. No charge.'

I started to walk away.

'Dr. Cross?'

When I looked back, I saw he had my card out and was playing with it in his fingers. 'Yes?'

'I . . . ' He paused to look at his bourbon. 'Do you think people like me, addictive personalities — do you think we can ever stop our obsessions?'

'If you're sufficiently motivated to change, yes,' I said.

'So someone else can't stop you?'

'When it comes right down to it, change has to come from within.'

Winters nodded and pushed the bourbon away from him. He gazed at me and said, 'Thanks.'

'Anytime.'

As I turned to go again, he said, 'I tried to change Kaycee, or whatever her name really is.'

I paused, unsure of what to say. 'Didn't work?'

He shook his head. 'She's crazy. Crazier than I ever was.'

82

Pablo Cruz was nothing if not patient.

On the second full day of martial law, President Hobbs's assassin waited until darkness had fallen before slipping out from beneath the protective cover on a Bertram offshore fishing boat moored in a slip at the Hope Springs Marina in Stafford, Virginia. He still wore the dry suit, and he attributed the fact that he was still alive to the suit and to the belt he'd used as a tourniquet.

The wound wasn't as bad as it could have been, given the number of shots that had been fired at him at the confluence of the flooding Rock Creek and the surging Potomac River. The slug had hit him in top of his left forearm, just below the elbow, and broken bone before exiting.

The pain had been excruciating enough to send even the most seasoned veteran to the surface and sure capture. But Cruz had embraced the pain and used it to drive him to swim harder and deeper into the main channel, where the current was swift and growing stronger with the rain and the tide. He was swept fast and far downstream as he felt water seeping through the holes the bullet had made entering and exiting the suit. He reached up and clamped his gloved hand over them.

After staying under for more than two minutes, he surfaced, saw lights on the shore, and ducked under again. Cruz kept on in this manner, swimming farther and farther toward the center of the river, always underwater.

After coming up for air the sixth time, he'd floated on his back, letting the river take him as it flowed toward the sea. He'd probed the wound, cleaned it as best he could, and applied the tourniquet.

Then he dug in the thigh pocket of the dry suit for the patch kit that came with it. The suit had been designed by cave divers, people who knew a torn suit could kill them.

It was a struggle, but he got two glued patches over the holes and then cinched the belt harder around his bleeding arm.

The assassin had swum on and floated for almost seven hours with the current, releasing the tourniquet every fifteen minutes to avoid cutting off the blood flow for too long and heading consistently southeast, downstream. When he'd climbed into the boat before dawn that Saturday, Cruz was forty-six miles from where he'd entered the river.

He'd found a cabinet with canned food and water in the fishing boat's cabin. Knowing he risked serious infection, Cruz had forced the antibiotics into him before the painkillers. He'd eaten and slept fitfully with the Ruger in his good hand all day, setting his wristwatch to wake him every twenty minutes to briefly loosen the tourniquet.

Even so, when Cruz stepped down on the dock, he felt feverish and light-headed. He needed to put as much distance as he could between himself and Washington, DC, he decided. But seeing a doctor came first.

Cruz was halfway down the dock to shore when he saw a light go on in one of the marina offices. It went off a few moments later, then another one went on and off, and then a third.

That works, the assassin thought.

Without hesitation, he hurried forward and was hiding in the bushes outside the main door to the marina office when the security guard, a scrawny kid in his early twenties, exited. He had a thin caterpillar-like mustache and carried a flashlight in his hand and a small can of pepper spray in a holster on his hip. Cruz waited until the guard walked past before stepping out behind him.

He stuck the Ruger against the back of the kid's head.

'Stop,' he said. 'Do as I say, and you'll live to see another day.'

The guard froze and then, trembling, raised his arms.

'Please, man,' he choked out. 'I got no money. And there's no money in any of the offices. Nothing worth nothing at all.'

'You have a car?' Cruz asked.

The guard said nothing. Cruz poked the back of his head.

'Answer me.'

'I just bought it.' He moaned. 'I worked overtime on this shit job just so I could — '

'I don't care,' Cruz said. 'Where is it?'

The kid cursed before nodding toward the side of the marina offices. 'Over there. The maroon Camry.'

336

'Keys?'

He hesitated, then said, 'Front right pocket.'

'Keep them,' Cruz said. 'We're going for a drive.'

'I can't leave.'

The assassin jabbed his head with the pistol's muzzle. 'You must.'

The guard had stumbled forward, and now he looked over his shoulder at Cruz. He saw his battered, swollen, and stitched face. He saw the dry suit, had a moment of realization, and then lost it.

'Oh, man,' he said, holding out his palms. 'Please, just take the car. I promise you I won't say a thing. I'll just say someone knocked me out and stole my car.'

'This isn't a negotiation,' Cruz said. 'Toss the pepper spray and move, or I'll shoot you for spite.'

The kid resigned himself to his fate, pulled out the pepper-spray canister, lobbed it toward the water, and then trudged around the building to a small gravel parking lot.

When they reached the Camry, Cruz said, 'Give me your coat.'

The guard removed the jacket and handed it to him. Cruz put it on. 'Get in. You're driving.'

After the guard was behind the wheel, the assassin took the seat directly behind him and tapped the back of his head with the gun barrel. 'What's your name?'

'Jared,' he said, flinching. 'Jared Goldberg.'

'Nice to meet you, Jared,' he said. 'Now drive.'

83

Back at Joint Base Andrews, as well as across the nation, anxiety was building. Despite the imposition of martial law, protests had broken out at peace vigils held in New York, Dallas, Los Angeles, Portland, and Seattle.

No country had lobbed a nuclear warhead at us, but the threat remained. You could see it was on everyone's mind. Agents were calling home as often as they called for investigative leads, and I didn't blame any of them for it.

But I simply refused to let the possibility of a world war dominate my thoughts. If I did, I knew I'd be useless in my new role.

When I returned from talking to Dr. Winters, Carstensen, the FBI deputy director, had asked me to move to the team that was synthesizing information. I'd started to protest that I was more useful in the field, but she'd cut me off and walked away.

So I'd kept my head down through the evening, focusing on the flow of evidence crossing my screen and desktop. Twice I'd tried to return Nina Davis's call, but I'd gotten no answer. But I couldn't pay attention to that. Every minute seemed to bring an update, a field report, or a result from Quantico's churning forensics laboratories.

We knew by then, for example, that, courtesy of a bright ER nurse at George Washington

University Hospital, we had DNA material and blood from the president's assassin and possibly his fingerprints off the rail of a hospital bed he'd used after the ambulance ride. We knew his blood type was O negative, but DNA testing still took several days. And so far, there were no matches to the fingerprints.

As I closed that file, I once again forced myself to consider who benefited the most from the assassinations.

Kasimov? I supposed if the Kremlin was behind the killings, then Kasimov would benefit as long as he could disappear and as long as his Moscow handlers could keep him hidden from the long arm of U.S. law enforcement. But Kasimov had vanished. Maybe it didn't benefit him. Maybe his role in the plot was done, and some higher-up in Russia had ordered his plane shot down over the ocean.

Did Samuel Larkin still benefit? The acting president had been at an undisclosed location all day, huddled with a small circle of advisers, dealing with the existential threat to the nation and the constitutional crisis. Would Larkin, the former attorney general, agree that Senator Talbot, the Senate president pro tempore, was the right and legal person to be sitting in the Oval Office and calling the shots? If Larkin refused to cede power, wouldn't that be an indicator of his involvement and of his intent?

For his part, Senator Talbot had been interviewed several times since the Lester Holt story appeared. Talbot seemed genuinely daunted by the idea of assuming the presidency, especially given his age. There'd even been talk of his retiring before this sudden change of circumstances.

So, did Talbot benefit? All in all, it didn't strike me that way, but then again, I'd heard it said more than once that every U.S. senator fantasizes about becoming president. U.S. senators were powerful and influential in their own right, but for men and women of overwhelming ambition, being a senator wasn't powerful and influential enough.

But having fellow politicians murdered to become president?

Before I could give that further thought, more forensics and field reports blinked into my in-box.

From Quantico's ballistics lab: a report confirming Keith Rawlins's suspicion that the bullets used to kill President Hobbs and wound the secretary of defense were made of carbon and built on a 3-D printer.

The next report came from Rawlins himself, who had been writing programs and devising algorithms to filter the huge amounts of data flowing in the wake of the assassinations. He'd found an incredible amount of speculation about the assassinations by various conspiracy theorists on the internet and dark web. But so far he'd discovered little to suggest the intricate dance of people and events that had to have occurred before the coordinated killings.

Mahoney came up to my workstation.

'A man and a woman with horses rented a remote cabin about forty miles north of the ranch where the Speaker and the secretary of state were shot,' he said. 'They drove a heavy-duty green Chevy pickup with Wyoming plates, paid the landlord cash, and had cases that looked like they could have held rifles. Best part? They carried bogus Wyoming licenses in the names of Frank and Elizabeth Marker.'

'Do we have agents at the cabin?'

Mahoney's face fell. 'The landlord hadn't been out there since he'd gotten his money. He led two agents from Dallas into the middle of nowhere, and, surprise, they found the cabin burned to the ground.'

Carstensen, who'd just walked up, said, 'Nothing else?'

'The owner's working with a sketch artist.'

I thought of something, got up, and went over to Keith Rawlins. I asked him if it was possible to craft an algorithm to sift through the vast NSA records of phone calls and data transmissions by specific location.

The FBI computer wizard said he thought so, and I told him what locations I had in mind. Rawlins said it might take him several hours, but he'd try.

When I returned to my work space, Mahoney, Carstensen, and half the other agents in the hangar were on their feet, their attention glued once again to the big screens dangling overhead.

Lester Holt sat at his anchor desk. 'Acting president Larkin and Senator Talbot have agreed to let the chief justice of the Supreme Court decide who should lead the nation. In the meantime, Secretary of Defense Harold Murphy clings to life. If Murphy lives, he'll also have a claim to the Oval Office. Could the situation be cloudier?'

Carstensen's phone buzzed. She answered, listened, punched her fist in the air, and then looked at us and smiled. 'The CIA just snatched Viktor Kasimov from a brothel in Tangier. They're bringing him here.'

84

Following Cruz's instructions, the marina security guard, Jared Goldberg, had driven east by southeast, staying on residential and county secondary roads whenever possible. There were plenty of vehicles out after dark, which was a relief.

In the assassin's worst-case scenario, he'd imagined a roadblock at every main intersection in a sixty-mile circle around Washington, DC. But he guessed that would have required calling out the National Guard from five or six states. Maybe more.

According to the all-news satellite station Goldberg had turned on, that had not yet happened and was unlikely to, given the projected short period of martial law. *Three more days*, Cruz thought. *Three more days and I can make a real move.*

He shivered. He almost swooned. He needed a doctor. Fast.

The radio was saying that the curfew would be in effect again at nine p.m. Any vehicles found traveling afterward could be stopped and searched.

Cruz forced himself alert. He needed medical care and a place to hide until —

'Where now?' Goldberg asked, gesturing at traffic signs.

They were coming up on Virginia State Route

17, a four-lane highway that could take them west toward Storck or east toward Interstate 95 and the bridge to the eastern shore of Maryland.

'Go west,' Cruz said.

On the highway, they passed several dairy farms, one called Mill Creek, and then, a good ten miles on and set well back from the highway on a county road, they saw a ranch house and a steel outbuilding.

Cruz caught more than a glimpse, enough to know that the ranch house was lit and that the parking area near the outbuilding was empty save for a single pickup truck. He also saw the sign at the entrance to the drive before they went by it.

KERRY LARGE ANIMAL HOSPITAL
TWENTY-FOUR-HOUR EMERGENCY
SERVICE

It took a moment for that to alter his thinking. He glanced at his watch: 8:10.

'Get off at the next exit and go back one,' Cruz said.

Goldberg did. At the assassin's instructions, the security guard drove beyond the pickup in the animal hospital parking lot and stopped where their car would be shielded from view of the highway and County Road 610. As they passed the glass front door to the vet clinic, Cruz saw through it to an empty lobby that was dimly lit.

Someone, probably a veterinary tech, was on the overnight shift, Cruz thought. Well, it was better than nothing.

'You got a cow,' Cruz said to Goldberg after he'd turned the car off.

'What?'

The assassin jabbed the kid in the ribs with the gun barrel. 'You ring the bell, and you tell them you've got a cow calf that's birthing breech at Mill Creek Farm, and you need help.'

'I don't even understand that,' Goldberg said.

'You don't have to,' Cruz said. 'Just say it. A cow calf that's birthing breech at Mill Creek Farm.'

The security guard muttered something but climbed from the car. Cruz got out after him and followed him down the walkway toward the entrance. It was cold. Their breath clouded in the air.

The assassin stopped ten feet short of the entrance and aimed the gun low and from the hip at Goldberg, who'd halted at the door and glanced at him.

'Do it,' Cruz said. 'Or I'll shoot you.'

Looking miserable, Goldberg rang the buzzer and stood there expectantly.

A few moments later, a woman's voice came over an intercom.

'Kerry Hospital,' she said.

The security guard looked up at the camera and, to the assassin's surprise, said exactly what he'd told him to say.

After a pause, she said, 'I'll be right out. Why didn't Angelo call?'

'Cell tower's out,' Goldberg said, without hesitation. 'So they sent me.'

'I don't know you.'

'I'm the new hired hand, ma'am.'

'I'll be right out to follow you back.'

Although Cruz was impressed by how well Goldberg had ad-libbed in the situation, he felt suddenly nauseated; his skin got hot, and he felt dizzy.

He lowered the gun and rested against the wall so he wouldn't fall.

'She's coming,' Goldberg said.

'Step back and smile, Jared.'

Cruz heard a dead bolt thrown, and the door was pushed open. A stout blonde in her forties stepped out. She wore winter gear and carried a large bag.

'Dr. Kerry,' she said, holding out her mitten. 'You keep her on her feet? Or is she down?'

Goldberg looked confused.

'The cow?'

Cruz stepped up and aimed the gun at the vet from point-blank range. 'She's still on her feet,' he said. 'Get back inside, Doc. Now.'

85

Dr. Kerry's eyes widened in shock and fear. She stepped back, and then she saw his face and registered the fact that he was wearing a wet suit and booties. She turned, terrified.

'Now!' Cruz said.

The veterinarian was shaking, but she did as she was told.

'You too, Jared.'

'Haven't I done enough? Can't I just go, man?'

'No.'

Goldberg didn't like it, but he went inside. The assassin followed.

He turned the dead bolt, then looked at Dr. Kerry, who was summoning her courage. She stood straighter, said, 'What do you want?'

'You're going to take care of my left arm,' Cruz said. 'Gunshot wound.'

Her chin dipped. 'I'm not an MD.'

'Large-animal vet is close enough,' he said. 'Get it cleaned out and give me IV antibiotics and some painkillers, and Jared and I will be on our way.'

Forty minutes later, a grim-faced Dr. Kerry taped the last bandage in place.

'That's the best I can do,' she said. 'You'll need a real surgeon if you want to use that arm properly again.'

Cruz grunted and felt himself on the verge of nodding off, something he could absolutely not do. Not when the veterinarian or Goldberg might overpower him. He shook his head to clear it.

He'd refused general anesthesia, though he'd let the vet shoot lidocaine into the wound before she gave him IV antibiotics. But he'd taken less than half the dose of painkiller she recommended in an effort to stay conscious as long as possible.

Cruz motioned with the pistol in his right hand. 'I see zip ties all over the place. Get me six long ones.'

Kerry hesitated, then went to a closet and found six.

Cruz had her put zip ties around her ankles and the marina security guard's. Then he had them restrain each other's wrists. With the last two zip ties, Cruz bound their wrists low and tight to one of the steel bars that supported the kennel cages.

'I won't gag you,' he said. 'But if you start yelling, I'll kill you. Understand?'

Goldberg looked petrified as he bobbed his head. Dr. Kerry just nodded.

Cruz needed sleep desperately, but he had things to do first. He left them. He turned off the outside lights and found Kerry's personal office. He sat at the veterinarian's desk and used Goldberg's cell phone to dial a number from memory. He heard clicks and hissing before the man he knew as Piotr came on.

'Talk,' Piotr said in Russian.

'It's Gabriel,' Cruz said, also in Russian. 'I want payment.'

A pause. 'Are you insane? We had a deal. You were to wait until things cool down. Then you'll get exactly what we contracted for. Where are you?'

'If you don't put the money in my account, I will come find you,' Cruz said, and he hung up.

He looked at the couch in the vet's office and almost lay down.

But then he retrieved the little black book from his dry bag and made one more call, this time on the desk phone. A woman's automated voice answered and prompted him to enter a series of codes and passwords.

There was a short delay before a woman with an Eastern European accent said, 'Universal Rescue. How may I be of assistance this evening?'

'I need full service. These coordinates. Medical and relocation specialists.'

She was silent. Then: 'Given your location and the current circumstances thereof, that will be quite expensive, I'm afraid.'

'Two, six zeros, in BTC?'

After a longer silence, she said, 'Three point five, six zeros.'

'Three.'

'Agreed. Make the transfers. Expect delivery shortly after your curfew lifts.'

86

In the hangar at Joint Base Andrews, I glanced at the clock, saw it was almost midnight, yawned, and contemplated another strong cup of coffee.

My cell phone rang. It was Bree.

'Hey, you,' she said, sounding bushed herself. 'Coming home soon?'

'Looks like I'll be bunking here tonight. They put up a tent city for us in an adjoining hangar. Think I'll catch a few hours right now.'

'Me too. I'll miss you, but sweet dreams, and I love you.'

'I love you too, baby.'

I carried the warm memory of her voice over to the hangar next door and found a cot in the corner. After a few prayers, I lay down. I fell asleep the moment my head hit the pillow and slept dreamlessly until Mahoney shook me awake at four a.m.

'He's here,' he said. 'Viktor Kasimov.'

Ten minutes later, I was drinking coffee once again and listening to the brief on the suspect awaiting us in the same room where we'd spoken to Morris Franks.

When the briefing was finished, Carstensen said, 'You ready, Dr. Cross?'

'Yes,' I said. 'Cameras?'

She nodded. 'Running on the other side of the mirror, trained tight on his face. If the body-language experts catch anything, we'll call it in to you.'

'Translator?'

'There will be one in the booth with me, but you'll find he's fluent in English.'

In both English and Russian, Viktor Kasimov told us he was spitting mad when Ned and I entered the interrogation room and found him manacled and chained to the table.

'You!' Kasimov shouted at me and Mahoney. 'You two think crazy imbecile thoughts! Invent these things!'

'I could say the same about you, Viktor,' Ned said, unruffled.

Kasimov looked like he wanted to rip both our heads off, but he took several deep, trembling breaths before saying, 'I am a Russian diplomat, an envoy of the Kremlin, and there will be serious repercussions if — '

Mahoney cut him off. 'We don't care about your bona fides or your diplomatic passport.'

I said, 'We've gone far beyond the normal rule of law here, Mr. Kasimov. Martial law allows us to do pretty much whatever we want. And I can tell you that there could be painful and perhaps deadly repercussions *for you* if you don't start helping us right now.'

'I have no idea how to help you,' he snapped.

'Tell us about Sean Lawlor.'

There was a twitch at the corner of his lips before he said, 'Who?'

Over the earbud I wore, I heard Carstensen say, 'That's a lie.'

I said, 'Lawlor, Sean. The former SAS sniper

you hired to perform at least three murders in the past four years. Your name turned up in his Scotland Yard file after he was killed following the assassination of Senator Walker. But of course you know all that.'

'I do not know what you're talking about.'

Mahoney said, 'You understand that by refusing to cooperate, you are aiding forces hostile to the sovereign security of the United States?'

'I am not cooperating with any — '

'You could be taken out and shot or hung, Mr. Kasimov,' I said. 'It's not what we want, but it is what could happen if you don't start speaking truthfully.'

When Kasimov glared at us, we both returned flat gazes.

'Okay,' he said finally. 'I did know this Lawlor person. He did *two* jobs for me, not three. Both domestic affairs. *Russian* domestic affairs.'

We asked him how he'd contacted Lawlor. Through a middleman, a number he called when he needed such work done. He agreed to give the number to us but said the access code was usually changed every six months, and he hadn't needed any such services in more than a year.

'Beyond that, I tell you for certain, and on my mother's grave, I know nothing more,' Kasimov said.

'I think you're in it up to your eyeballs,' Mahoney said.

The Russian threw back his head and laughed. 'I am not that smart or cunning or ruthless, Mr. Special Agent of the FBI. Believe it or not, I think we should all coexist in peace. I mean, who needs war?'

'Right,' I said, 'who needs war if you can achieve the same ends through political assassinations?'

Kasimov sighed. 'Whoever are these masterminds you look for, they are playing games with you, I think. Yes, they are theorists, like the chess player. You know, somebody who thinks ahead twenty, fifty steps, this is the kind of person you search for, Dr. Cross. Me? My mind is simple. I do what I'm told.'

'Unless you're raping women,' Ned said.

He gave us a weary expression. 'I don't know how these lies follow me.'

I decided a different route might be more helpful. 'So what else do you think was behind the assassinations? Hypothetically. What's the purpose? A takeover?'

Kasimov perked up, thought about that, and then shook his head. 'If it was to be an attack on your shores, it would have happened already.'

'We had multiple cyberattacks coming out of your country and China and North Korea in the immediate wake of the assassinations,' Mahoney said.

'Just what you'd expect,' he said dismissively. 'The sudden shift in power leaves a vacuum and gives an excuse and opportunity to look around, to — how do you Americans say it? To see what's what? The U.S.A. would do the same thing if the situation were reversed. Look, in my humble opinion, the money is where you should focus your attention. The whole Russia thing? It's a dead end, I tell you. What did your Watergate Deep Throat teach you? Follow the money.'

It wasn't a bad idea, and I was thinking Bree had better get back on the phone with her contacts at Scotland Yard to find out if they'd managed to track down Lawlor's bank accounts. But then there was a knock at the door.

In my ear, I heard Carstensen say, 'Who the hell is that?'

I got up, opened the door a crack, and saw Rawlins standing there.

'Keith, I'm in the middle of — '

'Take a break,' he said. 'Your trap? It caught a bug, maybe two.'

87

When I looked up from the screens and data the FBI consultant had been showing me, it was 5:21 a.m. on Sunday, February 7, two days after President Hobbs and the others were assassinated.

'Do that second sweep we talked about, and I'll be right back,' I said, and I ran to the booth outside the interrogation room where Kasimov was still talking with Mahoney.

I knocked sharply, stuck my head in. 'Madam Deputy Director, I need to show you something ASAP.'

Carstensen looked annoyed at having to leave the Russian, who was explaining how he'd paid Lawlor for his services, but she came out into the hall.

'What is it?'

'Probably better to let Rawlins explain,' I said. 'Mahoney needs to see this too. Kasimov can wait a few minutes.'

Rawlins soon had the three of us looking over his shoulders at the trio of screens before him.

'The algorithm's function was Dr. Cross's idea,' the FBI consultant said. 'He asked me to write it to sift through NSA-gathered data limited to international phone calls and international data transmissions cross-referenced with proximity to eight specific locations and times.'

He typed on his keyboard. The screen changed

to a satellite image of the lower forty-eight states. Seven digital pins glowed on the map.

Rawlins zoomed in on each, and I identified them.

1. Senator Walker's murder scene in Georgetown
2. The murder scene of the assassin Sean Lawlor, a few blocks away
3. GW University Hospital, where the former Senate president pro tempore had died two mornings ago
4. The DC arena where the late president and the secretary of defense had been shot
5. The street where Bree and DC Metro SWAT had engaged in a firefight with West Coast gangbangers
6. The West Texas ranch where the Speaker and secretary of state were assassinated and, to the north of it, the site of the remote cabin that had been burned down
7. The motel room that Kristina Varjan had booby-trapped
8. Lower Manhattan, where the treasury secretary had been shot

'My idea was to look for commonalities in and around these areas,' I said. 'Phone numbers used or large data transmissions going to a specific site.'

'And?' Carstensen said.

Rawlins said, 'The algorithm found nothing unusual in Texas, around Senator Walker's home, by the DC arena, near the gangbanger scene, or around GW Hospital. But . . . '

He typed again, and a new file came up. He tapped on an international phone number: 011-7-812-579-5207.

'This number was called from inside or near Lawlor's death scene well before discovery of the body. The number was also dialed on Skype from inside the Mandarin Oriental hotel in DC two days before the assassinations, and on a phone in Lower Manhattan shortly after Abbie Bowman was shot.'

'The Mandarin Oriental,' Carstensen said. 'Kasimov *is* lying. He *is* the mastermind.'

'Or someone else staying at the hotel or working at the hotel was involved,' I said, thinking about Dr. Winters and wanting to go back to ask Kasimov about the makeup and masks the doctor had seen.

'Whose phone number is that?' Mahoney asked.

'Someone in St. Petersburg, Russia,' Rawlins said. 'Beyond that, I don't know yet. If we could get some cooperation from the Russians, it would be a bit easier.'

'Fat chance,' I said. 'Did you do that second sweep we talked about?'

'I started it but haven't taken a look at the results yet.'

The FBI contractor pivoted in his chair and started typing. Carstensen and Mahoney were puzzled.

I said, 'I asked him if he could look for that phone number being used in *any* call coming to or leaving the continental United States in the past ten days.'

'Bam!' Rawlins said. 'Look at that!'

The map of the U.S.A. now showed five glowing blue pins. One was in West Texas, not far from the burned-down cabin. Another was close to Varjan's motel in Gaithersburg, Maryland. The third was near Lancaster, Pennsylvania. The fourth was well south of Washington, DC, near I-95 in Ladysmith, Virginia. The fifth pin was not far away from the fourth, near rural Storck, Virginia.

'Can you give us the times with the locations?' Carstensen asked.

Rawlins nodded and gave his computer a command.

The screen blinked and showed dates, times, and whether the connection was incoming or outgoing beside the blue pins.

There was a call *from* the Russian number to a burn cell in rural West Texas that had occurred late in the afternoon a few days before.

There was a call *to* the Russian number from near Varjan's motel that was made the evening before she almost blew us up.

The call near Lancaster was also *to* the Russian number and had occurred the day before that in the afternoon. The fourth call was *from* the St. Petersburg number to a burn phone several hours later.

'Look at the one near Storck, Virginia, though!' I said. 'My God, that was outgoing to St. Petersburg last night! Less than seven hours ago!'

88

Seventeen minutes later, along with eight heavily armed and experienced agents in full SWAT gear, Mahoney and I boarded an air force helicopter. We were all harnessed into jump seats, radioed up, and in direct contact with Carstensen and Rawlins, who'd identified the final phone number as that of twenty-two-year-old Jared Goldberg, a resident of Stafford, Virginia.

'I wonder what Jared's doing down in Storck?' I asked.

Carstensen said, 'We've got agents working on Mr. Goldberg right now.'

'Any luck getting us a tighter location on the call? Or Goldberg's phone?'

'I've got you down to a five-mile radius,' Rawlins replied. 'Sorry, there are only two towers in the area. Meantime, I'll try to ping the phone.'

'Can you send that radius superimposed on sat images?' Mahoney asked.

'Already on its way to the pilot and to your e-mail accounts.'

We lifted off Mahoney had an iPad, and he called up Rawlins's link. The screen launched Google Maps and showed the circular search area, which was bisected by Virginia State Route 17, a four-lane highway.

Storck itself didn't look like much. No stores. No gas stations. It was all farmland, small subdivisions, and dense forest.

'I pinged Mr. Goldberg's number three times,' Rawlins said. 'It's been turned off.'

'We're going to need him to turn it on and make another call or we're looking for a needle in a haystack,' Mahoney said.

I said, 'Rawlins, can you further refine what we're looking at? Show us property ownership?'

'Give me a few minutes.'

The first gray light of a winter day showed in the east as we hurtled south beyond the nearly empty Beltway and over suburban sprawl that soon gave way to leafless wooded lots, farms, and the odd tract-home development. Shortly after 6:30 a.m., we passed Fredericksburg and flew over Civil War battlefields and then large stretches of forest broken up by farms.

'We're three minutes out from the perimeter,' the pilot said.

'What are we looking for?' one of the SWAT agents said.

'Something out of place,' Mahoney said. 'If we don't see it from the air, I'll fly in twenty agents and we'll hit the pavement and knock on doors until we find something.'

That didn't seem to satisfy the SWAT agent, nor did it satisfy me. Goldberg, or someone using Goldberg's phone, had called that number in St. Petersburg not eight hours before, and . . .

'Rawlins,' I said, triggering the mike. 'Can you do another sift? Seven to nine hours ago, any other international calls out of the Storck area?'

There was a pause before he came back,

sounding stressed. 'You're next, Dr. Cross. Sorry, this map's being a pain.'

We flew over Route 17 and headed west toward Storck. Out both sides of the chopper, I saw farms and cows and then, near the exit to County Road 610, a small business of some sort with a large steel building and a smaller structure set near a large paved parking lot.

There were two vehicles there. A wine-colored sedan was parked nose in to the smaller building. A tan panel van was parked a few feet away, pointing nose out. Its rear doors were wide open to a walkway and front door.

That was all there was to Storck. If I'd blinked, I'd have missed it.

We kept flying above the highway until we reached the southwestern edge of the search area. The pilot turned south, meaning to trace the perimeter so we understood the full lay of the land.

Our radios crackled.

'Link to the map with property owners on its way,' Rawlins said. 'And, Dr. Cross, yes, there was a call from a phone near Storck a few minutes following the one made to St. Petersburg. That second call went to Pretoria, South Africa.'

'Pretoria?'

'Affirmative,' he said. 'I'm trying to get a reverse ID on both the — '

Carstensen cut him off, excited. 'Stafford police just called our hotline. The owners of a marina on the Potomac there found drops of blood on their dock and no sign of their young security guard, *Jared Goldberg,* or his burgundy Toyota Camry.'

'The Frogman got him!' Mahoney said.

'There's a wine-colored car back there at that exit north of Storck,' I said, and I swiped Ned's iPad with my finger until I could see the parking lot and the buildings and the name of the property owner.

'If he's wounded, he's in there!' I said. 'It's an animal hospital!'

'That is where the second call came from,' Rawlins said over our headsets. 'Kerry Large Animal Hospital.'

Less than two minutes later, we circled high and well wide of the Kerry Animal Hospital. The tan van was gone, but the burgundy Toyota Camry was still there. We got an angle and binoculars on the license plate. It *was* the missing security guard's car.

'Land right in the parking lot,' Mahoney said.

'We lose the surprise factor,' one of the SWAT agents said.

I said, 'There was a tan panel van here when we flew by. I saw it. We need to know who or what's in it.'

Mahoney said into his mike, 'Cap, can you call Virginia State Police or the local sheriff? Get them to cordon off this area and look for a tan panel van? Don't have a license plate.'

'Done,' Carstensen said.

The SWAT team went first, storming the veterinary hospital from all four sides.

They threw flash-bang grenades the second they were all in position and then went in.

Thirty seconds after they entered, our radios crackled with urgency.

'We've got two alive,' the SWAT team leader barked. 'Goldberg and the vet. Rest of the place is clear.'

The pilot began to speak, but I cut him off.

'Get us back in the air!' I shouted. 'We've got to find that van!'

89

Early Sunday morning, Kristina Varjan was traveling north on County Road 610 in a black Audi Q5. She lowered the driver-side window and picked up a black Glock pistol with an after-market sound suppressor.

There was forest on both sides of the lightly traveled road. She waited until she could see a long empty stretch in the other lane before sliding the pistol out the window, resting the barrel on the side mirror, and stomping on the gas. The Audi roared and closed the gap between it and the tan van ahead of her in seconds.

Varjan knew she had one good chance of this working. If she missed the opportunity, the equation changed, tilted against her.

She drove up behind the van and weaved slightly right, toward the shoulder of the road, giving her a good look at the van's rear tires. Varjan shot them both out with hollow-point bullets.

She slammed on her brakes. The van swerved hard into the other lane, tires smoking as they disintegrated. The van's back end swung around almost a hundred and eighty degrees.

Varjan saw the horrified look on the driver's face before the van careered sideways off the far shoulder. It had smashed and rolled over twice before she brought the Audi to a screeching stop. The assassin jumped from her car and sprinted across the narrow road and down the short embankment.

There was tire smoke in the air, but no smell of spilling gas, so she went straight to the van, which had landed more or less upright. The roof and side door were partially caved in. Blood dripped down the driver's face as he lifted his head to look at her.

'Help,' he said.

She shot him between the eyes.

Varjan moved down the side of the van and around the back, seeing one door shut and the other almost torn off. Gun up, she looked inside and saw the ruins of a full ambulance setup. A woman was sprawled on the floor by an overturned gurney. She was bleeding and struggling to move. Varjan shot her through the top of her head before checking behind the closed door.

No one.

She heard a soft thump and a twig snapping. She jerked back, then took two cautious steps toward the opposite side of the van, where the sounds had come from. When she took a quick peek, she saw nothing but burned brush and the edge of the woods.

She pivoted back the other way, but it was too late.

Quiet as a leopard, Cruz had slipped up behind her, and now he stuck the muzzle of his pistol against her forehead.

'You didn't think it was gonna be that easy, did you, Varjan?'

90

Route 17, southeast toward the town of Brera and I-95, was my best guess of where the president's assassin was headed. Mahoney thought so too.

But when we lifted off, we immediately saw a plume of black smoke rising above the forest canopy not far to the northeast. Give credit to Ned's instincts. He told the pilot to check it out before we went all the way to the interstate.

We flew over a lumberyard and a farm toward a big chunk of forest. Within it, the black smoke had quickly become flames that fully engulfed the van, and now the fire was dying down.

'Get us on the pavement,' Mahoney said.

As we swung around to land, I punched in 911 and was surprised to be almost instantly connected to a dispatcher for Stafford County emergency services. After identifying myself, I reported the fire and asked that the Storck road be closed in both directions.

We touched down north of the van. The flames coming from it were all but done, leaving the smoking, scorched shell. Tendrils of fire were consuming leaves and pine needles but not spreading widely or rapidly; they were hampered by the recent wet conditions.

I went toward the burning vehicle, stopped at a safe distance, and used the pocket binoculars I always carry to study it.

'Body in the front seat,' I said.

Mahoney had already gone down the bank, and was looking at the van from behind through his own binoculars. 'And a second in the back here.'

We heard the first sirens in the distance. I knew the fire trucks would want to get close, and there'd be hoses, and water, and boots.

While Mahoney called for an FBI forensics team, I lowered my binoculars and got out my cell phone. I walked past the van and started taking pictures of the scene, especially the skid marks that told a story in reverse from the tire tracks in the softer soil on the shoulder where it left the road to the beginning of the skids a good eighty yards beyond.

Right away I saw that there could be two vehicles involved, the van and another one that had come to a stop almost parallel to the wreck. Was this second set of marks from before?

If the marks had ended anywhere but in front of the van, I might have discounted them. But they did stop by the van, so I went on the assumption that they were new.

Had someone seen the accident, stopped, saw the van was on fire, and left? Who? And why hadn't that person called it in?

I looked beyond the start of the van's skid, no more than forty feet, and saw what seemed at first to be a piece of tire rubber. I walked to it and realized that it was actually a shard of pavement about three inches long and the shape and thickness of my pinkie.

I saw the gouge in the road where the little finger had come from, and then behind that and to the left, I saw another gouge and two pieces of asphalt. As I photographed it all, I heard the sirens closing on our position from two directions. I looked north and saw the flashing red lights of a fire truck, followed by the lights of an ambulance.

I ran toward the smoking wreckage of the van. Mahoney had come back up the bank onto the road and was talking to Susan Carstensen on the radio.

The van was no longer burning, just belching caustic smoke.

'Anything?' Mahoney called to me.

'Don't let them spray down the van. I want a closer look at it just as it is,' I said. 'And let's keep them away from those skid marks until forensics gets here.'

Ned nodded and turned to meet the firemen. I scrambled down into the ditch and got much closer to the van.

The metal was still throwing enough heat that I had to stop a good fifteen feet away. After shooting a video and stills of the scene from that perspective, I used the binoculars again to study the corpse in the front seat.

The jaw was frozen open, not unusual for a burn victim. Though the face was charred beyond recognition, I could make out big fissures in the skin where it had split in the heat, several on what was left of his cheeks, and another that started between the eye sockets and ran up onto the forehead.

Something about that one looked strange, but I couldn't tell why. I shifted the binoculars lower and adjusted the focus so I could peer at the ground between myself and the van.

The forest floor was a tangle of old leaves, dormant vines, and thorny stalks that were charred close to the vehicle. Behind me, up on the road, I could hear the firemen calling out to one another.

Two of them looped around me and the van with axes and shovels, heading toward the trees. More firemen maneuvered a hose across the ditch and sprayed down the struggling blaze in the woods.

I kept moving around the van, fifteen feet back, peering at the ground through the glasses. I'd taken six or seven steps counterclockwise before I spotted something that made me lower the binoculars.

I couldn't make it out with the naked eye, so I looked again with the glasses and figured out exactly what it was. Holding my arm up to protect my face from the heat, I hurried to within six feet, squatted, and pushed aside a singed leaf that half covered a nine-millimeter shell casing.

Of course, it was a rural area. The brass could have been there from something unrelated, but I didn't think so. Leaving it in place, I went around the smashed front end of the van to look in at the corpse from the passenger side.

At a glance, I was positive. After walking to the rear of the van and peering inside with the binoculars, I was dead certain.

'What are you seeing?' Mahoney called from the road.

I went around and climbed up to him. 'This wasn't an accident, Ned. And neither of them is Hobbs's assassin.'

'Okay?'

I gestured south. 'There are gouges in the pavement over there that I think were made by bullets, two of them. Someone very good shot out the tires, which sent the van into this curving skid and off the road. The shooter skidded to a stop right there, climbed out, went into the ditch, and shot those two.'

After that I described the position of the spent shell casing, the weird fissure between the driver's eye sockets, and the hole the size of a fist in the back of his skull.

'The corpse in the rear has a head wound too,' I said.

Mahoney looked beyond frustrated. 'But how do you know neither of them is Hobbs's assassin?'

'The one in the rear's too small in stature to match Bree's description of him,' I said. 'I'm guessing a woman. And the driver had all his teeth. The president's killer had knocked out or broken several. Remember?'

'Now that you reminded me. But I'm still confused. Did Hobbs's assassin go off with this shooter of his own free will? Or was he forced out of here?'

'One or the other. Unless he took off into the woods. We should check, but I don't think so.'

'Son of a bitch,' Ned said, furious. 'Now we

have no idea what kind of car we're looking for. We had him, Alex. We had him, and we let him slip away again!'

Part Five

STOP ME, PLEASE

91

On Sunday, as the sun was setting, Pablo Cruz plunged a thick knitting needle that he held with vise grips into the flames of a gas stove burner. He watched the metal tip turn a glowing red.

Cruz had given Kristina Varjan no chance to try to overpower him once they were in her car. He'd disarmed her right away. Then, at every stoplight or stop sign, he'd pressed the muzzle of her Glock into her side and given her directions that took them across one arm of the Chesapeake Bay and onto Maryland's Eastern Shore.

According to the satellite radio, they'd gotten across the bridge just in time. News reports said the president's assassin had been hiding in a veterinary hospital west of there and had managed to elude federal agents once again.

Cruz smiled. He liked elusion. He took pride in staying ahead of the dogs. It was an art form, as far as he was concerned, and he was the master of it.

Like his choice of safe house. He'd spotted the shuttered beach cottage from the road and had Varjan park the car behind an outbuilding. After looking for signs of an alarm system and finding none, he had her crowbar the back door open.

Cruz turned from the stove in the cottage's kitchen with the glowing knitting needle before him and looked at Varjan, who was tied to a chair and eyeing him like she wanted to rip his throat out.

'I'm going to ask you again,' Cruz said. 'Who hired you to kill me?'

She sneered. 'I'm going to tell you again: I don't know. He calls himself Piotr.'

'A Russian?'

'Who knows.'

'I don't believe you,' Cruz said, bringing the still-glowing knitting needle by her cheek. 'There is more you are not telling me.'

'I don't have to tell you anything.'

Cruz dropped the nose of the needle to her collar and pushed it aside. Fabric burned before he touched her skin, right above the carotid artery. Her skin sizzled, and she shrank back, gritting her teeth.

He said, 'A second or two longer and you'd be bleeding out, Varjan.'

Her pained expression returned to a snarl. 'How do you know my name?'

'I make it my business to know my competitors,' Cruz said.

'Who are you?'

'Me? I am nobody, nowhere, in no time.'

'What the hell does that mean?'

Cruz did not answer. He returned to the rustic kitchen and put the knitting needle back in the flame, saying, 'I have nowhere to go, Varjan. I have nothing to do, and so I will do this until you tell me what T want to know.'

She said nothing, but watched him sidelong.

A few moments later, he came at her again.

Varjan raised her head in contempt.

He stopped, laughed. 'You don't think you're going to somehow reverse this situation and kill me, do you? Who hired you?'

Varjan did not reply and would not look at the red-hot knitting needle that he brought toward her neck again.

Cruz stopped the tip less than an inch away from her skin so she could sense the heat. Then he poked it through her shirt and bra into the side of her breast.

She screamed and cursed at him in Hungarian. He went back to the stove, saying, 'Even if you could have somehow managed to kill me, Piotr wouldn't have paid you. My payment request upon completion of task? Delayed, which is as good as denied in my book. Think about that. If I'm expendable, you are too.'

Varjan stayed mute, but something changed in her carriage. She'd relaxed slightly, a small reaction, but he'd gotten her attention.

'Think about it,' he said, watching the needle tip begin to glow again. 'They're stiffing me *and* trying to kill me. What do you think they'll do to you? Pay? No way. You *will be* expendable, and dealt with appropriately. In our profession, to believe otherwise would be . . . well, stupid. And I know you're not that.'

Varjan tried to remain contemptuous. He touched the needle to the collar of her shirt again, let the singed smell reach her nose.

'Where will it go next?' he asked, and he glanced down the front of her body.

After a pause, he gazed into her eyes. 'But it

doesn't have to be like this. There's another choice here.'

She twitched, and he knew he had her properly leveraged.

'What's that?' she asked.

Cruz took a step back, set the knitting needle down. 'I propose we join forces, find out who is behind this plot, and go get our money. Does that work? Or do I continue to knit?'

Varjan glanced at the needle, then at the floor, then up at him.

'We don't need to find out who's behind the plot,' she said evenly. 'I already know. I laid a trap and caught them in it right from the start. They haven't got a clue.'

92

Saskatoon, Saskatchewan

Dana Potter paced in the hallway outside his son's hospital room. Every two minutes, Potter thumbed Redial on his phone. SpoofCard, an app that disguised a caller's number, took over and placed the call.

He heard ringing somewhere in St. Petersburg, Russia, but he got no answer and no voice telling him to leave a message. Hanging up, Potter wanted to hurl his phone against the wall, see it shatter into a million pieces.

But anger was useless, he told himself. Anger said you were out of control and feeling like you were cornered.

I am cornered, Potter thought. *They've got all of us cornered.*

Fighting against that idea, willing himself to be brave, Potter entered the hospital room and tried not to weep at the sight of his son wasting away in bed. Jesse's eyes were closed, and Potter thought once again how much his boy resembled a baby bird fallen from its nest, all skin and sinew.

He looked to his wife, who sat by Jesse's bed. She gave him a questioning raise of her eyebrow. Shaking his head, he wondered if God had inflicted this punishment on the poor innocent boy as payback for his father's sins.

Jesse had been born just fine, ten fingers, ten toes, a healthy cry when the midwife delivered him. And he'd thrived through the age of five.

Then he started falling a lot for no apparent reason. Soon after, he was diagnosed with Duchenne muscular dystrophy. Duchenne, the deadliest form of muscular dystrophy, caused muscles to waste away. Boys around five or six were the most likely group to develop the disorder, and those boys usually died in their early twenties.

If we had until his early twenties, we could beat this thing, Potter thought bitterly. *But here's my Jesse dying at fifteen, and there's hope, but there's nothing I can do about it. Nothing.*

Potter cursed himself for a tactical error. He should have insisted on more of a payment up-front, enough to hire a private jet to fly his son to Panama and pay a doctor millions to administer a radical, controversial, and illegal stem-cell treatment that some said could stop the muscle wasting in its tracks. Even give Jesse back his strength.

Potter went to his son's side and stroked his face before looking at his wife. 'I don't know how to think of life without him,' he choked out. 'And they won't answer the phone. They're leaving us hanging in the wind, and I don't know what to do.'

Mary had tears in her eyes when she nodded. She was barely able to say, 'I know.'

Potter took his attention off his son. He could not bear to watch him just slip away in his sleep.

He glanced at the television on mute. His wife had it turned to CNN.

The anchorman was jazzed up about something, but Potter had no idea what until a chyron appeared on the screen:

CHIEF JUSTICE RULES TALBOT RIGHTFUL SUCCESSOR TO PRESIDENCY. LARKIN MUM.

Potter looked over at his wife in disgust. 'Was it for nothing?'

Before Mary could answer, their son moaned and stirred. The burn phone in Potter's pocket began to buzz.

He yanked it out, saw a number like the one from St. Petersburg, and surged toward rage as he stomped back into the hallway and answered.

'My son is dying,' Potter said in a tense whisper. 'We had a deal, and you aren't paying, and — '

'Is this Mr. Marston?' a woman said in a slight Eastern European accent.

He stopped ranting. He'd never talked to a female before.

'Who is this?' Potter said.

'The woman hired to eliminate you and your wife. I suggest you destroy the phone you are using, find another, and call the number I'm about to give you if you want any chance of saving your son.'

93

At seven thirty on Monday morning, February 8, three days after the assassinations and almost twenty-four hours since we'd lost our chance at the president's killer, I sipped coffee and poked at the plate of scrambled eggs, bacon, and toast Nana Mama had set before me.

I'd had less than ten hours of sleep in the past seventy-two, and we were no closer to the killers still at large. I was feeling grumpy, if not downright cranky, as I ate and gazed dully at the morning news on the television screen.

Anderson Cooper was up early, standing on the White House lawn and struggling to explain, first, the violent events that had seen President Hobbs and several successors assassinated and, second, the constitutional mechanics that had resulted in Attorney General Larkin assuming leadership. Then he began discussing the chief justice's ruling that the Oval Office rightfully belonged to Senator Talbot.

'Will there be a power struggle?' the CNN anchor said. 'Will we see yet another constitutional crisis if Larkin refuses to step down?'

The former attorney general, Cooper noted, had not been seen since the ruling had come down the evening before. He was rumored to have been flying in his airborne command post out west for the past two days, landing only to refuel at various air force bases across the country. But that was unconfirmed.

For his part, Senator Talbot had been holed up in his office on Capitol Hill all night while a steady stream of advisers had come and gone.

Cooper touched his earbud, then bobbed his head vigorously and stared into the camera with the peeved look of a man in the wrong place at the wrong time. 'Evidently, Senator Talbot has a statement to make live outside his office on Capitol Hill.'

The screen jumped to an image of the Nevada senator fighting not to look like a deer in the headlights as he went to the microphones.

'My fellow Americans,' Talbot said, sounding like someone's nice old uncle. 'I am as surprised as you are by these strange turns of events. But the chief justice has ruled, and I am not one to question the Founders of our nation, men like Jefferson and Adams and Franklin, who anticipated these kinds of difficult days. The Founders believed in an order of succession. They crafted that order into our Constitution, the precious document that is the basis of our unique form of governance. And I, as a mayor, a congressman, and a senator, have long sworn allegiance to God, country, and our remarkable system of laws.'

Talbot paused and stood taller. 'So, forthwith, I *will* assume the office of the president of the United States, and I want to assure every American that while I might be an old dog, I can certainly learn new tricks. I feel deeply humbled and honored to lead you in this time of crisis. My first act is to lift martial law. I want people to resume their lives. We must go on.'

I set my fork down.

Nana Mama said, 'Did he say no more martial law?'

'He did.'

My grandmother threw her arms overhead. 'I've got serious shopping to do.'

I laughed. 'You sound like we've been imprisoned for months.'

'Feels like it to me.' She sniffed. 'You know I like ingredients fresh.'

'I know you do,' I said, taking my plate to the sink and pecking her on the cheek as I passed.

'He doesn't sound too bad,' Nana said. 'That Talbot. Means well.'

'I get that sense too,' I said. 'But then again, I thought Larkin was a natural leader until he taunted the Russians and the Chinese like that.'

'Any chance Larkin fights it?'

'What's there to fight?' I asked. 'The chief justice ruled.'

'But not the entire court,' she said. 'I think it could be appealed on that basis.'

'I'm sure someone in Washington's looking at the idea,' I said.

I didn't want to go upstairs to shower yet. Everyone else was still sleeping. Even Bree, who'd been working just as hard as I had, if not harder. It was too cold to sit outside, so I went into the television room and sat with my coffee. I shut my eyes and let my thoughts roam.

Once again, I asked myself, *Who benefits from the murders? What about in light of recent events? Talbot, of course. He benefits. But he'd* struck me as a reluctant leader, someone who had never seen himself as presidential timber. And yet, now that he was called, he was willing to do his duty.

But what about Larkin? Why hadn't he come forward to give the country his reaction to the ruling? For that matter, where was he? The last we'd heard he was at an air force base in Kansas. Doing what? Trying to figure out his next move?

If Larkin was involved in the assassination plot, I decided, he would emerge to fight tooth and nail to stay president. He would do as Nana Mama had suggested, at the very least: appeal to the full Supreme Court.

But until then, what was *my* best course of action? For several minutes, I couldn't come up with a clear way forward. But then, as I opened my eyes to drink more coffee, I remembered something Viktor Kasimov said.

Follow the money.

94

I was back in the hangar at Joint Base Andrews less than two hours later, standing with Ned Mahoney and Susan Carstensen. We were all once again looking over Keith Karl Rawlins's shoulder.

The FBI cybercrimes expert was hacking into bank accounts that, according to British intelligence, belonged to Senator Walker's killer. The accounts in Sean Lawlor's name — gleaned upon request from British MI6 — were all in known money-laundering centers: Panama, Seychelles, and the Isle of Jersey.

'There we are,' Rawlins said when the screen jumped to the electronic ledger on Lawlor's account in Panama.

He scrolled down. 'Empty.'

'Find recent transactions,' I said.

He did and we saw that more than a million euros and a million British pounds had been transferred out the same day Lawlor was strangled.

'Where'd it go?' Mahoney asked.

'Bank in . . . ' Rawlins said, typing frantically. 'El Salvador.'

'Can you hack it?' I asked.

He looked at me as if I'd insulted him and soon had the account open on the screen. It, too, was empty.

'Whose account?'

'Esmeralda del Toro,' he said. 'Address in Madrid.'

'Send it to me,' Carstensen said. 'I'll dispatch agents.'

Rawlins did, and then Mahoney said, 'Where'd the money go from there?'

'Probably another empty account, probably belonging to a shell corporation, and on and on,' Rawlins said. 'I'm betting Esmeralda is not at home in Madrid.'

'Or that she even exists,' I said.

'Humor me,' Mahoney said. 'Push the ball ahead a few times.'

Rawlins sighed and gave his computer an order. Nothing. He gave another order. The screen didn't budge.

'Interesting,' he said. 'There's a firewall around recent transactions that . . . '

The FBI contractor cocked his head, rattled away at his keyboard, and hit Enter. The screen didn't change at first, but then it blinked to a new document.

'Ahhh,' Rawlins said. 'The money went to an account on Kraken. It's an exchange for cryptocurrencies in . . . Singapore.'

'Can you hack that account?' Mahoney demanded.

He cringed a little. 'That will take time. Those crypto-exchanges have hired the best in the world to build their security systems.'

'I have faith in you,' Mahoney said. 'Alex?'

I was staring off, blinking, trying to see what was bothering me through the fog of fatigue and ignorance. And then I flashed on the inner back cover of that Bible and saw a glimmer of hope.

'Can you call up the Kraken Exchange home page?' I said.

Rawlins did, and I saw more than hope. I saw possibility.

'What are you thinking, Cross?' Carstensen asked.

'Forget following the money,' I said. 'Let's play follow the Bitcoin.'

95

Four hours later, with the help of Rawlins, Mahoney, Carstensen, and a dozen others assigned to the investigation, I believed I knew who and what was behind the plot to overthrow the U.S. government by assassination.

'Who does that?' FBI director Derek Sanford said, shaking his head after I'd explained my theory to him in the conference room. 'Is there no end, no bottom?'

'We can't prove it beyond a doubt yet, sir,' Carstensen said. 'We've still got a lot of legwork to do before we know the details. In the meantime, I wish we were still under martial law. It would make things easier.'

Sanford paused, then said, 'I can offer you extraordinary powers for now. Mirandize when you have to. Otherwise, do what you need to do.'

I heard his cell phone buzz. The FBI director glanced at the screen, said, 'Larkin petitioned the full Supreme Court over the validity of Talbot's claim to the Oval Office.'

'He's still flying around?' Mahoney said.

'At his home in Kansas awaiting the court's decision,' Sanford said. 'Whatever. That's outside our purview. Go make real arrests. When you've got the lot of them in custody, I want the perp walk to end all perp walks.'

'What about their homes? Offices?' Mahoney said.

'Search warrants will be executed within the hour. Once that has happened, I'll contact my Russian counterparts and Interpol. They'll handle everything outside our jurisdiction. And when it's appropriate, I'll personally notify the Secret Service of our intentions.'

After Sanford left the conference room, Carstensen pointed to me and then Mahoney. 'You two are coming with me.'

'By car?' Ned asked.

'Helicopter,' she said, heading to the door.

'SWAT?' I asked.

Carstensen paused to check her watch. 'What time did you say it started?'

'Seven p.m.'

'I'll put a full SWAT team on standby,' she said, opening the door. 'I'm hoping that given the setting and occasion, our targets will be easy to locate and subdue.'

96

At six p.m., Kristina Varjan got out the carbon knife Pablo Cruz had given her and slid it up her sleeve, then she slipped through a throng of people packing a long, wide concrete hallway.

The assassin barely noticed them. She was focused. Prepared.

'Coming from the southwest,' she said, her voice picked up by and transmitted from the sensitive Bluetooth mike taped to her throat and hidden beneath her shirt.

'Coming from northwest,' Cruz said over a small earbud.

'Cutting east to west,' Dana Potter said. 'I'll approach up the near staircase.'

'Muscle?' Varjan said.

'Unseen,' Potter said. 'But I'm sure it's there.'

'No blood if possible,' Cruz said.

Varjan did not reply. She'd spotted a woman coming at her through the crowd. She was looking at her phone with a worried scowl on her face and had a VIP pass hanging around her neck on a lanyard.

Putting on sunglasses, Varjan looked down at the VIP pass she held and felt confident. She climbed stairs to a higher floor and ran into a security guard at the top who was looking at his phone. She smiled, then held out her VIP pass.

'The lanyard broke,' she said, acting embarrassed.

The guard appeared bored, waved her on, and went back to staring at his phone. Varjan went around him into a long hallway and saw Cruz coming at her from the far end, also wearing a VIP pass.

Between them stood a big white guy with a military haircut and military bearing. He was leaning with his back to a door. She noted a gun bulge, chest-high, under the suit jacket.

The muscle's head swiveled, took them both in.

Varjan went by a staircase to her right, saw in her peripheral vision that Potter, the Canadian assassin, was climbing with a VIP badge around his neck.

She smeared an easy smile across her face and acted a little tipsy as she ambled to the security guy.

'This where the VIP bash is at?' she asked shyly.

'No, ma'am.'

'That right?' Cruz said, also acting like he'd had a few. 'I was told this was the place too.'

'Me three,' Potter said behind her.

The bodyguard seemed relaxed, in control, not bothered by them or the odd outfits they wore.

'Well, I'm Philip Stapleton, director of security for Victorious, and I can tell you there's no party up here. Yet.'

'Yet?' Varjan said, lifting her VIP pass to show him as she slid closer.

'So we're early?' Cruz said.

The question distracted Stapleton just long

enough for Varjan to spring at him and get the blade of the carbon knife up against the side of his neck, right under the jawbone and across his carotid.

'One wrong move, and I'll bleed you right here,' Varjan whispered.

Cruz came in beside them, took the pistol from Stapleton's chest holster.

'Open the door now,' Varjan said.

Cruz set the muzzle of the guard's pistol against his temple. 'Your call.'

'It's coded,' the guard said. But he gave them the number.

Potter keyed the code into the pad by the door. They heard the door lock click open. Knife blade still tight to Stapleton's jaw, Varjan pushed him through. The other two assassins followed her, stepping inside fast.

'Nobody move,' Varjan said to the people in the room as Cruz kicked the door shut behind him. 'Or this man dies.'

97

We reached the outskirts of Atlantic City at 6:40 on Monday evening. Out the window and far below the FBI helicopter, life was going on. From that height, you'd never have known that the country had been under martial law and in the grip of one constitutional crisis after another for the past several days.

My cell phone buzzed, alerting me to a text. It was Nina Davis again.

Please, Dr. Cross. I need your help. I think someone is stalking me, not the other way around. And I'm scared.

I stared at the text, and then answered: Still tied up in the investigation. Stay home. If you feel threatened, call local police. I will call as soon as I can.

Rather than wait for an answer, I turned the phone off.

'Police lights,' Carstensen said, looking out the window on her side of the chopper. 'Heading toward our landing zone. Pilot, can you find out why?'

'Roger that,' the pilot said.

Now I could see the police cars, five of them, racing east toward the ocean.

The pilot came back on. 'Police in Atlantic City say there was a murder and a vicious assault and robbery in the Tropicana garage. Three victims, three assailants, all dressed in costumes.'

'As long as it's not about us,' Carstensen said.

'Put us on that roof.'

'What did they steal?' I asked.

'VIP passes to the big show.'

'What kind of costumes?'

'Didn't say,' the pilot said. 'But I'll ask.'

We circled, the helicopter shuddering in the wind before landing on a helipad atop the Tropicana casino. We jumped out into a chill, raw sea breeze.

Carstensen spoke with the casino's head of security while Mahoney and I hustled to a hatch and a stairway. We waited for her outside, and then we all walked together north several blocks toward Boardwalk Hall, a famous sports and entertainment venue where some of history's greatest boxing matches had been held.

That night, however, the marquee read

VICTORIOUS E-SPORTS
WORLD CHAMPIONSHIP FINALS.

The three of us went to the main gate and showed our badges and credentials to security. Carstensen quietly told the guard in charge to let us in and keep our presence to himself or she'd have him arrested for obstruction of justice.

The lobby and the hallways of the venue were jammed with video-gamers, most dressed as Victorious avatars, all pressing toward the event hall itself.

'Ten thousand five hundred capacity,' Mahoney said.

'Narrow the search,' Carstensen said. 'We're not looking in the cheap seats.'

We split up. Mahoney headed north, and Carstensen went south. I climbed as high as I could go and came out in the nose-bleed section. The auditorium was already more than half full. There was rap music playing and a festive atmosphere around a large wrestling ring that filled the center of the floor. Inside the ring, there were six empty gaming stations, and television cameras on arms swung around above them.

I got out my pocket binoculars and used them to peer beyond the ring to a stage at the other end of the hall where a band was setting up. I scanned everyone on the stage but did not see who I was looking for.

Remembering Carstensen's remark about ignoring the cheap seats, I looked all around the wrestling ring, the first ten rows, best seats in the house. Nothing.

But then I looked directly across the auditorium and one deck down, toward a row of skyboxes. Most were dark, which surprised me. Maybe e-sports weren't a big enough business yet to attract a skybox sort of corporate clientele.

Whatever the reason, there was only one that appeared occupied. The lights were on. I moved over until I was directly across from that box and looked through the binoculars.

The first thing I saw was a woman with her back to me. She wore a glam outfit and a black wig, like the avatar Celes Chere. Beside her, also with his back to me, stood a big lanky guy wearing a black cowboy hat and the sort of long, hemmed duster that horsemen wear in the rain.

Just like the avatar Mr. Marston.

I almost took my attention off the skybox but then noticed movement beyond the two. I moved another five feet to my left and saw Austin Crowley and Sydney Bronson, the wunderkind founders of Victorious Gaming, and Philip Stapleton, the company's director of security.

Crowley was sitting forward in a club chair, fingers pressed in a steeple pose, staring through his thick black glasses at Bronson, who had his head down and was working furiously on a laptop. Stapleton was slumped in a chair behind Crowley. His eyes were closed and he was bleeding profusely from a head wound. Standing behind Bronson was a man wearing the white robes of the Victorious avatar Gabriel.

I could see only part of the angel. The cowboy blocked my full view of his head.

'Cross?' the pilot called. The static was heavy.

'Copy.'

'You asked how the assailants at the Tropicana were dressed. A cowboy, an angel, and a punk rocker.'

In the skybox, Bronson took his attention off his computer, looked toward the big cowboy, and nodded.

The cowboy walked away from the window and straight across the room to Bronson, then paused, his back to me. Bronson handed the cowboy his computer, and the cowboy left the skybox.

But if I hadn't been standing in that exact spot, I might have missed the latex mask the guy dressed as Gabriel wore, the way his left arm dangled oddly, and what looked like a pistol in his right hand. The veterinarian and Jared Goldberg both said that the president's killer had been wounded in the left elbow.

I fiddled with the focus, trying to make sure. But then the woman dressed as Celes Chere turned to peer out the window and down on the building audience.

I lowered the glasses and triggered my mike, trying to remain calm.

'This is Cross. I've got Bronson, Crowley, and Stapleton in the middle skybox, south side of the auditorium. If I'm right, there are three assassins in there with them, including Kristina Varjan and possibly the president's killer.'

Before Mahoney or Carstensen could reply, I raised my binoculars again and found Varjan, hand to her brow to cut the spotlight glare, staring right back at me.

98

My earbud crackled.

Mahoney said, 'Alex, repeat the location, you're garbled.'

Varjan had seen enough. She spun around and headed away from the window fast. Before following her, Gabriel clubbed Bronson across the back of his head with the butt of his pistol, sending him sprawling.

'Cross?' Carstensen said. 'Repeat?'

I jammed the binoculars in my coat pocket, pivoted, and headed for the exit. When I hit the hallway, I hesitated, knowing the skyboxes would be closer if I went left. Instead, I went right and broke into a dodging run through the growing crowd of fans, triggering my mike as I did.

'This is Cross,' I said. 'Repeat, we've got two, probably three of the assassins right here in the building. The president's killer and Varjan. She just made me. They're fleeing the sky-boxes. Look for a glam girl, a cowboy in a black hat and a long brown duster, and an angel in white robes and a latex mask. The angel has a clipped left wing, like the president's assassin, and he is armed. Assume others are as well.'

'Copy,' Mahoney said. 'I'm heading toward the closest exit to the skyboxes.'

Carstensen said, 'I'm calling in SWAT, sealing the entire venue.'

I spotted a stairway finally and wanted to

bound down it, but there were too many people coming up. I had to squeeze hard right against the flow, which cost me more time.

When I made it to the skybox level, I decided to keep going down. There was no doubt in my mind they were trying to get the hell out of the venue.

Varjan saw me just now. She saw me at the motel, and again the first day of the e-sports championships. She knows I'm FBI. They'll all be on high alert.

I reached the hall's lowest level and almost went toward the west entrance where Mahoney had gone in anticipation of the shortest line of flight from the skyboxes. But something told me to do the opposite, to double back and go east.

Moving as fast as the crowd would let me, I kept one hand ready to draw my service weapon and swiveled my head as I ran, scanning the faces and costumes.

I got a look at several girls dressed as Celes Chere and two cowboys in black hats. But they weren't wearing the horseman dusters, and —

An alarm began to whoop.

Diversion, I thought. *Just like the last time.*

Fans froze in place, not knowing what to do. Several panicked and I heard people saying, 'Fire?' Then I heard screaming ahead of me.

I yanked out my badge and gun and yelled, 'FBI! Get down!'

People started running away instead of getting down, but it opened up a path through the crowd that allowed me to quickly round a curve in the passage and to see a red light flashing below an emergency exit sign. A security guard was lying in a pool of blood below the flashing light in front of an emergency door that was ajar.

'Help's on the way,' I shouted at the wounded man as I vaulted over him, seeing that his pistol was missing from his holster before I threw my shoulder into the door.

It flew open, revealing a steel staircase landing and a short flight of stairs leading down to an empty ambulance parked in a bay.

Behind the ambulance, the overhead door was up. I ran toward it. Two EMTs carrying cups of coffee appeared.

'FBI!' I shouted. 'Did you see people come out this door?'

'Two of them, a guy dressed as an angel and a glitter girl,' one of them said. He gestured with the coffee cup. 'They ran like hell toward the boardwalk.'

99

I sprinted along the north side of Boardwalk Hall and triggered my mike.

'This is Cross again,' I said, gasping. 'Two of them have escaped the venue. Repeat, escaped the venue. Get that helicopter in the air. They're on the boardwalk somewhere ahead of me. Male in angel costume. Female dressed glam.'

'Copy,' Carstensen said.

I reached the boardwalk with a stitch in my side but managed to calm down enough to look through the binoculars south toward the Tropicana.

Despite the raw conditions, there were knots of people along the boardwalk, some coming at me, some walking away. No angel. No glam girl. No cowboy either, for that matter.

I swung around to look north along the boardwalk and saw similar small groups of pedestrians braving the —

'I got a visual!' I barked into the mike as I took off again. 'Heading north on the boardwalk, two blocks north of the hall, near the pier!'

I'd caught a solid look at the back of a man dressed in white robes far ahead of me, and I'd gotten a glimpse of a woman at his side. There was no chance they were getting away again, I told myself, and I picked up the pace.

For the better part of a block, I couldn't locate either of them ahead of me, and I was starting to doubt what I'd seen. But then I spotted the angel again, still with his back to me, still heading north, going past Bally's Beach Bar.

He was alone now and no longer running. His left arm looked useless. Sirens began to wail to my west, north, south.

My earbud crackled with static. I could tell it was Carstensen, but I could not tell what she was saying.

I hit the mike, said, 'Suspect dressed as angel heading north on boardwalk north of Michigan Avenue toward Brighton Park. Suspect is alone now.'

I could barely make out Mahoney saying, 'Copy.'

I ran on, trying to keep the few people on the boardwalk in front of me so the assassin wouldn't see me gaining ground if he happened to look back.

I was less than half a block away from him when the tragedy happened.

A young Atlantic City uniformed police officer came out of the park in front of the killer. The patrol cop was moving quickly, and when he saw the angel, he started to skid down into a combat shooting position, his hands and pistol already rising.

The assassin was quicker; he threw up his gun and fired, hitting the officer square in his bulletproof vest. As the cop staggered backward, he pulled the trigger on his pistol. The bullet went wide, hit the boardwalk, and ricocheted out to sea.

The angel's second shot caught the young

policeman through the throat and dropped him in his tracks.

I was closing fast on him then. Two hysterical young women in raincoats were fleeing toward me.

'FBI!' I yelled to the angel. 'Drop your gun! Put your hands up!'

The two girls dived to either side of me. The president's assassin had already looked over his shoulder and started to spin in his tracks, his gun up.

He wasn't quite fully turned when my first shot — in my off hand, and shaky — slapped him across the ham of his left leg. He jerked as he shot. I heard his bullet crack by my left ear, rattling me.

Because a trained assassin was not going to miss twice at this distance, I pointed the gun at him and fired again, just hoping to put him on the defensive.

But by some miracle, it center-punched him just below the sternum. He hunched over and then fell hard onto his side, gasping for air.

I ran up. When he tried to raise his gun, I kicked it out of his hand.

I squatted, pulled off the mask so he could breathe. His face was a swollen mass of stitches.

'Who are you?' I said. 'Who hired you to kill Hobbs?'

He blinked at me dully, then shuddered and, through the blood that began to seep out his mouth, croaked, 'I am . . . nobody . . . nowhere . . . in no — '

The assassin convulsed then, choked, and

404

coughed up a gout of dark blood. He died quivering on the boardwalk.

I stared at him, hearing sirens closing on my location and a helicopter approaching, then turned to check on the two young women in raincoats.

Kristina Varjan was standing twenty feet behind me, squared off and looking at me over the barrel of a pistol.

100

'Drop the gun, cross,' Varjan said. 'Or die.'

I let go of my weapon, heard it strike the concrete.

'There's an army coming, Kristina,' I said. 'You'll never get out of here alive.'

I noticed her expression tightened when I said her name.

'I'll take my chances,' she said. 'I just wanted you to know I had nothing to do with the president's death or the death of any of the others. I was a maid. Cleanup. That's all.'

'Maid for who, Kristina?'

'You saw,' she said, angrier but glancing around.

'What did I see, Kristina?' I asked, hitting her given name hard.

'Stop that,' she said, shaking the gun at me, 'or I'll kill you anyway.'

Behind her in the sky, I saw the helicopter coming. And patrol cars had squealed to a stop back on Michigan, their bubbles flashing blue. From behind me, from the park, I heard tires skidding to a halt and sirens dying.

'It's over, Kristina,' I said. 'Drop the gun.'

Varjan looked at the beach and the water.

'They'll get you out there too. Save yourself. Drop the gun.'

'The CIA takes me. No one else.'

'I can't promise that.'

406

She processed my response, and then all the tension in her shoulders seemed to vanish, as if she'd come to some decision and was resigned to her fate.

'Then I take it all back,' Varjan said, her voice flat. 'You'll just have to die before me, Cross. You'll have to lead the way into hell.'

'No — ' I managed to blurt out before she pulled the trigger.

Her bullet blasted into me eight inches below my Adam's apple.

I was hurled back and off my feet. I landed hard, choking for air in a whirling daze. I heard another shot and a third before a barrage of gunfire that was the last thing I remembered before everything vanished into darkness.

101

Dana Potter moved at a steady clip west from Boardwalk Hall, forcing himself to exude easy confidence and showing only passing interest in the police cars that blew by him, their sirens singing.

After he'd left the skybox, his business done, Potter had gone out a service entrance and immediately saw a garbage truck backing up to a full trash container.

He tossed the cowboy hat, the duster, and Sydney Bronson's laptop computer into the bin just before it was lifted and dumped into the truck.

Both identifying articles of clothing and that weasel's computer were leaving the area even before Potter reached the entrance to Caesar's Palace and went inside. He strolled to a souvenir kiosk he'd scouted earlier in the day and bought a hooded sweatshirt with the casino's logo on it.

He pulled the hoodie on and left the casino just in time to hear shots to the northeast, back toward the boardwalk and the beach, three in a cluster, and then four more shots in rapid succession. There was a break, and then a shot, and then another shot a minute later, and then multiples, a firefight.

But since then, as Potter walked farther and farther west, he'd heard only the sirens. When he saw a bus about to pull into a stop, he ran to catch it.

Potter took an empty seat, yawned, and shut his eyes. Ten stops later, he got off, went into a corner store, and bought a Bud tallboy. He drank it as he walked the seven blocks to the train station, where he bought a ticket to Newark Penn Station.

Eleven minutes passed. He was aboard the train and it was pulling out. Two stops later, he got off. He watched everyone else who'd exited the train until he was satisfied there was no tail. Then he bought another ticket, this time to Hoboken.

While he waited for that train, Potter walked down the platform, away from all the commuters. Only then did he pull the burn phone from his pocket and punch in the number of another burn phone.

'Paul?' Mary said, using the code they'd agreed on.

'Right here, Sal,' he said. 'We're good. Get him out of that hellhole now.'

He heard her break down crying.

'C'mon, now,' he said. 'I need you to be strong. We've done it.'

'I'm just so relieved, so hopeful, is all.'

Potter smiled. 'Me too.'

'You following?'

'I'll be there as soon as I can. But do not wait for me to start the therapy.'

'What about payment?'

'I got it. Now get to work.'

'I love you.'

'Love you too,' he said. He clicked off and broke the phone in two before tossing it in a trash can.

Potter pulled a USB drive from his pocket, looked at it, and imagined his son healed, on his feet, and walking again.

That will be worth the risk, he thought. *Jesse is worth every risk.*

He could even acknowledge that, sooner or later, U.S. federal agents would track him down. Sooner or later, he'd have to tell them he'd done the job in Texas alone, that his wife had no idea he'd assassinated the Speaker of the House and the secretary of state using two identical rifles set side by side on bipods.

Mary had no idea what Jesse's stem-cell treatments cost. He'd been the one to go to Panama to learn about it. His wife had zero to do with any of it.

He'd say all that, and then he'd die somehow, death by cop or suicide to seal the deal and keep Mary free to raise Jesse.

As his train pulled into the station, Potter was at peace with his fate. He stuck the USB drive in his pocket and got on board. He could see Jesse walking in his mind, and for that, he would accept every punishment that might come his way.

102

My head spun a bit as the FBI helicopter lifted off from the beach by the boardwalk where Varjan had shot me high in my Kevlar vest.

The bullet at short range had been enough to knock me down and out.

But not for long. I'd come around within seconds and saw Carstensen, Mahoney, and a small army of Atlantic City police officers swarming past the bullet-ridden corpse of the Hungarian assassin.

They'd tried to make me lie still and wait for the medics, but I refused and was getting woozily to my feet when Philip Stapleton, Victorious Gaming's director of security, staggered up to us. His face and suit were covered in blood. He held a wad of bloody napkins to his head.

'Arrest him,' Carstensen said.

'No,' Stapleton said. 'I had nothing to do with this.'

'Arrest him and his bosses,' she snapped.

'They're gone,' Stapleton said. 'That's why I came to you. They left me there for dead. I came straight here after they left.'

'Where'd they go?' Mahoney demanded.

'The airport,' Stapleton said. 'They have a jet.'

'Arrest him anyway. Get him to a hospital.'

'No! Believe me. I served my country. I love my country. I would never ... I faked being unconscious in there. I heard everything they said. Everything.'

Which is how Stapleton came to be sitting in the jump seat across from me and Mahoney, his wrists in handcuffs, and an FBI SWAT medic working on his head wound.

'Talk,' Carstensen said.

Stapleton didn't stop talking as we picked up speed, and the pilot attempted to call the air traffic control tower at the Atlantic City airport. I admit to being fuzzy on that flight, but everything the security director was saying fit with what we'd suspected.

The pilot called out, 'Are they in a Gulfstream?'

'Yes,' Stapleton said. 'Don't let them off the ground. They can fly more than six thousand miles in that thing.'

'That's them,' the pilot said. 'They are taxiing toward the runway and ignoring air traffic control orders to turn about.'

'Move!' Carstensen shouted.

The pilot juiced the chopper to its limits, one hundred and forty-five miles an hour. Then he dropped speed and swung the bird past the airport tower.

The Gulfstream was just making the turn onto the runway when the pilot flew over the top of the jet, passed it, and hovered broadside over the runway. The jet kept coming. Carstensen slid back the side door of the chopper. Five FBI SWAT agents aimed automatic weapons at the cockpit and the pilot.

The jet stopped. The engines died. The jet's

pilot put his hands up.

We landed. The SWAT officers surrounded the jet.

'This is the FBI; open the door and come out with your hands up,' Carstensen said over the helicopter's loudspeaker. 'Now.'

Two minutes later, the airplane door slowly opened and let down the staircase.

Austin Crowley came first, blinking nervously behind his thick glasses, the fingers of both hands interlaced on his head. Crowley's partner, Sydney Bronson, had his hands up but was openly defiant.

'What the hell is this?' he cried after agents grabbed Crowley and slammed him facedown onto the tarmac. 'Why are you — '

Two agents dragged him off the staircase, threw him down beside his partner, and restrained his wrists behind his back.

I looked at Carstensen, who nodded and said, 'All yours, Dr. Cross.'

'Austin Crowley, Sydney Bronson,' I said. 'You are both under arrest for conspiracy to overthrow the government of the United States.'

103

At ten o'clock the following morning, outside the northeast gate to the White House grounds, Bree and I met Mahoney, Carstensen, and FBI director Sanford. After presenting our credentials, we were waved in and soon found ourselves standing in the hall outside the Oval Office.

'You good?' Bree whispered to me.

'Slight headache.'

'I didn't mean your head.'

'I know. I'm good.'

I don't know why, but I was good, strangely calm when the door opened and we walked in. The room was fairly crowded with people I recognized. Some were cabinet members. Others were leaders from both houses of Congress and from both sides of the political aisle.

All nine Supreme Court justices were there as well. And Secret Service special agent Lance Reamer, and Lieutenant Sheldon Lee of the Capitol Police. Bree went and stood by them.

President Talbot was on his feet behind the Lincoln desk, looking grim.

'What the hell happened in Atlantic City? No one will tell us anything.'

'We've been sorting that out all night, Mr. President,' Director Sanford said. 'It seemed easier to brief everyone who needed to know at once.'

'Well, then,' Talbot said, irritated, as he sat

down. 'Get on with it.'

Sanford glanced at Carstensen, who said, 'Two of the assassins are dead.'

That set off a hubbub that lasted several moments before she continued, 'They were killed on the boardwalk in Atlantic City last night.'

Chief Justice Watts said, 'Who were they?'

I said, 'One was a notorious Hungarian contract killer named Kristina Varjan. The other, who we believe was President Hobbs's killer, is as yet unidentified.'

The Senate majority leader said, 'Explain how you caught up to them.'

'A fluke, Senator,' Mahoney said. 'We were up in Atlantic City following a different thread of the investigation, and we spotted them.'

'Doing what?' the House whip asked.

Carstensen said, 'They were shaking down their employers.'

'You mean whoever hired them to do the killings?'

'That's correct,' the FBI director said.

'So who are they?' the secretary of the interior asked.

'Austin Crowley and Sydney Bronson, co-founders and owners of the largest e-sports company in the world.'

That set off another animated reaction in the room. *E-sports? What?*

'You're sure about this?' the Senate majority leader said.

'Yes,' I said. 'When I spotted the three assassins in Crowley and Bronson's skybox, they evidently were there demanding payment for the killings. They got Bronson to transfer millions of dollars in Bitcoin to so-called hard wallets — small, densely encrypted thumb drives — that the killers took with them.'

I could see skepticism on the faces of many in the room, including the president.

'They told you this?' President Talbot said. 'They confessed?'

Sanford said, 'No, Crowley and Bronson tried to tell us the three were just sophisticated robbers who'd heard about the purse for the tournament being in Bitcoin and taken advantage of the situation.'

I said, 'That was nonsense. Stapleton, their director of security, was beaten by the assassins, and he overheard the conversations that occurred in that skybox. When we hit Crowley and Bronson with what Stapleton told us, they denied it and said they'd sue us and him.'

Carstensen smiled. 'Until we showed them that Stapleton had recorded almost the entire thing on his iPhone. Then they caved, admitted they were the masterminds.'

The chief justice said, 'Why in God's name would they do such a thing? These are video-game people, right?'

'Sophisticated video-game people,' I said. 'Expert coders. MIT- and Harvard-smart. And arrogant about it. I think they thought they'd never get caught, that they knew enough about the dark web to get away with playing behind the scenes, anonymously hiring assassins to topple the U.S. government.'

'But why?' the chief justice said again, growing irritated.

Carstensen told him that Bronson and Crowley said that they hadn't planned to kill the president. Not at the outset, anyway. They had been spending more and more of their time exploring the dark web, doing research for future games, and they'd come upon a site that offered killers for hire.

'They claim they got on the site to see if a game they were designing was plausible,' Mahoney said.

'I'm confused,' Talbot said. 'This was a game? A goddamned game to them?'

'At first, sir,' I said. 'Then President Grant died. And someone made them realize they had a unique opportunity.'

'What opportunity?' the House whip said.

'Ultimately?' I said. 'The opportunity to make Bitcoin, lots and lots of Bitcoin.'

104

Most of the people in the Oval Office that day had vaguely heard of Bitcoin and cryptocurrencies, but we gave them a crash course in the so-called block-chain technology that underlies digital money and keeps trade in it relatively anonymous.

'A lot of very smart people think this is the radical future of money,' Director Sanford said. 'So ask yourself: What would you do if you were Crowley and Bronson, two of those very smart people who think Bitcoin is the future, and you owned a huge e-sports company? Being entrepreneurs, you're looking to the future, trying to tie your company to potentially radical change. What business would you want to be in? What business would it make sense to be in?'

No one in the room said anything. Sanford looked to me and nodded.

'Gambling,' I said.

'What?' the chief justice said.

'Consider these facts,' I said. 'E-sports are the fastest growing participatory and spectator sport in the world. The only thing that isn't happening there is what has happened with all other sports in the world: Betting. Wagering. Gambling.'

Carstensen said, 'And now imagine a time in the not-too-distant future when you could bet on e-sports, all digitally, potentially from any computer in the world. And every smartphone.

And every tablet. And all of the betting is occurring via hard-to-trace Bitcoin.'

Director Sanford said, 'We're talking billions upon billions upon billions of untraceable dollars. If it had worked, Crowley and Bronson could have been among the wealthiest people on earth, if not *the* wealthiest.'

'Who would take such a chance?' the House minority leader said, disgusted.

'Two super-nerds, young brilliant dropouts with no social skills and zero empathy for their fellow man,' Carstensen said. 'They see little difference between real-life humans and game avatars. They're all expendable. And they believed that they were so good at game theory and design, at thinking their way through the ramifications of every possible move, that they could cover all their bases. Only they didn't. Evidently, the first time Varjan, the Hungarian assassin, was contacted by them anonymously, she attached some kind of electronic bug to her reply that followed it to the source. She knew who they were from the start.'

'Fatal mistake on their part,' Mahoney said. 'I mean, they were good enough hackers to know the itineraries of every one of their targets, but they missed her bug.'

The Senate majority leader said, 'Idiots. Congress would never have allowed uncontrolled gambling like that.'

I shrugged. 'Congress might have if the president thought it was a good idea.'

All around the Oval Office, brows knitted and then heads turned to look at President Talbot, who appeared puzzled. 'What are you saying?'

'I said that, hypothetically, sir, if the president thought unfettered gambling on e-sports was a good idea, their scheme might have worked. Such a president could have lent his popularity and influence to see it through Congress, sold it as a way to bring in new sources of revenue to do governmental good.'

'Well, hypothetically or not, I don't support anything like that,' Talbot said. 'Never have. Never would.'

There was silence in the room.

Director Sanford ended it by saying, 'I'm sorry, Mr. President, but you must know that's not true.'

The president raised his head and glared at Sanford. 'How dare you tell me what I support and don't.'

Carstensen said, 'The Senate bill that would have allowed digital gambling as a means to collect tax revenues and so decrease the national debt. You're familiar with it, aren't you, Mr. President? You're listed as a co-sponsor.'

Talbot laughed. 'Young lady, do you know how many cockamamie bills a senator will cosign in a career? Hell, half the time you don't know what it is you're supporting. You're just doing a colleague a favor. Making him look good.'

Sanford said, 'So you don't support digital gambling, sir?'

'I just said that, didn't I?' Talbot snapped. 'Frankly, I think this is outrageous. You don't honestly think I colluded with these two clowns on the autism spectrum to overthrow the government just so they could make billions, do you?'

105

There was another long, tense silence in the room, with everyone either looking at us or at Talbot.

I cleared my throat, said, 'Well, sir. There's also the presidency. The ultimate office. The dream of every senator. Even you, sir.'

'Bull turd,' Talbot sputtered. 'I have never — ' He laughed caustically and shook his head. 'How in God's name do you think this all happened? I mean, I became Senate president pro tempore by accident. My good friend and colleague Senator Jones — who was expected to recover just fine after his heart operation — died before he even got on the operating table. Explain that.'

Bree said, 'Senator Walker was assassinated, sir, and if she hadn't died, she'd have been in line to take Senator Jones's place as Senate president pro tempore. Not you.'

His face reddened and tightened. 'And who are you?'

'DC Metro chief of detectives Stone, sir,' Bree said. 'I solved Senator Walker's murder. And again, if Walker wasn't dead, she would have been standing where you are now.'

'Exactly right, but so what?' Talbot said dismissively. 'Arthur wasn't killed. He just died. Things happen randomly.'

'They do sometimes,' I said. 'But not in this

case. Senator Jones did not just die. He was helped.'

Mahoney held up a photograph of Kristina Varjan in death. 'We showed this picture to Senator Jones's sister, who was in the room when he coded. We also showed it to the night nurse on the cardiac unit. Both women identified this assassin as the phlebotomist who was with the Senate president pro tempore shortly before his *heart attack*.'

I said, 'Which put you behind Abraham Lincoln's desk, sir. The most powerful man on earth. Capable of bestowing unfathomable wealth on a favored few.'

Talbot shook his head like a horse at biting flies. 'This is not true. You will not find any tie between me and — '

The door to the Oval Office swung open. Samuel Larkin walked in.

'Larkin?' Talbot said, growing furious. 'What in God's name are you doing here?'

'I'm here to place you under arrest for treason,' the former acting president and attorney general said, unruffled. 'I've seen the interrogations of Stapleton, Crowley, and Bronson. They all say it was your idea, cooked up the day after President Grant died. You and Bronson and Crowley were eating at a restaurant in Reno and talked out the whole thing.'

'That's not true!' Talbot said.

'There's security footage of you all together.'

'It's fabricated! Fake news!'

'You'll get your day in court to prove that. A lot more than your victims got,' Larkin said, nodding to Secret Service agent Reamer. 'Arrest him,'

Reamer smiled, said, 'With pleasure, Mr. President.'

'What?' Talbot shouted, backing up. 'They're giving the presidency back to you, Larkin? This is illegal! *This* is a coup!'

'I'll be taking over temporarily,' Larkin said. 'By all accounts, Harold Murphy is going to live and make a full recovery, thank God. The secretary of defense is the rightful successor to the office and will take over as soon as he's physically able.'

'No!' Talbot said when the Secret Service agent came around the desk. He stormed over to the French doors that led to the west colonnade of the White House, threw them open, and stepped outside. He looked ready to try to make his escape, but he froze when two Marine MPs walked up and blocked his path.

'Stand aside,' Talbot said. 'I'm your commander in chief!'

'Not anymore, you're not,' Agent Reamer said from behind him, and he roughly snapped the cuffs on the former leader of the free world.

106

Six days later, six riderless black horses clip-clopped down Pennsylvania Avenue, followed by six coffins on horse-drawn caissons, all draped in U.S. flags.

Once again, I stood with my family at the corner of Constitution and Louisiana. Well, most of my family. Damon had exams, and Bree had just been called away.

'I can't get over this,' Nana Mama said as the funeral cortege approached. 'Crowley and that Bronson, they didn't think twice about taking all those brilliant lives to gain control of the presidency and make billions. Who thinks like that?'

'At least three people do,' Ali said.

'All it takes, I guess,' Jannie said. 'If you can work the dark web.'

Later, during the eulogy he gave at the service for the fallen leaders at the National Cathedral, the acting president, Larkin, talked about the fragility of life. He also spoke of the strength and resiliency of our nation.

'The simple fact about our country that has been undervalued time and again is that we are by design a government that continues to function no matter the tragedy or turmoil,' Larkin said. 'If you kill one of our leaders, another rises, and the country goes on. If you assassinate two, three, or even six of our leaders, there is a natural succession laid out by the Framers, and the country and the government go on.

'These gifted, patriotic men and woman who lie before us lived in service to the people, and I believe they did not die in vain,' he said. 'They are martyrs, and I will always think of them as such, martyrs to the ideals of our country as laid out in our brilliantly conceived Constitution.'

I left the service thinking how right Larkin was. We had just endured one of the biggest upheavals in our country's history, but life would continue. And America would go on trying to create a more perfect union of the people, by the people, and —

My cell phone buzzed. Bree.

'Funerals done?' she asked.

'They all left for Arlington a few minutes ago. Figured it was for family. I'm heading home.'

'Not so fast,' she said. 'I need you to come see something. Right now.'

'I told Jannie we'd go for a run. Can't it wait?'

'I'm sorry, baby, but no.'

She gave me an address in Foggy Bottom that sounded familiar, but I couldn't place it. I called an Uber, and even with the traffic, I got there fifteen minutes later.

Bree met me outside an old restored town house with a freshly painted green door. 'You've never been here, right?'

I shook my head. 'No. I don't think so. Why? Who lives here?'

'I'll show you.'

She gave me blue booties and latex gloves. We

walked inside a few feet to a steep narrow staircase. Bree went up it before I could look around.

I followed. We reached a narrow landing and entered a bedroom.

I took one look and felt my knees wobble.

My patient Nina Davis, Justice Department attorney and stalker of men, was naked and hanging by her neck from a rope tied through an eyebolt screwed into a beam above the bed. Her wrists were handcuffed in front of her. She had a red ball-gag strapped into her mouth. Her eyes were open, bulging, and dull.

Sprawled in an overstuffed chair to the right of the bed, Dr. Chad Winters wasn't breathing either. His eyes were rolled up in his head, and his jaw sagged open. An Hermes silk scarf was cinched around his neck.

There were mirrors on the ceiling and above the headboard.

In scrawled lipstick on the mirror behind Nina Davis's body, someone had written this:

I asked you to stop me, please, Alex Cross. And you didn't. Now look what I've gone and done. — M.

427

Books by James Patterson
Published by Ulverscroft:

WHEN THE WIND BLOWS
BLACK MARKET
CRADLE AND ALL
THE JESTER (with Andrew Gross)
THE LAKE HOUSE
SAM'S LETTERS TO JENNIFER
HONEYMOON (with Howard Roughan)
JUDGE AND JURY (with Andrew Gross)
BEACH ROAD (with Peter de Jonge)
SUNDAYS AT TIFFANY'S
(with Gabrielle Charbonnet)
SAIL (with Howard Roughan)
THE MURDER OF KING TUT
(with Martin Dugard)
SWIMSUIT (with Maxine Paetro)
WORST CASE (with Michael Ledwidge)
THE BLACK BOOK (with David Ellis)
THE STORE (with Richard DiLallo)
HAUNTED (with James O. Born)

THE ALEX CROSS SERIES:
CAT AND MOUSE
POP GOES THE WEASEL
ROSES ARE RED
VIOLETS ARE BLUE
FOUR BLIND MICE
LONDON BRIDGES
THE BIG BAD WOLF

MARY, MARY
CROSS
CROSS COUNTRY
I, ALEX CROSS
CROSS FIRE
KILL ALEX CROSS
ALEX CROSS, RUN
MERRY CHRISTMAS, ALEX CROSS
CROSS MY HEART
HOPE TO DIE
CROSS THE LINE
THE PEOPLE VS. ALEX CROSS

THE WOMEN'S MURDER CLUB SERIES:
3RD DEGREE (*with Andrew Gross*)
4TH OF JULY (*with Maxine Paetro*)
THE 5TH HORSEMAN (*with Maxine Paetro*)
THE 6TH TARGET (*with Maxine Paetro*)
7TH HEAVEN (*with Maxine Paetro*)
9TH JUDGEMENT (*with Maxine Paetro*)
10TH ANNIVERSARY (*with Maxine Paetro*)
11TH HOUR (*with Maxine Paetro*)
12TH OF NEVER (*with Maxine Paetro*)
UNLUCKY 13 (*with Maxine Paetro*)
15TH AFFAIR (*with Maxine Paetro*)
16TH SEDUCTION (*with Maxine Paetro*)
17TH SUSPECT (*with Maxine Paetro*)

We do hope that you have enjoyed reading this large print book.

Did you know that all of our titles are available for purchase?

We publish a wide range of high quality large print books including:
Romances, Mysteries, Classics
General Fiction
Non Fiction and Westerns

Special interest titles available in large print are:
The Little Oxford Dictionary
Music Book
Song Book
Hymn Book
Service Book

Also available from us courtesy of Oxford University Press:
Young Readers' Dictionary
(large print edition)
Young Readers' Thesaurus
(large print edition)

For further information or a free brochure, please contact us at:
Ulverscroft Large Print Books Ltd.,
The Green, Bradgate Road, Anstey,
Leicester, LE7 7FU, England.
Tel: (00 44) 0116 236 4325
Fax: (00 44) 0116 234 0205

HAUNTED

James Patterson & James O. Born

Detective Michael Bennett is ready for a vacation after a series of crises pushes him and his family to the brink. He settles on an idyllic small town in the beautiful Maine woods. But just when Bennett thinks he can relax, he gets pulled into a case that has shocked the tight-knit community. Children are disappearing with no explanation — until several bodies turn up in the woods. Far from the city streets he knows so well, Bennett is fighting to protect a town, the law, and the family that he loves above all else.

THE STORE

James Patterson & Richard DiLallo

Imagine a future of unparalleled convenience. A powerful retailer, the Store, can deliver anything to your door, anticipating the needs and desires you didn't even know you had. Most people are fine with that, but not Jacob and Megan Brandeis. New York writers whose livelihood is on the brink of extinction, they are going undercover to dig up the Store's secrets. But after a series of unsettling discoveries, their worst fears about the Store seem like just the beginning. Harboring a secret that could get him killed, Jacob has to find a way to escape the Store's watchful eye and publish his expose — before the truth dies with him.

THE BLACK BOOK

James Patterson & David Ellis

Being a cop runs in Billy Harney's family. The son of Chicago's chief of detectives, whose twin sister Patti also followed in their father's footsteps, Billy would give up everything for the job, including his life. After a brutal shooting, Billy is left for dead alongside his tempestuous former partner and an ambitious assistant district attorney out for blood. But somehow Billy survives. He remembers nothing about the shootout, and is charged with double murder. Desperate to clear his name, Billy retraces his steps to get to the bottom of what happened. He must find the little black book; it could either set him free or confirm his worst fears.

17TH SUSPECT

James Patterson & Maxine Paetro

A reluctant informant puts her trust in Sergeant Lindsay Boxer, and the tip leads her to disturbing conclusions. Her friends in the Women's Murder Club warn her against taking the crimes to heart, but with lives at stake, she can't help herself from venturing into ever more terrifying terrain. Meanwhile, when ADA Yuki Castellano learns that a man is seeking to press charges of rape against his female superior, she's intrigued. Believing that she can make the case, Yuki puts all her efforts into selling it. But the evidence begins to muddy the original narrative, and she is left wondering if she made the right choice. With Lindsay and Yuki both facing personal issues of their own, they cannot let their home lives cloud the cases before them, for they refuse to be victims . . .